A NEW DAWN AT OWL'S LODGE

JESSICA REDLAND

Boldwood

First published in Great Britain in 2024 by Boldwood Books Ltd.

Copyright © Jessica Redland, 2024

Cover Design by Lizzie Gardiner

Cover Photography: Shutterstock

The moral right of Jessica Redland to be identified as the author of this work has been asserted in accordance with the Copyright, Designs and Patents Act 1988.

All rights reserved. No part of this book may be reproduced in any form or by any electronic or mechanical means, including information storage and retrieval systems, without written permission from the author, except for the use of brief quotations in a book review.

This book is a work of fiction and, except in the case of historical fact, any resemblance to actual persons, living or dead, is purely coincidental.

Every effort has been made to obtain the necessary permissions with reference to copyright material, both illustrative and quoted. We apologise for any omissions in this respect and will be pleased to make the appropriate acknowledgements in any future edition.

A CIP catalogue record for this book is available from the British Library.

Paperback ISBN 978-1-80162-504-3

Large Print ISBN 978-1-80162-505-0

Hardback ISBN 978-1-80162-503-6

Ebook ISBN 978-1-80162-506-7

Kindle ISBN 978-1-80162-507-4

Audio CD ISBN 978-1-80162-498-5

MP3 CD ISBN 978-1-80162-499-2

Digital audio download ISBN 978-1-80162-502-9

Boldwood Books Ltd
23 Bowerdean Street
London SW6 3TN
www.boldwoodbooks.com

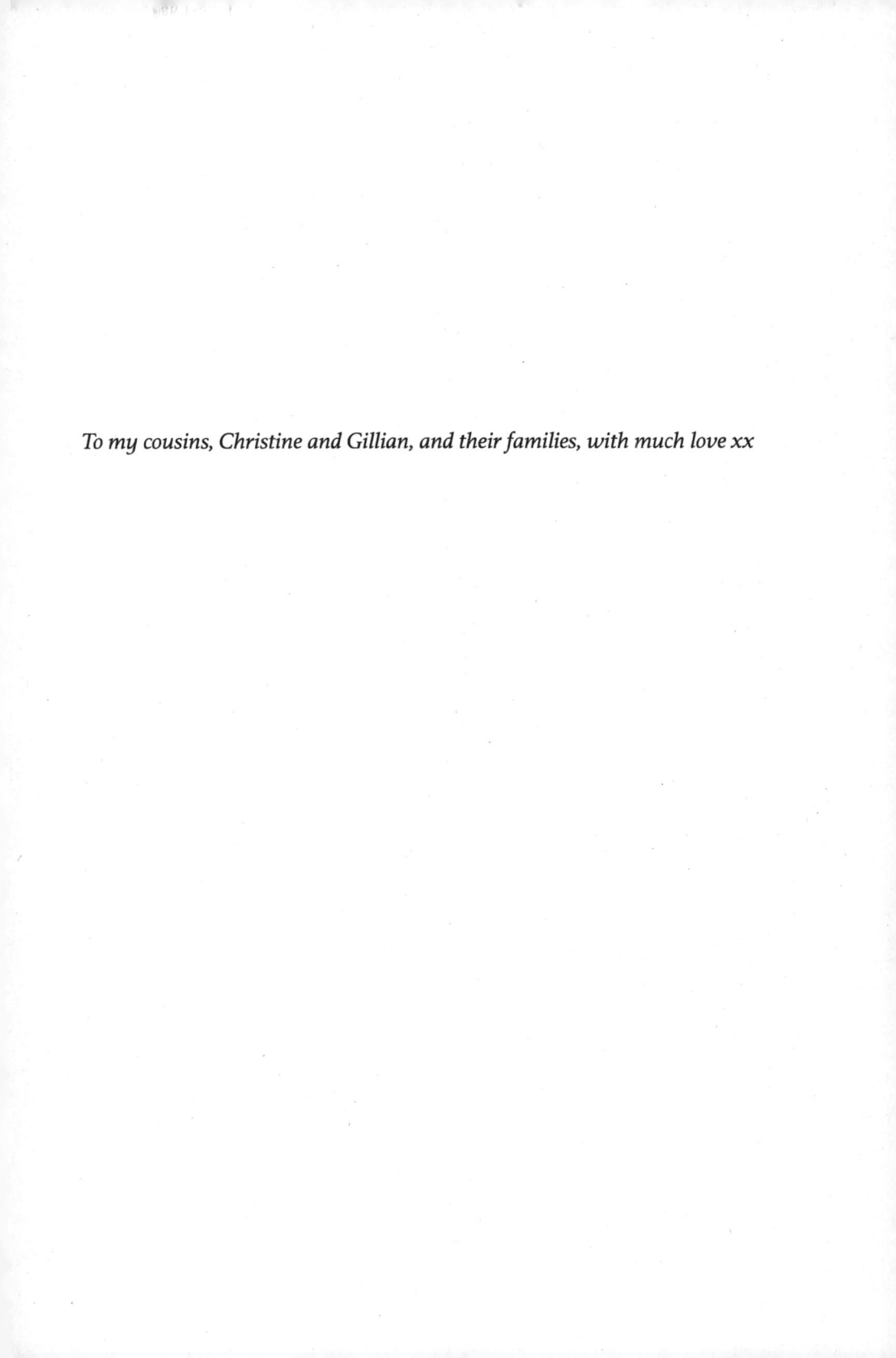

To my cousins, Christine and Gillian, and their families, with much love xx

1
ZARA

'I haven't been to a carol service since I was little,' I told Amber as I slipped my feet into my boots. 'And I don't think I've *ever* been to a candlelight one,' I added, standing up and wrapping my scarf round my neck.

'Really? Ooh, you're in for such a treat.' Amber smiled at me as she pulled a bobble hat down over her long auburn hair. 'It's magical.'

It was Saturday evening, eleven days before Christmas. We were staying in a holiday cottage in a village near Alnwick in Northumberland while filming the first half of the winter season of *Countryside Calendar*. Amber was the producer and I was her assistant on the family-friendly seasonal-based television programme which aired on Sunday evenings, showcasing the highs and lows of living and working in the UK countryside. She'd recruited me when she started on it six years ago and I worked directly for her rather than the show, supporting her with other projects between filming.

This morning, we'd been up early to film the sunrise with a local farmer and to explore what Christmas Day on a farm looked like. There'd been some set-up footage of the family opening gifts and having Christmas dinner and when they were asked about their favourite Christmas traditions, tonight's candlelight carol service was mentioned.

Amber and I had already booked a table in The Golden Lion – the pub a few minutes' walk from our holiday cottage – but the service sounded lovely, so we'd pushed the timing back to do that first.

'I hope we sing "Ding! Dong! Merrily on High",' Amber said after we'd set off. 'Brad, Sophie and I used to compete with each other to see who could sing the word "Gloria" for the longest.'

All of Amber's family had careers in television, although she was the only one who worked behind the camera. Her dad, older brother Brad and younger sister Sophie were all actors and her mum was a brilliant chef and gardener, presenting long-running programmes showcasing both talents. They were enthusiastic but terrible singers with the exception of Sophie, who was what was known in the business as a triple threat – able to act, sing and dance.

We both burst into song, trying to work down the scales while singing 'Gloria' for as long as we could before taking a breath. If I wasn't laughing so much at Amber's caterwauling, I might have won the impromptu contest, but I had to concede, fingers in my ears.

'You win!' I cried. 'Is it safe to let you loose with a song sheet tonight?'

'I promise to keep the volume down,' she said, laughing. 'Funnily enough, Barney said the same thing when I told him about the service.'

During the spring, we'd worked on a reality TV show called *Love on the Farm*, aimed at finding love for farmers around the country. Barney Kinsella of Bumblebee Barn in East Yorkshire had been the third farmer for whom we were hoping to find a happy ever after and we'd succeeded – just not with one of the show's contestants. Barney and Amber couldn't have been more perfectly matched and I was still pretty chuffed with myself that I'd spotted the attraction before either of them had.

The only downside to Amber finding her dream man was that it made me so much more aware of my hopeless singleton status. I didn't have a great track record with relationships. I seemed to be a magnet for treat-'em-mean-keep-'em-keen bad-boy types who always let me down, like Declan with whom my six-month relationship had ended in mid-April. We were meant to be celebrating my twenty-sixth birthday with a romantic weekend in the Cotswolds but he was a no-show and I spent the weekend on my own. Turned out he'd been seeing someone else most of the time we'd been together and I genuinely hadn't a clue. I was brilliant at spotting the early signs of chemistry or the cracks in relationships for others, but had blinkers on when it came to mine.

I hadn't dated since Declan, although there was somebody I desperately wanted to be with. Miraculously, he wasn't a bad boy. Unfortunately, he was with someone else and seemed really happy with her and, until I got over him, I couldn't imagine even looking at anyone else.

'Speaking of Christmas,' Amber said, bringing my thoughts back to the present and away from my fruitless crush, 'have you decided which day you're heading home?'

'I'm still torn,' I said, opening up the calendar on my phone. 'I want to say Christmas Eve but the traffic'll be hideous.'

There really wasn't a great day to travel unless I headed down to Lincolnshire extra early before the schools broke up, but there was no way I could face staying with Mum any longer than I needed. Too much time at home wasn't good for either of us.

'Maybe I'll brave the twenty-third,' I said. 'With any luck, those who have Christmas week off will have done their journeys over the weekend.'

My official home was Thorpe on the Hill – the small village where I'd been raised, five miles from Lincoln city centre – but the reality of a job where I travelled so much was that 'home' was wherever we happened to be filming. *Countryside Calendar* had taken me all over the UK, my capsule wardrobe prepared me for every eventuality, and living out of a suitcase had never bothered me, although Amber's decision to share a holiday cottage or Airbnb rather than stay in hotels had certainly helped that, making our time away more homely.

I loved my job. It played to my strengths of organising, project managing and solving problems. There was lots of variety, I saw places I'd never have discovered otherwise, and met the most amazing people. But the greatest pull of all was working with Amber. As well as being an amazing boss, she was my closest friend, the transition from colleagues into friends being a natural byproduct of so much time away together. I didn't need to accompany her all the time but we got more work done that way and we both enjoyed the company.

'How long will you stay?' Amber asked.

I glanced at the calendar again. Christmas Day was on the Wednesday and Mum had all the weekdays off, returning to work on the Saturday and working right through until the end of New Year's Day. She worked exceptionally long hours as the manager of Sycamore Beck Golf Club on the outskirts of Lincoln. She'd been there for as long as I could remember, working her way up to manager after Dad left.

'I'll see the week out and drive back on the Friday afternoon, if that's okay with you and Barney. I don't want to be in your way. If you want more time on your own, I can—'

A playful nudge from Amber cut me off. 'Seriously, Zara, you'd be welcome to stay at the farm for the *whole* of Christmas and New Year if you wanted. And don't worry for a moment that you're in our way. Do you think we'd have given you your own room if you weren't welcome?'

Shortly after Amber moved into Bumblebee Barn, I went home to celebrate my stepdad Owen's birthday and returned to find that Amber, Barney and his sister Fizz had redecorated the spare bedroom I'd been staying in. It was exactly to my taste, using my favourite colours, and they told me the room was now exclusively for my use.

Staying at the farm was heaven. I'd always thought I loved a country/city balance until I started working on *Countryside Calendar* and now I struggled to spend any significant time in a city. As well as the stunning views at Bumblebee Barn, I loved the sounds and smells. Barney had pigs, sheep, goats and horses, two gorgeous Border collies, and three cats. Growing up, I'd never had pets, but we'd had the beautiful Whisby Nature Park on our doorstep. There was something about being around nature and animals that brought me such a sense of peace and, if there were tensions at home, a visit to the nature park always calmed me down and gave me perspective.

'There's a big difference in me staying at the farm between filming and me spending the holidays there too,' I said.

'Not to me there isn't, and Barney feels the same. And I know it's so much better for you. I hated seeing how tense you'd get towards the end of filming but, since you've been staying at the farm instead of going home, that's stopped. It's obvious how much happier you are.'

'I do feel lighter for not going home so often,' I admitted. 'It shouldn't be like that, should it?'

'No, but families can be complicated and if seeing less of each other means you're actually closer, why fight it? Although I bet you miss Owen.'

I sighed. 'I do. That's the downside of going home less.'

Owen had married Mum when I was twelve, four years after she and Dad split up. I loved him so much and was frequently prodded by the sticky fingers of guilt because I didn't share the same closeness with my parents, but I couldn't help it. Owen had always been there for me when they hadn't.

'Don't forget the other big plus,' Amber prompted. 'Less time at home is also less time around Roman or having to listen to your mum extolling his virtues.'

She gave me a sideways glance and a raise of the eyebrows. Very true. If I had a difficult relationship with Mum, I had an impossible one with my brother. He was invariably the cause of the tensions between Mum and me too. She couldn't seem to accept that there'd been irreversible damage done to our relationship long ago and kept trying to push us into being the best of friends.

'I'll message Mum and confirm the Monday to Friday and then that's sorted.'

I clicked into the WhatsApp group I shared with Mum and Owen.

> TO MUM AND OWEN
>
> I've been looking at the calendar and I'll come home on Monday 23rd and drive back on Friday 27th. Hope that's OK x

I switched my phone to silent and returned it to the zipped pocket inside my coat.

'Back to the farm,' Amber said. 'As far as Barney and I are concerned, you're not just a friend – you're part of our family. I know you're saving for a house deposit but, until you're ready to buy, we want you to think of Bumblebee Barn as your home and, if you ever wanted to pack up your stuff in Lincolnshire and officially move in, you'd be very welcome.'

Tears rushed to my eyes and I tried to thank her but the ball of emotion caught in my throat stifled the words.

'Are you okay?' Amber asked, shooting me a concerned glance.

I nodded and took a couple of deep breaths.

'I'm fine,' I finally managed. 'Just a bit emotional. You've already done so much for me.'

'And you've done the same for us. I couldn't do my job without you, the time on the road would be lonely, and you're the one who helped me go for it with Barney.'

The sat nav announced that we'd reached our destination – a car park a short walk from the church. As Amber reversed into a space, I pondered on what she'd said about packing up my room in Thorpe on the Hill. Should I? Although Mum had never suggested she wanted me to move out, was it fair of me to hog a bedroom when I was hardly ever there? She'd converted Roman's room into a home office for her, and Owen might like my bedroom as his office/man cave. Perhaps I'd sound them out about it when I was home for Christmas, although I could already hear Mum's response in my head now: *You're moving into Amber's spare room? Really? What about your own home? Why aren't you on the property ladder like your brother? First thing he did when he started earning was invest in bricks and mortar.*

Maybe I'd leave that conversation until another time. Being compared to my brother had never made anyone happy.

2

ZARA

Amber had been spot on about candlelight carol services being magical. The large church was heaving with people of all ages and every pew was packed full. Wooden stands above the pews held hundreds of white candles. At 6 p.m. the lights dimmed and several people appeared at the front, each with a lit taper on the end of a pole. The opening verse of 'Once in Royal David's City' was sung by a lone choirboy as they lit the candles. The choir joined in with the second verse onwards and the congregation were invited to sing the final verse before the minister welcomed us to the service.

The candles and the beautiful singing made me feel quite emotional, especially when the children in the congregation gathered at the front to sing 'Away in a Manger'.

The minister announced the number in the song sheets for the final carol and Amber and I laughed as we turned to 'Ding! Dong! Merrily on High!' As we sang – completely off-key in Amber's case – the candles were extinguished.

After a final prayer, we were asked to leave the carol sheets in our pews and wished a safe journey home and a happy Christmas.

'You're not going to sneak one out for your scrapbook?' Amber asked.

'The order of service will do.' I waved the A5 leaflet at her.

'I'm so glad we went to that,' Amber said as we stepped out of the warm church into the cool night air.

'Me too. I'm feeling so Christmassy right now.'

When Amber pulled out of the car park, I removed my phone from my pocket to switch it off silent.

'Oh, that's weird!' I said.

'What's up?'

'Three missed FaceTime calls from my mum. She *never* FaceTimes me. I'd better call her back. Do you mind?'

'Go for it.'

Amber switched the radio off as I FaceTimed Mum.

'Sorry for all the missed calls,' she said as soon as she answered. 'I wanted to catch you before you went out to eat.'

'We've been to a candlelight carol service.'

'Oh, how lovely!' she said, smiling at me. 'Was it good?'

'It was amazing. We're on our way to the pub now, though.'

'In that case, I'll get straight to the point. There's a change of plan. Owen and I are working over Christmas now and having New Year off instead.'

'But you've had Christmas booked off all year.'

She shrugged. 'I know, but it's Roman.'

My jaw tightened. I should have known. Every time Mum changed plans she'd made with me, I could guarantee my brother was the reason.

'What's he done now?' I asked, struggling to keep the frustration out of my voice.

'He's cancelled his holiday. He realised a nine-hour flight with his leg in plaster wasn't such a good idea and he's celebrating his thirtieth with a black-tie do in Lincoln instead so, to Howard's delight, we've swapped shifts.'

Her deputy manager, Howard, might have been delighted to unexpectedly be spending Christmas with his family, but I wasn't so enamoured.

'So you're saying I can't come home for Christmas,' I said, my voice flat.

'Of course you can! I'm just warning you that we won't be there.'

'There's no point coming home for Christmas if you're both working. I'll stay at the farm.' I glanced at Amber, hoping that was okay, but she caught my eye and nodded vigorously.

'We've got a wedding on the twenty-eighth,' Mum said, 'so I'm covering that too and I'll need to go in for a couple of hours on the Sunday. When do you think you'll drive down? And please don't say New Year's Eve. Don't want you hitting traffic and being late for the party.'

I frowned at her. 'I won't be down for New Year.'

She looked taken aback. 'Why not?'

'Because I have plans.'

'Then you'll have to change them. You can't miss your brother's milestone birthday.'

'Mum! I can and I will. It's not like he'll miss me.'

'Of course he will. He wants *all* his family there.'

'Really? Because I don't remember being invited to Saint Lucia to celebrate his birthday.'

The smile was gone, replaced by that familiar look of disappointment that I didn't idolise my brother and fall over myself pandering to his needs.

'Don't be facetious, Zara!' she snapped. 'You know the holiday was a kneejerk reaction to his accident and can you blame him? What that man did to him was horrific. He should have a life ban if you ask me. What he's put my boy through is...'

She tailed off and took a deep calming breath, clearly not wanting to go down that route again, which was just as well as she'd only work herself up into a frenzy. Granted, 'horrific' wasn't an understatement as I'd seen the footage online and it was sickening. Roman was a striker for Lincoln City Football Club and, a few weeks ago, he'd been stretchered off the pitch in agony after a bad tackle. A couple of leg fractures meant he was in plaster and unable to play for the rest of the season. He'd never been able to celebrate his New Year's Eve birthday in style as there were so many matches across the festive period, but his accident had changed that this year, hence the now-cancelled holiday.

'Anyway,' Mum said, composed once more, 'your brother's struggling with not playing and this party will be the lift he needs. You don't need to confirm the date you're coming down tonight, but let us know when you've decided so we can adjust the online food order.'

'You don't need to adjust anything,' I said, shaking my head. 'I'm not coming. I'm going to a masked ball at Hedgehog Hollow. I told you about it weeks ago.'

She scrunched up her forehead, looking confused. Evidently, she hadn't remembered that conversation, despite me detailing what I'd be wearing and how excited I was. I should have known she hadn't been paying attention.

'Are you sure you told me? I don't—'

'I *definitely* told you,' I said firmly, cutting her short. 'So I won't be back for Roman's party.'

'He'll be really upset.'

I have no idea how she managed to say that with a straight face. 'We both know that's not true,' I said gently. 'He wouldn't notice if I wasn't there.'

'He would, and so would Owen and I. Please reconsider, Zara.'

I couldn't help noticing Amber's hands tightening on the steering wheel and it comforted me knowing that she didn't appreciate the emotional blackmail either.

'I'm sorry Roman got injured but I made my New Year's Eve plans before that happened and it's not fair to ask me to change them.'

'But that would mean we don't see you at all.'

I didn't think it would help to point out that I wasn't the one who'd changed the plans, so I just shrugged apologetically.

'I'm in Northumberland for another week and your presents are at the farm,' I said. 'I'll give you them next time I see you, although I've no idea when I'll be able to squeeze in a visit. We've got a busy start to the year filming the docuseries at Hedgehog Hollow.'

I expected her to express some disappointment in not being able to see me for ages, and perhaps even to offer to drive up to visit me but, no, the conversation was still about my brother.

'There'll be an invitation waiting for you when you get back to the farm.'

Amber glanced at me and rolled her eyes.

'There's no point sending it. Tell Roman he can save himself the postage.'

The humour of that – saving the cost of a stamp when my brother earned a six-figure salary – was lost on her.

'It's already gone,' she said. 'Look, I know you and your brother don't get on, but he really wants you there.'

'I'm not going.'

'Please, Zara. You could see this as him waving the white flag. I think the accident has made him re-evaluate a few things.'

'I'm pleased for him, but it's still a no.'

'If not for him, what about for me? It breaks my heart that the pair of you don't get on. Please.'

I'd had such a lovely time at the carol service and had felt all warm and festive, but now I just felt irritated and manipulated.

'We're nearly at the pub,' I said. 'I'll look at my filming schedule for the next few months and see when I can fit in a visit. Bye, Mum.'

I ended the call before she had a chance to guilt trip me even further and smacked my head back against the headrest with a heavy sigh. This was so typical of my brother. The cancelled holiday and replacement party I understood, but why rope me into it? He had a phenomenal number of friends – albeit some not as genuine as others – and I knew for a fact that he'd much rather spend time with them than me, so why should I change my plans?

Before and during the filming of *Love on the Farm*, Amber and I had stayed in the holiday cottages at Hedgehog Hollow and befriended the owners, Samantha and Josh, as well as Barney's sister Fizz, who worked there. Four years ago, they'd hosted a big New Year's Eve party to test out the suitability of Wildflower Byre – the converted dairy shed on the farm – as a wedding reception venue, after which they'd become licensed to host weddings. They'd decided it was time they hosted another New Year celebration – a masquerade ball. I'd never had a big circle of friends but I finally had one in East Yorkshire and was really excited about seeing the New Year in with them all.

After that, Amber and I would start filming for *The Wildlife Rescuers* – an eight-part docuseries exploring a year in the life of running a rescue centre. Hedgehog Hollow was going to be the main focus but we'd be visiting another four centres around the UK, filming between *Countryside Calendar* episodes. Everything had been looking so good, but that one conversation with Mum had just blighted it all.

'Are you okay?' Amber asked when I hadn't spoken for a minute or so after hanging up.

'Not really.'

'Do you want to talk about it?'

'What's there to say? We both know I'm going to go to Roman's party because that's what I do.' I sighed once more and added in a weary tone, 'It's what I've always done.'

3
SNOWY

I pulled my beanie hat down lower over my ears and turned up the collar of my jacket as Harrison and I stepped into Bloomsberry's – the garden centre nearest our home and the place where my nine-year-old son had a very special appointment.

'There's a sign!' Harrison said, pointing to a large glittery arrow with *SANTA THIS WAY* on it.

He tugged my arm and we followed further arrows. All the while, my eyes flicked around me, cautious as ever.

'Do you think Santa will remember me from last year?' Harrison asked.

'I'm sure he recognises all the children he sees, but his focus will be on finding out what you want this year.'

'He already knows that. I wrote to him and he wrote back.'

'I think the elves help with the letters, so you'd better tell him when he asks, just to be on the safe side.'

'Okay.'

We turned to our left and joined a glittery pathway weaving through artificial trees draped with fairy lights. Plush toy deer peeked between the trees and smaller woodland animals gathered round them.

'There's an owl!' Harrison cried, pointing to a fluffy white owl with dark spots on its wings nestling halfway up one of the taller trees. 'It's a snowy owl. They don't live in England.'

'Ah, but we're not in England anymore,' I said, smiling at him. 'Where are we?'

He grinned at me, his pale blue eyes sparkling. 'The North Pole! And the snowy owl lives there.'

'Can you remember what continent the North Pole is in?' When Harrison hesitated, I added, 'The clue is in one of the snowy owl's other names.'

'The Arctic!' he declared proudly. 'They're called Arctic owls, white owls and polar owls.'

'Well remembered.'

Snowy owls mainly lived and bred on the tundra and their hardiness to survive there never ceased to amaze me. They also lived in North America and could occasionally be seen in the northern parts of the UK but as migratory visitors, typically during very cold weather. I'd only seen a few in my lifetime, but what a special gift those moments were.

Harrison gave the owl a gentle stroke before moving on. Further along the path, the branches were sprayed with fake snow – small amounts at first but soon whole trees were frosted and there were boxed gifts rather than animals round the bases. We rounded a final turn and spotted a small queue just ahead.

A young woman dressed as an elf bounded up to us and beamed at my son. 'Welcome to Santa's Grotto! What's your name, please?'

'Harrison Oakes. I'm here to see Santa.'

She glanced down the list on her sparkly clipboard and ran a highlighter pen through his name. 'And Santa is very much looking forward to seeing you. You're his last visitor today. Have you been a good boy this year, Harrison?'

'I think so.' He glanced up to me for confirmation.

'Very good,' I said, smiling at him.

'In that case, let me give you one of these.' She reached into the pocket of her green apron and handed Harrison a large chocolate coin. 'Santa has a few children to see before you, but you shouldn't be waiting long.'

We both thanked her and she returned to the front of the queue where another elf had appeared to take a small group into Santa's Grotto.

Harrison pocketed the coin, saying he'd eat it after tea. He reached up to his bobble hat and I gently batted his hand away.

'My head's warm,' he objected.

I crouched down beside him. 'I know, but we don't want to lose your hat, do we? It's your favourite. Why don't you keep it on for now and remove it when we meet Santa?'

That seemed to placate him as he left the hat alone and unzipped his coat.

'Can I take some photos for Pops?' he asked, removing his phone from his pocket.

'Yes, but don't go far. We don't want to keep Santa waiting.'

'I'll just get the trees and animals.'

He backtracked along the pathway and I kept an eye on him, a familiar guilty feeling churning my stomach. I felt like I was forever battling with Harrison to keep his hat on in public. *You don't want to burn your scalp*, I'd say in the summer when he wore a baseball cap and *You don't want to get cold* was the counter-argument in the winter with the reserve about it being his favourite and not wanting to lose it when he protested he was too hot. Fortunately he liked hats, probably because I wore one nearly all the time and he was at an age where he thought it was cool rather than embarrassing to dress like me. I'd never told him the real reason we both wore hats and he'd never asked. I wasn't sure what I'd say the day he inevitably did.

It seemed that there was a different exit point from Santa's Grotto as the group who'd gone in hadn't reappeared but the second elf came out to guide another family in. One more after them, then us. I shuffled forward and checked my hat again.

Harrison re-joined me as the final family went into the grotto, flakes of fake snow on the knees of his jeans where he must have knelt down to get the photos of the animals.

'I got a close-up of the owl,' he said as he showed me his photos. 'Do you think Pops will like it?'

'He'll love it.'

Pops was my grandpa, but saying 'great-grandpa' had been a bit of a mouthful for Harrison when he was younger and the shortened version of Pops had stuck. The three of us lived together at Owl's Lodge. Originally a working farm called Maplewick Farm, Grandpa had sold off the livestock and most of the fields when I was little, retaining the outbuildings, a paddock and the woodland. He'd knocked down the farmhouse and re-built it as an impressive stone, wood and glass lodge, and had changed the name in honour of the many owls living on the property – a bird we were all passionate about. Although he'd transferred ownership of Owl's Lodge to me when Harrison was born, I still thought of it as his.

As we followed the elf into the grotto entrance for Harrison's appointment, he pulled his hat off and handed it to me. I stiffened as I gripped onto it.

We stepped into a room done out like a living room with a fake fire crackling beneath a mantelpiece draped in stockings, a large decorated tree on one side and Santa in a high-backed armchair on the other, surrounded by hessian sacks bursting with presents.

'Ho! Ho! Ho! Merry Christmas!' Santa boomed. 'And who do we have here?'

'This is Harrison, Santa,' the elf said, 'and he's been a good boy this year.'

'Indeed you have, young man,' Santa said. 'I know you from my list. Come and sit beside me.'

He patted a red velvet ottoman and Harrison settled onto it.

'And how old are you, Harrison?'

'I'm nine. I'll be ten in April.'

'Goodness! Nearly double figures. What would you like me to bring you for Christmas this year?'

'Please can I have a painting easel and some canvases?'

'You're a budding artist?'

'I love drawing and I want to get better at painting.'

'Marvellous! One of my elves, Sketchy, is fabulous at painting. Such a wonderful skill to have.'

'My pops is a brilliant artist.'

'Pops?'

'My dad's grandpa,' Harrison said, glancing towards me. 'He's ninety-two. We live with him and he draws all the wildlife that visit us but his favourite thing to draw is owls. We all love owls.'

'Did you spot the snowy owl on your way in?'

Harrison nodded and whipped out his phone to show Santa the photos he'd taken.

'Budding young photographer too,' Santa observed. 'You'll have to see if you can paint our owl from one of those photographs. Now, is there anything you'd like to ask me while you're here?'

Harrison studied Santa's face for a moment and I found myself doing the same. He was a jolly-looking elderly man, in his early seventies at a guess, and the white hair and beard weren't fake.

'Were you born with white hair like me?' Harrison asked and my stomach tightened. Of all the questions Harrison could have asked, I hadn't considered that one.

'I had no hair at all when I was born!' Santa declared, laughing. 'Not even a bit of fluff. It took a while to come through. It was more blond than white when I was little, but I love my white hair. Owls are one of my favourites too and I like how my hair's the same colour as the snowy owl's feathers. And I'll tell you something else, young man. One of my elves has pure white hair like yours and mine and we all call him Snowy, just like the owl.'

'Pops calls my dad Snowy!' Harrison cried, his grin showing that he was clearly delighted with Santa's answer. 'Thanks, Santa.'

I released the breath I'd been holding. Nicely handled, Santa. Thanks from me too!

Santa handed Harrison another chocolate coin for asking a great question, and a gift which made Harrison's smile widen. There was a discussion about going to bed in decent time on Christmas Eve, not rising too early on Christmas Day – accompanied by a wink in my direction – and what to leave out for Santa and his reindeer before the elf showed us out via a door opposite where we'd entered.

'That was awesome!' Harrison declared as the door closed behind us. 'He said my hair colour's like the snowy owl's feathers and he's right. Is that why Pops calls you Snowy?'

'Actually, no. It was your mum who first called me that and it was after her pet rabbit.'

He studied my face for a moment and I could tell he had questions, but there was also something he wanted and that took priority.

'Do you think they sell those snowy owls here?'

'Probably.'

'Can we get one?'

We'd emerged into a large area full of Christmas decorations, divided into bays according to colour. I'd deliberately booked the last Santa appointment of the day in the hope that it wouldn't be too busy by then. It appeared to have worked as there were people around but nothing like the throngs there'd have been earlier.

'Okay. We'll try that white section but, if we can't find it quickly, we have to go.'

Harrison raced over to the white section and I glanced around me once more but nobody was paying us any attention, so I joined my son in the search for a snowy owl.

* * *

'Wow! What a stunning pair of snowy owls,' Grandpa gushed, holding one in each hand after Harrison thrust them at him the moment we arrived home.

The owls at Bloomsberry's hadn't taken much finding, but they'd come in three different sizes including a two-feet-high one. Harrison had wanted the entire owl family but I'd told him to pick between the two smaller ones. After ten minutes of chopping and changing his mind, I caved and said they could both come home with us.

'Were these from Santa?' Grandpa asked.

'No, but my present from Santa is awesome. Look!'

Harrison took the jigsaw from me. 'Can you spot the owls?'

He'd been delighted when he opened the gift in the car. The jigsaw was of a snowy scene outside Santa's workshop with the elves loading up the sleigh. A snowy owl was flying in the inky blue sky and another was perched on one of the reindeer's antlers.

'Oh, yes! I see them,' Grandpa said, pointing. 'And where are your new owls going to live?'

Harrison turned in a circle, looking round the room. 'In the Christmas tree?'

'The little one will fit in the tree,' I said, 'but the other's too big.'

'They need to stay together,' Harrison responded.

'Why don't you put them on the coffee table for now?' Grandpa suggested. 'You can help me prepare tea and tell me all about your visit with Santa and, after we've eaten, we can find somewhere to put them. Sound good?'

Harrison shrugged off his coat and followed Grandpa into the kitchen. I picked up his coat and hung it with mine in the cloakroom. Pulling off my beanie hat, I dropped it into a crate full of hats with a slow breath of relief. *Another outing survived.*

4

SNOWY

Tea was bangers, mash and garden peas and I laughed as Harrison placed my plate in front of me.

'That's brilliant, but I don't know whether to frame it or eat it,' I joked.

The mash was in the shape of an owl with long slices of sausage as wings and peas for the eyes, beak and claws.

'Eat it!' Harrison cried, picking up his fork and stabbing one of his sausage wings on his owl.

I'd heard Harrison and Grandpa chatting about our visit to Santa's Grotto while they peeled the potatoes and the topic had spawned a new game – coming up with elf names based on appearance, personality traits, hobbies or occupation – which continued across teatime with much hilarity. My favourites, none of which I could take credit for, were Neigh-o-mi (the elf who loved horse riding), Doug (the gardening elf) and Fiery-Pants (the elf who told fibs).

While I cleared the table after we'd eaten, Harrison toured the room with his owls, perching them on various shelves and removing them again. By bedtime, he still hadn't decided so I suggested he take them upstairs and keep them in his room for now.

'Are you reading to me tonight?' I asked when he was settled under his duvet a little later.

Harrison devoured novels, particularly fantasy ones, which would have delighted his mum, Eliza, who'd loved reading. I'd never been into books and, although Grandpa was a big reader, it was always non-fiction.

'Will you read to me?' Harrison asked, handing me the novel from his bedside drawers.

'You don't think you're too old for that?'

He shook his head. 'Please, Dad. I'm too tired to read.'

I couldn't resist those puppy-dog eyes so I perched on the end of his bed and we were soon both lost in a world of good versus evil where unicorns, dragons and other mythical creatures took centre stage.

Realising Harrison had drifted off, I put his owl bookmark back a few pages, closed the book and watched him sleeping for a few minutes. I'd enjoyed reading to him tonight, creating voices for the different characters, just like Eliza used to do and like my grandma had done for me when I was young. I didn't recall my dad ever reading me bedtime stories and I doubted my mum, who'd cleared off when I was three, had ever bothered.

Rising from the bed, I placed the book back on the drawers and gave Harrison a light kiss on the forehead. I switched his lamp off, leaving the room bathed in the gentle light from a projector which cast stars on the walls and ceiling.

'That's Harrison settled to sleep,' I said, joining Grandpa in the lounge a few minutes later. 'Shattered after the excitement of meeting Santa.'

Grandpa looked up from his book about tawny owls and peered at me over his glasses. 'How was it really?'

'Harrison loved it.'

'That's not what I asked.'

I busied myself adjusting the cushions on the sofa so I wouldn't have to make eye contact.

'Would I have preferred to stay here? Of course I would! But I can't let my fears and hang-ups rob my son of every aspect of his childhood. A Santa visit each year is the least I can do.'

I finally looked up to catch Grandpa narrowing his eyes at me. 'That statement suggests that you think you're depriving him of other aspects of his childhood. Like what?'

I raised my eyebrows at him, astonished he was even asking that when the answer was so obvious.

Grandpa closed his book – a sign that he meant business. 'Don't you dare say his mother because you did *not* deprive him of her.'

'My actions did. If it wasn't for me, she—'

'No! I'm not having that.' He sat forward and slammed his book down onto the coffee table, making me jump. 'We've been through this before, Snowy. You cannot spend the rest of your life blaming yourself for her death. It was *not* you. It was a tragic accident. Do I make myself clear?'

'Yes, Grandpa,' I said in a small voice, a little alarmed at the volume and tone, so unlike him.

'I'm sorry for raising my voice,' he said, his voice soft once more. 'But you know how I feel about this. It's not good for you or Harrison. If he picks up that you blame yourself for Eliza's death, he could start believing it and grow to resent you, which is the last thing any of us need. Parts of this family are already broken beyond repair and you know what that feels like. Don't ever risk that happening to you and that boy. The pair of you have an incredible bond. Promise me you'll keep nurturing it.'

His pale eyes were shrouded with such sadness as they held mine and I nodded. 'I promise.'

'Pleased to hear it. So you're good?'

'I'm good.'

He picked up his book and settled back onto the sofa, signalling the end of that conversation, which was a relief as I really didn't want a deep discussion about how else I feared I might be failing Harrison.

I put my EarPods in and streamed the latest episode of my favourite podcast, *CLASS*, which stood for 'Creating a Life After Sporting Success'. Run by former US Olympic figure skater Brent Starkey and his wife Kimberley, a motivational coach, they had guests from around the world representing every sport you could imagine who'd achieved varying levels of success in their field. The podcast explored what life looked like when the guest's sports career ended. It was fascinating hearing the journeys, the different reasons for careers ending and the struggles most guests had experienced to find a place of contentment after the one thing that most of them had trained for pretty much the whole of their life was no more. Every single episode lifted me and filled me with inspiration to finally get my act together and yet, somehow, it never translated into actions.

About eight months ago, I'd received an email from the *CLASS* researcher about appearing on the podcast as a guest. I'd ignored it. What did I have to offer the listeners when I hadn't succeeded in creating a life after my sporting success? Nearly thirteen years down the line, I was still floundering. Would that ever cease?

5
ZARA

It was late morning the following Saturday, four days before Christmas, when Amber turned onto the track to Bumblebee Barn. It was a cool, still day with wispy clouds stretching across a pale blue sky.

'Feels like we've been away for way longer than a fortnight,' Amber said. 'I wonder why some trips feel like that.'

'It's since you met Barney. You've got someone to rush home to now.'

As we pulled to a stop in the farmyard, Pumpkin jumped up onto the bonnet and mewed at us. One of three stray moggies who'd made Bumblebee Barn their home, she was an affectionate ginger tabby. Radley, a grey and black tabby boy, liked the occasional fuss but mainly did his own thing. My favourite was Socks, a younger black cat with white socks and a white face. Barney said they'd appeared across a two-year period and, although he'd welcomed them into the house, they'd chosen to settle in one of the outbuildings, only coming into the house when they wanted affection or during colder weather. Since I moved in, Socks seemed to favour the farmhouse and specifically my room. It had started out with him lying on my floor, then on the end of the bed, then in the empty space beside me. While I was away, I missed the comfort of reaching out and sinking my fingers into his soft fur and hearing his purrs as I drifted off to sleep.

Barney appeared round the corner on his quad bike with his Border collies Bear and Harley in the basket on the back. Seeing Amber's face light up at the sight of him gave me the warm and fuzzies.

'Perfect timing!' he called, removing his helmet as the dogs jumped down and raced over to greet us.

I said hello to Barney before bending down to stroke the dogs, allowing the couple a moment to themselves. I sensed I was being watched from across the yard and spotted a white face in the shadows.

'Socks!' I called. 'Hello, sweetie.'

He ran over, scooted through Bear's legs and weaved around my legs.

'I've missed you,' I told him, stroking his tail. 'Have you missed me?'

He looked up at me and released a plaintive mew. He'd never let me pick him up before but it felt like he was asking for a hug so I gave it a go and, sure enough, he settled into my arms with a contented purr.

'He's definitely been missing you,' Barney said. 'He's been padding round the house like a little lost soul.'

'Aw, bless him. I've missed you too, Socks,' I said, scratching his belly. 'I'm sorry I was away for so long.'

We removed our cases and bags from the boot and headed into the kitchen with the dogs.

'There's some post on your bed,' Barney said.

My stomach lurched. The invitation to Roman's birthday would be among it and I'd done my best across the past week to shove all thoughts of it out of my mind. Mum had messaged to ask if I'd decided which day I'd travel down but I hadn't responded.

Socks raced upstairs ahead of me and, when I pushed my bedroom door open, he launched himself onto the bed. I left my luggage by the door and sat beside him, stroking his back, a tension knot building in my stomach at the sight of the small pile of post, on top of which was a thick cream envelope. There was no point putting it off, so I ripped it open and removed the invitation. A pale yellow rectangular Post-it note was stuck on top of it in Roman's messy scrawl.

Z

Sorry it's last minute & messes up xmas.

Really hope you can come!
R

I raised my eyebrows, surprised to see both an apology and an acknowledgement that he'd messed up my Christmas plans. In fact, him bothering to scribble a note at all was unexpected. I peeled off the Post-it and scanned down the invite itself – the usual gubbins about date, time, venue, dress code and a request to RSVP to his girlfriend Portia's email address. They'd only been together for about four months and I hadn't met her yet.

There was a gentle knock on the open door. 'Thought I'd bring this up for you,' Amber said, handing me a mug of tea. 'Is that the invite?'

'Yeah.' I stuck the note back on it and handed it to her.

'Where's your head at now?' she asked after she'd scanned down it.

'Same as before. Don't want to go but feel like I should. Do you think I could do both? Show my face at Roman's then hoof it up the A15?'

'You could, but would you want to spend a couple of hours driving? And would leaving so early cause more problems than not going at all?'

I clapped my hands to my cheeks and exhaled loudly. 'I'll have to go. I'll never hear the end of it if I don't and it's just not worth the grief. I'm sorry.'

'Hey, don't apologise to me. We'll miss you, but we get to keep you for Christmas and we'll have a great time then. I promise.'

I gave her a weak smile. 'Thanks for letting me stay.'

'Like I said last weekend, you're welcome here any time you want for as long as you want. It's your home.' She headed for the door and paused. 'What if you stuck by your guns and said no? Even your brother acknowledges it's last minute and he's messed up your Christmas plans. I'm sure he'll understand if you tell him what you already had planned.'

'Roman *would* understand. I doubt he could care less either way. In fact, he'd probably prefer it if I wasn't there because that would save him five minutes of awkward conversation. The issue is Mum. I've been treading a thin line for years, refusing to watch him play or go to any events connected to football and I've just about got away with it because she knows how much I hate the game, but this is different. This is the only occasion he's been able to celebrate his birthday on the actual day and if I don't go, it won't just cause problems between Mum and me – it'll cause problems between Mum and Owen and I can't do that to him. He's fought my corner pretty much from the moment I met him. I wouldn't be doing it for Roman or Mum. I'd be doing it for Owen.'

'I'm sure there'll be other Hedgehog Hollow balls,' Amber said, her voice full of positivity. 'And as your brother's do is a black-tie one, you'll still get to wear that gorgeous dress.'

My work wardrobe was jeans or leggings and T-shirts so it had been a special treat to splash out on the most stunning dress for the Hedgehog Hollow Masked Ball. It was a deep purple halter neck, cut above the knee at the front and dipping down to the floor at the back with layers of tulle. I'd bought silver sparkly strappy sandals and a lacy silver and purple mask to accompany it. Barney and Amber had gone historical as a highwayman and a bejewelled damsel in distress. The pair of them had looked so amazing when they tried on their costumes that I wondered if I'd been too hasty with my dress choice and should have gone historical too, but Samantha's cousin Chloe, who'd made costumes for Samantha and Josh, had kindly offered to make me a hooded cloak. It was black with a silver lining and it was amazing how that and a pair of long silver gloves transformed my dress into something quite remarkable. Except I wasn't going to be able to wear all the extras. Or was I?

I smiled at Amber. 'I might still go for full-on masquerade. I could be this mysterious raven-haired masked woman who strides into the room, swishes her cloak and bewitches all the guests.'

'Loving the sound of that. And if anyone can pull it off, you can. If you're going, you might as well go all out to have a brilliant time.'

As she disappeared downstairs, I felt a lot more positive about Roman's birthday. It was one night. Yes, I was gutted to be missing out on New Year's Eve with my friends, but I could turn an evening with my family into something special too. Or that was what I'd keep telling myself.

And while I was searching for the positives, missing the masked ball meant avoiding further heartbreak from watching the man I'd fallen for completely loved up with his girlfriend. Silver linings.

6
ZARA

I woke up early on Christmas Day with a buzz for what I knew was going to be an amazing day. The excitement had been building since Sunday when Amber's parents, Cole and Jules, had arrived. I knew them well and they'd always treated me as though I was part of their family. Enveloping me in an enormous bear hug, Cole told me how delighted he was to finally be spending Christmas Day with me and, when she hugged me tightly, Jules reiterated it.

The next day, Amber's brother Brad and his long-term partner Tabs arrived and yesterday – Christmas Eve – Cole and Jules drove across to York to collect their youngest daughter Sophie from the train station.

Last night, we'd gathered in the lounge in front of the real fire, the dogs sprawled across the floor and all three cats draped over a chair arm or favoured human. I marvelled at how, despite awards, fame and an impressive circle of A-list friends, Amber's family were so down to earth. They were truly the warmest, friendliest and most genuine people. Between them, Cole and Jules seemed to know everyone in showbiz and kept us entertained with hilarious and heart-warming anecdotes. Cole had a gift for impersonations and it was like having the celebrities in the room with us.

'Good morning, Socks,' I said, scratching his soft belly. 'Happy Christmas!'

I opened my bedroom door and almost tripped over a Christmas gift bag. The top was sealed with sticky tape and there was a message on the gift tag.

Happy Christmas, Zara!
  Please wear these
  Santa xx

Unsealing the bag, I lifted out a pair of Christmas pyjamas. The long bottoms were navy and red tartan and the short-sleeved top was navy with a cartoon gonk on the front and my name on its hat. I smiled as I cuddled the PJs to my chest, appreciating how soft and snuggly they were. Presumably we all had a pair and would be posing for a group photo in them later. Such a Cole and Jules thing to do.

As I padded downstairs a little later in my new PJs, Socks trotting beside me, the smell of bacon drifted up to me and I could hear laughter.

'Zara! Happy Christmas!' Jules cried, rushing to hug me as soon as I entered the kitchen.

Brad and Tabs were with her and they hugged me too.

'Amber, Cole and Sophie are out with Barney but they're due back any minute now to get changed,' Jules said. 'They've been told the rules – no PJs, no breakfast.'

'Thanks so much for these,' I said. 'I love them.'

'Not from me,' she responded, grinning. 'They're a special delivery from Santa!'

And so began a magical, laughter-filled, incredible day. The others returned and were sent upstairs to put their PJs on and even Bear and Harley had matching gonk jackets with their names on which were completely adorable.

We breakfasted on bacon, fluffy pancakes and maple syrup and toasted to a wonderful Christmas with champagne flutes of Buck's Fizz before moving into the lounge for gifts. 'Santa' had been at it again with joke presents for everyone among the proper gifts.

This was what Christmases should be like – happy families playing silly jokes on each other. In my twenty-six years, I'd only come close to a Christmas like this once. I barely remembered Christmases with Dad. He'd moved out when I was eight and I'd never been invited to spend Christmas Day with him. He had Charlotte and his new family in London and his late-afternoon 'Merry Christmas' phone call had always felt like an afterthought.

My strongest memories were of Christmases with Owen. He'd always dreamed of having a family of his own but his ex-wife Esther had announced on their first wedding anniversary that she didn't see children in her future after all. Knowing him as well as I did, I could imagine he'd thrown everything into making their marriage work despite that bombshell, but it sounded like she'd checked out early on – had possibly never checked in – and had bided the time over the years until she found a suitable replacement, breaking his heart once more.

Even though Roman and I weren't little kids anymore – I was twelve and Roman was fifteen when Owen moved in – he dressed up in a Santa costume and went all out to make Christmas special for us all. He insisted on making Christmas dinner while Mum put her feet up with a glass of bubbly and he'd secretly made a giant cracker full of silly gifts, sweets and forfeits which kept us entertained for hours. For once, Roman and I actually got on. If only I could have bottled whatever magic Owen brought to our lives that day and had a different relationship with my brother.

A few years later, Roman was playing for Lincoln City FC, had moved out and only made a fleeting visit on Christmas Day to exchange gifts, not wanting to indulge in any food excess with so many sporting fixtures approaching. Over Easter that year, I'd secured a job washing pots in the village pub and had saved hard to buy Mum, Owen and Roman thoughtful gifts. Roman, already on a weekly wage which eclipsed my annual one, bought me nothing and didn't even have the decency to look embarrassed about it. I was in my bedroom at the front of the house with the window ajar when he left and Mum's voice drifted up to me, questioning him about the lack of gift.

'I'm eighteen now,' he'd said. 'Nineteen next week. Seemed a good age to stop with the presents.'

'But your sister's only fifteen and she saved for ages to get you that gift.'

'I never asked her to.'

'You're missing the point.'

'If it's that big a deal, I'll get her a gift voucher when I've got time.'

He never found the time and muggins here had still bought him a birthday and Christmas gift every year since. I suppose it was my futile attempt at a peace offering. Or perhaps it was my even more futile attempt at trying to prove to Mum that I wasn't the bad guy here. I never had been.

After several years of quiet Christmases, often on my own because Mum was working, spending this year with Amber's family was exactly what I needed to restore my bruised and battered Christmas spirit. I couldn't wait to see what happened when Barney's parents and grandma – equally warm and fun-loving – joined us for lunch. The noise level would be through the roof. Although I was also nervous about lunch because there'd be one more joining us – Barney's best friend Joel. The object of my affection.

* * *

With twelve of us for lunch, there wasn't enough room in Barney's oven to cater for everyone so his parents, Hadrian and Natasha, were expected at half twelve with the turkey. They were bringing Barney's grandma, Mary, who was cooking a joint of gammon. In the meantime, it was all hands on deck preparing the vegetables and setting the table. I had my back to the farmyard so hadn't noticed Joel's car pulling in. When he pushed open the door, placed a stack of gift bags on the floor and started dishing out hugs, my stomach did an enormous loop the loop and my heart thudded.

'Happy Christmas!' he said, kissing me on the cheek before embracing me.

He smelled divine – like pine trees – and I fought hard to keep my eyes open rather than close them and drink him in.

'And to you. Good to see you.' I released him much sooner than I wanted to.

Joel had been Barney's best mate since school. I'd liked him from the moment I first saw him in this very kitchen on the first day of filming for *Love on the Farm*. He'd been here that day for the friends and family soundbites but had stuck around for most of the filming, helping keep the farm running while Barney was otherwise occupied.

Joel and I had got along well and I'd thought the attraction was mutual, but I was still licking my wounds after it ended with Declan so I hadn't made a move or given out any signals that I was interested. Even if I hadn't been on the rebound, there was the impracticality of distance. At the time, I was expecting to leave the area, only returning to film the follow-up programme three months later. By the time Amber and Barney got together, it was too late. Joel had started seeing Marley, one of the contestants from *Love on the Farm*. I'd never have put them together and assumed it would fizzle out after a few dates but, six months on, they were still going strong.

Being Barney's best mate, Joel was a regular visitor to Bumblebee Barn and, every time I saw him, my feelings seemed to intensify. It was hard enough having him pop by at least once and sometimes up to three times a week, but it was even worse when Marley was with him. And why did she have to be so goddamn likeable? I hadn't been sure about her when Amber and I had interviewed her as a *Love on the Farm* contestant but when she'd had her day of filming, we'd both warmed to her. She was smart, funny and beautiful and it really shouldn't have been a surprise that Joel asked her out when it was clear that she wasn't attracted to Barney or vice versa.

'What can I help with?' Joel asked, looking round the hive of activity.

'I'm about to wrap the pigs in blankets if you fancy that,' I said, cursing myself for inviting him to huddle up close to me as we wrapped the bacon round the sausages.

I was all fingers and thumbs and kept dropping the cocktail sticks, feeling ridiculously giddy in Joel's presence, but I was aware that I was also giggling and flirty, fuelled by several glasses of Buck's Fizz, and it needed to stop. The only way to do that was to focus on Marley.

'What's Marley doing today?' I asked.

'Her grandparents have a huge house near Inverness and the whole family fly up there every Christmas.'

'Weren't you invited?'

'I was, but I can't miss out on seeing Imogen over Christmas.'

'Of course! Are you seeing her later today?'

He sighed and shook his head. 'Tilly's being awkward as usual. Refused to let me see her today. Says it's too disrupting doing the two-parent thing. I'm permitted to pick her up in the morning.'

'Aw, Joel, I'm so sorry.'

'It is what it is and I pick my battles carefully. In my mind, it's better for Imogen and for me that we have a full day together tomorrow – including a sleepover – than an hour or two today.'

'I like your thinking.'

Tilly was Joel's ex-fiancée and, even though she was the one who'd ended the relationship and had since moved on to find happiness with a new husband and more children, she seemed intent on making Joel's life a misery when it came to spending time with their six-year-old daughter. I'd never met Tilly but Joel brought Imogen to the farm when he could and that little girl was a ray of sunshine.

'I've got a present for Imogen,' I said. 'Make sure you don't leave without it.'

'That's good of you. Thank you.'

'It's a pleasure. I don't have many people to buy for and she's such a sweetie that I couldn't resist.'

Joel hugged me to his side and my heart raced once more. So much for changing the subject!

* * *

Before long, Barney's parents and grandma had arrived and we were soon sitting down to a loud and chaotic lunch. Somehow I ended up next to Joel. Fortunately, there was so much conversation and laughter that I had plenty to distract me from his close proximity although, occasionally, his leg pressed against mine or his hand brushed against me and my heart leapt.

When everyone had finished eating, our drinks were topped up and Barney tapped his knife against his glass, silencing the chatter as he stood up.

'I don't normally do a Christmas dinner speech but we've never had such a big gathering before so I feel it deserves one. Thank you for all being here today and making this the best Christmas ever. For me, this past year has been unbelievable. At the start of it, if somebody had told me that I'd find love on a reality TV show, I'd have thought they were mad but, thanks to my crazy sister, that's exactly what happened. Nobody will ever get to see that TV show, which is probably a very good thing, but you just have to look around this table to see what it brought to my life.' He looked round everyone smiling before settling his gaze on Amber, the look of adoration passing between them making my heart melt.

His smile faltered as he lifted up his drink. 'The only downside to this year has been that we lost my amazing granddad, Frank. So can we raise our glasses to absent friends.'

We followed his guidance, toasting to Frank, who'd sadly passed away during filming.

'Finally,' Barney said, his voice bright once more and the smile back on his face, 'I'd like to say a huge thank you to you all for helping create this delicious meal. Merry Christmas, everyone. I hope all your Christmas wishes come true.'

We toasted to that and I closed my eyes. I'd never made a Christmas wish before. What would mine be? Joel's hand brushed against my arm and I knew what it had to be. *I wish I could get over Joel. Or that he'd get over Marley and pick me instead!* My stomach lurched. No, that was an awful thing to say and I definitely didn't want that. *Kidding! I wish to only see Joel as a friend but, if I can be super cheeky and make two wishes, I'd love this to be the year where I finally find someone who's nothing like the wasters I've hooked up with in the past. Please!*

I crossed my fingers on both hands under the table. Was it too much to ask? I hoped not.

7

SNOWY

'Oof!' I opened my eyes with a start as my bedroom light flicked on and a child landed on me.

'Has Santa been?' Harrison demanded, bouncing up and down beside me.

I rubbed my eyes and squinted at my bedside clock. 'It's not even five o'clock yet. It's too early.'

'But I'm excited.'

'I understand that, but you'll be asleep by teatime if you get up now. Back to bed. Half six is the earliest, please.'

With a groan, he slithered off the bed and padded back to his own bedroom, switching the main light off on his way out.

I plumped my pillows and closed my eyes but, annoyingly, I was wide awake with an active mind. This would be the fourth Christmas Day without Eliza. One more week and it would be five years since she'd gone. How had so much time passed?

Eliza had loved Christmas. There were many who grumbled about it being 'too early' when Christmas cards and chocolates appeared in the shops from August but not Eliza. She'd rush home, eyes shining, announcing that she could smell and taste Christmas. She loved romance novels and couldn't wait until the festive reads were released in

September, devouring all the early titles and clamouring for more. The tree would go up in mid-November and she'd work her way through a phenomenal number of Christmas films. Christmas itself was a three-day event with activities planned for Christmas Eve through to Boxing Day and I have to admit her enthusiasm was infectious.

If I'd known that that Christmas was going to be her last with us... I shook my head. Grandpa often said that the avenue of regret was a dark place to travel, especially alone, and he was right.

I didn't remember much about our last Christmas together. I didn't remember much about that whole year or the one after, but I'd resolved to make every Christmas since extra special for Harrison. Okay, so we didn't put the tree up until the start of December and Boxing Day was permitted as a day to relax and unwind but, with Grandpa's help, I made sure Christmas Eve and Christmas Day were memorable. I'd organised a treasure hunt round the grounds yesterday morning with small gifts for each clue solved, Grandpa had baked and decorated gingerbread shapes with him during the afternoon, and we'd all watched *The Christmas Chronicles* in the evening.

Pulling on a hoodie, I tiptoed downstairs, made myself a herbal tea and sat looking out over the veranda. Staring into the darkness, I tried to remember previous Christmases with Eliza but so much of it was a blur and the scene I kept picturing was from much further back when I was Harrison's age. I'd woken up and rushed downstairs to see what Santa had brought. I'd placed a hessian sack on an armchair the night before and it was now stuffed full of gifts with more on the armchair and floor. I knew better than to open anything without everyone around, but I couldn't resist reaching out and stroking the shiny paper. My arm was grabbed roughly from behind and I was yanked backwards.

'Who gave you permission to open them?' Dad yelled.

'I wasn't! I was just—'

'I saw you touching one!'

He shoved me and I stumbled, landing in a heap beside the sofa. A voice in my head told me to apologise, but that's not what came out my mouth. 'I was stroking the paper.'

His eyes flashed angrily. 'You were being impatient. You were ignoring what you'd been told. This is why you'll never be an Olympian. You don't listen. You try to do it your way as though you know best. Well, you don't. I do. Get your damn kit on. Work before pleasure.'

I stared at him, shocked.

'See! Not listening! Gym kit on now.'

Legs shaking, I sprinted upstairs, pulled on my leotard and tracksuit as instructed and raced back down. It wasn't physically possible for me to have done it quicker but he was standing by the door, tapping his wrist with his finger, lip curled.

Grandpa found us in the gym an hour later. He and Grandma had assumed we were both still in bed and had come to tell me Santa had been.

'For God's sake, Iain, it's Christmas Day and the lad's ten,' Grandpa said. 'Can't you let him be a boy instead of your protégé for one day?'

'Can't you keep your nose out of things for one day?' Dad snapped back and stormed out. We didn't see him for the rest of the day and, although my grandparents tried their best to make Christmas Day a happy one, Dad had ruined it. He did that a lot.

* * *

Grandpa, always an early riser, joined me shortly after 6 a.m. and, when Harrison hadn't appeared by seven, having clearly needed the extra sleep, I lightly shook him awake.

'Santa's been,' I said, gently. 'Do you want to come down and see what he's brought?'

He leapt out of bed and raced downstairs, grinning. The tree lights were on, the fire was lit, there was Christmas music playing and a note from Santa wishing him a Merry Christmas and thanking him for the milk and mince pie and the carrots for the reindeer. Eliza would have been proud of me.

The next couple of hours flew past as gifts were opened and admired. One of them was a Lego Hedwig from the *Harry Potter* books so, after lunch, the three of us crowded round the dining table constructing the owl.

'Can we watch a film now?' Harrison asked after he'd proudly displayed his completed Hedwig in the centre of the mantelpiece.

'If you like. What do you want to watch?'

'What was Mum's favourite?'

'*The Muppet Christmas Carol*,' I said without hesitation. She'd had many favourites but that was the film she liked to watch first each year. 'We can watch that if you like.'

'Are you sure?' Grandpa whispered while Harrison searched for it on streaming.

'I think so. Even if I find it hard, it's right that he gets to see it.'

Grandpa made mugs of hot chocolate while I opened a box of Christmas chocolates and we all settled on the sofa to watch the film.

I hadn't expected so many memories of Eliza in the space of eighty-five minutes but I could vividly picture her expression at so many points in the film. I knew where she laughed, where she teared up and where her heart was captured. And even if I hadn't been able to recall those moments, they were right in front of me because Harrison reacted in the same way at the same parts.

As the closing credits rolled, a tide of emotion washed over me and I needed a moment on my own. Grandpa caught my eye and nodded his understanding before I even said a word.

'I'm going to head over to The Owlery,' I said, rising to my feet.

'Can I come?' Harrison asked.

'I was hoping you'd help me make the pastry for tomorrow's turkey pie,' Grandpa said. 'You can make some shapes with the leftovers.'

Harrison loved playing with pastry and didn't need any further convincing. I smiled gratefully at Grandpa.

It was late afternoon and already dark. The cold air rushed at my cheeks the moment I opened the door, pulling my beanie on. Solar lights illuminated my route down the track to The Roost – a large stone and wood barn which Grandpa told me had originally been used for lambing.

At the back of The Roost was The Owlery – a well-equipped hospital for sick and injured owls and other birds of prey. Inside, I administered medication and fed my four patients – a long-eared owl, a little owl, a barn owl and a kestrel. When I was done, I locked up and walked round to the front of The Roost and paused there for a moment, hoping to catch a glimpse of one of the barn owls in flight.

Although barn owls did hunt at night, they were mainly a crepuscular species – most active at dusk and dawn. They could also be seen out during the day, mainly during winter when food was more scarce or after prolonged rainfall as their feathers weren't waterproof, preventing them from flying in the rain. I stood near the entrance for fifteen minutes, but there was no sign of them this evening, so I returned to the lodge.

* * *

'A successful Christmas Day?' Grandpa asked after Harrison had settled down to sleep later that evening.

'I'd say so. Harrison enjoyed it.'

'Did you?'

I contemplated that for a moment. 'Mostly. I was determined to make the day about the three of us in the here and now instead of constantly thinking what would be different if Eliza had been here.' I rolled my eyes at him. 'Which worked really well until we watched *The Muppet Christmas Carol*. Seeing his reactions as he watched it for the first time...' I shook my head. 'It was like Eliza was right beside me.'

'That's why I asked if you were sure about it,' Grandpa said, his tone soft with understanding. 'I thought you might not make it to the end, but I was proud of you that you did.'

'Really?' I fixed my eyes on his, genuinely touched by that comment.

'Really. If you had a visit tonight from the Ghost of Christmas Present, I think he'd be impressed with how far you've come to this point, particularly across this past year. You might not feel like you've made much progress but I've noticed it. Keep going because you're doing great.'

His voice cracked and he blinked rapidly, as though pushing back tears. I had a lump in my throat and didn't trust myself to speak so we simply nodded at each other and Grandpa grabbed the remote control and switched the TV on.

His words meant so much to me because I often felt like I was stuck on a treadmill set on the steepest incline, battling to stay onboard. I certainly hadn't felt like I was moving forward but Grandpa never said anything he didn't mean.

Grandpa selected a documentary about sea otters and I managed to focus on maybe the first ten minutes before my mind drifted to what he'd said about the Ghost of Christmas Present. If I was visited by the three ghosts from *A Christmas Carol*, I knew which echoes from the past the Ghost of Christmas Past would present to me but, like Scrooge, it was the Ghost of Christmas Future I feared the most. What would he show? A reclusive man who'd cut off his friends, retreated from society and hidden from the world? But what if I was elderly and I was also cut off from my son? I'd made my world Harrison's world and he was happy in it right now, but was it what he'd have chosen if he knew what the alternatives were? And would he remain happy as he got older and started questioning the way we lived? He had the sort of bedroom most boys his age would dream of, he could roam freely through woodland and build dens and treehouses, he had 1:1 coaching in a state-of-the-art gym and he was excited and challenged through his home schooling. He had everything... except friends. So far, it hadn't been an issue. We went out for plenty of day trips where he interacted with other kids. Poppy and Dexter – the grandchildren from the neighbouring farm – played in the woods with him when they stayed with their grandparents during school holidays, but that wasn't the same as regular friends who he saw from week to week and one day, probably soon, he was going to challenge me on that.

I stood by home schooling but should I have bitten the bullet and got him into a gymnastics club before now? I couldn't put it off forever. If he was going to start on the competition circuit – something he was absolutely ready to do – he had to be enrolled with a club.

I picked up my phone and stared at it blankly for several minutes before composing a text.

TO ASHLEY
Got any spaces at your club? Need to get Harrison enrolled

I shook my head with a sigh and deleted it. What a woefully inadequate opener.

> **TO ASHLEY**
> Happy Christmas! Hope you and Kendra have had a great day and

I stopped typing once more. I hoped they were still happily married but what if they weren't? And what right did I have to blow in with a 'Happy Christmas!' out of the blue? *Try again.*

> **TO ASHLEY**
> I know it's been far too long and that's all on me but

But can I have a place at your club for my son please? I put the phone down with another sigh, drawing a concerned look from Grandpa. I gave him my *nothing-to-see-here* smile and muttered something about clickbait news headlines before venturing into the kitchen for a glass of water. What had I been thinking? Who in their right mind thought it was acceptable to send a text on Christmas Day to their best mate who they hadn't spoken to for over four and a half years asking if they could bump their son to the top of the waiting list?

8

ZARA

I leaned over the dressing table in my bedroom in Thorpe on the Hill and pushed open the window. It was early evening on New Year's Eve and close to freezing so the air rushing into the room instantly covered my bare arms in goose pimples. I didn't care about the cold as I listened intently and was soon rewarded with a gorgeous *Hoo!* call from an owl drifting through the darkness. It was followed by three speeded-up cries, making me smile contentedly and, for a brief moment, push aside the grimness of the evening ahead at Roman's party. The call of an owl was one of my favourite sounds and one of the few things I loved about coming home.

'Zara!' Mum shouted up the stairs. 'Have you got a window open up there?'

'I'm listening to the owls,' I called back.

'It's freezing! Get it closed and focus on getting ready. We're leaving soon.'

With a sigh, I pulled the window shut and closed my bedroom door too, cursing myself for not doing that first, although Mum would likely still have felt the draught. She had a nose for these things.

I gazed at my dress hanging from my wardrobe and wished for the umpteenth time that I'd been strong enough to put my foot down and refuse to come. But what Roman wants, Roman gets. It had been like that ever since Dad left and maybe I'd have understood it if he'd been the younger sibling and had struggled with the split, but he was older than me by over three years and both of us had come through the divorce relatively unscathed. Dad had, after all, been absent for most of our lives, frequently working away in London.

I pulled the dress on and sank down onto my bed with a weary sigh. I'd had messages from various friends across the afternoon, all saying how much they'd miss me tonight and hoping I had a good time. Not much chance of that.

'It'll be all right,' I muttered under my breath. 'It's just one night. Duty done. Mum happy. Owen not caught in the middle.'

I fastened the straps on my sandals then stood up to look in the full-length mirror on my wardrobe, tweaking a few tresses of my dark brown hair. I'd had the same style for years – shoulder-length choppy layers with a full fringe – but I'd let it grow this year and was enjoying the extra length. It had delighted Mum, who'd always proclaimed that I looked better with long hair – softened my cheekbones, apparently – and she'd gone a bit over the top with the hairstyling gifts for Christmas, getting me some expensive straighteners and some scary-looking spinning contraption which sucked your hair in and somehow curled it. I couldn't see me ever using that – visions of getting it hideously tangled and never being able to release my hair – but I'd used the straighteners this evening and was blown away by the results. I usually wore my hair full and messy and barely recognised myself with smooth, glossy locks. If it wasn't for the trademark black eyeliner I always wore, I'd swear I was looking at a stranger.

I picked up my phone and was about to put it in my clutch bag when I spotted a WhatsApp notification.

> **FROM AMBER**
> Hope Roman isn't too much of an arse tonight.
> Happy New Year!

She'd added the blowing a kiss emoji and several celebratory themed ones.

> TO AMBER
> Unless Santa delivered a personality transplant for Christmas, I can guarantee he will be! Heading out soon. Deep breath! Happy New Year to you too! x

There was a gentle knock on the door, which I guessed would be Owen, sent by Mum to chivvy me along.

'Come in!' I called.

Owen poked his head round the door, an apologetic expression on his face. 'Sorry, but your mum's keen to get away early in case the traffic's bad. I don't suppose you're nearly ready?'

'Already working on Mum Time,' I said, rolling my eyes at him. 'Tell her I'll be down in two minutes.'

Mum Time meant taking the time Mum had told everyone to be ready to leave the house, then chopping fifteen minutes off it because she always had an eleventh-hour fear of being late. I dread to think how many hours of my life I'd wasted sitting in car parks, scrolling aimlessly on my phone because we were far too early.

'I knew I could rely on you.' Owen smiled at me warmly. 'You look lovely.'

I gave him a twirl so he could see the back too.

He shook his head, tears in his eyes. 'I know I've said this before, but I genuinely don't know where the years have gone. It seems like only yesterday that you were my little Tigger.'

'I'm still your little Tigger,' I said, my voice catching in my throat. 'And I still love bear hugs.'

Owen laughed as he hugged me, trying not to rumple my dress.

'I'll see you downstairs shortly, Tigger.'

My beautiful mask sparkled at me from the dressing table and, taking care not to mess up my hair, I slipped it over my head. I draped my cloak round my shoulders and lifted up the hood.

'I love this outfit,' I muttered, gazing at myself in the mirror. Swishing the cloak, a streak of rebellion ran through me and I smiled. 'And I'm going to wear it tonight. All of it.'

I clicked a photo and sent it to Amber.

TO AMBER
Wrong place, right costume. Should I?

FROM AMBER
Hell yeah! DO IT!!!!!!

As soon as I opened my bedroom door, Mum's voice drifted up to me from the lounge.

'I thought you said she was ready, Owen! We're going to be late!'

'We're *not* going to be late,' he reassured her.

'We are. What sort of impression does that make?'

The high pitch of her voice told me she was in full-on anxiety mode. She never used to be this bad and I had to assume that the pressure of her job had spilled over into everyday life. Time off was typically spent at football matches, cheering on my brother but, with him not playing at the moment, I'd have thought she'd have more time and be less stressed. Apparently not.

'I'm ready!' I called jovially, setting off down the stairs.

'At last!' she said, exiting the lounge, already wearing her best coat.

Without pausing to look at me, she opened the door and stepped out onto the drive. Owen turned to me, his expression sorrowful, and I simply shrugged. I was used to it by now and the way forward was to be quiet and compliant. Once we were close to the hotel and assured of being early, she'd relax and conversation would be possible.

'I love the mask,' Owen said as we walked out to his car. 'Very mysterious.'

Mum turned round, her eyes on stalks when she saw me. 'Why are you wearing that?' she snapped.

'Because it's the outfit I bought for this evening,' I said, keeping my voice calm and steady.

'Why?'

'Because I was meant to be going to a masked ball.'

We bundled into Owen's car and I hoped that was the end of the conversation but, as soon as he pulled off the drive, Mum resumed it.

'This isn't a masked ball so take the mask off,' she said without turning round in her seat.

I didn't respond.

'Take it off now,' she said, her tone steely.

'I'd rather keep it on, if you don't mind.'

'I *do* mind. Ditch the mask. That's an order, not a request.'

'Oh, come on, Jenna,' Owen said, his voice light and breezy. 'She's twenty-six. She's old enough to decide on her own wardrobe.'

'Great! So you're on her side as usual.'

'It's not about sides. Zara had plans – exciting plans – with her friends and she agreed to change them for Roman. It's not our place to start dictating how she dresses and, personally, I think she looks smashing.'

'You would, wouldn't you?'

Tears burned at the back of my eyes and I closed them tightly, refusing to cry. Mum and Owen at loggerheads over me was the last thing I wanted. I'd agreed to come to avoid this exact scenario but had still managed to cause problems.

'It's okay, Owen. I'll take it off.'

I lowered my hood and reluctantly removed my mask. Owen caught my eye in the rear-view mirror and I gave him a weak smile.

'And the cloak,' Mum added, still not looking at me.

'No. It's too cold without it.'

She didn't respond to that.

I gazed out of the car, counting how many Christmas trees I could see in the windows as we passed through the village. I remembered doing that with Roman when we were little, before my parents divorced. Before the world revolved purely around Roman and I slipped through the net.

The journey into the city was silent and I wondered whether Mum regretted pushing me into coming. We were a few traffic light junctions away from the hotel when she twisted round in her seat.

'I trust you'll be nice to your brother tonight.' Her tone was so steely that she might as well have started the sentence with *I demand* rather than *I trust* – another order rather than a request.

'I'm always nice to him. He's the one who starts it with the snide comments about—'

'Enough!' she cried, the volume of that one word clearly startling Owen as much as it did me because he swerved the car.

'It's his thirtieth birthday,' she said, her voice much softer, 'and he's had a tough year with Amy leaving him like that.'

'That was in March and what do you expect? Poor girl stuck with him for over a decade while he repeatedly cheated on her. You surely can't blame her for walking away.'

'Perhaps not, but you have to understand it's difficult for him being so famous. He has women throwing themselves at him.'

'Yes, but here's an idea. He could say *no thank you, I've got a girlfriend* and keep it in his trousers.'

'Don't be so crude!'

It was the truth, but I wasn't going to try to defend myself. In Mum's eyes, Golden Boy could do no wrong. Even though Dad having an affair had caused the breakdown of her own marriage, Mum refused to put Roman in the same camp. The first time she gave her often-repeated excuse for Roman's behaviour – *it's not adultery if you're not married* – we had a huge row, but she refused to accept my counter-argument of *yes, but it's still infidelity and the behaviour is the same*.

I'd really liked Amy and was sorry that they'd split up. She'd made spending time with my brother tolerable, but ending her twelve-year relationship with Roman had absolutely been the best thing for her. I was amazed that she'd put up with his philandering for as long as she had, but that's easy to say when you're not the one in the relationship.

'Is he really still pining over Amy?' I asked, wondering if my brother had finally realised what he'd had with her now that he'd lost her. 'It's been nine months.'

'He's still hurting,' Mum said, snippily.

'That's not strictly true, is it, Jenna?' Owen said, his tone teasing. 'He's happy with Portia and there were at least two more before her.'

Mum sighed. 'Okay, so he's moved on with Portia now, but it doesn't mean he wasn't hurt. He's a sensitive young soul.'

Roman was a lot of things but sensitive wasn't one of them.

'How many are invited tonight?' I asked, feeling the need for a subject change.

'Three hundred, I think.'

I emitted a low whistle. Wouldn't like to see the bar bill for that.

* * *

We'd been there half an hour when I spotted Roman across the other side of the dance floor. I knew from Mum that he'd had one of the trouser legs of his fancy designer tux cut off and taken up at the knee so he could still wear it with his plaster cast.

Best get this over with. I knew that Mum wouldn't fully relax until she'd seen me engaging in a pleasant conversation with my brother. I wasn't much of a drinker and alcohol loosened my tongue quickly. I'd therefore restricted myself to half a glass of welcome champagne so far to make sure I didn't say something sarcastic.

Roman was laughing with a couple of his friends as I approached, but his smile slipped when he spotted me. He said something to them which was clearly derogatory because they both turned round and looked at me then patted him on the shoulder as they walked away. Nice.

'Happy birthday, Roman,' I said brightly, giving him a kiss on each cheek.

'Zara! I didn't think you were coming.' The tone translated as *I hoped you weren't coming*. That made two of us!

I matched his fake smile with one of my own. 'I RSVPd to say I was.'

He shrugged. 'Portia was keeping track. So...' Roman tailed off, evidently having no idea what to say next.

'Good Christmas?' I asked.

'Yeah. You?'

'Good, thanks.'

Silence.

I glanced at his crutches. 'How's the leg?'

'I won't know until the cast comes off.'

'Did it hurt?'

Okay, so it was a stupid question, but it didn't warrant a loud tut and a roll of the eyes.

'I'll take that as a yes,' I said, wishing I could walk away from this awkward conversation but knowing I couldn't because Mum was watching us from across the room.

'So…' I said again, immediately tailing off when I had no words to accompany the sentence-starter.

'Still directing films?' Roman asked.

How many times? Smile. Be polite.

'No, not directing films because that's not my job. It's TV production and I'm the producer's assistant.'

But he wasn't listening, his eyes scanning the room. He smiled genuinely this time, flashing a Hollywood-style set of white teeth, and waved someone over.

'You need to meet Portia,' he said.

A heavily made-up young woman in a dress cut down to the navel staggered over to us on impossibly high heels. I couldn't take my eyes off her dress and how the limited material was managing to contain her sizeable breasts. One sudden movement and it would be game over.

'Hey, babe,' she gushed, slipping her arm round Roman's waist. 'I was missing you.'

She kissed him full-on and I turned away, cringing, as I spotted tongues. Ew! No need! I was about to make myself scarce when they broke apart, laughing.

'Sorry,' Roman said, smiling sheepishly at me. 'I can't get enough of this girl. This is Portia. Babe, this is my sister, Zara.'

Portia's eyes widened – no mean feat with all those layers of lashes. 'Shut up! The film director?' She gripped my forearm. 'I've always wanted to be an actor.'

'That's great,' I said, smiling back, 'but I'm not a film director. I'm the producer's assistant on *Countryside Calendar*.'

She removed her hand and curled up her lip. 'Urgh! That boring programme about farming?'

Keep smiling! 'Our seven million regular viewers would probably disagree with the *boring* tag.'

An apology would have been nice, but it wasn't forthcoming.

'What does a producer's assistant do?' she asked.

'Anything that's needed. I compile the production schedules, keep track of the budget, arrange filming permits—'

'So you're an administrator?' she said.

'That's right.'

'Then why did you say you're the producer's assistant?'

'Because I *am* the producer's assistant. That's my job title.'

'Isn't that like a binman saying they're a waste management and disposal technician?' She patted Roman on his chest and the pair of them laughed together.

It pained me to keep smiling, but Mum was watching us like a hawk. I was determined to make an effort and not come out of this like the bad guy as usual, especially after that spat in the car. A few more minutes wouldn't kill me and then my duty would be done for the evening. I could order a large drink and find myself a quiet corner in which to hide.

'What do you do, Portia?' I asked, trying to sound interested. She looked a lot younger than my brother – late teens or very early twenties – so I couldn't imagine she was high up the ladder with whatever career choice she'd made.

'I'm between jobs at the moment. It's been so full-on organising this party for Roman.'

'Oh! I thought Mum said you'd used a party planner.' It just slipped out and the stony look on Portia's face told me I'd said the wrong thing.

'I still needed to liaise with her,' she snapped, her eyes flashing. 'Party planners don't just magic a concept out of thin air.'

I wasn't aware that there was a concept. The invitations had said black tie but that was a dress code, not a concept. Unless she meant the giant balloon display with the number thirty and the outgoing and incoming years, which were surely a given for a thirtieth birthday falling on New Year's Eve.

Roman and Portia were both staring at me, evidently expecting me to say something.

'It's a great party,' I gushed. 'You've clearly got a talent for these things.'

Portia gave me a withering look. 'I see what you mean about her, babe.' She stroked Roman's arm before shooting me another dirty look and teetering off across the dance floor.

'What did you go and do that for?' Roman hissed at me.

'Do what?'

'Belittle her.'

'I didn't! I complimented her on a job well done.'

'Sarcastically.'

I couldn't defend myself there. I had meant it sarcastically, but I'd never have said a word if she hadn't taken the mickey out of me for being an administrator. As if there was anything wrong with that. I loved what I did.

'What did she mean by *I see what you mean about her*?' I asked.

'This! Snide remarks, sarcasm, making it all about you as usual.'

'All about me? It's *never* about me!'

'It's *always* about you.'

I planted my hands on my hips and glared at him. 'Name a time when it's been about me, when *I've* been put first, when *I've* got what I wanted.'

'All the time.'

'When? Seriously, Roman, when has it *ever* been about me? Name one occasion.'

He glared back at me. 'I can't think of a specific one right now.'

'Because there aren't any. You can't accuse me of something without evidence to back it up.'

'So you're the police now, are you?'

'All I'm asking for is one occasion where it's been about me rather than you.'

He clenched his fists and fixed me with a hard stare before lowering his voice. 'I'm *not* doing this with you. Not tonight.'

'Fine, but you started it.'

'*You* did.'

'I didn't! I—' I sighed and shook my head, adding in a lighter tone, 'Can I buy you a birthday drink?'

He scowled at me. 'It's a free bar.'

'I know that. It was meant to be a peace offering.'

'You know what, Zara? I don't want anything from you. I don't even know why you're here.'

I reeled back at the contempt in his tone. 'Because you invited me. You wrote me that sticky note.'

'Only because Mum made me.' He looked me up and down, lip curled. 'I didn't want you here. I never do.'

With that parting shot, delivered with such venom, he stormed off across the dance floor towards Portia.

The chill in his tone made me shiver. I looked around me and, despite so many people in the room, I felt suddenly alone and vulnerable in an unfamiliar place, surrounded by strangers.

The bar was to the right of me and the exit to the left. Should I get that drink and hide or should I do a runner? Mum was standing on the other side of the dance floor, not too far from where Roman was hugging Portia, and the look she gave me made me shiver once more. She couldn't have overheard my exchange with Roman but she'd have been able to read the body language and, from the shake of the head before she turned away from me, she clearly believed I was the one at fault. I wasn't proud of myself for the exchange but the difference between Roman and me was that I never made it personal. I could easily have thrown out *I'm only here because Mum made me come*, but that wasn't who I was. I questioned, I teased and I was prone to the occasional sarcastic remark, but I never said or did anything that would hurt.

Still undecided as to what to do next, my stomach did a backflip when I spotted who'd just entered the room – my ex, Declan. What the hell was *he* doing here? My stomach did another backflip when Candi joined him – the one with whom he'd been two-timing me – recognisable from the photos I'd seen of them together on social media after I was unceremoniously dumped.

Portia let out a squeal and the two women tottered over to each other, dishing out air kisses. They were obviously friends, which explained how Declan had got an invite. This evening appeared to be the gift that was going to keep on giving and I couldn't face it. I might not have any residual feelings for Declan but that didn't mean I wanted to spend the evening in his company. Time to go.

I was on my way to the cloakroom when someone grabbed my arm and I released a surprised yelp.

'Don't be so dramatic,' Mum hissed. 'I'm barely touching you.'

It didn't feel like 'barely' as she steered me towards a pair of armchairs in a dark corner and shoved me down onto one.

'What the hell was that all about?' she demanded.

At five foot three, I wasn't particularly tall and Mum was only one inch taller than me but, my goodness, did it feel like she was six foot as she towered over me, hands on hips?

'What was what?' I asked in a small voice.

'You know exactly what I mean. It's his thirtieth birthday, for crying out loud. Would it kill you to be civil to your brother for one night?'

I wanted to stand up so I was on her level but she was so close that, if I tried, I'd headbutt her. I straightened up instead and pushed my shoulders back.

'I *was* civil to him, but it wasn't reciprocated by Golden Boy or his girlfriend. They laughed at my job.'

'Oh, grow up, Zara! You're not in primary school anymore. Stop with all the petty squabbling and name-calling.'

'Are you going to tell him that too?' I stared at her defiantly. 'No, of course not because, as usual, it's all my fault and he can do no wrong.'

'He's going through a rough time and he needs our empathy. Or did you not notice the crutches?'

'The crutches are recent. The bad attitude isn't and I'm sick of him treating me like crap.'

'Then maybe you shouldn't be here.'

'Exactly what I've been saying all along but you *made* me come.'

'Made you? How? Did I threaten you? Did I hold a gun to your head?'

'Mum! You said...' I stopped abruptly, aware of guests staring in our direction. Mum had evidently noticed too as she backed away a few paces, which meant I finally had the space to rise.

'I think we'll all have a much better evening if I'm not here,' I said, my voice low so nobody could overhear. 'Happy New Year, Mum!'

I strode towards the cloakroom, head held high, hoping she couldn't see my hands shaking as I fumbled with the clasp on my bag to retrieve my ticket. Feeling sick, I couldn't face turning round while I waited for my cloak. She'd accused Owen of taking my side but he only ever stepped in as the voice of reason when she'd gone too far. The only one who took sides was Mum and it was always Golden Boy's. He'd never done anything wrong in her eyes and I was always unfairly labelled as the troublemaker. It was a constant source of friction between Mum and me and I was exhausted by it.

Fastening my cloak round my neck, I released a shaky sigh. I wished I hadn't said *Happy New Year* in such a sarcastic tone, but I hadn't been able to help myself. How could she possibly see my presence here tonight as anything other than her making me come?

The lobby doors swished open and I stepped out into the cold night air. A couple had just exited a taxi and the driver switched his light on to hire. I ran down the steps to his open window.

'Thorpe on the Hill?' I asked, relief flowing through me when he told me to get in.

'Zara!'

Owen was running down the steps as I pulled on my seatbelt.

'Can you give me one minute?' I asked the driver, not wanting to snub my stepdad.

'Where are you going?' Owen asked as I wound the window down.

'Home.'

'No! Please stay.'

'I can't. Mum and I have had a massive argument and Roman made it clear I wasn't welcome, so I'm not feeling in much of a party mood right now.'

'Then let me drive you home.'

'And cause even more problems between you and Mum? I'm fine with the taxi. I'll see you later.'

'Promise you'll still be there when we get back.'

The minute he said that, I knew I wouldn't be.

'I'll speak to you soon. Happy New Year, Owen.' I gave him a weak smile, wound the window up and instructed the taxi driver to drive.

I hadn't been planning to leave but, other than Owen, what reason was there to stay? I couldn't face going into a New Year in a hostile environment. I'd only had half a drink so I could pack my bag, drive back to Yorkshire and make it to Hedgehog Hollow in time to see the New Year in with people who wanted me there. My stomach lurched. Damn! My mask was still on the back seat of Owen's car. But a masked ball without a mask was better than a non-masked ball where I'd had to wear a virtual happy-to-be-here mask.

9

ZARA

As soon as the taxi driver dropped me back in Thorpe on the Hill, I raced upstairs to start packing. This evening could still be salvaged. I was in the bathroom when I heard keys turning in the front door and froze, my pulse racing. If that was Mum – not that I could imagine her abandoning Golden Boy's party – I really wasn't in the mood for another ear-bashing.

'Zara?' Owen called. 'It's only me.'

I cautiously stepped out onto the landing. 'Are you alone?'

'Yes.'

He took the stairs two at a time and stopped at the top, his expression sorrowful as he took in my attire of jeans and T-shirt and the washbag in my hands.

'Please don't leave.'

'It's for the best. I don't think I've ever seen Mum so angry with me.'

'Did you tell her what happened with Roman?'

'I tried to, but you know she never listens. In her eyes, *he* can do no wrong.'

I crossed the landing to my bedroom and packed the washbag in my travel bag. Owen hovered in the doorway.

'I'll make her listen. I'll tell her it wasn't your fault.'

'Thanks, but I've already caused enough friction between you tonight. I'll suck it up as usual.'

'No, you won't. I was at the bar. I caught the full conversation including what he said about your mum forcing him to invite you. That was bang out of order.'

I zipped my bag closed, sighing. 'It doesn't matter, Owen. Even if you were to relay the conversation word for word, I'd still be in the wrong. She'll believe what she wants to believe and it's easier to accept that than fight it.'

I heaved the bag off the bed.

'I understand you escaping the party, but are you sure about leaving without resolving things with your mum?'

'You didn't see her earlier. It was bad. Really bad. So, believe me, it's better for all of us that I go. I've spent years doing everything Mum wants just to keep the peace and maintain some sort of relationship with her. Ditching my plans tonight was yet another example and, seeing as it's gone horribly wrong, I'm going to do what I want to do for once. Long overdue, don't you think?'

He nodded slowly. 'I'll miss you.'

'I'll miss you too. And you know I hate goodbyes so give me a hug and get yourself back to that party before you're in trouble too.'

Owen wrapped his arms round me and held me tightly. I hoped Mum wouldn't be annoyed with him for chasing after me. If she even noticed he was missing. A massive football fan, she loved Roman's world and everyone in it and they loved her back. It just wasn't a world I belonged to and never had.

I waved Owen off and returned to my bedroom feeling weary. Moments later, I heard a key in the door again and the sound of someone running up the stairs.

'You might need this,' Owen said, handing me my mask.

'You absolute star. Thank you.'

Another hug and he was gone.

I loaded my dress, cloak and mask onto a strong hanger and carefully packed them inside a carrier which I hooked over the door. I reached for my bag but paused to look around my room at the lilac walls and the peeling 'Groovy Chick' decals. I'd been seven when we'd had a massive family decorating session. I remembered laughing as Roman and I raced each other to get the most paint roller coverage while Mum and Dad did the cutting in. We sang and danced and flicked paint at each other – a perfect snapshot of a happy family life. Only it clearly hadn't been happy because, a few months later, Dad moved out and, not long after that, my relationship with Roman started on its downward trajectory.

I unfurled the edge of a large decal in which the blonde-haired cartoon character was sitting cross-legged. Nearly twenty years had passed and my room had remained the same. During my teens, I'd asked several times if we could redecorate and had always been fobbed off – *too much hassle, too busy*. I'd offered to do it myself in my early twenties but the excuse had been – *you'll move out eventually, so what's the point?*

I crossed the landing to the much larger bedroom which had been Roman's. I flicked the light switch on and gasped. It had been decorated yet again. There was a bright red feature wall and three white ones – the colours for Lincoln City FC – although the paint was barely visible past the memorabilia. Highly polished trophies vied for shelf space and shiny medals dangled from hooks. Framed newspaper clippings and photographs boasted some of the key moments in my brother's career to date, and several white ring binders in red magazine racks held copious other clippings and copies of programmes. Mum was a one-woman archivist when it came to my brother's career.

Two large frames containing signed football shirts dominated one of the white walls above a large sofa bed – one from Roman's final year in the youth team and another from five years ago when the first team were promoted from League Two to League One.

My throat tightened as I took it all in. Roman had moved out years ago and his bedroom was an immaculate, frequently redecorated shrine to his greatness. Officially, this was still my home, yet my bedroom was tired and neglected. Each room highlighted the very different ways Mum treated us.

I switched off the light, sighing heavily as I closed the door, and returned to my bedroom. On the far wall was a solitary pine shelf where a handful of small trophies and medals from my limited sporting achievements languished in a bed of dust. I pictured my room at Bumblebee Barn, decorated exactly to my taste. Amber's words about being welcome there if the time came to officially move out of my childhood home echoed round my mind.

'It's time,' I whispered.

My belongings needed a good sort out but, if I did that, I'd still be here way past midnight so I quickly stuffed everything into bin bags and a couple of cardboard boxes I found in the garage, determined I'd make it to the masked ball for at least the last half an hour.

I loaded my bedding and towels into the washing machine and set it away before scribbling a letter which I'd been composing in my head the whole time I'd packed.

Dear Mum

Happy New Year! I hope you were able to celebrate in style, despite how the evening started.

I know you never believe me when I say it wasn't me but I wouldn't keep saying it if it wasn't true. I didn't deserve your reaction earlier.

I know you want Roman and me to have a relationship but it's time we all accepted it's not going to happen and that's okay. Lots of siblings don't get on. Every time I see him, it's bad, but tonight was off the scale horrendous and I'm not willing to put any of us through that again.

This has to be the end of the line for Roman and me which, after what he told me tonight about never wanting me there, is going to be as much of a relief for him as it is for me. My only regret is the damage it's done to you and me. I really hope the two of us can find a way back to a positive relationship.

Because of how angry you were with me, the next move has to be yours. To be clear, I'm not asking you to choose between Roman and me. You can have us both in your life – just not at the same time!

I've cleared my room to give you space to think. You know where I am when you're ready to talk... and to listen. I hope you don't leave it too long.

Zara x

I read the letter several times over, wondering how Mum would react to it. Should I scrap it in favour of a short and sweet note wishing her a Happy New Year and saying we'd speak soon? But where would that get me? Tonight had genuinely been one of the worst nights of my life and I wasn't going to brush it under the carpet. Every time I tried to talk to her about the issues with Roman, her defences rose and she shut me down. The written word was all I had left and was what I'd written really that bad? Yanking out my drawers and tipping the contents into bin bags had defused the anger, leaving me with calm and considered statements. I'd leave it and face the consequences.

Back outside, I placed my bags in the passenger side footwell and draped my dress carrier over the seat before returning to lock the front door. I backed away and took one last look at the house I'd grown up in. Would I be welcome here again? I hoped so, but that was up to Mum. I couldn't keep putting myself through this.

Leaving the village boundary and approaching the A46, my stomach churned and my eyes glazed with tears. I jabbed the hazard lights on and tightly gripped the steering wheel, fighting the urge to turn around.

'You can do this!' I muttered. 'You have to.'

I felt really shaky and realised I'd barely eaten all day. Among my Christmas gifts in the boot was a selection box so I jumped out, ripped open the cardboard and grabbed the first chocolate bar I came to, feeling much better once I'd eaten it.

Setting off once more, I turned my music up loud, not wanting the headspace to replay any part of tonight. I only turned it down after I'd crossed the Humber Bridge and was on the home stretch.

I wondered what Mum would do with my bedroom. Redecorate and keep it as a spare bedroom so I had somewhere to stay – assuming she wanted to make peace and I was still welcome there? Let Owen have it? Or turn it into an overspill shrine to my brother? One thing for certain was it wouldn't turn into a shrine to me as I'd never been given my opportunity to shine. I'd done nothing to make Mum proud. A thought struck me. Roman thought I was a film director. Was that his lack of interest in me, meaning he only half-listened to conversations, or was Mum telling people fibs about my job? *My son's a professional footballer and my daugh-*

ter's a film director. She'd often asked me about my plans to move up the career ladder and I'd brushed it off with a laugh, saying I loved what I did and didn't have any plans to progress. Was my lack of ambition a disappointment to her? Was I a disappointment? I couldn't shake that thought as I continued towards Hedgehog Hollow.

10

ZARA

It was 11.18 p.m. as I pulled into the farmyard and found a space among the many vehicles parked there. There was nobody about so I stood in the gap between my car and the next one, whipped off my T-shirt and pulled on my dress. I wiggled my jeans down to my ankles and plonked myself down on the driver's seat to remove them completely and fasten my sandals. Finally, I ran a brush through my hair, applied a slick of lip gloss and pulled my mask into place. *Four hours late but better late than never.*

Wildflower Byre was a short walk past the rescue centre and holiday cottages and my cloak fanned out around me as I followed the lit path down. I could hear peals of laughter over the bassline of the music. *Forget about what happened earlier this evening. Focus on now.*

There were a few people milling around outside, but nobody I recognised. As soon as I stepped into Wildflower Byre, my spirits rose. The place looked incredible with black, gold and royal blue balloons and garlands. The tables had elaborate gold candelabras, draped with beads and a mask with feathers protruding from the middle. At one side of the room was a giant gold photo frame decorated with masks, flowers and feathers which guests could pose inside for photos. I wished I had time to fully drink it in, but my priority was to find my friends. I craned my neck but, even in heels, I wasn't tall enough to spot them through the throng on the dancefloor. Thankfully Amber spotted me.

'Zara! What are you doing here?' she squealed, rushing up to me, arms outstretched.

'You know how bad I thought it would be? Multiply that by twenty.'

'Oh no! I'm so sorry.'

'Did you mean what you said about me properly moving in?'

'Of course.'

'Good, because I've emptied my room and my car is jammed.'

'You're in the right place,' she assured me, drawing me into another hug. 'We're all here for you.'

'You look amazing,' I said when we pulled apart.

'I'm a bit dishevelled now. Been dancing all night. You look amazing too. I'm so glad you got to wear...' She broke off with a squeal. 'We've been waiting for the DJ to play this all night. Come on!'

I laughed as I recognised the eighties tune 'Stand and Deliver' by Adam and the Ants, which was all about a highwayman. Amber grabbed my hand and pulled me through the crowd to where Barney was dancing with Fizz, her girlfriend Phoebe and Phoebe's adopted daughter, twelve-year-old Darcie. My heart began racing. Joel. Of course he'd be with them.

While Barney and Amber re-enacted a highwayman hold-up, each of the group gave me a welcome hug and we exchanged compliments about costumes. Fizz was dressed as the Snow Queen, Phoebe was a butterfly, and Darcie was a fairy. Their outfits were stunning, but I had to laugh at Joel's.

'Batman?' I asked. Not a contemporary contoured version but the original sixties TV-show variation.

He swished his cape. 'It was all I could borrow at the eleventh hour.'

I was sure Amber had told me that Marley had organised *Alice in Wonderland*-themed costumes for them but there'd evidently been a change of plan. Was Marley even here?

When the track ended, I went in search of a drink and Joel caught up with me at the bar.

'Marley not here tonight?' I asked him.

'She's at her auntie's annual shindig. She was meant to be coming here, but I could tell her heart wasn't in it, so I suggested we do our own thing. By that time it was too late and too far to drive for my costume, so I put out a plea on the socials and one of my brother's mates offered me this.' He swept his hands down the tight grey top. 'Beggars can't be choosers and I've had enough beers not to care.'

To be fair to him, he wore it well, although I really shouldn't be looking, especially as I could feel a wave of heat sweeping through my body.

Fizz appeared and pulled us both back onto the dance floor and, before I knew it, there was a countdown to midnight and celebratory cheers all round. Joel hugged me and kissed me on the cheek, making my heart pound. *Stop it! He's with Marley.*

I needed some air and slipped outside and into a nearby deserted field. Over the music, I could hear the bangs of distant fireworks and the occasional explosion of colour in the sky.

Remember your Christmas wish? Make that your New Year's resolution too! Bumblebee Barn is your official home now and Joel Grainger is a regular visitor and Barney's best friend. Completely and utterly off limits. Get over him. Fast!

My cloak didn't provide much protection from the cold and I was soon shivering, but I felt sufficiently in control of my feelings to venture back into Wildflower Byre and continue celebrating. My head was in charge and continuing on the soft drinks until the party wound up at 1 a.m. would ensure it stayed that way.

'Where did you vanish to?' Amber asked as I joined her at the bar but, before I had a chance to make up an excuse, Samantha and Fizz appeared and we were swept onto the dance floor.

'Final song of the night,' the DJ announced a little later, 'and we're going to slow it down.'

He played a recent ballad. All around me, guests were coupling up and I had that uncomfortable moment of acknowledgement that I didn't have anyone. I was about to scuttle off the dance floor when Joel caught my eye and put his hand out.

'Batman and the mysterious lady?' he asked, laughing.

A slow dance with Joel? No! But if I refused, would Amber notice and guess the reason? She knew I'd been attracted to him when I first met him and, when he started seeing Marley, she'd asked if I was okay with that. I'd assured her it had been an initial stab of attraction and nothing more, but she might see through that lie if I said no to Joel. She might equally see through it if I said yes.

'Holy slow dance, Batman!' I said, taking his hand. But, thankfully, it turned out to be a fast dance as Joel twirled me round the floor in a kind of polka which had us in peals of laughter. No chance of anyone guessing that I saw him as anything more than a friend.

Barney was the designated driver but, as I had my car here too and had been on the soft drinks, he suggested I take Amber back to Bumblebee Barn while he took Joel home.

'I'm glad you could make it tonight,' Amber said as we set off down the farm track after I'd transferred some of my bags into Barney's car to make room. 'But I'm sorry for whatever happened at your brother's do.'

'I'll tell you all about it in the morning. I'm feeling all relaxed and happy now and I don't want to kill that buzz.'

I hadn't had high hopes for New Year's Eve and it had been far worse than anticipated but, while the end to last year had been sour, the start to this one had been sweet. Whatever happened next with Mum, I had much to look forward to this year. We had some great locations lined up for *Countryside Calendar* and I was really excited about filming *The Wildlife Rescuers*. I had a lovely group of friends, and I'd found somewhere I wanted to set down roots. I'd been a nomad for a long time, on the road with work and never feeling like Lincoln was truly my home. The Yorkshire Wolds felt like home. This was the year of focusing on me in which I stopped tying myself into knots trying to please Mum.

Back in my bedroom at Bumblebee Barn, I sank onto the bed and opened my bag, my stomach churning as I removed my phone. I hadn't looked at it since leaving home, not wanting the ugliness of the first party to creep into the second one. Would Mum have left a message or even tried to call? I cautiously turned it over. No missed calls. No messages from Mum either, but there was one from Owen.

FROM OWEN

Hope you made it back to Yorkshire in plenty of time for a great evening with your friends. It was a shock to discover you'd properly moved out, but I do understand why. I suspect you'll be worried your mum is angry with you so I wanted to reassure you that she isn't, but she does need some time to think about things. Your letter was very moving and I believe the whole situation has been a wake-up call. Hang on in there, Tigger. She'll be in touch soon xx

Socks leapt onto the bed and sprawled across my lap. I stroked his ears as I replied to Owen's message.

TO OWEN

Relieved to hear that. Sorry about the shock. It wasn't planned but I think it's what was needed. Speak soon xx

'I wish Owen didn't have to be tangled up in this mess,' I told Socks. 'Sounds like Mum's calmed down, though.'

As I'd put in my letter, the next move was up to her. I just hoped it wasn't too long before she made it.

11

SNOWY

From my position on one of the wooden chairs tucked away in the front corner inside The Roost, I heard the distant bangs and pops of fireworks signalling the arrival of New Year's Day and another whole year slipping by without Eliza. I'd held it together throughout Christmas and, from what Grandpa said, I had perhaps turned a corner this year but, with the arrival of the anniversary, tears spilled down my cheeks and I slumped forward, that familiar cloak of guilt and desolation wrapped tightly around me as my body shook with silent sobs.

When the wave of grief finally passed over me, I straightened up and wiped my cheeks with the back of my gloves. Hopefully that was the end of it and I could remain strong throughout New Year's Day, especially during the afternoon when we visited the paddock where we'd scattered Eliza's ashes.

My cheeks felt tight and uncomfortable from the tears and I longed to splash some warm water over my face, but I hadn't seen the barn owls yet – my reason for being here. We had a pair of barn owls who'd made it their home, roosting in one of the nesting boxes which Grandpa had built in his workshop. I'd seen one of the owls peeking out a couple of hours ago, but it seemed I'd been a little ambitious in my hope to see one of them in flight.

I was about to call it a night and took one more longing glance towards the nesting box where my patience was rewarded with what I considered to be the most spectacular sight in the world. It didn't matter how many times I saw a barn owl in flight, the silent majesty of its glide completely captivated me, the white face, body and underside of the wings giving the appearance of a ghost floating past. I watched it fly out of The Roost and ran to the open doorway to catch it disappearing into the night.

I must have been about six the first time I saw a barn owl but I'd assumed it was a snowy owl because of the colour. Grandpa explained that, while the snowy owl had white feathers, they were covered in brown and black markings, giving it a speckled appearance. It was also quite rare to see one in the wild in England. By contrast, the barn owl was one of five owls native to this country. It appeared to be white when in flight but its coloured feathers were revealed when it perched. The markings on its back and the top of its wings were beige, brown and grey, with the females distinguishable as having darker markings.

I loved all owls but had particularly been fascinated by barn owls ever since and was fortunate that so many had made Owl's Lodge their home.

When I couldn't see the owl anymore, I returned to my chair with a smile. That was exactly how I'd hoped to begin the New Year.

Grandpa crept into The Roost, placed a flask, mug and a pair of binoculars on the table, and settled down onto the second chair.

'I thought I'd find you in here.'

He lifted up my mug and sniffed the dregs of cold tea before he tipped them away. I was four years sober, but I couldn't blame him for checking. He probably wasn't aware he was even doing it, the habit so strong from the dark years when I'd lied to everyone.

He poured us both a fresh steaming tea from his flask. 'It's nippy tonight. Thought you might need warming up.'

I pulled my gloves off and cradled the mug, savouring the heat. 'Cheers.'

He placed a thick blanket over his knees and took a sip of his tea. 'Much movement tonight?'

'You've just missed one going out but quiet otherwise, although I saw a tawny in the woods earlier.'

Grandpa and I sat in silence for a few minutes, sipping on our drinks.

'How's Harrison?' I asked.

'Tucked up in bed and sound asleep.'

'I knew he wouldn't make it to midnight.'

'He barely made it to ten o'clock.'

'Thanks for keeping an eye on him.'

'It's never a bother,' Grandpa said. 'Especially at this time of year.'

He looked at me meaningfully, the unspoken question evident.

'I had a moment earlier,' I admitted, 'but I'm all right. Doesn't feel like five years.'

'Doesn't feel like fifteen since I lost my Shirley.'

I'd been approaching seventeen when Grandma was diagnosed with an aggressive type of motor neurone disease. Less than eighteen months later, she was gone. It was perhaps a blessing that she left us before my decline. She'd have been heartbroken and so very ashamed.

Grandpa finished his tea and wiped his mouth with the back of his fingerless gloves.

'It's a bit too chilly for me tonight, lad. You coming back in?'

'I might give it another half hour. See whether the barn owl returns.'

'Okay. I'll see you in the morning.'

He dropped the blanket over my knees and held a hand up to silence me when I protested that I didn't need it.

'You'll take it and quit your mithering,' he said.

To be fair, it did feel warm and comforting.

'Night, Grandpa.'

'Night, lad.'

He left the barn and I topped up my mug with the last of the tea from his flask. I ran my thumb over the faded lettering on the blue mug. *World's Best Daddy*. Eliza had presented me with it to announce her pregnancy with Harrison. But I hadn't been the *world's best daddy* at the time. I hadn't been the best anything. Except maybe liar.

12

SNOWY

I was eating my breakfast when Harrison launched himself at me.

'Happy New Year, Dad,' he said, stealing a slice of banana from my bowl and popping it into his mouth.

'I didn't think we'd see you until this afternoon,' I said, smoothing down his dishevelled bed-hair. 'Thought you might be shattered from staying up until... what was it? Two hours before midnight?'

'Pops snitched on me?' Harrison cried. 'It got boring staying up so long. Where is he?'

'Putting some fat balls out for the birds. He should be back soon.'

Although owls were our shared passion, Grandpa loved birds of all varieties. He spent hours each day in his workshop making or repairing nesting boxes and feeders which he positioned all around the lodge and throughout the woods. Every morning, he walked round them all, topping up the feeders with nuts and seeds and stringing up his home-made fat balls and seed shapes. He probably got in more steps doing that each day than most people half his age managed across a week, and I swear it was what had kept him so agile into his nineties.

Harrison's shoulders slumped. 'He said I could help.'

'Don't panic. He's saved the ones you made so you can do those together.' The pair of them had spent most of yesterday afternoon at the dining table rolling out a sticky seed concoction and using pastry cutters to cut out the shapes. Grandpa had gone traditional with circles but Harrison had insisted on using the Christmas cutters so there were Christmas trees, angels, reindeer, snowmen and stars ready to be strung up.

Placated, Harrison helped himself to a bowl of cereal.

'Are we going to the gym today?' he asked as he added the milk.

'I'm going down shortly, but you'll be going out with Pops.'

'When are we going to see Mum?'

It was such a casual question, spoken as though we were a divorced couple and she was living in the next village.

'We need to be there for half two,' I said, 'so we'll leave here at ten past.'

It was always half past two and Harrison had never asked why. He knew it was today because that was the day we lost her, but I don't think he realised the time was because 2.34 p.m. was the moment Eliza had drawn her final breath.

Feeling melancholy taking hold, I changed the subject.

'I saw one of the barn owls flying last night, and a tawny in the woods.'

'Any little owls?'

Little owls – smaller and fluffier than barn owls – were Harrison's favourites. We had several who'd made the grounds their home. Although the species had many habitats, all of ours had chosen to nest in the hedgerows which I'd grown high for maximum privacy.

'No little owls,' I said. 'Why might that be?'

'Oh, yeah! They're only out in the day.'

'And can you remember the word I taught you for that?'

He scrunched his face up and I didn't think he was going to get it, but then he grinned at me. 'Diurnal.'

'I'm impressed,' I said, giving him a fist bump.

I'd finished my breakfast but I stayed at the table while Harrison chatted to me about where he was going to hang his feeders. My eyes drifted to the clock on the wall behind him. *Quarter past ten – the time Eliza left the house with Harrison to search for me.* I fought hard to concentrate on what Harrison was saying instead of measuring every minute of that fateful day.

* * *

I dismounted the pommel horse later that morning, my landing solid, my arms in the air. I could still hear the roar of the crowd, feel the elation of a near-perfect routine and the thrill that I might have just clinched an Olympic medal.

A loud, slow clap startled me and I twisted round towards the gym entrance. A man was standing there, dressed in jeans and bundled in a thick puffer jacket and a beanie hat.

'Still got it,' he said, sauntering towards me. It was only when he pulled off his hat that I recognised him and my stomach plummeted to the floor.

'What are you doing here?' I demanded, grabbing a towel and wiping my face.

'That was the winning routine, wasn't it?' he said, shooting me his most charming smile.

'You haven't answered my question.'

'Aw, come on, Snowy.'

'Only my friends call me that. It's Nathan to you.'

'Don't be like that, Na-than.' He drew out my name as though it was two words. 'It hurts that you don't think of me as a friend when you and I go back such a long way. Happy New Year, by the way. Or is that the wrong thing to say in the circumstances? Five years ago today, wasn't it?'

'What do you want?'

'To give you a chance to share your side of the story.'

'Really? You weren't so interested in my side back then. Wrote what the hell you liked.'

'It's not like I didn't try to get your side, but you had a couple of gate-keepers who wouldn't let me close.'

'My wife had just died. What did you expect?'

He held his hands up in a surrender pose. 'I don't want to fall out with you, Snowy. I want us to be friends again.'

I couldn't be bothered to correct my name, but I was going to correct his statement. 'We were *never* friends.'

'Aw, you're not still angry with me for a little bit of teasing at school.'

'A little bit? You called me Freak Show.'

He winced – completely fake, of course. 'We were kids. I didn't know the nickname would catch on.'

'Sure you didn't. Just like you didn't know that your filthy little exposés on me would make the front page of all the tabloids.'

'I was only trying to help. It's not my fault that the attitudes towards mental health weren't what they are now. But if you work with me on a piece now, I'm sure you'd get a positive response.'

'Get lost, Parnell.'

He removed a business card from his coat pocket and held it out towards me. When I made no move to take it, he placed it on the pommel horse and patted it. 'For when you change your mind.'

'I'm not going to change my mind.'

'How's that young lad of yours getting on?'

'None of your business.'

'Harrison, isn't it? He'll be, what? Nine?'

I slapped the towel onto the pommels, sending his business card fluttering to the floor. 'Do I need to escort you out?'

He held his hands up again. 'It's all right. I'm going.'

But in a predictably overly dramatic move, he paused before he reached the door. 'Harrison's home schooled, isn't he? Is that because he's inherited your looks and you're scared he'll get called Freak Show too?'

'Leave!' I yelled.

The gym door opened. 'What's going on?' Grandpa cried, looking from me to Parnell. 'You!' He practically spat the word when he realised who it was. 'This is private property. Out!'

'I'm not here to cause trouble. Just want to give Snowy a chance to tell his story.'

'If he wanted to tell his story, you'd be the last person he'd tell it to. Should we call the police or are you skedaddling?'

'I'm going.'

As the door to the gym closed behind him, I rested my elbows on the pommels and sank my head into my hands with a deep sigh. I caught sight of his card face-up on the floor.

'Elliot Parnell, Investigative Journalist,' I read. 'Is that code for making shit up?'

'Don't give him another thought,' Grandpa said, now by my side. 'He's not worth it.'

I stood up and shook my head. 'I wouldn't care if it was just me, but he asked if Harrison looks like me.'

'He's fishing and trying to get a rise from you. It's what scum like him do.'

'Can you believe the nerve of him, showing up on the anniversary?'

'Again, purely to get a reaction. He knows it's an emotional day. Probably hoping to find you've slipped.'

'For once, I'm glad to be a disappointment.'

'You might be a disappointment to him, but you're not to me. You never have been. You know that, don't you?'

His voice cracked and I felt the weight of his suffering too. He'd loved Eliza like a granddaughter.

'Are you doing anything more in here?' Grandpa asked.

'It was the vault next, but he's put me off my stride.'

'In that case, Harrison has a special request. He wants to go on the trampoline.'

I frowned, confused. We regularly used the trampoline to practise tumbles before taking them to the floor. 'And that's a special request because...?'

There was a pause before Grandpa answered. 'Because he wants you to show him Eliza's routine.'

My heart sank. I'd met Eliza at Campion's Gymnastics Club in Wilbersgate. I'd been going since I was a toddler but she'd moved into the area when she was nine and we'd become instant friends. Her floor skills were incredible but her favourite apparatus was the beam and I'm convinced she'd have gone all the way to the Olympics if it hadn't been for a fall when she was twelve. It had been so unexpected and on a simple move she'd done hundreds of times before, but she fell off and landed really badly on the mats below, fracturing both her wrists. Not only was professional gymnastics off the radar from that point but she lost her confidence doing gymnastics for fun, too afraid of further injuries.

Even though she left the club, we stayed friends and, when we were fifteen, it became more. Over the years, I tried to coax her back into the sport, but she wasn't interested. One day, shortly after we were married, she announced that she'd like to go on the trampoline. It took a long time to build her confidence but we eventually developed a routine. She hadn't quite perfected it when she discovered she was pregnant. When Harrison was two, Eliza decided it was time to get back on the trampoline and master the routine. Except she hadn't been able to because I hadn't been there to help her. She'd never asked much of me, never demanded my time, but I hadn't been able to give her the one thing she really wanted. And now Harrison wanted to learn his mum's routine on the anniversary of her death of all days.

'Did you tell him I would?' I asked Grandpa.

'I said I'd ask.'

'I'm not sure.'

'It's just a routine.' He winced. 'That came out wrong. I know it's not any old routine – it's Eliza's and I know you're angry with yourself for not helping her perfect it – but that's your issue, not his. The lad's curious about his mum. He only has vague memories of her and they're already fading. He's seen all the photos, watched the videos and heard the stories. This is something new.'

'I wish she'd let me video it. I could have shown him that.'

'She didn't want you to until she'd perfected it, so either you perform the routine for him or he never gets to see it.'

I looked across at the trampoline and could picture Eliza on it so clearly, fits of giggles as she struggled in the early days to trust herself with the basics through to jubilant bounces with her fist in the air when she mastered each new move.

'I will show him, but not today.'

Grandpa placed his hand on my shoulder and gave a reassuring squeeze. 'If not today, when? Look, I know it's a tough day for you, but don't forget you had many happy years with her and he didn't. As I keep telling you, you had no control over what happened that day, but you *do* have control over what happens next and the legacy that young lad has. Show him the routine. Teach him it if that's what he wants. Let him finish what she started, eh?'

He gave another squeeze of my shoulder, then released his hand with a sigh. 'Sorry for lecturing you.'

'You're not lecturing. You're speaking sense.' I ran my hands through my hair, my thoughts in turmoil. 'Okay. Give me half an hour then bring him down.'

'Good decision,' he said.

'Good coaxing.'

Grandpa left and I shivered in the cold draught from the opening of the door. I pulled on my tracksuit top, zipped it up and took a swig of my drink. Grandpa was right to have called me out on this, but he shouldn't have had to. I should have been the one to realise it was important to Harrison. I should have been the one who suggested teaching him Eliza's routine. Was I so consumed by guilt around her death that I'd forgotten how to celebrate her life? Four years ago, on the one-year anniversary of losing her, I made a New Year's resolution never to drink again. It hadn't been easy and I'd come close to falling off the wagon several times, but I'd stuck to it. This year, it might be time to make another resolution to live in the moment instead of forever dwelling on the past. I couldn't change what had happened but I could change my reaction to it, especially if my behaviour was affecting my son. Harrison and Grandpa were my world and I needed to do everything I could to make them always feel part of it and never push them away. I'd made that mistake before.

13

SNOWY

'I can't believe he's that good already,' Grandpa said as Harrison landed the final twist on Saturday, just three days after I'd first shown him Eliza's routine. 'Men's trampoline for Brisbane instead?'

He said it in jest, but it gave me a jolt. Our goal was the thirty-fifth Olympic Games in Brisbane in 2032, at which point Harrison would be seventeen – a year younger than I'd been when I competed in Beijing. The focus for Harrison had always been my discipline of artistic gymnastics, but there was no denying that he had a gift for the trampoline which I'd never registered until now. We'd used the trampoline frequently for practising tumbles as well as for a bit of fun, but the focus he'd shown while learning Eliza's routine and the speed at which he'd picked it up was quite astonishing.

'What did you think, Pops?' Harrison asked, lowering himself down from the trampoline.

'I think you must have been sneaking in here every night for the past four years to practise because that was incredible, young man.'

'Thanks, Pops. Do you think Mum would have liked it?'

'She'd have loved it.'

'Can I do it again?' he asked me.

'One more time and then we'll call it a day.'

Harrison scrambled back onto the trampoline and started bouncing to gain height.

'You might be right,' I murmured to Grandpa.

He grabbed my arm. 'It was a joke.'

'I know, but look at him. I need to keep an open mind.'

* * *

'I didn't think he'd settle this early,' I said to Grandpa, plonking myself down onto the corner sofa in the lounge, 'but he's spark out.'

'All that bouncing's worn him out.'

Bedtime during the school holidays and weekends was anywhere between nine and ten depending on what we were doing, but Harrison's eyelids had been drooping all evening. We'd spoken extensively about how important it was for an athlete to listen to their body and get plenty of rest, but I couldn't imagine there were many nine-year-olds who'd pay much heed to that. I'd therefore expected protests when I suggested bedtime at 8.15 p.m., but Harrison had agreed he was tired and toddled off to get ready. When I went into his bedroom to say goodnight, I held the back of my hand against his forehead to make sure he wasn't coming down with anything.

'I'm not poorly, Dad,' he'd said. 'I'm just tired and I want to make sure I've got lots of energy for the trampoline tomorrow.'

So my task for this evening was to do some research into men's trampoline at the Olympic Games. Although artistic gymnastics had been part of the programme since the first modern Olympic Games in 1896 trampoline was a fairly recent addition to the Games, first appearing at Sydney 2000. I wanted to understand the route to selection and what was required of the competitors.

Grandpa looked up from the bird book he'd been flicking through.

'Searching for anything interesting?' he asked.

'Trampoline. It's too early to talk to Harrison about it. He might decide he's mastered the routine and that's that, but I want to be clued up on what's needed if he does show interest in going down that route.'

There wasn't much online yet about Brisbane but we'd had the Paris

Games in the summer and Los Angeles was next, so there was plenty relating to both those Games for me to read and watch.

It was quiet in the house except for the occasional crackle from the log burner. Grandpa added another log at one point but otherwise we remained silent, absorbed in our activities. By 10 p.m. I'd had enough and closed down the laptop.

'Found what you wanted?' Grandpa asked.

'Enough for now. I hadn't paid much attention to the scoring system before so that was useful.' I placed the laptop beside me and stretched out my back.

'Are you going down to The Roost tonight?' Grandpa asked.

'I can't decide.'

I wasn't sure if I could be bothered to go out, which wasn't like me. I normally went owl-spotting in all weathers and temperatures, no matter how warm and cosy it was in front of the fire. I wandered over to the bifold doors and looked out across the veranda towards the trees. Being remote, we rarely drew the curtains. If it was windy, maybe I'd stay inside, but the dark shapes of the trees were still.

'I might sit out on the veranda for a bit,' I said.

'Temperature's dropped so make sure you wrap up warm.'

'I will. No need to worry about me.'

'Do you ever stop worrying about Harrison?' he asked.

'No.'

'Then I'll never stop worrying about you. It's what family does.'

Some of them. But I didn't vocalise that. Parenting wasn't easy. Making the decision to bring a child into the world meant making sacrifices and the jury was still out as to whether Dad had been selfish or selfless by leaving. Most of the time, I leaned towards the former. What was it they said? *Don't judge a man until you've walked a mile in his shoes.* Well, I'd walked a hell of a lot further than a mile, Dad's shoes were the same size as mine, and I'd stayed.

'Something's bothering you,' Grandpa said.

I turned my attention back to him. 'What makes you say that?'

'Because I know you too well. Something's been bothering you for a few days now and it's not Eliza's anniversary. It's different.'

'It's nothing.'

'I believe you. Thousands wouldn't.' He closed his book and put it down beside him. 'It's that Elliot Parnell, isn't it?'

I sighed as I plonked myself back down on the sofa. 'He was the last person I wanted to see on the first day of the year. Can't stand him.'

'Neither can I, but that's nothing new. What did he say to you?'

'Usual crap like I told you. Wants my side of the story. Like I believe that.'

Grandpa studied my face for a moment before shaking his head. 'That's not it. What else did he say because whatever it was, it's got you rattled?'

'He mentioned home schooling Harrison and asked if it was because I was bullied at school. Obviously I didn't rise to it, but he's hit a nerve. Did I make the right decision for Harrison, or was it for me?'

Grandpa ran his hand across his beard.

'Are those two decisions mutually exclusive?'

I shrugged. 'I guess not.'

'It goes back to what I said just now – always worrying about your family. Your choice for Harrison was what you considered to be best for both of you.'

'It was definitely best for me, but was it best for him? If he'd been blond like Eliza, would I have even considered home schooling?'

'Don't forget you didn't make the decision alone. It's what Eliza wanted too.'

'Because she saw what school did to me and she didn't want that for our son. But were we both projecting our fears onto him?'

'Probably, but show me a parent who doesn't.' He stood up and rolled his shoulders. 'I'm making a brew before bed. Do you want one?'

'Nah, I'm okay, thanks.'

'Don't let that idiot Parnell get to you, but if you genuinely are having second thoughts about whether home schooling is right for Harrison, why don't you ask him? Because, to my knowledge, he's asked why he doesn't go to school like next door's grandkids but he's never said he wishes he did.'

With a shrug, Grandpa shuffled out of the lounge. I glanced out into the darkness once more. I *would* venture into the woods after all. The cold night air should help clear my head. Five minutes later, I'd layered up, and pulled on my thick boots and a beanie hat.

'I'm taking my brew to bed with me,' Grandpa said, 'so I'll say goodnight for now. Don't let that jumped-up little squirt get to you.'

I smiled at the expression I hadn't heard in years. 'Night, Grandpa. Sleep well.'

* * *

The trees silently welcomed me under their canopies. Even as a small lad, I'd never felt afraid of the darkness or the shadows. The woods felt safe and it was out there beyond the boundaries of Owl's Lodge to be feared.

The white hair ran through the male side of my family as far back as I could tell. Dad had it, Grandpa had it and he'd told me his dad and grandfather had too. We all had fair skin and pale blue eyes so anyone we met assumed we had albinism, but Grandpa had done some research and reckoned the genetics didn't work for that to be the case. My brain had hurt when he'd tried to explain it to me.

From an early age, I was aware that I looked different. Dad and Grandpa looked like me, but nobody else did. The only people with white hair on television or in my picture books were old. At primary school, none of the kids had pale skin and white hair. There were a few redheads but even their fair skin looked pink against mine.

I wasn't teased from the start. I think really young kids tend to be accepting of looks and it's only when older siblings or parents point something out that they begin to notice and label differences. And judge them. It was Elliot Parnell who kicked it all off for me. His family moved to the village where I attended primary school when we were eight and I vividly remember that day.

'Let's all welcome Elliot to our class,' Miss Maughan had said, beaming at us all. 'There's a spare seat next to Nathan there.'

Parnell glanced at the empty chair then his eyes locked with mine and he shook his head vigorously.

'No way! I'm not sitting with that freak show!'

By the end of the day, everyone was calling me Freak Show. I told Dad. He told me, *Suck it up and toughen up. A bit of teasing never hurt anyone.* He couldn't have been more wrong about that. That hideous nickname followed me to senior school and I found myself an outcast because word had also spread that I did gymnastics. *Only girls do gymnastics. Are you a girl, Freak Show?*

A shriek overhead returned my thoughts to the woods and I looked up through a gap in the trees in time to see the ghostly barn owl soaring overhead, its catch in its claws, heading for The Roost. Absolutely stunning. Some would say that that particular call was chilling because it was reminiscent of a human scream, but I loved it as it meant home. Barn owls used to be thought of as bad and, in the Middle Ages, they were known as screech owls, their cry believed to herald death or disaster. Over the centuries, there'd been all sorts of superstitions connected with the barn owl including the Yorkshire one that whooping cough could be cleared up by barn owl broth. Thankfully attitudes had changed when farmers realised that barn owls were their friends rather than foe, eating the mice who dined on their grain. As well as finding the barn owl mesmerising to watch, I felt drawn to it as my spirit animal. It was notoriously unsociable with only brief sightings of it beyond its home. Hard relate to that.

Another call lifted my spirits further – the long-eared owl. It sounded like an adult taking a mouthful of helium from a balloon and crying out *whee!* The long-eared owl's song was the *hoot* sound that many people associated with owls, not realising the differences between species. Even within a species, the male and female calls could differ, and most owls had several sounds depending on what they were trying to communicate.

Leaning my back against an old oak, I kept my eyes focused above me. Owl's Lodge was well away from the light pollution of the closest large towns, meaning we were treated to a spectacular show of stars. Gazing up at the inky vastness and the blanket of stars was so calming. The universe was so much bigger than me and my problems and five minutes of stargazing helped put everything into perspective.

I lowered my head and closed my eyes, focusing on the sounds. The branches creaked, the leaves on the evergreens rustled, as did the wildlife through the undergrowth. We had a lawn out the back of the lodge but otherwise kept our land wild to encourage wildlife to make Owl's Lodge their home.

I heard a noise nearby and opened my eyes. A hedgehog was snuffling through the undergrowth, unaware or unafraid of my presence. A rabbit peeked round a tree trunk, sniffed, then bounded out of sight. This place was so magical. Could there be a better place to live? It had everything I needed – a comfortable home, a state-of-the-art gym, my family and nature. My stomach lurched. But was that enough for Harrison? I'd already been thinking about getting him enrolled at my former club but did that go far enough? I'd made the decision to live my life reclusively but Harrison hadn't. I hated that it was Elliot Parnell – that *jumped-up little squirt* – of all people who was making me question all my choices.

14

ZARA

Sunday arrived – the fifth day of the New Year – and I hadn't spoken to Mum yet, although I knew it wasn't personal. Owen had phoned late on New Year's Day to say it had been a disastrous start to the year at the golf club and Mum was up to her neck trying to sort out a couple of major incidents – a golf buggy accident and a break-in.

'She really does want to talk to you,' Owen had said, 'but she doesn't want that conversation to go badly because she's not in the right frame of mind.'

Tomorrow, we were kicking off three weeks of filming for *The Wildlife Rescuers* at Hedgehog Hollow so my weekend was fortunately hectic with final preparations, meaning no time to dwell on when I might finally hear from her. Amber and I had spent yesterday afternoon at Hedgehog Hollow, running through the plans with Samantha and Fizz for the first week of filming. It had been fabulous to be back at the rescue centre, hearing all about their gorgeous admissions and seeing a few receiving treatment. This afternoon, we were going back to meet with our crew. Starshine Productions – the production company who'd commissioned the docuseries – specialised in documentaries and factual shows for television. They were responsible for *Jules in the Garden* and *Jules in the Kitchen* – the two hugely successful long-running TV shows fronted by

Amber's mum. We hadn't even started filming yet but, so far, the experience couldn't be more different than working for Clementine Creates, who'd been behind *Love on the Farm*. Talk about two completely different approaches – professional and ethical versus completely unscrupulous.

The CEO of Starshine Productions, Róisín Brennan, had stipulated that we needed to work with their crew. Amber already knew the two videographers – husband and wife team Jackie and Shane – and the sound mixer Ishaan from her mum's shows. There was flexibility on the director so we'd jumped at the opportunity to work with Matt Hambleton again – the first of three directors during our time on *Love on the Farm*. Matt and the crew were all staying in Hedgehog Hollow's holiday cottages for the next three weeks, which made it convenient to film sunrises and sunsets and be on hand if an animal was admitted outside of the filming schedule. There'd already been a change of plan for tomorrow because minus temperatures were predicted. The farm would look beautiful covered in a blanket of frost and, as the series was about showcasing rescue centres across the seasons, we were keen to capture the wintry look while we could. This afternoon, we'd take the crew on a tour so they could decide on locations for capturing a (hopefully) frosty farm early tomorrow.

This morning, I had a stack of admin tasks so I'd taken over the kitchen table at Bumblebee Barn while Amber was out on the farm with Barney, Bear and Harley. It was shortly after eleven and I'd just wandered over to the sink to fill the kettle when a knock on the door startled me. I put the kettle down and gasped as I answered it.

'Mum!'

'Surprise!' She smiled but it was uncertain, as though she wasn't sure if she was welcome. 'Can we come in?'

'Of course! Yes!' I stepped back to let her and Owen pass. Mum wasn't a hugger – never had been – but Owen gave me a bear hug.

'I was about to make a coffee,' I said. 'Do you want anything?'

They gave their orders and, as the kitchen table was littered with paperwork, I directed them into the lounge to make themselves comfortable while I made the drinks. Mum had never paid a surprise visit to anywhere I'd been working and this was actually her first visit to

Bumblebee Barn. That in itself made me nervous, but my biggest fear was the conversation that lay ahead. Now that she'd had the time to reflect, would she accept that she'd treated me unfairly for years or would she be firmly on Golden Boy's side? Would she think me leaving his party and packing up my room was another example of my 'childish' behaviour? Only one way to find out.

'Here you go,' I said, pasting a smile on my face as I carried a tray into the lounge and placed it down on the coffee table.

'Filming starts tomorrow, yes?' Mum said once we were all settled with our drinks, Mum and Owen on the sofa together and me on one of the snuggle chairs.

I nodded. 'I'm finalising a few details this morning and we're off to Hedgehog Hollow this afternoon to meet the crew.' I kept my tone light as I didn't want Mum to think she wasn't welcome, but it was important she knew I had commitments and wasn't free for a long conversation poring over every past incident.

'We won't stay long as I know you have things on, but we need to talk about what happened at New Year and I thought it was best to do it face to face.'

'Okay.' The word came out a bit squeaky as my stomach tightened.

Mum glanced at Owen and he nodded at her encouragingly.

'I want to start with an apology about Roman's party,' she said. 'I was in the wrong. I jumped to conclusions based on what I saw and that was unfair of me. Owen filled me in on the conversation and I've told Roman in no uncertain terms that I'm not impressed with his behaviour or with Portia's.'

Wow! Giving Golden Boy a dressing down was a first.

'I know you believe I always think the worst of you and the best of him,' she continued, 'but that's really not how it is.'

I could sit there meekly and let her get it all off her chest, which would likely make her feel better, but would it really help me? This was my opportunity to calmly put across how her constant favouring of my brother made me feel.

'Then why does it feel like that all the time?' I asked, my voice strong, my expression questioning.

Mum lowered her eyes and stared into her mug, her shoulders slumped.

I took advantage of the silence. 'I'm not saying I can't give as good as I get, but nine times out of ten, it isn't me who starts it. You seem to think the sun shines out of his backside and it doesn't. Sure, he's a talented footballer who's done some amazing things with his career, but he's not a very nice person. Every success has made him more arrogant and self-centred and the adoration he gets on the socials feeds into that. I understand that you want us to get on but, like I put in my note, it's never going to happen. We've got nothing in common and he's never shown any interest in my life. When we do see each other, it's either awkward silences or he goes on and on about what he's been doing but is never interested enough to ask about me. He doesn't know what my job is or where I live, for God's sake, but I know everything about him.'

Mum's head shot up. 'No, you don't,' she snapped. 'Nobody does.'

The volume evidently surprised her as much as it did me – and Owen by the startled look on his face – and she softened her voice as she spoke again.

'I just mean that nobody really knows what's going on in another person's life. They might think they do, but they don't. However, I take the point you're making and I know it's partly my fault. I saw your relationship deteriorating when you were younger and I did nothing to stop it. Hands up, I did wrong by you when you were little, Zara. I didn't cope well with your dad leaving.'

That was also unexpected. My parents had a surprisingly cordial relationship considering Dad had left her for another woman. And not just *any* woman but one he'd been seeing for years and who already had a child by him and was expecting another! I wouldn't go so far as to say that my parents were friends, but there'd never been any worry that things would kick off between them on the few occasions when they were in a room together. It probably helped that they were both happier with their new spouses than they'd ever been with each other. Mum had never given any indication that she found it tough without Dad, although we had been young, so she'd likely covered it up.

Mum sipped her tea. 'It was hard trying to hold down a job, get you both to school and keep your clubs going when your dad was frequently working away, but he wasn't away all the time and took up some of the slack when he was home. When he left, it was impossible for me to keep all those plates spinning and I had some tough decisions to make. You didn't show the same enthusiasm for gymnastics as Roman did for football, so I prioritised his club over yours.'

'But I loved gymnastics. I was gutted when I couldn't do it anymore but you told me off every time I mentioned it, so I learned to put up and shut up.'

Mum winced, but she couldn't deny that was how it had been.

'If I could go back, I'd do it differently,' she said, holding my gaze. 'I don't know how, but I'd somehow find a way for both of you to do what you wanted and I'd have done what I could to make the pair of you friends instead of enemies. I should have and could have stepped in sooner and I realise I've been trying to make up for that over recent years when the damage was already done. You've accused me of not listening and I see that now, so I've listened carefully to what you said in your letter. Even though it breaks my heart to say it, you're right about me accepting that I can't keep pushing you two together because all that's happening is that I'm pushing a wedge between you and me, which is the last thing I want to do.'

Tears glistened in Mum's eyes. She was a practical woman who didn't tend to show emotion. I couldn't remember ever seeing her cry and certainly didn't want my spat with Roman to be the cause of her breaking down, but that didn't mean I should brush over how deeply her actions had wounded me.

'It's been tough living in his shadow,' I admitted, 'and it's been even worse being seen as the troublemaker all the time. You accepting that I wasn't in the wrong at his party means a lot to me and I hope you realise now that it hasn't been my fault on countless other occasions.'

'I do. I genuinely am sorry.' She took Owen's hand as she fixed her gaze on him. 'And to you too. I'm embarrassed about the number of times I got angry with you and accused you of taking Zara's side when all you were doing was trying to show me what was really going on.'

'I'm fine,' he assured her, squeezing her hand and giving her a gentle smile. 'We can talk about it at home if you want, but let's focus on you and Zara for now.'

Mum turned back to me. 'I realise now that I talk to you about Roman far too much, usually with an instruction for you to try harder with him, so I'm going to step back and stop meddling. I'd love for you to have a relationship with your brother – a good one – but you're both old enough to make your own decisions about who you want in your life. Having said that, I'd love it if you didn't write him off just yet. Your brother is...' She broke off and bit her lip, evidently searching for the right words.

'It's complicated,' she said eventually. 'He's complicated. I can't go into it at the moment, but things aren't always what they seem.'

That all seemed very cryptic and the puzzled expression on Owen's face suggested that he might be as much in the darkness as me as to what was *complicated* about my brother's situation.

'I can't promise that,' I said. 'Truth is, I don't like him. I'm sorry if that sounds harsh, but it's fairly obvious he doesn't like me either, especially when he didn't want to invite me to his party and told me you made him write the note.'

'I'm sorry,' she said, looking at me sadly. 'I can't... There's nothing I can say to make that sound better.'

'It's fine. I understand why you did it, but it proves my point about it being the end of the line. It's not like I haven't tried over the years. I changed my plans to be there for Roman's birthday and for what? I cancelled a great night with my friends to spend half an hour at a party I wasn't welcome at. Fortunately I made it back here in time to see the New Year in and salvage part of the night, but I'm not cancelling anything for Roman in the future and I'd really appreciate your support and understanding on that and no more pressure. You said you hadn't forced me to go but I need you to accept that you did by emotionally blackmailing me.'

It was a strong term but it was appropriate for what she'd done and I held my breath, wondering how she'd react. The pause was excruciating but, eventually, she exhaled loudly, nodding.

'That's a fair point. I do accept it so, from now on, I promise you have my support and understanding. No more pressure.'

'Thank you. I really appreciate it.'

Mum took another sip on her tea. 'I have a question for you. I understand you leaving the party. In your shoes, I'd have done the same. Not staying the night, I also understand – of course you'd want to be with your friends after what happened. But you emptied your bedroom. You moved out. I have to say, that was a shock for both of us. Why did you do that?'

'It wasn't the plan. I left the party intending to pack my bag and drive to Hedgehog Hollow but I looked in Roman's old bedroom and you'd redecorated again. He doesn't even live there but—'

'You do and you saw the state of your bedroom,' Mum finished for me, grimacing. 'I never even thought about what sort of message that must have sent to you.'

'Nothing new. Same message I'd been getting all my life – that my brother was important and I wasn't.'

I bit my lip wondering if I'd gone too far with my honesty, but we weren't a family who talked about emotions. I therefore couldn't help thinking that this was a conversation that wouldn't be revisited so I had to take my chance while I could. Owen caught my eye and he looked heartbroken. I talked to him more than I talked to Mum, but I'd never admitted that to him. How could I? I didn't want to be the cause of conflict. He made Mum happy when I didn't, and he made me happy and I'd never wanted to jeopardise that.

I watched in alarm as a couple of tears tracked down Mum's cheeks. 'I didn't say that to upset you,' I cried, jumping up and offering her a box of tissues.

'I'm so sorry. I've had my head in the sand about this whole thing. I'm amazed you're still talking to me after I failed you so badly. You just always seemed so on the level whereas Roman...' She tailed off and wiped her eyes. 'I'm sorry. I know it doesn't change anything, but I really do regret how I've handled it all and I wish it hadn't taken you moving out to make me face up to things.'

Owen placed his hand on her thigh and she took hold of it, linking her fingers through his.

'It is what it is,' I said softly. 'And, as you say, you can't change the past so let's not let it affect our future. Line in the sand?'

'I'd like that.'

'And no more nagging me to be there for Roman when it's not reciprocal.'

'No more nagging.'

We all sipped on our drinks in silence.

'How long are you planning to stay here?' Mum asked eventually, her voice brighter.

'I'm not sure. It makes sense for this to be my base while we're filming at Hedgehog Hollow and we'll be on the road in between that to film at the other rescue centres and for *Countryside Calendar*. Beyond that, I don't know.'

'I hope you know you'll always be welcome back home.'

I smiled at her gratefully. 'Thank you, but I'm nearly twenty-seven so I think moving out is overdue. I really love it round here. If I can afford to stay in this area, I'd like to.'

'Is it expensive to rent or buy around here?'

'I've never looked into it. If it is, maybe I'll become a permanent resident at Bumblebee Barn.'

It was meant as a joke, but Mum clearly hadn't taken it that way.

'You can't live forever in the spare bedroom on your boss's boyfriend's farm. That's no way to live. You need your own home. And if the problem's money, maybe it's time to think about a promotion. I know you love working with Amber but you've been doing the same job for six years. You've surely learned everything you're going to learn by now. What about becoming a producer? Or moving into films? Surely that pays better than television.'

And it had been going so well.

'I don't want to be a producer,' I said, fighting hard to keep the frustration out of my voice. 'I've *never* wanted to be a producer, or a director, or any other roles in TV and I certainly don't want to move into film. I don't love my job because it's television. I love it because it plays to my skills. I love organising things, solving problems, sorting out messes. The bonus of doing that for television rather than an office job is all the travel. I've been to amazing places I'd never have discovered otherwise. Every day's different and I get to work with my best friend.'

'And what if Amber decides it's time to have a family? What if she hangs up her producer's hat to become a farmer? What happens to you then?'

'I look for another job, but neither of those things are imminent. *The Wildlife Rescuers* is Amber's pet project. It's being filmed over a year and there's no way she won't see it through to the end. I'm therefore guaranteed a job until next spring which, in the current climate, is better than many people face.'

'You were guaranteed a job filming that dating show but didn't it get pulled after a couple of months?'

'That was a completely different set of circumstances.'

'I'm just looking out for you. I really like Amber – you know that – but I'm worried you've put all your eggs in one basket with your home, your job and your friendship all tied to one person, especially when that person's at a point in her life where she's found someone to settle down with.'

'Is this about me being single?' I cried, my frustration spilling over.

'I know it's harder than ever to meet a suitable partner these days, especially when you have a job like yours with so much travel, and I know you've been let down badly by previous boyfriends. I'd love you to meet someone, as I'm sure you would, but it's important to be self-sufficient. I realised that too late when your dad left. My wages from the golf club went from being pocket money to being the only source of income and it was hard. I set my sights on the manager role and did everything to make sure I got it because I never wanted to be in a position again where I was having to count every penny. I can't emphasise enough the importance of a good job and a decent salary.'

I might not earn a lot – we couldn't all be professional footballers on six-figure annual salaries – but I didn't need a lot because I spent so much time working away with my travel and food covered by expenses. I therefore saved most of what I earned. If Amber and Barney did start a family next year and my job circumstances changed, I had a sizeable financial buffer while I decided what to do next. And Amber wouldn't leave me high and dry anyway – she'd give me plenty of notice.

'I didn't know things were tough for you financially when Dad left,' I said, 'but I'm not broke and I'm not stupid. I can look after myself whether I meet the man of my dreams or not. Roman's life might be complicated, but mine isn't and I like it that way.'

Mum studied my face for a moment before smiling. 'You always were the sensible one. Promise me that, if anything changes and you need somewhere to stay, you will consider coming home.'

'I promise, but I need to put down some roots somewhere.'

'I'm sorry if you think I was lecturing you about your job.'

'Apology accepted and, from me, I'm sorry I moved out in anger. I hadn't driven far when I realised it maybe wasn't my best move.'

I put my empty mug down on the tray and stayed sitting forwards.

'You've promised not to nag me about Roman, which should do wonders for our relationship, but I need you to promise me something else.'

'I'm listening.'

'Can we not replace that with nagging me about my job, getting a house of my own, finding a man? That doesn't mean we can't ever talk about those subjects – just that I want you to trust me to know and do what's right for me from now on. I might make some mistakes, but they're mine to make. It's my life and I don't need anyone else trying to take control of it, no matter how well-intentioned.'

'Sorry again. I promise.'

I stood up. 'I know you're not a hugger, but I am, and I could really use one right now.'

Mum rushed round the coffee table, arms outstretched, and held me tightly. I blinked back tears, not wanting her to feel worse than she already did, and I hoped for the sake of our future relationship that not interfering was one New Year's resolution that didn't fall by the wayside before the end of the month.

15

SNOWY

We'd survived the first week of home schooling after the Christmas break and Harrison had thrown himself into his studies with enthusiasm, as always. We spent time outdoors every day in forest school, learning about nature combined with practical skills like map reading and how to build a shelter and fire. There was no legal obligation to follow the national curriculum, but it made sense to me to roughly follow it as I wanted Harrison to gain the same knowledge from his home education as his peers.

Forest school automatically covered subjects such as geography, science and art, and I loved finding ways of relating the outdoors to others. For English, there were lots of opportunities for creative writing but we also practised different grammatical terms by walking through the trees and talking about what we saw. I found ways to develop maths skills and Grandpa took Harrison into his workshop once a week for design and technology.

All week, I kept asking myself whether Harrison would have a better experience in school. My gut told me it was a no as far as learning was concerned. At home, he had one-to-one attention, he was learning valuable practical skills and, while we had a plan for each week, we retained flexibility depending on the weather and Harrison's engagement with the learning. If something wasn't sinking in, we'd put it aside and come back to it later and, if he was loving something else, we'd give it more attention. He wouldn't get that in a school setting. My main concern was about socialisation and whether I was projecting my own negative experiences onto him.

It wasn't like we lived completely reclusively. I might have wanted to hide away forever and forget about the rest of the world – and I did manage that for the first year after losing Eliza – but getting sober brought with it clarity of thought. Harrison deserved better than an isolated existence, so I incorporated days out to the coast and the countryside to continue learning about nature in different settings. We went to the local towns of Reddfield, Wilbersgate, Claybridge and Whitsborough Bay and our two nearest cities of Hull and York to study urban geography and architecture. We visited museums, parks, playgrounds and swimming pools. Granted, we did it all during normal school hours when there weren't as many children around, but Harrison would talk to and play with any kids he did encounter. Surely that, combined with the visits from next door's grandkids, was enough to keep developing his social skills.

Although it wasn't unheard of to go out and about during a weekend, I preferred to stay at home. Harrison typically had a lazy morning on Saturday and Sunday, watching television, playing computer games or reading while I spent time in the gym with Grandpa as my spotter as I worked on the rings, parallel bars and high bar. Harrison would usually join me after lunch to work on his skills.

This morning I'd been in the gym on my own and, while I was on the vault, I'd experienced that weird sensation of being watched. The windows were high up, their sole purpose being to let in light, so nobody outside could see through them. The only way for anyone to watch me was to come through the door, and that had stayed firmly closed, so I put it down to me being jittery after Parnell's unwelcome appearance. His business card was still on the floor by the pommel horse and there was no way he'd leave it at that. If he wanted a story, he'd keep pestering me until I relented or until he found an angle and wrote what the hell he liked.

* * *

'Can I do Mum's routine first?' Harrison asked me as Grandpa led the way down the steps to the gym after lunch.

'You're not bored of it yet?' I teased.

'No, but can we make it longer?'

'If you like. We could practise a few more different moves and you can have a think about where they can go.'

'It's important you keep up your floor skills,' Grandpa said. 'And the other apparatus too.'

'I will. I promise.'

Grandpa's mobile phone rang.

'It's Desmond,' he said before answering it.

Desmond was Grandpa's best mate. He lived in the nearby village of Fimberley and the pair of them frequently met up to go freshwater fishing.

'I'll have to go back up to the house to check my diary,' Grandpa said. 'Give me five minutes and I'll call you back.'

'He wants to confirm a date for Scotland,' he told me after he'd hung up. 'You know what he's like. If I don't sort it now, he'll only keep calling me.'

A group of them had an annual week of salmon fishing in Scotland each spring and Desmond was the self-appointed tour manager for it.

'We'll see you later,' I said, running down the steps after Harrison, who was already pacing by the gym door.

Harrison must have taken heed of Grandpa's words as he announced that he'd go on the trampoline last. After we'd warmed up, there was still no sign of Grandpa. Safety came first when coaching my son and, even though we weren't a club and therefore not tied by the same rules, I did try to adhere to the safety guidelines from British Gymnastics to have a second responsible adult present. Sometimes it wasn't possible – like when Grandpa was away fishing – but there were some exercises that carried less risk which I tended to focus on if I was alone with Harrison.

'Floor or vault?' I asked Harrison, already knowing what the answer would be.

'Vault.'

It was his current favourite. Before Christmas, we'd worked hard on sprinting to improve his power and speed for the run-up. I had that same sensation of being watched but I couldn't tear my eyes away from Harrison until he'd completed each vault.

'Are you looking for Pops?' he asked, pausing to have a drink after his fifth go.

'Erm, yeah. I thought he'd be here by now.'

'Desmond will be talking his ear off,' he responded.

Hearing Grandpa's phrase coming from a nine-year-old made me laugh. I glanced towards the entrance again, but there was definitely nobody there.

'Give me a second,' I said, shaking my head as I power-walked to the door. Outside, I looked around and shook my head. This was ridiculous. There was nobody here and I had to get Parnell out of my mind.

'I thought I heard someone at the door,' I said to Harrison. 'Ready to go again?'

Desmond was definitely talking Grandpa's ear off as we'd finished with the vault and moved onto some floor exercises and he still hadn't appeared. Harrison had completed several tumbles across the diagonal when I heard raised voices outside.

'Stay here!' I instructed, rushing towards the door.

'...nothing to say to you!' Grandpa bellowed as I thrust the door open. 'Clear off before I call the police.'

'You!' I cried, running towards Parnell, who hastily backed away. 'Leave us alone!'

'I'm not here to cause trouble,' he said, holding his hands up. 'I wanted to see if you'd reconsidered telling your story.'

'Listen to me very carefully,' I said, squaring up to him. 'It's not just a no, it's a never. If you show your face on our land again, I'll have you charged for trespassing. Do I make myself clear?'

'No need to be so touchy,' he said, haughtily. 'I'm going. Enjoy the rest of your weekend and tell your kid from me that he's got some impressive skills. Are you hoping he'll do one better than you and bring the gold home at Brisbane?'

'Have you got your phone on you, Grandpa?' I said.

Grandpa held it up. 'You want me to call the police now?'

'I think you'd better because somebody's not listening.'

The threat had finally hit home and Parnell sauntered off down the track. Presumably he'd parked his car further down to avoid us seeing or hearing his approach.

'Do you think it's time we got an entry system for the gate?' Grandpa asked.

I sighed and shook my head. 'My feelings haven't changed on that. This is Harrison's home.'

We'd discussed it after Eliza died and again each time Parnell or another reporter came sniffing around but, for me, the negative message it sent to Harrison outweighed any positives. I didn't want him living in a fortress, feeling like there was a threat in the outside world from which we needed to protect ourselves. Even if I frequently felt like there was.

'I think he's been hanging around for a few days now,' I said as Grandpa and I set off back to the gym. 'I've had this repeated sensation of someone watching me. Where did you spot him?'

'He came round from the south side of the gym.'

Instead of going inside, I walked round the perimeter and gasped. A metal ladder was propped up against the far end of the wall.

'The cheeky blighter!' Grandpa cried.

He strode towards it but I stopped him. 'There might be fingerprints. I can't believe the nerve of him.'

I'd been busy looking at the windows and door and it had never entered my head that Parnell would have the audacity to climb onto the roof to watch us through the skylights.

'My phone's inside,' I said to Grandpa. 'Can you take a couple of photos on yours?'

'Are you calling the police after all? Because I think you should.'

'Yeah, I've had enough of this. I'll ring Mike.'

Mike Sunning was the constable at Reddfield Police Station who'd handled the original problems with Parnell and had said never to hesitate to call him if I had any more trouble.

'What's going on?' Harrison asked when I returned to the gym to retrieve my phone. 'Who was shouting?'

'Nothing to worry about. You know that reporter I don't like? He came to visit but he's gone now. He knows we don't want to talk to him.'

'Pops!' Harrison called as Grandpa returned. 'You were gone ages.'

Grandpa smiled at him. 'You know what Desmond's like. Could talk the hind leg off a donkey, that one.'

'I need to make a call, Harrison. You can get on the trampoline and do the basics but no tricks until I'm back, okay?'

'Okay.'

I wandered over to the far end of the gym with my phone, out of earshot, and called Reddfield Police Station. My timing was fortunate, catching Mike on shift and at his desk.

'Did you actually see him up the ladder?' Mike asked after I'd brought him up to speed.

'No.'

'And is there any sign of a break-in or attempted break-in?'

'Not as far as I can see.'

'Any CCTV covering that area?'

I sighed, knowing where this was heading. 'Only round the door. Nothing on the side of the building.'

'Then I'm going to struggle to get the ladder tested for prints because there's no evidence of a break-in or of him using the ladder.'

'Can't you do him for trespassing?'

'We've talked about this before, Nathan. It's not a criminal offence.'

'But he keeps harassing me.'

'Harassment and stalking is another matter but there needs to be repeated unwanted incidents.'

'There's been more than one occasion.'

'And has his behaviour been antisocial or bullying?'

'No.'

'Has it made you feel scared, distressed or threatened?'

I sighed once more and reluctantly said, 'No.'

'Then the best I can do for you is to pay Mr Parnell a visit the next time I'm passing his home or workplace and make a friendly suggestion to stay away before his behaviour does start to scare or distress.'

'If you could, that'd be good.'

'I'm sorry I can't do more. I know it's frustrating. If you find any footage of him on your property, hang onto it in case his behaviour escalates but, if you've told him you're contacting the police, I suspect that'll be enough for him to leave you alone.'

'Let's hope so. Thanks, Mike.'

I took a few deep breaths after I'd hung up, forced myself to smile, and returned to Grandpa and Harrison. Grandpa raised his eyebrows and I discreetly shook my head.

'Ready to do Mum's routine?' I asked Harrison, my voice sounding much brighter than I felt.

As he bounced and twisted, I realised that Elliot Parnell's presence today had helped me with the dilemma his last visit had kicked off. I *would* continue to educate Harrison at home because, that way, I kept him safe from bullies like Parnell. For socialisation, I couldn't keep putting off the obvious solution. It was all very well having our sights set on an Olympic gold but we had no chance of being part of Team GB if I didn't get Harrison into the competition system. And the only way to do that was for him to be part of a gymnastics club, which meant I had to make contact with that world again. I had to reach out to Ashley.

16

ZARA

We were halfway through our three weeks of filming at Hedgehog Hollow and I couldn't believe how quickly the time had flown. It had been frosty for the first couple of days and, as hoped, our videographers had gathered some beautiful wintry footage. I was impressed by the little details like a frosty spider web outside the barn which housed the rescue centre, and a frozen puddle reflecting the sky.

Last week, we'd interviewed Samantha about the origins of the rescue centre and how it developed from just helping hedgehogs into accepting all wildlife. This week, our focus was on Fizz, who was the only other full-time paid member of staff, and, next week, we'd be visiting Alderson & Wishaw Veterinary Practice, which Samantha's husband Josh ran with her dad, Jonathan.

'Good morning!' Amber and I chorused when we arrived at the rescue centre on Wednesday morning.

'Morning!' Fizz and Samantha called.

'All set for your turn in the spotlight today, Fizz?' Amber asked.

'I think so. Can we record it again if I fluff it up?'

'That's no problem at all.'

Matt looked up and down the room. 'We did Samantha's interview at the treatment table,' he said, 'but I'd like to do yours in the rest area, Fizz, if that's okay with you.'

While Jackie and Shane set up the cameras, Ishaan passed me a mic pack from his bag to hook Fizz up. After a quick sound check, we were good to go. Fizz had only uttered one sentence when the door opened and a woman rushed in holding a sandcastle bucket. She stopped dead, eyes wide, when she saw the cameras.

'Everything all right?' Samantha asked, heading towards the door.

'I found a hedgehog on the path outside my house. I nearly stood on it.' She thrust the bucket at Samantha. 'I thought it was dead but I picked it up with my scarf and it moved.'

This was the first time during filming that a rescue had been brought in, so Jackie was quick to focus her camera on the woman. I grabbed my iPad but, before I could even open a release document to obtain the woman's permission to use the footage, she put her hand up in front of her face.

'You're not filming me. I've got to go. You can keep the bucket.'

'But—'

But it seemed the woman couldn't get out of there fast enough. Samantha shrugged and Matt indicated for Jackie to keep filming while Samantha brought the bucket over to the treatment table and removed the hedgehog from it.

'Autumn juvenile,' she said. 'Still alive but freezing.'

Fizz grabbed a crate, plugged in a heat pad which she covered with a towel, and added a couple of pieces of fleece to the crate. Samantha placed the hedgehog on the heat pad while Fizz gathered various supplies. They each pulled on a pair of gloves.

'Can we get Samantha miked up?' Matt said, but Ishaan was already on the case with a mic pack ready.

'Fizz, can you explain what you're doing?' Matt asked while I was attaching Samantha's mic.

'We've had an autumn juvenile brought in,' Fizz said, looking into the camera. 'A woman found it lying on the path outside her house and was worried it might be dead until she saw it move, so she scooped it up and brought it straight here. With an admission like this, our priority is to get the hedgehog warmed up and some fluids into it.'

She pointed to her side. 'I've set up a crate with a heat pad to warm the hedgehog while we've gathered everything we need, but we'll transfer it into an incubator as soon as we've got some fluids into it. The incubator is much better because the whole space is warm in there rather than just the area covered by the heat pad.'

While Samantha weighed the hedgehog and scribbled a number down on a chart, Fizz talked us through the supplies on the treatment table.

'We have a boy here,' Samantha said, lifting the hedgehog off the scales when Fizz had finished. 'He's cold, dehydrated and far too small. As Fizz said, he's an autumn juvenile. Baby hedgehogs – hoglets – who are born in the spring have plenty of time to gain weight before the winter, but this second round of autumn births don't have that advantage. They need the weight to see them through winter, particularly if they hibernate.'

Fizz, who'd filled a syringe with subcutaneous fluids while Samantha was talking, took over the commentary.

'We start with an injection to get the fluids straight into the hedgehog to counteract dehydration. It's no good trying to apply fluids through the mouth when a hedgehog is this bad. We couldn't get sufficient fluids into him quickly enough and an unresponsive hedgehog like this probably won't swallow anyway.'

Samantha held the hedgehog in a towel while Fizz injected him. He didn't even flinch. I hoped the woman had found him in time and that he was going to make it.

'It's important to give the right amount of fluids,' Fizz said. 'We calculate that on the basis of the weight and the level of dehydration, which we can assess by looking at the hedgehog. This little one has collapsed, will be in shock and, unfortunately, is at death's door so we give him the maximum fluids for his weight.'

'I've just done a quick visual inspection,' Samantha said. 'I wanted to check for ticks, injuries and infection. There's nothing I can see externally but that doesn't mean there's nothing sinister going on internally. When he leaves us a sample, we'll test that under a microscope. For now, he'll go in the incubator. Pieces of fleece in there give extra warmth and are great for hiding under.'

'We won't put any food in with him for the moment,' Fizz added. 'If you feed a dehydrated hog, the digestive system takes fluid away from the vital organs and it can be fatal. He won't be given food until his hydration level is good.'

'What's the likelihood of survival?' Amber asked after Samantha and Fizz had settled the hedgehog in the incubator, cleared their supplies away, wiped down the table and washed their hands, all the while being filmed by Jackie and Shane.

'Impossible to say,' Samantha said. 'He was in a bad way and it very much depends whether there's anything going on internally. If he has parasites, he has a bigger fight on his hands and he might be too weak to make it, but we continue to be surprised. We've had hedgehogs in much worse states who've pulled through although, equally, we've had ones we expect to fully and quickly recover who haven't.'

'How do you feel when they don't make it?' Amber asked.

Fizz and Samantha exchanged looks and both shook their heads.

'It's the worst part of the job,' Fizz said. 'My grandparents had a farm which my brother now runs so I've always been around animal life and death. I went into this career knowing I'd have to deal with loss of life regularly, but it doesn't make it any easier. We're here to save lives and make sick and injured animals better so, when we can't do that, it hurts. We have a shelf full of boxes of tissues and we get through a lot of them.'

'My dad's a vet,' Samantha said, 'so, like Fizz, I've been around that reality all my life too, although I wasn't directly dealing with it. When I opened Hedgehog Hollow, loss was my biggest struggle. Josh once said to me—'

But we didn't get to find out what Samantha was about to say because the door opened and an elderly man appeared.

'Got an owl for you,' he called and, before anyone could respond, he crouched down, opened up the towel he'd been holding and released a clearly distressed owl. It flapped its left wing but was evidently struggling to move the other one.

'Where did you...?' Samantha started, but the man was gone. What was it with people vanishing today?

17

ZARA

I'd seen owls in the distance at Whisby Nature Park back home but I'd never seen a wild one up close and I felt an unexpected surge of emotion.

Samantha grabbed a pair of thick gloves and slowly approached the owl, scooping it up from behind.

'Hello, my lovely,' she said in a gentle voice. 'What's happened to you? Don't be afraid. We're here to help.'

Fizz placed a pet carrier on the treatment table, adding a small towel into the bottom of it. 'This is our first owl,' she said as Samantha carried it over to the table.

'What type is it?' Amber asked.

'It's a tawny owl,' Fizz said.

It was beautiful. Its feathers were a mix of white, brown and a caramel colour, it looked quite fluffy, and it had the most gorgeous face with big dark eyes. I was completely captivated and couldn't stop gazing at it.

Samantha sat down at the treatment table with the owl's back against her stomach, one gloved hand holding its feet. She picked up a small piece of fleece and placed it over the owl's eyes.

'We want to alleviate as much stress as possible,' she said. 'As with any wildlife, covering its eyes helps. Owls have extremely sharp claws so you'll notice I'm holding our tawny's feet to ensure I don't get hurt. The man who dropped him off clearly didn't want to stay and that often happens, like you saw with our hedgehog earlier. People are in a rush, perhaps on their way to work or the school run, and finding a sick or injured animal means an unexpected detour for them. Sometimes they've been involved in an incident with the animal and they're worried they'll be in trouble so they drop and run. It's not ideal because we're left trying to work out what might have happened and, if we don't know where they found an animal, we have no way of returning it to its original habitat.'

She slowly opened out the left wing which had a huge span when unfurled. She repeated this with the right wing and it was clear to even an untrained eye that there were breaks.

'My guess is that our tawny has flown into a vehicle and fractured its right wing. Tawny owls aren't normally out during the day unless they're feeding their young and, as it's not breeding season, this probably happened last night or even before that. Anyway, it needs treatment and I'd rather it goes to an owl expert. We have a place locally, although I've blanked on the name.' She looked questioningly at Fizz.

'Owl's Lodge,' Fizz said. 'It's not far from here.'

Samantha carefully placed the owl in the pet carrier and removed the eye covering. 'I'll give them a call.'

* * *

Filming at Owl's Lodge would have added fabulous footage to *The Wildlife Rescuers* but Samantha came off the phone and told us that the owner, Snowy, had point blank refused access to the cameras. Amber, noting how smitten I was with the owl, suggested I accompany Samantha there.

'You haven't met this Snowy before, then?' I asked Samantha as we set off in her jeep with the pet carrier secured on the back seat.

'No. I don't know anything about him and neither does Fizz. When we were looking into expanding, Phoebe did some research into what other rescue centres there were in the area and Owl's Lodge came up, so we hung onto the details in case we ever had an owl admitted.'

'It's a shame he won't be filmed.'

'Yeah. He wasn't nasty about it – just very absolute that it wasn't an option.'

'Fair enough. It's not for everyone.'

It took us about twenty minutes along country lanes to reach our destination. A pub-style sign read 'Owl's Lodge' above a beautiful painting of an owl perched on a branch. I hopped out and opened the wooden gate, closing it and clambering back into the jeep once Samantha had driven through. We set off up a long winding track with trees on either side.

'He said he'd meet us outside the first building on the left,' Samantha said, peering through the trees as she drove slowly.

The track was only wide enough for one vehicle but there were several passing points. On the right was a large modern-looking building with aged wooden cladding round the outside and high windows. It didn't look residential but it didn't look like a farm building either.

'This must be it,' Samantha said, pulling into a passing point on the left and parking.

To the left was a more recognisable farm building – a stone and wood barn with an open doorway and small unglazed windows. Samantha removed the pet carrier and we headed towards the entrance. A wooden sign above the door read 'The Roost' but it was in darkness and we were debating whether we were in the right place when we heard a man calling, 'Hello,' behind us.

We both turned. A short man dressed in jeans and a fleece and wearing a navy beanie hat was crossing the track.

'Are you the ones with the owl?' he asked as he joined us.

'Yes, hi. I'm Samantha, this is my friend Zara, and we have a tawny owl for you.'

Snowy – assuming that's who he was – barely glanced at either of us but he did look into the crate and nodded. 'Yep, that's a tawny.' He straightened up and glanced down the track. 'I'm not being filmed, am I?'

'We've left the film crew at Hedgehog Hollow,' Samantha assured him.

The tension visibly eased from his broad shoulders. 'Thank you. I can't be... I appreciate you listening. Do you want me to take the crate?'

Samantha handed it over and we followed him round the side of the barn. There was a door at the far end with 'The Owlery' carved into a wooden sign above it.

Snowy opened the door and flicked a light on. 'Come in. Let's take a look.'

We stepped into a large room which I suspected was the full width of the barn. Sturdy metal shelves to the right held pet carriers like the one our tawny owl was in as well as plastic crates containing equipment and medicine, the contents of each one clearly labelled. There was also a large fridge freezer. Snowy placed the tawny's carrier on a table beside the shelves and pulled on a pair of thick gloves.

'Do you know what happened to him?' he asked as he reached into the crate and carefully lifted out the owl.

'A man dumped him and fled,' Samantha said. 'I'm guessing he's been hit by a car. His right wing looks broken but we've never treated an owl before and, as you have...'

'You did the right thing bringing him here,' he said.

He perched on a stool and held the owl the same way that Samantha had earlier but he pulled the bottom of his fleece over the owl's head. I emitted a surprised gasp and he looked directly up at me. I was always drawn to eyes and Snowy's were quite beautiful – really pale blue with slightly darker rims. His skin was really pale too and his cheekbones chiselled like a model's. His hat was pulled down over his eyebrows so I couldn't see what colour his hair was although, with that pale skin and pale eyelashes, I guessed he was a redhead or strawberry blond.

'Stops him being scared,' Snowy said, a defensive tone to his voice.

I felt really bad. He must have thought I was judging him, and I felt I needed to explain myself.

'I don't work at the rescue centre. I'm part of the film crew, although I'm not here filming you, obviously. I wanted to come because I've fallen in love with that owl and I wanted to make sure it was okay. I didn't mean to gasp. Samantha put something over the owl's eyes earlier and she explained why, but I was just surprised to see you stuffing it up your jumper. And now I'm talking too much and making it worse.' I gave him an apologetic shrug and hoped he had a sense of humour.

Fortunately he did, smiling as he ran his fingers down the owl's belly. I had no idea what he was doing that for, but I didn't like to question him. He poked and prodded in silence, all the while with the owl's head under his fleece. It looked ridiculous and I wanted to laugh but it didn't feel appropriate when the poor creature was injured, so I turned my gaze away to study the room further. There was another desk on the opposite side of the room and, at the far end, there were some much larger crates and I did a double take when I realised that several of them contained owls.

'You're right about the broken wing,' Snowy said, pulling my attention back to him.

The door opened and a young boy of maybe nine or ten wearing a bobble hat poked his head round it.

'Can I see it, Dad?'

'Come in and close the door,' Snowy said, his tone so much warmer than the one he'd used with us.

'It's a tawny,' the boy exclaimed.

'Male or female?' Snowy asked him.

'Male. Much smaller than the female.'

'Good lad.'

'The male's really smaller than the female?' I asked, surprised. 'I thought males were always bigger.'

'Urban myth,' Snowy said. 'There are lots of species where males and females are a similar size and many where the female's bigger.'

'Wow! Every day's a school day,' I said, impressed.

'What's happened to him?' the boy asked.

'Broken wing, probably hit by a car. I can see a clear break here where there's a tiny spatter of blood but there could be other breaks so what do we need to do?'

'Put him to sleep and do an X-ray,' the boy said.

'Should I have taken him straight to a vet after all?' Samantha asked.

'No. I've got the equipment here. Thanks for bringing him in. If you get any others, give me a shout.'

If we hadn't already realised that was our cue to leave, his next statement confirmed it.

'Harrison, can you show our visitors out?'

Samantha handed over a business card for Hedgehog Hollow. 'We take all sorts of injured wildlife if you ever find anything other than an owl in need of help. As you can probably tell from the name, hedgehogs are our speciality.'

He placed the card on the desk with a nod.

'Thanks for rescuing the tawny,' Harrison said, opening the door for us. 'Dad loves owls and he's amazing with them. He'll make him better.'

'Pleased to hear it,' I said as he walked along the side of the barn with us. 'Do you love owls too?'

'They're my favourite birds, but my favourite animal's a dragon.'

'You mean a reptile like a bearded dragon?'

He shook his head, his expression deadly serious. 'Like a huge dragon with wings which breathes fire. Have you ever rescued one of those?'

Samantha and I exchanged glances and Harrison burst out laughing.

'Got you!' he said. 'I do know dragons aren't real. I like reading fantasy books and there's lots of dragons in those. Not sure I'd want to meet one in real life, unless it was soft and cuddly and I don't think there are many like that.'

We'd reached the jeep.

'You had us going there for a moment,' I said, smiling at Harrison. 'My name's Zara, by the way, and that's Samantha. Please tell your dad we're grateful to him for looking after the owl. If he has time to let us know how it gets on, I'd really appreciate it.'

Harrison cocked his head to one side and studied my face. 'You love him, don't you?'

My mouth dropped open. Where had that come from? Was Snowy a single dad and his son was trying to matchmake for him?

'Your dad?' I said, my voice a little high. 'I've only just met him! We've barely said five—'

'Not my dad!' Harrison cried, his shoulders shaking with laughter. 'I meant the tawny owl. You love him.'

I could hear Samantha's giggles as she got into the vehicle.

'Yes. I love the tawny owl,' I said, relieved to clear up that misunderstanding. 'He took one look at me and captured my heart.' I made a heart shape with my fingers to show him and he smiled and copied me.

'Owls do that. Got to go and help Dad. See ya!'

And he ran off back to The Owlery.

'That was hilarious,' Samantha said, when I clambered into the jeep beside her.

'It was embarrassing! I can't believe I thought he was asking me if I was in love with his dad. Of course he was talking about the owl. Kill me now!'

Samantha was still laughing as she turned her jeep round and we set off back down the track while I sat shaking my head, cringing.

'I can't believe he has his own X-ray equipment,' she said, finally composed. 'That's an expensive outlay. Explains why he said to bring the owl direct to him, though.'

'Did you notice the other owls?'

'Yes. Looks like he has a few patients.'

'I wanted to ask about them and find out what'll happen to the tawny.'

'Me too,' Samantha agreed, 'but I don't think he was very talkative. You could always come back in the next couple of days, saying you need to know what happened for the documentary. You could ask again about filming. He might feel more comfortable about it now he's met us.'

I pondered on it. 'It's worth a try. You don't think it's better to ring him instead of just turning up?'

'You're more likely to get a yes if you do it face to face. I think he liked you.'

I laughed. 'I think he thought I was a gibbering idiot.'

'He smiled at you. He'd barely glanced at either of us until that point.'

'I still maintain he thinks I'm an idiot, but I'll see what Amber and Matt think.'

We reached the end of the track and turned onto the country lane. Owl's Lodge was more remote than Hedgehog Hollow and Bumblebee Barn and I rather liked it. The track had been sloped and, if it continued to incline, the house must be on an amazing elevated position with spectacular views across the Yorkshire Wolds. I hadn't seen the house, unless that building on the right was it and had been designed with all the windows on the other side. I'd have to ask about that if I had the chance to return and, as that owl had completely captured my heart, I hoped I'd get that chance.

18

SNOWY

The tawny owl's wing had three fractures – all on different bones but all clean so he should heal nicely. With the help of my medical assistant, Harrison, I'd splinted them and would need to keep the tawny in The Owlery for two to three weeks while the bones repaired.

I wished the person who'd found him hadn't scarpered without handing over any information. There'd be a female out there somewhere wondering what had happened to her mate and, while I could do nothing about that while his wing was healing, I could have returned him to the same area when he was better. Tawny owls were territorial and tended to stick to their homes so there was every chance they'd have tracked each other down through their calls. I could try releasing him at or near Hedgehog Hollow and hope he'd been hit close to there, or I could release him on my own land and wish for him to find a new mate. Why were people so thoughtless sometimes?

Harrison wanted to name the owl and, while I preferred not to name wild animals, I gave in to him as usual. I could never resist his puppy-dog expression. He'd liked the name of one of our visitors – Zara – and would have named the owl after her if it had been a female but, as it was a male, he adjusted it to Zorro.

Damaged wing aside, Zorro appeared to be in good health and had eaten well across the two days he'd been with us so far. Harrison and I had spent the morning so far in The Owlery using Zorro as inspiration for our lessons. Starting with art, we'd drawn pencil sketches, Harrison going for the full owl and me focusing on his head. Taking after Grandpa, Harrison had shown a strong aptitude for art since he could hold a pencil so his sketch was far superior to mine, although I was pretty proud of how much my drawing had improved through watching online tutorials.

'It's really good, Dad,' Harrison assured me. 'You should put it on the board.'

'I'll put yours up, but I think mine needs to go in the recycling.'

He wouldn't hear of it, insisting I sign and date it before attaching them both to the whiteboard with magnets.

'We'll nip up to the lodge for a quick break, then come back for some creative writing before lunch and, as you've worked so hard this week, we'll leave your school work there and spend this afternoon in the gym.'

'Yay! Thanks, Dad.'

My phone rang on the way. It was a local number but I didn't recognise it.

'It's Mike Sunning,' the caller said after I'd answered.

I indicated to Harrison that he should run on ahead. 'Hi, Mike, how's it going?'

'Good. Just letting you know that I caught up with Elliot Parnell yesterday. He's assured me he won't be paying you any more visits. I'm assuming you haven't seen him since we spoke?'

'No. I've had a couple more cameras installed but it looks like he's stayed away.'

'Good. Hopefully that's the end of it.'

'Fingers crossed. Thanks for having a word. I appreciate it's difficult when he hasn't directly broken any laws.'

'It was no bother. Give me a shout if you have any more problems.'

I thanked him and hung up. I hoped it was over, but I knew Parnell too well. He didn't give up on things and, if he wanted a story, he'd get it – even if he made some of it up.

I ran up to the lodge where I found Grandpa and Harrison in the kitchen.

'Harrison tells me you both drew pictures of Zorro and you decided yours should be confined to the bin,' Grandpa said.

'It wasn't nearly as good as his.'

Grandpa raised a bushy eyebrow at me. 'Since when was your success defined by someone else's? Was it better than the last thing you drew?'

'Yes.'

'Then it's a success. Can't believe I'm having to remind an elite athlete of that.'

I couldn't either!

'How's Zorro doing?' Grandpa asked, handing me a mug of green tea.

'Good. They're all doing well. The long-eared owl is ready for release tonight so we'll do that at dusk.'

'Will Zara and Samantha come back when we release Zorro?' Harrison asked.

'No,' I said, surprised he'd asked. 'It'll just be us three as usual.'

'But Zara loves owls. She told me. Please invite them, Dad, or just Zara if you don't want too many people here. I really liked her.'

'Sounds like a date,' Grandpa said, barely stifling his grin.

'It's not a date and it's not... We're not talking about this. I'm taking my tea onto the veranda. Be ready in fifteen minutes, Harrison.'

I headed back out into the cold and rested my elbows on the wooden ledge on top of the glass balustrade, my hands cupped round the mug. A date? Where had that come from? Going on a date couldn't be further out of my comfort zone than spending a night in the pub playing darts with Elliot Parnell. Grandpa had never mentioned dating before but maybe he thought that five years was enough time to 'get over' the loss of my wife and find someone else. If so, he could think again. I'd never get over losing Eliza and I certainly wasn't going to take advice on moving on from a man who'd been widowed for fifteen years and whose only dates during that time were fishing ones with Desmond and his gang.

But as I gazed out over the tops of the trees, trying to focus on the beautiful view, Zara's face swam into my mind and I chuckled to myself as I pictured her squirming when she thought she was digging herself into a hole. Admittedly, she was extremely attractive and when my eyes caught hers, there had been the briefest stirring of something in the pit of my stomach, but it meant nothing. We didn't get many visitors at Owl's Lodge – intentionally so – and we certainly didn't get attractive women with an obvious fascination for owls.

I sipped my tea, trying to focus on the creative writing exercise for Harrison, but my thoughts kept drifting back to Zara, which made no sense. She'd been here less than ten minutes and I'd spent most of that time looking at the owl rather than her, but there was something magnetic about her.

Placing my tea down on the table, I ran my hands through my hair. Why was I even giving any headspace to this? I wasn't going to phone Hedgehog Hollow and invite either of them back and I doubted they'd rush to visit after the cool reception I'd given them. 'We've still got ninety minutes of school left,' I muttered under my breath. 'Focus!'

19

ZARA

I usually woke up each morning when Barney rose. Even though he wasn't particularly noisy, the sound of doors opening and closing and the dogs scampering around seeped into my consciousness. Most mornings I fell back to sleep but, this morning, I felt wide awake.

The heating hadn't yet kicked in and there was a chill in the air so I pulled on a soft oversized hoodie and snuggled down under the duvet to watch Fizz's interview on my laptop.

The camera loved Fizz. She looked fabulous with her pink hair in space buns and she came across as enthusiastic, which was exactly how she was in real life. We'd met plenty of bubbly people before who'd frozen in front of the camera and become monotone, so it wasn't a given that their personality would translate.

She talked about how she'd first encountered Hedgehog Hollow – a tale I already knew. Her cat had brought a hoglet into the house and Fizz had found more in her garden so she took them to the rescue centre, helped Samantha feed and toilet them and completely fell in love with hedgehogs.

'You were training to be a veterinary nurse at the time,' Amber said. 'Presumably you were planning to work in a veterinary practice.'

'That was the goal but I was smitten with the hedgehogs so I started volunteering here around my studies. I loved the work and really didn't want to leave but I needed to earn a wage when I graduated. Fortunately that coincided with the changes to the rescue centre – becoming the charitable arm of Josh and Jonathan's practice and expanding beyond hedgehogs.'

'You couldn't see yourself moving into a veterinary practice in the future?'

Fizz shook her head. 'This is my dream job. Money's not my motivator. I've no desire to climb the career ladder. What's important to me is having a job where I get to work with animals every day, which I'm good at, and where I know I'm making a difference. I can see myself working here forever. Every day is so varied. I arrive for work and I've no idea what animals will be admitted and what will be wrong with them. How exciting is that? Why would I want to leave?'

Viewers would be left in no doubt about Fizz's passion for her job. It shone from her eyes and bounced off every word. Her view on work was the same as mine – not motivated by a big salary or progression but by being good at the job and having variety. I sank back into the pillows. I loved variety but was my job really that varied after six years on the same programme? I closed the lid of my laptop, my thoughts whirring. Was that a bad thing? An element of repetition was good, familiar. It meant I could do those parts of the job easily and give more attention to anything new or unexpected. *I can see myself working here forever*, Fizz had said. Could I see myself doing my job forever?

'It's Mum's fault,' I muttered to myself. She was the one who'd questioned my career and now had me questioning it. I *did* love what I did and hadn't had any doubts about the longevity until Mum had talked about Amber and Barney having a family and casting doubts on my long-term future. Yes, I'd had those thoughts myself but having someone else voicing them made them all the more real.

I watched the rest of Fizz's interview and responded to a few emails. I'd settled into a routine of rising at half seven, having a shower and getting dressed before breakfast. With being awake so much earlier this morning, my stomach was growling by 7 a.m. so I pulled on my slipper boots and padded down to the kitchen in search of sustenance.

The LED lights under the cupboards were on as usual, bathing the kitchen in soft light, and I froze as I spotted Amber and Barney locked in a passionate clinch. His T-shirt was discarded on the floor and he was slipping Amber's dressing gown off her shoulders as he kissed her neck. Holding my breath, I stepped backwards and crept up the stairs, praying I wouldn't land on a creaky board and alert them to my presence.

I made it to the top, creak-free, and slipped into my bedroom, softly closing the door. That had been close! I'd walked in on them kissing before but what I'd just witnessed had been several heat levels up and, if I'd been a minute later, I might have caught the full floor show. My cheeks burned at the thought. Thank God they hadn't seen me.

I sank down onto the edge of my bed. What was I doing here? Amber and Barney had been nothing but kind and welcoming, but three was a crowd. I hadn't felt that way until Mum planted the idea and now I was increasingly conscious of me being the third wheel. They were still in the early days of their relationship and they were very likely holding back on their passion because I was here. That wasn't fair. It had to be frustrating for them knowing that, if anything did get spicy between them, they had to cool it down because I could walk into the room at any moment and catch them. They'd likely only got carried away in the kitchen just now because my routine dictated that I wouldn't appear until later.

Feeling restless, I wandered over to the window and parted the curtains. My bedroom looked out over the farmyard, but it was still dark outside and I couldn't see much more than the dark shapes of the barns and the sky lightening on the horizon.

I had some big decisions to make. As Mum had pointed out, I did have all my eggs in one basket with my job, my home and my strongest friendship all tied to Amber and that was risky. There was no reason for our friendship to falter but, if Amber did have a family, the other two connections would be impacted. The production company didn't employ me – Amber did – and she wouldn't need to do that if she was on maternity leave. I needed a contingency plan. But what?

* * *

Matt and Amber liked the idea of me returning to Owl's Lodge so we drove to Hedgehog Hollow in separate cars that morning and, at half one, I said goodbye to everyone and drove to Owl's Lodge. It was a beautiful day with a clear blue sky, a few wispy clouds and a nip in the air. A strong desire to take a walk pulled at me so I parked in one of the early passing points and set off up the track.

What a beautiful setting Snowy had. I loved how the long track meandered between the trees and I could imagine the woods being packed with wildlife. I was probably being watched by some deer right now.

The Roost was empty and I tried The Owlery, but it was locked. I crossed the track and paused, looking at the modern building. Stone steps ahead of me led down to a wide door with obscured glass either side. To the left, another set of steps inclined, but I couldn't see where they went. I turned in a circle but, with no signs of life in any direction, I set off towards the building. There were lights on inside, so hopefully I'd find Snowy there.

I'd only descended a few steps when my mobile beeped with a message which I stopped to read.

> **FROM AMBER**
>
> Hope Snowy is OK with you being there and you have a great afternoon. Last minute evening plans – Joel & Marley are coming over and Joel's picking up an Indian takeaway on the way. Aiming for 7pm. Any special requests?

Yes. Not to be there. But I could hardly reply saying that, especially when I hadn't confided in Amber about my feelings towards Joel. I wasn't faring particularly well with my Christmas wish or New Year's resolution to get over him and move on. He'd visited the farm a couple of times since the ball and I was still as smitten as ever. It was bad enough seeing him, knowing my feelings weren't reciprocated, but I really didn't want to spend an evening with him and Marley. Being single had never bothered me but, when I wasn't working, it was all I seemed able to think about at the moment. I blamed that on the conversation with Mum.

Would it be too sneaky to make alternative arrangements for tonight and reply to say I'd already got plans? But what? I'd been to the cinema with Phoebe and Fizz last night so I couldn't contact them to suggest something and... I gasped as I realised they were yet another couple with whom I was third-wheeling, often with Phoebe's friend Leo and his boyfriend.

None of my friends had ever made me feel uncomfortable or like the odd one out, but it seemed that everyone in my life wasn't just in a relationship – they were all completely loved up. They'd found the one. I'd never come close. I'd never told a boyfriend that I loved him because I'd never fallen that deeply. I'd come close with Declan, but something had held me back. I liked to think it was because there was something deep down in my gut telling me I couldn't trust him, but what if it was me? What if I was someone who didn't fall in love? What if all I ever felt was physical attraction and lust? But it wasn't just physical attraction and lust with Joel. There was something so much more with him – a friendship and deeper connection. If only he was single and it was reciprocated.

I re-read Amber's message. I could either reply with my food choice, give myself a stern talking to and enjoy the evening, or I could ignore the message for now. I hadn't clicked into it so Amber had no indication that I'd even read it.

'Can I help you?'

I looked up to see an elderly man with white hair and a white beard halfway down the other set of steps, glaring at me. As I was there without invitation and didn't know who this man was, I found myself lost for words.

'I said, can I help you?' he demanded in a gruffer tone, coming closer.

'Hi... erm, sorry. My name's Zara Timmins. I was looking for Snowy. I brought him an owl to be fixed.'

I cringed inwardly. *I brought him an owl to be fixed?* What sort of nonsense was that?

The man stopped a few paces away from me and his stony expression softened. 'Ah! You must be the owl's namesake.'

'Sorry?'

'I'm Eddie Oakes, Snowy's grandpa.'

'Hi! Nice to meet you. How am I the owl's namesake? I thought it was a male.'

'Young Harrison thought you had a pretty name but, as you say, the tawny's a boy so he tweaked it to Zorro.'

'Aw, bless him. That's so sweet.'

'Is Snowy expecting you?'

'No. I called on the off-chance. I wanted to find out how the owl was doing and to ask him if I could bring the crew up to film it if we promised not to film Snowy.'

'Film crew?' It was Eddie's turn to look confused and it seemed Snowy hadn't told his grandpa about the docuseries.

'I'm the producer's assistant on a docuseries about rescue centres. We're mainly filming at Hedgehog Hollow and Zorro was brought in while we were filming but when Samantha, the owner of Hedgehog Hollow, mentioned the film crew to your grandson, it was a definite no.'

'Yeah, I'm not surprised. Fiercely private, that one, and you can't blame him after everything he's been through.'

His tone was very conversational, as though we were old friends and I knew exactly what he was talking about. It didn't feel appropriate to ask him to expand.

'So how is Zorro?' I asked, getting back on track.

'You can ask him yourself. Snowy, that is. Not the owl. Come with me.'

I followed him down the steps towards the door.

'Your ears must have been burning,' he said. 'We were just talking about you earlier.'

'You were?'

'Harrison took quite a shine to you and asked whether you'd be coming back for Zorro's release.'

'Oh my gosh, I'd love to! When's that likely to be?'

We'd reached the door and he paused with his hand on the handle. 'About two to three weeks.'

I grimaced. 'I'll be away in Scotland filming *Countryside Calendar* then. Shame, as it would be amazing to see one released back into the wild.'

He smiled at me. 'Then you're in luck, because we're releasing one tonight. We've got a long-eared owl ready to fly if you fancy sticking around.'

I gasped, thrilled by the idea. 'Can I? Really?'

Eddie pulled on the door and I followed him inside and gasped once more as we stood in the entrance. I had *not* expected this. It wasn't a house or an office. It was an enormous fully equipped gymnasium with all the gymnastics apparatus, mats and foam pits I'd expect to see in a proper club. My attention was drawn to Harrison, who was sprinting towards a vault. He leapt off the springboard and executed a front handspring with a full twist, landing perfectly on both feet. Wow! He was good.

Snowy had his back to us and was wearing a tracksuit top. I did a double take at the Olympic rings on it and glanced at Eddie, eyes wide, so many questions in my mind.

His pale blue eyes twinkled as he smiled. 'He didn't tell you who he is, did he?'

'No. Who is he?' I whispered.

'I'll leave that to him.' He raised his voice as we started down the steps past several rows of staggered seating. 'Snowy! Visitor!'

Snowy spun round and it was only when he was facing me that I registered his hair colour now that he wasn't wearing a hat – pure white like his grandpa's. Harrison's hair was white too.

'Zara!' he said, shock evident in his expression as he grabbed a beanie hat which had been dumped on the floor near him and pulled it on. 'What are you doing here?'

'I wanted to see how the owl was doing and I bumped into your grandpa outside.'

'I named him after you,' Harrison said, rushing over to me. 'Well, nearly after you. He's called Zorro cos he's a boy.'

I smiled down at him. 'So I hear. I'm very flattered. How's he doing?'

'He had three broken bones but Dad put a splint on him and he's going to be fine, isn't he, Dad?'

Snowy was still staring at me, as though in a trance.

'Dad?' Harrison prompted.

'Sorry, yes. It was clean breaks. Erm... sorry. We don't get many visitors.'

I'd already guessed that from his reaction to Samantha and me on Wednesday and, given how uncomfortable he looked now, tugging his hat further down over his ears, I wondered whether I should have phoned ahead after all. Putting people at ease was part of my job and a compliment was often a great opener.

'This is a seriously impressive set-up,' I said, sweeping my arm round the gym. 'And that was some seriously impressive vaulting, Harrison. How long have you been doing gymnastics?'

'Since I was a baby,' he said. 'I want to compete in Brisbane 2032.'

'The Olympics? Wow! How old will you be then?'

'Seventeen. Granddad was twenty-two when he got the bronze at Montreal and Dad was eighteen when he got the silver at Beijing, so I'll be the youngest in the family to compete.'

I glanced from Harrison to Snowy. 'Oh, my God! You're an Olympian?' I was very aware that I sounded all fan-girly about it but who cared? I was awestruck.

Snowy's jaw clenched and his nod was barely perceptible. Why wasn't he owning it? Why wasn't he smiling and offering to show me his medal? Okay, so Olympians probably didn't whip out their medal at every opportunity, but they were surely extremely proud of their achievements. The dedication and expertise needed to even get on the team was phenomenal.

'Dad's a brilliant gymnast,' Harrison gushed. 'He's my coach.'

'Hoping for the gold this time, aren't we?' Eddie said, ruffling his great-grandson's hair.

'What did you get your silver in?' I asked Snowy.

'We need to get back to Harrison's training,' he said, pointing his thumb in the direction of the vault behind them.

'Okay. Can I watch?'

'I don't think—'

'Please, Dad!' Harrison interrupted. 'I want Zara to stay. Nobody ever comes to watch me.'

Snowy said nothing for a while, but then his shoulders relaxed and he sighed. 'Okay, just this once.'

'Yes!' Harrison said, punching his fist in the air. 'She can spot for me on the trampoline too.'

'You've got a trampoline?' My eyes flicked round the room and I couldn't believe I hadn't clocked it when I walked in. 'Wow!'

'Yes, but don't feel you need to stay for that too,' Snowy said, in a tone which made it clear he'd rather I didn't.

'She's in no rush,' Eddie said. 'She's staying for tea.'

Snowy frowned. 'Tea? Why's she staying for tea?'

'Because I invited her to join us for Tufty's release and it would be rude to send her home straight after. She might as well join us for tea. Be nice to have a guest for once.'

I hadn't thought about the invitation extending to food but it solved my dilemma about this evening, giving me the perfect excuse to avoid being around Joel and Marley.

'When did this happen?' Snowy asked.

'Outside. I invited her, she said yes, end of story. Come on, Harrison, show us what you've got.'

Snowy opened his mouth as though he was going to protest, but he closed it again, put his arm round his son's shoulders and guided him over to the vault. Eddie led me back up the steps and along a row of benches.

I so badly wanted to see that owl released and Harrison and Eddie were so warm and friendly, but Snowy was obviously not a fan of visitors.

'Eddie, if me being here's a problem...' I began.

'It's not. You're my guest and he can stop his mithering. It'll do him good to have some company. Can't hide away from the world forever.'

I wanted to ask what he meant by that, but Snowy turned round and stared fixedly at his grandpa.

'No talking,' Eddie whispered to me, holding his hand up to indicate to Snowy that he'd got the message.

Although I had stacks of questions, I was happy to remain quiet for now and take it all in. I could ask my questions over our evening meal.

The gym was as big as the one I'd attended as a child, if not bigger. The family must be loaded to be able to set up and run something like this privately. At the opposite side of the gym was a three-lane running track which would be used for sprinting and drills to build speed and technique for the vault. The full-size trampoline was to the far right along with a mini trampoline. At the end to the left were the type of weights machines typically found in a recreational gym, along with free weights. Most of the space was given up to the sprung floor, the tumbling track, the big artistic gymnastics apparatus – rings, parallel bars (known as p-bars), high bar and uneven bars – and the smaller apparatus of balance beam, pommel horse and vault, the latter two in different sizes to suit adults and children.

The uneven bars and balance beam were used in women's gymnastics rather than men's, the floor and vault being the only apparatus in common. Did this mean there was a woman who trained with them – Harrison's mum or perhaps a sister? If there was a sister, where was she now? School? Come to think of it, why wasn't Harrison at school? I glanced at my watch – 2.27 p.m. Schools would have another half an hour or so before finishing for the day so he clearly hadn't been to school today or when we brought Zorro over on Wednesday, so he must be home educated. Was that because it was easier to fit his training in or was there some other reason? The questions kept on coming!

Harrison did several vaults before moving onto the floor. It had been a long time since I'd stepped inside a gym and, as I watched Harrison, memories flooded back to me about how much I'd loved gymnastics. And how, because of Roman, it had been taken away from me.

20

ZARA

Eighteen years ago

I wasn't a happy nine-year-old. It was Bonfire Night and my best friend Suzie Thomas had invited me to a bonfire with her family but Mum had said no. She said inviting me with two hours' notice was far too late when we already had plans, so now we were on our way to yet another stinky football match.

'Stop sulking, Zara!' Mum snapped, glaring at me in the mirror stuck to the windscreen.

'I'm not!' But I was. I couldn't help it. I glanced across at my brother sitting in the back seat beside me. He gave me a smug grin and stuck his tongue out, so I poked him in the ribs. The dobber yelped.

'Mum! Zara's hitting me.'

'Right! That's it!' Mum slammed on the brakes. 'Out you get, Roman. You can sit in the front after all and you, Zara, can explain to Owen why he has to sit in the back.'

Roman stuck his tongue out again as he jubilantly settled into the front seat but I didn't care because it was a win for me too. I was delighted not to share the back seat with my brother and I had no problem sitting with Owen. My parents were now divorced and Mum had introduced us to Owen a few months ago. He played golf at Sycamore Beck where she worked and they'd become friends because they were both going through divorces, and then he'd become her boyfriend. Roman wasn't keen on Owen because he wasn't Dad. I liked him even more because Roman didn't.

We set off again and, a couple of turns later, stopped outside Owen's flat. Without a word, Mum got out and stomped up to the door, getting there just as it opened. She must have blurted out about me wanting to go to the bonfire because she kept pointing towards the car. Owen hugged her and it must have made her feel better because she didn't seem quite so angry when she returned.

Owen gave me a warm smile as he sat beside me and fastened his seatbelt. 'Lucky me, getting to share the back seat with you.'

'I have to tell you it's because Roman stuck his tongue out at me so I poked him. Sorry.'

'It's no problem,' he assured me as we set off again.

'Mum says I have to stop sulking but I can't help it. It's Bonfire Night and I wanted to go to a bonfire but Mum said I have to watch Roman playing football instead. Bonfire Night is only once a year. Football is three times a week, sometimes four.'

'You're not a football fan?'

'I hate it.'

'Zara!' Mum snapped. 'That's not a nice thing to say.'

'But it's the truth and you say we should always tell the truth! Football's just a bunch of smelly boys kicking a ball about and shouting at each other. It's so boring. Bonfires and fireworks are exciting.'

'We're not going through this again,' Mum said. 'I've told you several times that it's an important match for your brother tonight.'

'The scouts are going to be there,' I told Owen. 'I don't understand why.'

'Not *the* scouts. *A* scout. A talent scout.' Mum was obviously angry with me again. I probably should have listened harder but I always switched off during conversations about football. And there were a lot of conversations about football in our house so I spent a lot of time drifting off.

'A talent scout is a person who looks for talented footballers,' Owen said, his voice calm and gentle. 'In this case, they're looking for potential in young players. All big football teams have youth teams who they train. Some of those boys might go on to play professional football for that team or another.'

'Do you like football?' I asked him.

'I think that's plenty of chatter for now,' Mum said. 'Roman needs some quiet so he can focus before his match.'

I looked up at Owen and he winked at me. 'We'll talk later,' he mouthed, making me feel really special. People weren't usually interested in what I had to say.

When we arrived at the floodlit football pitch, I wrapped my scarf round my neck and pulled on my thick coat but I struggled with the zip.

'It's hard because I've got three jumpers on,' I told Owen as he helped me.

'That's a lot of jumpers.'

'It's always cold watching the football. It wouldn't have been cold at the bonfire.'

'Don't start that again,' Mum warned. 'I can't be in two places at the same time.'

'But you weren't invited.'

'I don't want to hear another word about it, Zara. I mean it.'

I slipped my gloved hand into Owen's as we crossed the car park. There was a high-pitched screech followed by several explosions in the air above us. I looked up at the colourful fireworks but didn't say anything about how pretty they were. I was sick of being told off.

* * *

Roman's team won their game 3–1, with him scoring two of the goals. I was pleased for my brother because he'd done well in front of the scout and I was pleased for me because he was always foul to me when he missed a goal or his team lost. Me saying *it's just a stupid game* never went down well.

Afterwards, the coach told Mum that the scout wanted to speak to her and Roman. My feet were so cold I could hardly feel them and I wasn't looking forward to waiting for them, but Mum handed Owen her car keys.

'I'm not sure how long we'll be so why don't you take Zara back to the car and pop the heating on?'

'Did you enjoy the game?' Owen asked as we briskly strode across the car park.

'I watched the fireworks instead, but don't tell Mum. Football's so boring.'

'Are there any sports you like?'

'Gymnastics.'

'Do you go to a gymnastics club?'

'I used to but Mum made me pack it in when Roman changed football club because his football nights were the same as my gymnastics ones.'

It used to be all right. I went to gymnastics twice a week and Roman went to football practice on a different night with matches on a weekend but then he went up to senior school and his PE teacher told Mum my brother had a gift. He got all big-headed and never stopped going on about that. He was invited to join his teacher's youth football club on the other side of Lincoln. They trained three nights a week and two of them clashed with gymnastics. I was told I'd have to miss one week while Mum and Roman checked out this new club. They both loved it. One week became two, then three, and I never returned to gymnastics. Nobody checked if that was okay with me. Every time I asked when I could go back, Mum said *I can't be in two places at the same time*. I didn't understand why Roman and I couldn't take turns with our clubs. Why was his football more important than my gymnastics?

Owen and I had arrived back at the car and clambered inside out of the cold.

'I loved gymnastics,' I continued. 'And I'd finally got a place to start trampolining. I'd had my name down for ages but it was really popular so I had to wait. But trampolining was on a Monday after gymnastics so I couldn't do that either cos of Roman's football. That's not fair, is it?'

'I'm sure your mum has her reasons.'

'She does! It's because she thinks Roman's better at football than I am at gymnastics.'

Owen raised his eyebrows at me. 'She said that to you?'

'Something like that. And that's not fair either because he's nearly three and a half years older than me and if I'd been going to gymnastics for another three and a half years, I might have been really brilliant and my teachers might have said I had a gift too.'

'That's a good point. It takes a long time to get really good at something.'

'Mum only cares about Roman.'

'Aw, that's not true, Zara. When we became friends, she told me how wonderful you both were.'

'Yeah, well, that was before Roman was told he had a gift and started at his new club. She likes Roman best now and I don't get to do anything because it's all about him and his stupid football. She only loves him now.'

And, with that revelation, I burst out crying. Owen hugged me and did his best to console me, but this had been building up for well over a year now and the tears wouldn't stop coming.

'Your mum's coming back,' Owen said. 'I'll have a quick word with her.'

I don't know what Owen said to Mum, but there were lots of glances in my direction from both of them. Roman ran across the car park and clambered into the front seat.

'The scout says I've got a gift too,' he said, twisting round with a big grin on his face. 'I've got a try-out for Lincoln City Academy.'

I knew that this was brilliant and I was about to congratulate him, but then he waved his arms in the air and added in a sing-song voice, 'I'm better than you,' really dragging out the 'you'.

* * *

Present day

I continued to watch Harrison while my thoughts about my own experiences at his age whirred round my mind. That declaration by my brother that he was better than me was the moment it properly fell apart for the pair of us. That evening was meant to be about him – I knew that – but he managed to turn it into a competition against me. Granted, he was only twelve, but I was only nine and already feeling vulnerable that Mum always put him first. If Mum and Owen hadn't got back into the car at that point, I'd probably have thumped him.

I never found out what Owen said to Mum that night or afterwards but, in the New Year, I returned to gymnastics and Owen was my taxi service. I'd lost my trampolining place but another one came free in the September so I started then and loved it.

Things improved with Mum because I wasn't sulking and stressing her out, but we never got back that closeness we'd had when I was little. She wasn't my hero anymore – Owen was. Still is. When they got married, my face hurt from smiling all day. Obviously I was pleased that Mum had found happiness again, but I was more pleased that I had a stepdad who meant more to me than either of my biological parents. And I still felt guilty every day about that.

While Harrison paused for a drink, I looked round the gymnasium once more. I remembered the moves and apparatus I'd found it easier to master, and those which had felt like my nemesis. I recalled that feeling of immense satisfaction when, after weeks or even months of practice, I finally mastered them. And with those memories came further regrets. While I certainly hadn't had the talent or mindset an elite athlete required and the Olympic Games wasn't on my radar at any point, I had been good. I'd won a few medals and could have added to my haul... if I hadn't gone and thrown it all away.

I drew my thoughts away from the past and focused on Harrison and Snowy. I longed to see Snowy demonstrating some moves. I put him at five foot six, a few inches taller than me. He was broad-shouldered and I bet that tracksuit was hiding impressive muscles. With his physique, I imagined he was best on the floor, vault and pommels and I was dying to know what he'd won his silver medal for.

Despite my love for gymnastics, I'd never actually followed the sport.

I didn't watch the Olympic Games or any other competitions and I didn't know any of the gymnasts' names. Unlike Roman, who'd lived and breathed football. His bedroom walls were covered in posters of his favourite footballers and if he wasn't playing, he was watching the game. Mum had, of course, taken that as further evidence that I wasn't serious about gymnastics.

Harrison stood at the edge of the floor, bowed to Eddie and me, then ran over to us. Snowy stayed where he was.

'Thanks for letting me watch,' I said, smiling at Harrison. 'You're amazing. How old are you?'

'Nine. I'll be ten in April.'

'Unbelievable. I can already picture that Olympic gold round your neck.'

His smile widened. 'I'm going on the trampoline now. Will you spot me?'

'I will if it's all right with your dad.'

I looked in Snowy's direction for affirmation. He nodded and walked towards the trampoline without a word.

'What's your favourite apparatus?' I asked.

'Trampoline at the moment. I've been learning my mum's routine.'

'Your mum's a trampolinist?'

'No. She just did it for fun, but I never saw it cos she died when I was four.'

'Aw, Harrison, I'm so sorry.' I didn't know what else to say and glanced up at Eddie for support. He put his arm round Harrison's shoulders.

'It was the five-year anniversary on New Year's Day,' Eddie said. 'Harrison wanted to learn her fun routine as a way of feeling closer to her.'

We'd reached the trampoline and Snowy had already positioned himself on one side. Eddie indicated that I should stand at the opposite side, and he took one end. I wished Snowy would look at me but my presence either irritated or unnerved him. I'd see how the trampolining went but if there were no signs of warming to me, I'd call it a day. Much as I wanted to see the long-eared owl released, I'd rather spend an evening squirming as Joel and Marley acted all cute together than make this widowed former Olympian feel uncomfortable in his own home.

21
SNOWY

Zara squealed and applauded loudly when Harrison landed Eliza's routine.

'That was fantastic!' she cried. 'You've really only been doing that since New Year?'

'I'm a quick learner,' Harrison said.

'I can see that. It looked like you were having fun.'

'It's brilliant,' Harrison said. 'So much fun. Are you wearing socks?'

'Yes, why?'

'You should have a go.'

'I'd love to!' Zara looked across at me and her smile faltered before she turned back to Harrison with a grin on her face. 'But this isn't about me. This is your practice time and I'm honoured to be able to watch. Will you show me it again?'

I felt terrible. She'd clearly been excited about having a go and I'd stomped all over it. Kudos to her for recovering so well in front of my son and not making me the villain. It would have been easy for her to say something like, *I don't think your dad wants me to.*

Harrison returned to the middle of the trampoline and gained some height before executing another immaculate routine. I couldn't wait to see where he took it when we worked on more difficult elements.

When he'd finished, Zara applauded enthusiastically again which, from the beam across his face, clearly made Harrison's day. I praised and encouraged him – of course I did – but I hadn't considered the impact of him missing out on peer adulation. I might have been picked on at school but my gymnastics clubs had provided a safe space where we all loved what we did and encouragement was plentiful. Getting used to performing in front of others was vital for competition success, so I had to pick up that phone and call Ashley before the month was out. But, after all this time, would he be willing to speak to me?

Harrison had wandered over to Zara to give her a fist bump. She said something which made him and Grandpa laugh and I felt strangely left out all alone on this side of the trampoline. I didn't like it and grappled for something to say to make me part of their group.

'Why don't you take a turn now?' I called across to Zara. I winced inwardly, thinking that might have sounded more like an order than the friendly invitation it was meant to be.

She looked uncertain. 'Oh, I don't think...'

'Come on. You can do it,' Harrison said, lowering himself to the floor.

'You'll need to remove your jewellery and anything that would snag,' I said.

'Just as well I put leggings on this morning,' she said, pulling her boots off.

She unclasped a necklace, removed several earrings and rings, a watch and a charm bracelet and placed them on the floor a little way from the trampoline. She was wearing a long-sleeved checked shirt over a T-shirt, buttoned at the bottom, and I was about to ask her to remove her shirt too in case the buttons snagged, but she was a step ahead of me. The T-shirt was actually a tight-fitting white vest top and I couldn't help noticing her arms were toned.

'I think I'm ready,' she said, 'although I'm probably going to embarrass myself by getting on here without any grace or style.'

She didn't embarrass herself at all. She pulled herself up with ease and walked confidently to the centre of the trampoline, which made me think this might not be her first time. I couldn't help noticing her colourful pink and purple socks and Harrison evidently spotted them at the same time.

'You've got owls on your socks!' he cried.

'I've got animals on most of my socks and it had to be owls for coming here. Have you ever seen a pink and purple owl, Harrison?'

'They don't exist,' he said, laughing.

'Oh, they do,' she responded, sounding deadly serious. Then she winked at him as she tapped her head with one finger. 'In here.' She wiggled her toes. 'And here.'

She bit her lip and screwed up her nose as she looked round the three of us. 'Promise me you won't laugh at me when I'm terrible.'

'Just enjoy it,' Grandpa said. 'You're among friends here.'

Zara looked nervous and I feared my far from welcoming reception wouldn't have helped. It wasn't her fault I was wary around visitors and it certainly wasn't her fault that Grandpa had got me flustered by referring to her as a date. I wondered what her personal circumstances were. When she'd removed her jewellery, I'd noticed there was no wedding or engagement ring but that didn't mean she didn't have a boyfriend. And even if she was single, there was no way she'd be attracted to me. The *Freak Show* taunts from school circled round my mind and I pushed them aside. My appearance didn't actually bother me. Grandpa had taught me to be strong and embrace my uniqueness. I couldn't do anything to change my appearance, so why not just accept it? Admittedly, there had been a few dabbles with the hair dye during my teenage years which had ended up looking worse rather than better. It was the taunts themselves which had bothered me because they'd led to me being an outsider and being alone like that *had* hurt. It still did.

I focused my attention back on Zara, who was doing a really great job of staying in the centre of the trampoline with each bounce. I needed to tell her that. I needed to save face in front of Harrison, who probably thought I was being a right dick today.

'You're doing brilliantly!' I called.

She glanced at me, clearly shocked that I'd spoken, and it put her off her stride, bouncing all over the bed.

'Sorry,' she said, pushing her dark hair back behind her ears as she came to a stop. 'I knew I'd mess it up.'

'It was my fault,' I said. 'I distracted you. Please go again. You were doing great.'

Her eyes locked with mine and I felt something stirring inside me. They were really dark, like pools of rich melted chocolate. Dark eyeliner accentuated them and I found myself momentarily mesmerised.

'Really?' she asked.

'Really.'

'Dad only says something's good if it's good,' Harrison called. 'He's always honest.'

Not always. But I smiled at her encouragingly and she set off bouncing again. Her position on the bed was spot on and her technique was absolutely there. I wanted to encourage her to do some of the simple starter moves like a tuck and a pike jump but I equally didn't want to put her off again. She'd evidently found some confidence and pulled herself into a tight tuck position on her next bounce, followed by a forward pike and a straddle jump. They were basic moves but they were executed with perfection. This definitely wasn't her first time. She landed a seat drop, rising to her feet easily, and a seat drop with a twist. It was all great but what had me really captivated was the expression on her face. Her eyes were shining, her cheeks were pink and so much joy emanated from her smile.

She bounced several times, gaining height, then shocked me with a full twist before stopping. Harrison shoved his fingers in his mouth and released an ear-piercing whistle as Grandpa whooped loudly. Zara pressed her hand to her chest, her eyes wide. 'I can't believe I just did that. I had no idea I was still capable.' She sank down onto her backside. 'My legs are shaking now.'

I grabbed my bottle of juice. 'Have some of this. I haven't drunk any yet.'

She accepted the sports bottle with a grateful smile and gulped down several mouthfuls before passing the drink back to me.

'Thanks. Not sure why I've gone all shaky.'

'Probably the adrenaline. Do you need a hand down?'

'I'll be okay.' She shuffled on her knees to the edge of the trampoline but seemed hesitant about continuing. 'Might need some help after all,' she said, sheepishly. 'My legs have lost the ability to move.'

'Slowly lower your legs over the side,' I said. 'Place your hands on my shoulders and I'll put my hands round your waist, if that's okay.'

Her eyes met mine and I swear time stopped for a few seconds as my heart unexpectedly leapt. She placed a hand on each of my shoulders, I clasped my hands round her petite waist and she never broke her gaze as I lifted her off the trampoline and gently placed her on the floor in front of me. She only took her eyes away when Harrison rushed round to our side of the trampoline with her shirt and an exclamation of, 'That was awesome!'

'I think I got a bit carried away,' Zara said as she put her shirt back on and pulled it across her chest as though she was cold.

'How about we call it a day for now?' I said, raising my voice so Grandpa could hear. 'We were about done anyway. Anyone for hot chocolate?'

That was met with a resounding yes from Harrison and an appreciative smile from Zara. I watched her, heart still thumping, as she put her boots back on and scooped up her jewellery. What was happening to me? It was completely unnerving. She'd done a few tricks and now I had butterflies and couldn't take my eyes off her. I needed a few minutes away from her to get my head together.

'You all go up to the lodge and I'll finish off here,' I said. 'I'll be five or ten minutes behind you.'

Agreeing to that suggestion, they gathered up their coats and bundled out the building, laughing.

I rested my hands on the side of the trampoline, dipped my head and stretched out my back. I closed my eyes but all I could picture was Zara, her face so close, her body warm beneath my touch. Standing up again, I tried to push her from my thoughts but one glance at the trampoline and I could see her joyful expression as she presumably relived a childhood experience. A look towards the benches and I could picture her smiling and clapping for Harrison. There was no escaping it. I was extremely attracted to her, especially now that I'd seen the warmth and excitement that Harrison had clearly been drawn to from the moment he met her. Whether or not she was attracted to me was neither here nor there because I didn't need or want this sort of complication in my life. Eliza had been the love of my life and I'd let her down badly time and time again. It was my fault she was dead. No way was I going to let anyone in again and risk letting them down. The only people I needed in my life were Grandpa and Harrison, and I only had three objectives – to look after our little family, to get Harrison ready for the Olympics and to provide a safe haven for owls. Romantic love was absolutely off the cards.

Having got my head clear on that, I picked up my juice bottle, put the lights out and locked up. Just an owl lover sticking around for the release of an owl and having a bite to eat after that. Invited by my grandpa. Not here for me. Polite conversation and then we won't see her again. That's all.

But the thought of not seeing her again made me feel a little empty inside.

22

ZARA

I was in heaven. I loved the farmhouses at Bumblebee Barn and Hedgehog Hollow, which were both completely different from each other and both beautiful, but the house at Owl's Lodge was in a league of its own and captured my heart from the moment I rounded the stone steps and it came into view.

'That's your house?' I exclaimed to Eddie and Harrison. 'It's gorgeous.'

The three-storey building looked like something you'd expect to find in the wilds of Canada or Alaska – not in the East Yorkshire countryside. The ground floor was constructed from stone and the rest from wood, dark metal and stacks of glass. Ahead of us was a wooden deck and a fire pit surrounded by large boulders. It looked so homely and I imagined the three of them huddled round the fire, sitting on blanket-covered boulders, toasting marshmallows while the sun set behind the trees.

I followed Eddie and Harrison up some wooden steps onto a huge veranda with a glass balustrade. To the left was a table and chairs and, to the right, all-weather seating and a patio heater. While Eddie unlocked the bifold doors, I paused to take in the view. It was spectacular – gently rolling countryside stretching for miles on one side and woods to the other.

Inside was the open-plan living area, but the space didn't feel overwhelmingly enormous as there were clear zones within it, cleverly separated by the woodburning stove, pieces of furniture and a couple of pillars. Whoever had designed the interior had an eye for colours and patterns which complemented each other perfectly and managed to blend cosy and modern.

'Let me hang your coat up,' Eddie said. 'Harrison can give you a tour while I make the drinks.'

The lounge area had a squidgy-looking corner sofa which could comfortably have seated about eight people so I could imagine the three of them all stretched out on it during evenings. On the left wall was a floor-to-ceiling bookcase and a couple of mismatched high-backed armchairs facing each other, each with a footstool.

'Who's the book lover?' I asked Harrison, scanning along the predominantly non-fiction titles.

'The fishing books and most of the bird books belong to Pops. He reads them over and over. The gymnastics ones are a mixture of Dad's and Granddad's, although Dad doesn't read much.'

'Does your granddad live here too?'

'He used to but he lives in Mexico now so we never see him.'

Harrison said it in a very matter-of-fact way so I couldn't tell whether it was a good or bad thing that he wasn't present in their lives and I didn't feel it appropriate to start delving into their family history without Snowy or Eddie present.

'You mentioned being a big reader when you told me you love dragons,' I prompted.

'Yes, I love fantasy series.' He rattled off a bunch of titles but the only one I'd heard of was *Harry Potter*.

'Sounds impressive. Do your dad and great-granddad ever read novels?'

'Dad says he gets fidgety whenever he tries to sit still and read, but that's weird cos he'll sit still for hours in The Roost watching the owls. The barn owls live in there. They're his favourites but I like little owls best. What's your favourite?'

'I'm not sure. I don't know that much about owls and I can't tell the breeds apart. Samantha told me that Zorro was a tawny owl. I wouldn't have known otherwise.'

'My dad'll teach you. He knows everything about owls.'

A little earlier, I'd have been confident that Snowy would have hated the idea of spending time teaching me, no matter how passionate he was about the subject matter, but his frosty attitude towards me had seemed to thaw when I went on the trampoline. He'd properly looked at me for the first time and there was definitely a warmth which hadn't been there before. I was still reeling with the discovery that Snowy was an Olympian. And that gym was something else. Would he let me come back and have another go on the trampoline? Hopefully my legs wouldn't give up on me next time. What had possessed me to attempt a full twist like that?

'Come and see my bedroom,' Harrison said, tugging on my hand.

I followed him to a beautiful wooden staircase going up and down, and ascended the stairs. Light flooded onto a spacious landing through glass panels in the roof. Spread across the walls were five large photographs of owls.

'They're the five species of owls commonly found in Britain,' Harrison said, catching me looking. He pointed to one at a time. 'Tawny, barn, little, long-eared and short-eared.'

'They're stunning photographs.'

'They're not photos. They're drawings.'

'No way!' I cried, peering closer.

'Pops drew them.'

'You're winding me up.'

He pointed to the bottom right corner of the nearest one where there was a signature, clearly distinguishable as Edward Oakes.

'Wow! Your great-granddad has skills.' I still couldn't get over them not being photographs. The detail and colour were astonishing.

'He painted the picture on the Owl's Lodge sign,' Harrison said, crossing the landing and pushing open a door. 'And he did this.'

All four walls in Harrison's bedroom were covered with colourful illustrations of mystical lands and the characters who inhabited them. Unsurprisingly, several dragons featured.

'Wow! This is awesome, Harrison.'

'They're scenes from my favourite books,' he said as I slowly turned in a circle, taking it all in and smiling as I recognised Harry and Ron's flying car stuck in the Whomping Willow from *Harry Potter and the Chamber of Secrets*. The styles of illustrations were all different, presumably inspired by the book covers, showing Eddie's versatility as an artist.

'It must have taken him ages,' I said.

'It did. I helped with some of the bigger chunks of painting but Pops did most of it.'

Alongside the usual bedroom furniture, Harrison had a desk and a book nook where an armchair, a large beanbag and several floor cushions were positioned in front of packed bookshelves.

'Your bedroom is amazing,' I said. 'If it was mine, I don't think I'd ever want to leave.'

Eddie called up the stairs that the drinks were ready, bringing an end to the tour. I headed downstairs, leaving Harrison to change out of his gym gear.

'I'm in awe of your artwork,' I told Eddie as we settled on the sofa with our drinks. 'What a talent you have!'

'Thank you. It whiles away the hours, although that mural in Harrison's bedroom whiled away way more hours than I expected.'

'I can imagine. Your drawings must sell well.'

He shrugged. 'I wouldn't know. I've never tried to sell any. It's just a hobby.'

'Just a hobby? This isn't how you make a living?'

'I've always doodled but I only took it up properly when my wife, Shirley, took ill. I found it soothing to keep it going after she died. I mainly draw owls but I've done other wildlife.'

'I'm sorry about your wife.'

'Thanks, lass. It was fifteen years ago and there's not a day goes by when I don't miss her, but I'm grateful that we were blessed with fifty-nine happy years together. Shirley was a wonderful woman.'

We sipped our drinks in companionable silence, Eddie likely lost in thoughts about his wife. Nearly sixty happy years together. What must that be like? Across my disastrous relationship history, I hadn't even managed six happy months.

Harrison appeared, dressed in jeans and a hoodie, and plonked himself between us with his hot chocolate. I was about to ask him if he was excited about the owl release when Snowy returned.

'I was beginning to think we'd need to send out a search party,' Eddie teased.

'I had to do a few things,' Snowy replied, a slight edge to his tone.

'I wasn't sure if you'd want hot chocolate,' Eddie said, 'but I can soon make you one.'

'It's fine. I'll have a green tea.'

Snowy headed towards the kitchen and reappeared with a mug shortly afterwards, still wearing his beanie.

'Thanks for letting me go on your trampoline,' I said, once he settled on the end of the sofa. 'My legs are functioning properly again now.'

'That's good to hear,' he said, nodding. 'Did you enjoy it?'

'It was the best. I knew I loved it but I'd forgotten exactly how it felt. That sensation of flying is unbeatable.'

He smiled and nodded. 'It's pretty amazing. You've obviously done that before.'

'I used to go to gymnastics and trampolining when I was a kid, but I stopped both when I was fourteen.'

'Why?' Harrison asked.

'You don't have to answer,' Snowy said, seemingly picking up on my hesitation.

'But I want to know,' Harrison said.

'And Zara might not want to talk about it,' Snowy said, his voice conveying his understanding.

'It's fine,' I said. 'Long story short. My older brother, Roman, loved football and I loved gymnastics but Dad moved to London to be with someone else. Roman was talent spotted and changed football club but, on her own now, Mum couldn't get us to both of our clubs, so gymnastics stopped in favour of football.'

Even though I'd made my peace with Mum about it, I could still feel the emotion welling inside me and my voice started coming out hoarse. I needed to clear my throat before I could continue.

'My mum started seeing my stepdad, Owen, and he took me back to gymnastics. I started trampolining shortly after. Unfortunately, the time out had put me behind with my gymnastics and I never quite managed to catch up. Eventually I lost interest.'

My throat burned with emotion as I fought hard to push down a sob, blinking back the tears pricking my eyes. I caught Snowy's eyes and the empathy in them nearly broke me. I had to change the subject fast.

'So, erm, Eddie. If you're not an artist by profession, what did you used to do?'

'Pops invents things,' Harrison declared proudly.

Eddie smiled warmly at his great-grandson. 'I've always been good with my hands, forever tinkering with things. Car engines, clocks, broken appliances – you name it, I'd have it apart and mended. I worked in the mechanical department of a long-gone factory in the late fifties. The owners made a few bad investments and the factory went bust. I couldn't find any similar work locally and I didn't want to leave Shirley on her own with a young child so I did some farm labouring, continued tinkering and managed to invent a few useful things. I secured patents and, well, I made enough money off those things to buy this place and devote my time to my family and the wildlife.'

I loved how humble he sounded, lowering his eyes during that final sentence as spots of pink coloured his cheeks.

'That's amazing, Eddie! What was it you invented?'

He looked up with an apologetic shrug. 'If I told you, it'd mean nothing to you. I don't mean that as an insult. It means nothing to most people. Technical stuff.'

'Well, congratulations. Sounds like that factory going under was the best thing for you.'

'It was. Sometimes the darkest moments can pave the way for the brightest ones. And what about you? You mentioned filming *Countryside Calendar* earlier?'

'Yes. I'm the producer's assistant so I handle all the admin and I support the producer, Amber, on set. This year's my seventh on *Country-*

side *Calendar* and we're filming an eight-part docuseries about rescue centres around that, which is what I was doing when the owl was brought in.'

'Pops loves *Countryside Calendar*,' Harrison said.

Eddie nodded. 'Never miss an episode. I'll watch anything about the countryside, but that's my favourite programme.'

That warmed my heart, especially after Portia's *boring* accusation at Roman's party. 'That's lovely to hear. Thank you.'

Eddie stood up. 'How about we all zip it for now and we release an owl before it gets dark?'

'I'm so excited,' I said. 'Thanks for inviting me to do this with you.'

'I'll fetch him and meet you in the paddock,' Snowy said.

We bundled back into our coats and set off towards the paddock – a sloped field which stretched down beside the house and behind the gym. Eddie explained that the property had originally been a much bigger farm and he'd taken on a manager to run it for him. It ran successfully for decades but, when the farm manager retired, a neighbouring farmer made him an offer for the land and Eddie decided to sell it so he could step back completely. They still had a sizeable plot but it was mainly scrub and woodland. The paddock was the only field they'd retained, which they'd turned into a haven for wildlife.

As we entered through the gate, I could see that the grass had been left to grow and wildflowers encouraged. There weren't as many as in the beautiful wildflower meadow at Hedgehog Hollow, but it was still a pretty sight.

Eddie led us over to a trio of thick wooden posts bound together, standing about four feet high.

'We put this in especially for owl releases,' he said. 'We place the crate on the top, open the door and let the owl find its way out, although it sometimes needs a helping hand. The paddock's ideal for releases as the owl has space to spread its wings after some time in confinement. Usually they do a lap or two before disappearing into the woods.'

He pointed to a small stack of three haphazardly laid wooden pallets nearby. 'We've got a dozen or so pallet piles like that scattered around the field. They're great for encouraging bugs which the hedgehogs love to eat. We've got lots of log piles and hedgehog houses too.'

'Pops makes the houses,' Harrison said.

'You have a very clever great-granddad,' I said. 'Do you help him?'

'Sometimes, but I like drawing more than I like making things.'

We chatted about what Harrison liked drawing and were soon joined by Snowy holding a carry case in one hand and a pair of thick gloves in the other.

'This is Tufty,' he said as he placed the crate on top of the poles. 'If you look at her ear tufts, you'll see why.'

I bent down and peered into the crate. A stunning pair of round rusty orange eyes met mine. 'She's beautiful.'

'Although they're known as the ear tufts, they're actually just feathers. The ears are behind her face disc. The tufts stand up like that when the owl's on alert. If she was calm and felt she was safe, they'd be flat. Raising them makes her look bigger than she really is.'

The tufts were the cutest and I tried to imagine her with them flat. She'd look very different. The feathers on her face were pale but her body and wings were covered in mottled orangey-brown feathers.

'When the tufts are down, long-eared owls sometimes get mixed up with short-eared owls,' Snowy told me. 'They're not massively different in size, but the way to tell them apart is the eye colour. Tufty has these gorgeous orange eyes but the short-eared owl has yellow eyes and its feathers are paler.'

'I just want to give her a cuddle, but I know I can't. Wild animal and all that.'

Snowy nodded. 'I'll open the crate and give her a few moments. You're welcome to get your phone out and take photos or film it. Just avoid filming me. Oh, and don't stand directly in front of the crate or she might collide with you.'

I whipped out my phone, then put it back in my coat pocket. 'You know what? I'm *not* going to film it. I just want to watch and enjoy it. I think we miss out on so much when we watch life through a phone.'

Snowy smiled at me. 'I agree.' He stepped back from the crate. 'Everyone ready?'

'Ready!' we chorused.

'You're free to go, Tufty,' he said, opening the door.

Tufty evidently wasn't too sure about what was happening as she initially shuffled to the rear of the crate and turned her back on us, but we remained silent and it wasn't long before she turned round. A bit longer passed before she moved to the front and poked her head out, turning left and right. Next minute, she was out and off.

'Stay safe,' Snowy said, watching her intently.

Tears welled in my eyes once more as Tufty did a lap round the field, just as Eddie had predicted. I didn't know what the best conditions were for an owl release, but I couldn't imagine anything more perfect than right now. Just like when I'd arrived, the sky had only a few wispy clouds but, with sunset fast approaching, the blue had deepened and there was a band of peach and pink on the horizon. The air was still, the open space so tranquil, and the world felt magical as Tufty embraced her freedom.

'Can you hear her calling?' Snowy asked me, enthusiasm in his voice. 'The male call is like the sound you'd make if you blew across a glass bottle but the female call is like putting paper against a comb and blowing through that.'

I listened intently and smiled. Her call sounded exactly as he'd described.

Tufty finished a second lap and disappeared into the pine trees bordering the top of the field.

'Another satisfied customer,' Eddie said.

I glanced at Snowy, who was still gazing at the point we'd last seen her, contentment written across his face.

'Couldn't have gone better,' he said, placing his gloves inside the crate and closing it.

'Thanks for letting me be part of that,' I said. 'It was really special.'

'You're welcome.' The warmth and smile in his voice reassured me that he was okay with me being around now.

'I'm getting hungry,' Eddie declared. 'Snowy, why don't you take Zara to The Owlery and show her how Zorro's doing while Harrison and I make a start on tea?'

'I want to go with Zara,' Harrison said.

'Are you hungry?' Eddie asked.

'Yes.'

'Then you'll come with me because tea will be ready much sooner if I have my helper.'

My heart sank as I looked at Snowy. His smile had disappeared and his earlier tension had returned. So much for making progress! He definitely wasn't comfortable having visitors. Or was it just me? But I swear he'd warmed to me across the afternoon. Snowy Oakes was evidently a complex man.

I wanted to see Zorro so I could do what Eddie suggested and hope Snowy was really okay with it, or I could forget about the owl and insist on helping to prepare the meal. I'd test the water with Snowy.

'Is that okay with you?' I asked him.

'Yeah, fine. There's not much to see but, yeah, it's okay. It's...' He tailed off with a shrug and a half-smile. He wasn't exactly hanging out the welcome bunting but I wanted to see Zorro, so I'd take it.

23

SNOWY

It wasn't fine or okay or anything else I might have said. Zara and me in a small space all alone? What was Grandpa playing at? As if I really needed to question that. I knew *exactly* what he was up to and I didn't appreciate the meddling at all.

Harrison chatted to Zara as we crossed the paddock, asking her what she'd thought about Tufty's release, so at least I didn't have to try to make conversation just yet.

Zara and I said goodbye to Grandpa and Harrison at the lodge and continued along the track towards The Owlery. It was only a five-minute walk but those five minutes would be agonising in silence. I was racking my brain to find something to say, but Zara saved me the effort by stopping, which drew me to a halt too.

'I get the impression that me being here makes you uncomfortable,' she said, those dark eyes fixed on mine. 'I don't want you to feel like that so, if you'd rather I leave, that's absolutely fine. I promise I won't make an issue of it in front of your family.'

How crap did I feel? There was no judgement in her voice. If anything, she sounded like she understood exactly what I was feeling and she'd definitely picked up on the family pressure.

'It's not you specifically,' I admitted. 'You seem really nice and my family clearly think so too. It's just that we don't get many visitors and I...'

How could I put it into words? I don't trust people anymore. I feel sick with fear that they're only here to dish for dirt and rake up the past. And if that's not the motive, I don't feel worthy of genuine contact with the outside world because of what I did. I let people down – people who don't deserve it – so they're better off staying away.

Zara was looking at me intently and I needed to finish that sentence. The only way I could think of to avoid more questions was to tell her the truth without actually telling her the truth.

'After I was picked for London 2012, I injured myself doing something really stupid and that was the end of any further Olympic dreams.'

She pressed her fingers to her lips. 'I'm so sorry.'

'I didn't cope very well for a long time. I made lots of bad decisions which had serious consequences for the people I care about. I'd rather not say anything else about it but, if you want to know, it's all online, although don't believe absolutely everything you read.' I shrugged. 'Come on! Let's go and check on your owl.'

Even though I hadn't given any specifics, that was a lot more than I'd said to anyone else about what happened and the urge to flee was strong. I strode purposefully down the track but Zara kept pace.

We reached The Owlery and I unlocked the door and switched the light on. 'Zorro had three broken bones so I—'

Zara touched my arm, stopping me mid-flow.

'You can tell me all that in a minute. There's something I need to say first.'

I gulped. Was this the point when she revealed that she was actually working on a docuseries about athletes who'd screwed up their careers or, even worse, specifically about me and the owl rescue had simply been a ruse to get close to me?

'Whatever happened to you after your injury is your business and I've got no intention of trawling the Internet looking for gossip. I'm not that sort of person. The only way I'll find out what happened is if you decide at some point to tell me yourself, and I won't put any pressure on you to do that. I don't know what sort of visitors you've had in the past and what they've been trying to get from you but, believe me, I'm not one of them. Although I do have to confess that there was an ulterior motive for coming here today.'

My stomach sank. *Here it comes!*

'I completely respected your decision not to let the cameras come on Wednesday and, from what you've said now, I understand that more. My first and foremost reason for coming back today was to find out how the owl was doing, but the secondary reason was that I was hoping to persuade you to let us film Zorro without getting you or any part of your property in the footage. It would literally have been the owl in his crate or a hand shot of you treating him if he needed any treatment while we were here, but I'm going to report back that it's a no and everyone will accept that and leave it there.'

That was it? It really was all connected to the owl and nothing to do with searching for dirt on me? I perched against the edge of the desk, feeling bad for being so suspicious and unwelcoming. Of course it was all about the owls for Zara. One look at her tear-filled eyes when Tufty took flight earlier had told me that, but I hadn't accepted it because Parnell had me on edge.

'If I said yes to filming, you'd really keep me off camera?'

'Absolutely. You wouldn't have to speak either as you can give us the information for the voiceover. I'm more than happy to put that in writing for you. We're making a programme about rescue centres – not sensationalising a story about a former Olympian. I promise.'

There was something so honest and sincere about Zara. What harm could it do? My face, my voice and my home wouldn't be shown and she'd give me a written assurance about that.

'Okay. You've persuaded me.'

She grinned at me, but her smile faded and she shook her head vigorously. 'No! You're not comfortable with visitors so it's not right to turn up with a bunch of strangers. If we include the owl rescue in the series, we'll get an update from you about treatment and release and leave it at that. No filming here.'

I stared at her, surprised. I thought she'd have jumped at my agreement. The fact that she hadn't spoke volumes about her integrity.

'You're sure?' I asked, realising I was perhaps unfairly testing her now.

'Absolutely sure. So, after all that heavy stuff, can I say hello to Zorro?'

She smiled at me and it was infectious. I'd never met anyone who was quite so honest before or so perceptive. It was like she could see into my mind and suss exactly what was going on.

I moved aside. 'Be my guest.'

She approached the crates at the end. 'Aw, look at him! He's so gorgeous. It was three broken bones?'

'Yes. Your friend was probably right about him being struck by a car and that's often fatal. If the collision itself doesn't kill the owl, the prognosis might. Certain types of injuries mean that the owl will never be able to use their damaged wing again and, unfortunately, that's game over for them. Zorro here was very lucky. Three clean breaks and no soft tissue damage so I was able to splint the wing and put it in a wing wrap – a bit like us having a broken arm in a sling.'

'Is that fake grass on his perch?'

'It is! Owls spend a lot of time flying but, as Zorro can't do that, he's going to be standing a lot more than usual. Because he's not used to that, he could develop pressure sores on the bottom of his feet if he was standing on wood all the time, so we make the perch softer to avoid that.'

'Your grandpa said it would only be two to three weeks before he's ready for release. That sounds quick.'

'Birds have a better metabolism than mammals so they heal much more quickly. I'll remove the splint after twelve days and check how stable the fracture site is. If it's not quite ready, I'll re-apply the splint and give it maybe another five days. When it's fully healed, the next stop is our outdoor aviary round the back of this building. He'll be able to fly in there although, obviously, not far. It means I can monitor him to make sure everything has healed how it should and, assuming it has, I'll give him a final check before releasing him in the paddock.'

Zara nodded. 'That makes sense. If you released him into the wild immediately and there was a flight problem, it's too late as you're not going to be able to capture him again.'

'Exactly. While he's in the aviary, I'll put some mice in for him and keep an eye on his flight but he'll mainly be left alone. After all, interaction with humans isn't his normal.'

Zorro stared at Zara, turning his head occasionally. With what sounded like a contented sigh, Zara straightened up.

'Thanks for explaining all that to me. Do you mind if I take a photo of him to show the others? They'll be keen to hear how he's doing.'

With my agreement, she took several photos then studied the other crates.

'What's wrong with these other owls? Oh! That one's not an owl.'

'It's a kestrel with a broken leg. Grandpa found it hopping around in the paddock. We think it got tangled in something, managed to get free and fly for a bit, but the pain grounded it. That small one is a male little owl – Harrison's favourite type – called Squeak. He was found lying on his side in the woods, which is an instant alert that something's wrong. He had an infected cut, very likely from a predator attack. Little owls are small anyway but he was really emaciated so he's been on a diet of antibiotics and crickets and has been working his way through a mouse.'

'Ooh, yummy,' Zara said, laughing as she rubbed her tummy, her eyes sparkling mischievously. 'My favourite meal. Do you usually have this many patients at one time?'

'It varies massively. Sometimes there's weeks with none at all. I have space for ten and have only ever been full once. We typically have more patients during babies season. Owlets – like all young – are so vulnerable. I've hand-reared quite a few over the years.'

Zara crouched down to get a closer look at Squeak. 'Hello, beautiful. I'm glad they found you and they're making you better.'

I smiled at her words and the reassurance in her tone.

She turned back to face me. 'I love that there are people like you and the team at Hedgehog Hollow all around the country working hard to save our wildlife. What you do and the time you give is amazing.'

'I couldn't not do it. Look at them! Who wouldn't want to help?'

She was looking at me with such an expression of admiration and, for a moment, I felt like I deserved it. But, of course, the voice in my head had to sabotage it. *You don't deserve anyone's respect and admiration. Not after what you did.*

Zara now looked concerned. 'Everything okay? You look worried.'

'Erm, no... I mean yes. I just remembered something I was meant to...' I cleared my throat. 'Do you want to look in The Roost next door? We might be able to spot the barn owls.'

'Yes, please!'

I locked up The Owlery and led Zara round the building and into the barn where we sat down on the chairs.

'Look up at the beams,' I said in hushed tones. 'Can you see the various nesting boxes? We have a pair of barn owls who roost – rest and sleep – in the box on the beam closest to us. It's dusk now which is when they're most active. We should see their faces peeking out and we'll hopefully catch one of them flying.'

'I see a face!' she whispered after a few minutes.

'Keep watching.'

She sat on the edge of her chair but I relaxed back into mine. I'd intended to watch the owls but found myself studying her side profile instead. She'd put her earrings back in – a silver hoop and stud at the bottom of her ear lobe, another stud at the top and an ear cuff just below it. Her rapt expression reminded me of Harrison's when we'd visited Santa Claus. I loved that he was still a believer, which was something that he'd probably have had knocked out of him if he'd been going to school and surrounded by children anxious to ruin it for others after they'd had the magic ruined for them, typically by an older sibling.

That thought took me to what Zara had said earlier about her brother getting to play football and her having to give up gymnastics for him. It seemed very unfair on Zara, but who was I to judge? I was a single parent like her mum had been, but I only had the one child, I wasn't trying to balance his needs with a job, and I had no financial pressures thanks to Grandpa's technical brilliance. Zara's mum had clearly had some tough decisions to make but, from Zara's reaction, those choices had negatively impacted on her and they still hurt.

A gasp from Zara broke into my thoughts and I peeled my eyes away from her to see one of the barn owls taking flight, soaring through the barn and out into the open.

'Are you okay?' I asked, noticing tears shining in her eyes once more.

'I find it really emotional seeing them. I don't know why. They're so... what's the word?'

'Majestic?' I suggested.

'That's it! And also a little bit magical somehow. You probably think I'm soft in the head.'

I shook my head. 'I sometimes feel that way myself. The barn owl looks a bit magical because of that ghostly appearance, especially when it's properly nighttime. Do you want to go outside so we don't need to whisper?'

Zara followed me outside and I returned my voice to a normal speaking volume as we set off up the track towards the woods behind the lodge. It was a lot darker now but the solar lights meant we could still see where we were going.

'The long-eared owl like tonight's release, Tufty, is really shy and secretive,' I told her. 'The species has been around for millions of years but not much is recorded about it because of how secretive it is. Imagine that. Millions of years and you're still a bit of an enigma.'

How often had I envied the long-eared owl, wishing I could be an enigma instead of having my life splashed all over the front page of the papers?

'What about the short-eared owl?' Zara asked.

'Completely different kettle of fish. It's a diurnal owl, which means it's out during the day.'

'I didn't realise any owls were out during the day. I thought they were all nocturnal.'

'Most people think that but, of the five we have in this country, there's only the tawny and long-eared owls who are nocturnal. The barn and little owls are crepuscular – active at twilight – although that's not to say they won't hunt at night, especially at this time of year when it's dark for longer. They all have different looks, sounds and behaviours. They hunt differently. Some are territorial and others aren't. I could bore you senseless with all the details.'

Zara stopped walking and shook her head. 'I can't imagine anything you tell me being boring. I'm loving how much I've learned already. I'm a sponge, always eager to absorb new things.'

I laughed as she beckoned with both hands to emphasise her point.
'What else do you want to know?' I asked.
'Anything you want to tell me.'
'Don't say something like that! You'll be stuck here forever.'
'Like that would be a bad thing.'

She held my gaze once more and those butterflies took flight. Did she mean being here with me wouldn't be a bad thing?

'I mean, look at this place. It's absolutely stunning. The trees, the wildlife, the tranquillity of it all.' She closed her eyes for a moment, smiling. 'I just want to breathe it all in and keep it in my head forever.' She put her arms out to the side and sniffed the air several times before opening her eyes and laughing lightly. 'Am I weirding you out?'

'No.'

'Just say if I am. I'm the height of professionalism on set but when I get with other people, the part of me I keep under control at work sometimes bubbles over. My stepdad once bought me a poster of a roller-skating flamingo wearing a feather boa which says *be your own kind of weird* and he told me to never change. I got it framed.'

I smiled back at her and I hadn't expected to reveal it but it just popped out. 'The kids at school thought I was weird because of my looks. They called me Freak Show.'

'Oh, my God! Snowy! How dare they?'

'There was this one kid – Elliot Parnell – who started it at primary school and, before I knew it, everyone was calling me it. It followed me to senior school and the only place where I ever felt I could really be me – where hard work and talent counted and hair, eye and skin colour had sod all to do with things – was the gym.'

'That's awful. Trying to find a positive in it, did it spur you on to be even better at gymnastics to prove yourself to him?'

'Maybe at first, but then Parnell went down the *only girls do gymnastics* route and I realised he wasn't worth a second of my time.'

'Only girls do gymnastics? Seriously? Who thinks like that? Attitudes like that are so pathetic. Is that why...' She shook her head. 'Ignore me. Being too nosy.'

I hesitated. The friendly thing to do would be to welcome her wondering, but it might be something I'd rather not answer. My mobile ringing saved me from making a decision.

'Hi, Grandpa,' I said.

'Tea will be ready in ten minutes.'

'Okay. We'll head back.'

'Tea's nearly ready,' I said, steering Zara towards the lodge. 'If you don't have any plans, you're welcome to come back at some point over the weekend. I can show you around – tour of the woods – and give you some more owlish facts.'

'Really? That would be amazing. I need to do some work tomorrow, but I'm free on Sunday.'

'You can have another go on the trampoline if you feel up to it.'

'You're the gift that keeps on giving,' she said. 'Keep this going and I'll have to appoint you as my new best friend.'

I laughed with her and I felt a warm glow inside at the mention of 'friend'. It felt like a long time since I'd had any of those. But that warmth was swiftly replaced by a sinking in my stomach. Friend. Nothing more. It shouldn't bother me at all but it did. Why? I'd been frustrated earlier by Grandpa's not-so-subtle matchmaking, encouraging Zara onto the trampoline, inviting her to stay for tea and ensuring Harrison didn't join us in The Owlery, so having Zara only see me as a friend should be good news.

24

ZARA

Eddie and Harrison had made a delicious pasta bake for tea, followed by ice cream, but it was still only 6 p.m. by the time we'd eaten and cleared the dishes, which presented me with a dilemma. Eddie had offered me a cup of tea, which I'd accepted, but I couldn't really string my visit out much beyond that without potentially overstaying my welcome and encroaching on precious family time. However, leaving too early meant I'd get back to Bumblebee Barn before Joel and Marley even arrived.

'I have a cheeky request for you, Eddie,' I said when we'd all settled in the lounge. 'I took some photos of Zorro, but do you think you could do me a sketch of him? Just something small and simple. I'd pay you, of course.'

'You'd do no such thing,' he declared. 'It would be an honour. How small? Postage stamp small?'

I smiled at his cheeky grin. 'Maybe not quite that small. A5 or even half that, if that's not too much to ask. Say if it is. I can't draw so I don't know how long something like that would take.'

'Not too long. What will you do with it?'

'Put it in my precious pages. It's something my stepdad started. When all the attention was on my brother, he bought me a scrapbook and stuck a page to the front saying *Zara's Precious Pages*. He got me to stick in my gymnastics certificates and school reports and anything else I was proud of. I stopped doing it when I packed in my clubs, but I picked it up again after I started on *Countryside Calendar*, although it's not about personal achievements anymore as, oddly enough, nobody gives me a certificate for showing up to work. I've got some press cuttings from when the programme has won awards but it's mainly reminders of the places we film which capture a piece of my heart – anything with a happy memory attached like postcards, flyers, ticket stubs.'

'Do you put photos in it?' Eddie asked.

'Yes, but only Polaroids. Owen gave me a Polaroid camera and I like to annotate the thick strip below the photo. I'd like to create a page in honour of my first visit to an owlery so a sketch of Zorro would be perfect for that.'

'Consider it done.'

'Can I start a scrapbook?' Harrison asked his dad.

'If you like. We'll see if we can find one next time we're out.'

'When will that be?'

Snowy grimaced. 'I'm not sure yet, but I promise we'll get one.'

'If it's okay with your dad, I can bring you one when I come on Sunday,' I said, glancing at Snowy for approval. 'It can be my thank you for cooking that delicious meal.'

Harrison launched himself at me with a hug, which took me by surprise. 'Thank you,' he whispered in my ear and, for the umpteenth time that day, I felt overcome with emotion. What was this family and this place doing to me?

* * *

It was half seven when I drove up the farm track at Bumblebee Barn. I'd managed to eke out my stay after all when Eddie offered to show me his art studio on the ground floor. I'd happily have stayed for hours looking through all his paintings but I was still mindful of encroaching on family time and that I had to return to Bumblebee Barn eventually.

My heart raced at the thought of seeing Joel again. Why couldn't I just accept that he was happy with Marley and that he only saw me as a friend? My head was very straight on the need to get over him but my heart wasn't listening. When it came to romance, there always seemed to be a head and heart disconnect for me, with my head telling me it wasn't right and to walk away and my heart hanging in there, full of hope that things would change.

I parked in the farmyard and noticed that Marley's car was there as well as Joel's, which struck me as odd. Why hadn't they come together? As I neared the farmhouse, a burst of laughter drifted out to me. *Deep breath. He's just a friend and that's all it'll ever be. Smile!*

'Zara!' Amber said, as I pushed open the kitchen door. 'How did it go with Snowy?'

'Amazing,' I said, shrugging off my coat. 'I'll tell you all about it later.' I looked round the group, smiling warmly at them all, trying not to let my gaze linger on Joel. 'Sorry I couldn't join you for food. Smells good.'

They all talked at once, enthusing over the takeaway and how they'd missed me.

'Are you going to join us for a drink?' Marley asked.

'Sure. Give me five minutes to change my T-shirt – bit sweaty from trampolining earlier – and I'll be down.'

'You've been trampolining?' Amber asked, understandable surprise in her voice.

'Yeah. Snowy has one. Back down soon.'

After I'd changed my T-shirt, I sat on my bed psyching myself up to going back down. Eventually I stood up, shaking my head. *This is ridiculous! You're a grown woman, not a teenager. So the boy you fancy doesn't fancy you. That's life! Suck it up! Stop moping, get your backside downstairs and have a fun evening with your friends.*

I heard a scratching sound outside the door and opened it.

'Hi, Harley, have you come to fetch me?' I crouched down and stroked the Border collie's head and back, but it was another delaying tactic. 'Come on, girl, we'd better show our faces.'

She ran down the stairs ahead of me, pausing halfway and turning her head as though making sure I was following. They'd moved into the lounge and I'd expected to see Joel and Marley cosied up together in one of the snuggle chairs but Amber and Marley had a chair each and the men were seated either end of the sofa, which meant I needed to sit between them. The butterflies soared as Joel moved a cushion so I could make myself more comfortable. It was lucky I wasn't prone to blushing so there were no outward signs of how it felt to be in close proximity to him.

'So how's the owl?' Amber asked after she'd handed me a mug of tea.

I filled them in on Zorro's progress, the release of Tufty and what I'd learned about the work Snowy did with owls. I wished I hadn't mentioned trampolining earlier as I suspected Snowy would have preferred me not to tell anyone about the gym. If I kept talking about owls, the subject would hopefully change and it would be someone else's turn to speak. The tactic worked because Marley shared that there were barn owls roosting at her aunt and uncle's equestrian centre, which led on to her telling us about some plans they had for expanding the stables this year.

For the next ninety minutes or so, the conversation flowed and there was plenty of laughter. I kicked myself for making such a fuss earlier.

'We'd better hit the road,' Marley said, standing up at half nine.

'Are you on an early shift?' I asked Joel.

'No, but I've got Imogen tomorrow.'

I was about to ask why that meant they had to leave early, but I caught Amber's eye and she gave me a subtle shake of the head.

Barney and Amber walked them to the door and I gathered the mugs and glasses together. I waited until I heard the door close before I joined them in the kitchen.

'Did I nearly put my foot in it just now?' I asked Amber as I loaded the dishwasher.

Amber glanced at Barney.

'It's okay,' he said. 'Joel won't mind you telling her.'

'Marley hasn't met Imogen yet,' Amber said, 'and it's causing a few issues between her and Joel.'

'Tilly causing problems again?' I asked.

'Surprisingly, Tilly's not the problem,' Amber said. 'It's Marley. Tilly's decided that they've been together long enough for Imogen to meet Marley, but it's Marley who's saying no.'

'Marley told Joel it's too soon,' Barney said, 'but he's worried she doesn't want to meet Imogen at all. They had a row about it earlier so Joel was going to come over on his own. Marley changed her mind but told him she wouldn't be staying over.'

That explained the separate cars. 'That's not good,' I said. 'What's he going to do?'

'He's not sure yet,' Barney said. 'He's bringing Imogen over tomorrow and I'll see where his head's at then.'

Neither of them needed to expand as it was obvious where this was heading. If Marley didn't want anything to do with Imogen, there could be no future for her and Joel.

'I might head up for an early night,' I said. 'Lots of work to get on with tomorrow.'

Barney said goodnight and grabbed a cloth to wipe down the table, but Amber followed me through to the hall.

'Are you okay?' she asked. 'You seemed a bit quiet this evening.'

'Did I? I didn't mean to be. Nothing to see here.'

'You know you can talk to me if there's anything on your mind, don't you?'

'Yes! But there's nothing going on, so don't worry about me.'

She smiled, evidently placated, and wished me a goodnight.

In my bedroom, I went to close the blind and noticed that Joel's and Marley's cars were both still in the farmyard which meant... yep, there they were kissing. Either all was well between them and they were having a goodnight kiss or they'd had another argument and were making up.

Stomach churning, I closed the blinds and drew the curtains. I had thought it odd they hadn't been sitting together tonight as Marley was usually tactile, snuggled up to Joel, holding his hand or with her legs draped over his. That said, I hadn't picked up any tension between them earlier. Barney and Amber weren't prone to over exaggeration so, if they said there was trouble in paradise, there clearly was. Despite my crush on Joel, that didn't make me happy. He was a great guy and I liked Marley too. I wouldn't have put them together as a couple any more than I'd have matched Barney with Marley on *Love on the Farm* but it somehow seemed to work for them and I'd be sad for Joel if that fell apart when it was obvious he adored her.

25

ZARA

Amber and I were working at the kitchen table the following morning when Joel arrived with Imogen. She launched herself at Amber for a hug, then did the same to me.

'Have you grown again?' I asked her. 'Because you have to stop! You'll be taller than me soon.'

'Mummy says I've grown two centimetres.'

'That's amazing! You'll definitely be bigger than me, although most people are.'

I hadn't seen Imogen since before Christmas so, while Amber called Barney on the walkie-talkie to let him know that Joel had arrived, I asked Imogen what Santa had brought her. She rattled off a long list of presents with a few prompts from Joel.

'I've got a Christmas gift for you,' I said. 'I forgot to give it to your dad on Christmas Day.'

Joel slapped his palm against his forehead. 'You asked me to remind you, and I forgot to do that.'

'There was a lot going on. Wait here, Imogen, and I'll go and get it for you.'

Back downstairs, Imogen ripped off the cute polar bear wrapping paper.

'It's got me on it!' she exclaimed, gazing at the large spiral-bound book.

Imogen loved drawing and crafts so I'd been sure she'd like my scrapbooking gift. I'd printed off a gorgeous photo I'd taken of her cuddling a couple of Barney's Herdwick sheep in the summer and added the words *Imogen's Awesome Adventures* in glittery lettering.

'When I was a few years older than you, my stepdad gave me a scrapbook to stick all my precious things in and I still keep one now. I used to put my gymnastics certificates in it but I put postcards in it now.'

I'd brought my current book down to show her so I flicked through a few pages and explained why I'd kept the various items.

'These are pretty,' she said, pointing to the tape I'd used to attach items or as borders round the pages.

'It's called washi tape. It comes in various widths and patterns.'

'Can I get some washi tape, Dad?' Imogen asked.

I smiled at her. 'Do you really think I'd give you a scrapbook and nothing to use with it? Here you go.'

I placed a second gift on the table which she eagerly unwrapped, revealing a storage box with several tiers of compartments. I'd included a dozen rolls of washi tape, stickers, stars, glue and child-safe scissors. I could have kept going, but I was worried it might scream to Joel *I've got the hots for you so I'm spoiling your daughter to prove it* when that really wasn't what the gift was about.

Imogen cooed over the contents of the box and it gave me a little thrill to know that I might have found a scrapbook convert. Her positive reaction reminded me of Harrison's yesterday. Before I went to Owl's Lodge tomorrow, I'd nip into Wilbersgate and get a scrapbook and some supplies for him.

* * *

'That gift you bought Imogen was so thoughtful,' Joel said as we leaned on a gate after lunch while Barney and Amber led Imogen round their paddock on a pony. 'I didn't realise you were into crafts.'

'Only scrapbooking. I can sit for hours picking the right tape and the perfect angle to display something, but I can't be bothered with any other type of craft. She seemed to like it.'

'She loved it. She wanted to know why your photos had white borders so I've been explaining about Polaroid cameras. Guess what she wants for her birthday?'

'Oh, no! I'm sorry, Joel.'

He laughed and playfully nudged me. 'I don't mind one bit. It'll be nice to get her something I know she wants and which Tilly hasn't ordered me to buy after she's picked off all the best gifts.'

'Is that what she does?'

'Every time. I choose my battles and being the parent to give the *best* gift isn't something I'm bothered about competing over.' He used finger quotes to emphasise the word *best*. 'If Tilly thinks that's what's important to Imogen, she really doesn't understand our daughter.'

'Any luck with pinning her down to more time with Imogen?'

'I wish. Even if I did manage to get a promotion, kept regular hours and could commit to having Imogen set days of the week, Tilly would put up another barrier. I'll never understand how her mind works. It's not like I'm the one who ended our relationship and broke her heart. She's the one who called time and she's the one who got married and had another two kids and...' Joel laughed and shook his head. 'This was meant to be a simple thank you for your gift, not a rant about my problems with my ex.'

'It's fine. Sometimes an opportunity comes up for us to offload and it's good to take it.'

'Thanks for listening. Anything you need to offload?'

'If you'd asked me that a couple of weeks ago, you might have been here for hours while I bent your ear off about my brother and how my mum's always on his side, but things seem to have calmed down there. For now, anyway.'

'Aren't families complicated?' he said, rolling his eyes at me.

'Daddy! Look at me!' Imogen called from the pony.

'You look amazing!' he called back, clearly bursting with pride. 'Clever girl!'

'Good job my best mate has a pony and can give free lessons,' he said under his breath. 'A Polaroid I can manage. A pony? Unless it's got the words *My Little* in front of it, not so much.'

We continued to watch her in companionable silence and my thoughts drifted to the situation with Marley and Imogen. Tilly had broken Joel's heart and Marley could be about to do the same.

'I need to get back to work,' I said, standing straight and stretching out my back. 'Keep doing you, Joel. Anyone who sees you and Imogen together can see the special bond you two have. You might not get much time together but you always make the most of the time you do and that counts for a lot. When I was Imogen's age, my dad worked away a lot so I didn't see much of him. I'd get so excited about him being home but he'd barely give me the time of day and I soon learned that I wasn't a priority in his life.'

'You learned that when you were six?'

'Yep. Hard lesson early in life. Years on, we're in touch but we're not close. I think of Owen as my dad because he's the one who behaves like one. If I ever got married, I'd want him to give me away.'

I blew my fringe out of my eyes, wondering what had possessed me to start talking to Joel about marriage. 'Not that I'm about to get married,' I said, my voice a little squeaky, 'cos I don't even have a boyfriend. And now I'm wittering and I'm not getting my work done. See you later.'

'See you.'

But I was already hurrying away, longing to break into a run. *Not that I'm about to get married cos I don't even have a boyfriend.* Good grief! I'm surprised I managed to stop myself from adding, *but I'd marry you and have all your babies.* There was no future for Joel and me and I needed to accept that. I would *never* give him any indication that I was interested in him while he was seeing Marley and I had no intention of being a rebound fling if things fell apart.

Back in the kitchen, I folded up the discarded wrapping from Imogen's Christmas presents, dropped it in the recycling crate and messaged Snowy.

> **TO SNOWY**
>
> Hope your weekend is going well. Is it still OK to come over tomorrow? About 1.30? It's fine if you have other plans

It took him a couple of hours to respond but his reply really cheered me up.

> **FROM SNOWY**
>
> Sounds good. The trampoline is calling so bring your gym kit and prepare to get hooked again! See you tomorrow

> **TO SNOWY**
>
> Beyond excited! Although this could be me...

I added a GIF of someone doing a belly flop on a trampoline.

> **FROM SNOWY**
>
> You've got too much grace. This is more like you...

I laughed at a GIF of a brown bear bouncing on a trampoline in someone's garden.

> **FROM SNOWY**
>
> Look at the bear's face. So happy! That was you yesterday

He'd added several smiling emojis. The bear really did look like it was living its best life and I'd felt like that yesterday. For those few minutes, my mind had been empty of thoughts or worries about my future at work, where I'd live long term, unrequited love, my brother or my mum. The higher I'd bounced, the freer I'd felt. And, later, when I'd watched Tufty flying round the paddock, her freedom returned, I felt the same. I couldn't remember the last time I'd felt such pure, uncomplicated joy. Twice. In the same place. I couldn't wait to go back to Owl's Lodge tomorrow.

26

SNOWY

Grandpa tutted loudly. 'Snowy, lad! Will you sit down before you wear a hole in the rug?'

I did as he asked, but I couldn't settle and was on my feet again within a couple of minutes, this time looking out across the veranda.

'Zara's not due for another ten minutes,' he said. 'If you're that nervous, why don't you do something to distract yourself like tackling the filing pile in your office? That'll soon pass the time.'

'What makes you think I'm nervous?'

'Let me see. Could it be the pacing, staring out the window and constant checking of the time?'

'You keep munching your nails too,' Harrison added. 'People do that when they're nervous, don't they, Pops?'

'They certainly do.'

'Why are you nervous about Zara coming?' Harrison asked.

Grandpa didn't even try to disguise his snigger.

'Do you think Zara's scary? Cos I don't. I think she's really nice and she likes owls and dragons.'

'I'm not scared of Zara,' I said, truthfully. *But I'm absolutely terrified of these feelings she's stirring.*

Harrison disappeared into the kitchen with an empty glass. Grandpa caught my eye, nodded at me and tapped his head – a signal to remove my beanie.

'She knows who you are now. You don't need to cover up.'

I sighed as I slipped the hat off my head. Some habits were hard to break. Movement out of the corner of my eye drew me back to the window and a small red car approaching up the track, stopping beside mine. My heart leapt as Zara got out and stood there for a moment, hands on her hips, looking from one side to the other. What was she doing? Eventually she reached into the back seat and removed a bag with a colourful owl on it. She looked around her once more then turned towards the lodge – my cue to step out onto the veranda to welcome her.

'Hi,' I said, leaning over the balustrade. 'Long time no see.' I cringed inwardly. Such a British thing to say.

She smiled up at me. 'Couldn't stay away. It's so beautiful here. I needed a few moments to drink in the view just now. How do you get anything done?'

I'd never take what we had here for granted, but seeing Owl's Lodge through someone else's eyes was a useful reminder of how lucky we were.

'I spend as much time outdoors as I can,' I said as she ran up the steps. 'Harrison is home schooled and every day includes forest school.'

At that moment, he shoved past me and threw himself at Zara. I'd never seen him do that to anyone, although we'd never had anyone like Zara visit before.

'Dad says you're going on the trampoline again today,' he said, releasing her. 'Can I teach you my mum's routine?'

My stomach lurched. No! Teaching our son was one thing but... Zara raised her eyes to mine and that incredible perception of hers kicked in again.

'I'd love you to teach me some moves, Harrison, but your mum's routine is really special and I think it should belong to your mum, your dad and you. How about we create our own routine together instead?'

'Are you going to stand out there nattering all day?' Grandpa called from inside. 'It's freezing!'

Harrison ran back inside and I smiled gratefully at Zara and mouthed, 'Thank you.'

She gave me a discreet thumbs up and stepped into the lounge. I took a deep breath and followed her. Grandpa had stood up and was kissing her on each cheek. I'd never seen him do that to anyone either. After one afternoon and early evening with us, it was as though Zara had already been welcomed into the family. It could be down to her being so warm and friendly, drawing my family to her, but it could equally be my fault. Had my decisions starved them both of company so that they were eagerly clinging onto the first person who'd spent any significant time here since we lost Eliza?

'This is for you,' Zara said, removing a large paper carrier bag from her owl bag and handing it to Harrison.

'My scrapbook!' he cried. 'You remembered.'

'Of course I did!'

Harrison tilted the book to show me before removing some stencils from the bag and rolls of tape with patterns on them.

'It's called washi tape,' Zara said. 'There weren't many suitable designs in the shop so these can start you off but I've ordered some more online – including some dragon ones – which will come here, although they might take a couple of weeks.'

Harrison flung his arms round her again, thanking her.

'I found some things I want to put in it,' he said. 'Will you help me later?'

'If that's okay with everyone else. I've brought a couple of my books with me so I can show you some ideas.'

'Harrison, why don't we put our trainers and coats on so we can go down to the gym?' Grandpa said, ushering Harrison towards the cloakroom.

'You've made his day,' I said to Zara. 'He loves art and he loves organising things so this is right up his street. Thank you.'

'Absolute pleasure. I hope he has fun with it.'

'Did you get your work done yesterday?'

'Yes. Next week's the final week of filming at Hedgehog Hollow and then we're off up to Scotland, so I had some things to organise ready for that.'

'You're leaving the area?' My stomach lurched at the thought of her not being around – crazy when we'd only just met.

'Only for a fortnight, but that's why I'll miss Zorro's release. How's he doing?'

'Seems to be coping well with the confinement.'

Harrison and Grandpa returned so the four of us headed down to the gym.

'When we're done on the trampoline, Harrison and I are going to nip into Reddfield to get some fine-tip pens for his scrapbook,' Grandpa said.

I'd already bought Harrison a packet for Christmas and was about to say so when I realised this was Grandpa's way of meddling again, ensuring Zara and I had some time alone. Even though there was no way anything was going to happen between us, the thought of some time alone was appealing and, to be fair to Harrison, it had only been a six-pack and he'd want more colours if he was going to fully embrace scrapbooking.

In the gym, we warmed up and Harrison was the first on the trampoline, showing us Eliza's routine with ease. She'd have been so proud of him. Zara was up next, wearing another colourful pair of owl socks, this time in oranges and yellows. That same expression of absolute joy shone from her throughout and it gave me a bit of a jolt. I loved what I did, but I'd never done it just for the fun of it. My whole life had been about working towards competition success and an Olympic medal. Practice, improve, perfect. Again and again. And while I'd never have made it to the podium at Beijing without that mindset, what was my goal now? I couldn't compete professionally anymore but I still used the apparatus as though I had my next win in sight. Why? Because that was all I'd ever known? What must it feel like to bounce freely just for the fun of it?

'That was awesome,' Zara said to me as she lowered herself to the floor. 'I can't think of a better way to feel happy than that.'

'You barely stopped smiling,' I said.

'I was being like that bear on the GIF you sent me, completely living in and loving that moment. Nothing else mattered.' She smiled at me. 'I'd love to see you having a go.'

'Yeah, Dad!' Harrison echoed.

Me? For the first time ever, I felt nervous about performing in front of an audience. Well, one member of the audience. Doubts flooded into my mind. *What if I make a mess of it? What if I'm a disappointment? What if she isn't impressed?* And that was the reality. I wanted to impress Zara but I didn't want to show off. Where was the balance?

'Please,' Zara said, fixing her dark eyes on mine. 'Be the bear!'

'Go on, lad!' Grandpa encouraged.

'You need to give the people what they want,' Zara said, her tone teasing.

'Okay,' I said, removing my tracksuit top. 'If the people really want it, I'd better not disappoint them.'

As I pulled myself up onto the trampoline, I wanted to give a disclaimer that it might not be very good but what sort of message would that send to Harrison, contradicting my vow not to put myself down in front of him?

I made my way to the cross in the middle of the bed and rolled my shoulders and neck a few times. *Don't overthink it. It's just a bit of fun. Do a Zara. Live in and love every moment! Be the bear!*

27
ZARA

Wow! Snowy Oakes was seriously ripped, not that I'd have expected anything else from a former Olympian who clearly kept up his training. He looked set to take part in a competition, wearing gymnastics stirrups and a sleeveless leotard – like a tight Lycra vest top – which clung to all his muscles and revealed spectacular biceps.

But when he started to bounce on the trampoline, appreciating his physique was soon eclipsed by marvelling at his talent. I'd thought of searching for footage of him at the Olympics, but it didn't feel right. Snowy was clearly a private man with a complicated past. I'd told him I wouldn't search for any gossip, but it felt equally wrong to watch videos of him competing without making sure he was comfortable with it. Besides, if I searched on his name, it was perhaps inevitable that competition videos weren't the only thing I'd find and I had no intention of breaking my promise to him.

Watching him on the trampoline now, seamlessly gliding from somersaults to twists, I was glad I'd stopped myself and that my first insight into his athleticism was live and close-up. At first, his expression had been intense but, as he gained height, he started to smile and it was infectious. His smile slipped as he did each trick but was back again as he bounced a few more times, finishing off with some basic moves. Harrison, Eddie and

I all whooped and applauded when he stopped. Snowy laughed and took a bow.

'I've never seen you smiling like that,' Eddie said. 'It was good to see.'

'I've never felt like that before. I took inspiration from Zara.' He sat down on the edge of the trampoline beside me, legs dangling over the side, his eyes twinkling as he added, 'Living in and loving the moment. Being the bear.'

As his gaze held mine, it was hard to believe that this was the same man who'd barely glanced at me on Wednesday. Did he relax and show his soft, fun side once he got to know people a little better, or was it me specifically? The thought that it could be me gave me an unexpected thrill and I felt my heartrate speeding up.

'Your turn, Pops,' Harrison said as Snowy lowered himself off the trampoline and wiped his face with a towel.

'I'll pass on that one,' Eddie replied. 'My body would never forgive me. Zara, what was your favourite apparatus other than the trampoline?'

'The bars,' I said, without hesitation. The uneven bars were the two bars at different heights on which competitive gymnasts completed a timed routine of circles and turns, changing grip style and hand position, and transitioning between the two bars using various flips and twists.

'I have this thing about flying,' I added. 'That moment of weightlessness as you change bars or dismount did something to me. I was good at it, but...' I tailed off, shrugging. Had I really just referred to myself as *good* in front of a past and an aspiring Olympian?

Snowy tilted his head and narrowed his eyes, as though he was going to question me further but, if he was, he thought better of it.

'Fancy a go on the bars now?' he asked.

'Gosh, no! It's been far too long. I don't think I could even hold my body weight on them, never mind anything else.'

'I bet you'd be surprised. Look how quickly the trampoline came back to you.'

I looked over to the bars and, while it would be amazing to have a go on them again, I knew my limitations. A couple of tricks on the trampoline was one thing but the bars were a different type of apparatus and I'd get frustrated with myself if I tried. And not just because

I'd struggle to do it, but because I could have taken it so much further. If only I hadn't... I stopped myself going down that path and smiled at Snowy.

'Thanks, but I'll say no to the bars.'

'What about some floor work?' Snowy suggested. 'No pressure if you only want to do the trampoline.'

I looked round their eager faces and felt the encouragement emanating from them. 'Go on, then. That's not quite as scary.'

It turned out not to be scary at all and the next hour flew past in a blur of tumbles, jumps, leaps and a few wipe-outs on my part. There was no denying it was great fun to be doing gymnastics again, but the real joy for me came from watching Harrison and Snowy, especially when they performed a series of synchronised tumbles.

'You must be so proud of them,' I said to Eddie.

'Every single day,' he said, sounding a little choked up. I felt proud myself, which was strange when I'd only met them a few days ago.

'Right, young lad,' Eddie said shortly before 3 p.m. 'It's a Sunday and if we don't get into town right now, we're not going to catch anywhere open, so run up to the house and quickly change. I want to see you out at the car in five minutes.'

'You'll still be here when we get back?' Harrison asked me, taking a set of keys from Eddie.

I glanced at Snowy. I didn't need to rush back, but it was his decision whether I stayed. He smiled and nodded at me.

'Yes, I'll still be here. Happy pen-shopping.'

He ran off and Eddie followed him with a goodbye wave to us.

'And then there were two,' Snowy said. 'Do you want to do anything else in here?'

I cast my gaze round the gym, pausing at the bars, wondering whether I should just go for it.

'What's your favourite?' I asked him.

'Varies between pommels and vault.'

'What did you get your medal for? I was going to find your routine but I promised I wouldn't look up what happened before the London Games and I was worried it might come up if I searched on your name.'

'I don't think I've ever met someone with as much integrity as you,' he said, smiling at me.

'I'm all about being fair to people.'

He led me over to the front row of benches and we sat down with our drinks.

'I got silver on the pommels in the apparatus finals and bronze in the team final.'

'You got two medals? That's incredible! Where do you keep them?'

'In a drawer in my office.'

In a drawer? I'd have expected them to be framed, or at least hanging up. Although maybe having them on display was too painful after his career was cut short.

'Any chance I could see them later?' I asked tentatively.

'If you like.'

His tone was positive, so perhaps I was reading too much into the drawer thing.

'What did your dad get his medal in?'

'He got bronze for the vault.' His tone was flat as he said that. 'And as for Harrison, it's early days so far,' he added, his voice full of warmth once more. 'He's strong on them all and his favourite varies from month to month. He's really into the trampoline at the moment, but who knows what it'll be in February.'

'Are you a strict coach?' I asked, thinking about how the coaching styles at my gym had differed depending on whether the gymnast had the potential and enthusiasm to progress or was there for fun.

Snowy laughed. 'You'd have to ask Harrison that. I'd say I'm focused, but I know where the line is between pushing someone to unlock their full potential and just plain pushing. My dad didn't.'

He seemed to drift off for a moment and I hadn't missed the change of tone when he mentioned his dad. There was definitely a story there, but there was no way I was going to quiz him about it. He'd tell me if and when he wanted to.

'Do you want to...' Snowy tailed off, cheeks colouring.

'What were you going to ask?' I said when it was evident he wasn't going to finish that sentence.

'I was going to ask if you wanted to see my pommels routine with you not watching it online, but—'

'Oh, my God! Seriously? I'd love to.'

His smile returned. 'Give me a moment to warm up on it and then I'll show you.'

He pulled on a pair of wrist guards and chalked his hands before taking hold of the pommels – the two curved bars – on the horse. The warm-up was extremely impressive, so I knew I was going to be in for such a treat from the main routine. Sure enough, I couldn't take my eyes off him as he twisted his legs and trunk across the apparatus, seamlessly switching between supporting his weight by holding the pommels and by placing his hands on the different parts of the horse. The speed and grace had me mesmerised and all too soon, he was done, supporting his weight in the middle of the horse – the saddle – on one hand only and flicking his body in a dismount onto the mat.

I leapt to my feet, bouncing on the spot and applauding as loudly as I could. 'Gold from me!' I cried.

Snowy wiped his hands down his stirrups. 'I wouldn't make it to the Games with that now, but I'm pleased with what I can still do.'

'It looked flawless to me. Makes me want to take up gymnastics again.'

'You should.' He frowned, looking around him. 'Hmm. If only there was somewhere local you could train. Somewhere with all the kit you need and a coach on hand.'

'You'd coach me?' I could barely spit out the words.

'If you like.'

'Yes! One hundred per cent yes! But I wouldn't dream of taking your attention away from Harrison.'

'We build our training into the school day so, if you wanted to come on evenings after work, you could combine training with owl-spotting.'

Without even pausing to think about it, I lunged at him to thank him, wrapping my arms round his neck. He stiffened and didn't return the hug.

'Sorry!' I said, quickly releasing him and stepping away to give him space. 'I'd love to be coached and I promise not to hurl myself at you like that again. Put it down to momentary madness caused by some serious fan-girling over your moves.'

I kept my tone jovial and hoped I hadn't made a serious faux pas. Snowy had done nothing to indicate to me that he was a hugger but, because Harrison had hugged me several times and Eddie had kissed me on the cheeks, I'd felt welcomed into the brood and had mistakenly assumed a level of familiarity with Snowy.

His expression softened. 'No, it's me. Sorry. It's been... I shouldn't have... It's all good. Erm... why don't we go back to the lodge, I'll make some hot drinks and then we can visit The Owlery?'

'Sounds good to me.'

Snowy gathered his belongings together and I heaved a sigh of relief. What a muppet I was. I'd just made a new friend – the first one in the area who wasn't also Amber's and Barney's friend – and I'd nearly blown it by being too me. I'd better tone it down a bit from now on because I wanted to come back. The gymnastics coaching was a massive bonus but that wasn't why I wanted to keep returning. This place had a special pull. The surroundings were beautiful, but so was Snowy's family and I wanted to spend time with them and learn all about owls. I wanted something that was for me for once.

28

SNOWY

What is wrong with you? Someone you like hugs you and you freeze. Idiot! The speed at which she let go and stepped back suggested that Zara was mortified, despite hiding it well with smiles and apologies. It had taken me by surprise, that's all. The last woman to hug me had been Eliza and I'd been rigid in her arms and hadn't responded to her either. One of my many regrets.

I locked up and we set off up the steps towards the lodge. Worried I might have made Zara uncomfortable, I was eager to fill any silence and asked her where in Scotland she was going to film, which turned into a bigger conversation than expected, keeping us going throughout making drinks. Thankfully, she seemed unperturbed by the non-hug.

'Any chance of seeing your medals while the drinks are cooling?' Zara asked.

I led her up the stairs to my office. Opening up the top drawer of a tall chest, I removed a metal tin and lifted the lid, revealing the two shiny medals nestling in my folded leotard.

'That's the leotard I wore when I won the silver,' I told her. 'It did get washed first.'

She smiled as she took the box from me. 'Wow! First time I've ever seen one of these.'

'I used to have them displayed on the wall but...' I shrugged. 'It didn't feel right anymore.'

'Because of what happened after your injury?'

'Something like that.'

'Can I?' She flexed her fingers towards the silver medal, but didn't touch it.

'Help yourself.'

She removed the medal and ran her forefinger across the winged image of Nike – the goddess of victory, pictured in the Panathinaikos Stadium – the Olympic rings above her head, and the engraving around the top: *XXIX OLYMPIAD BEIJING 2008*. Turning it over, she ran her finger round the reverse side – a simpler design in the middle with a jade ring around it, and the name of the sport.

'It's heavier than I expected,' she said, turning it back and forth, letting it catch the light before placing the silver back in the box and admiring the bronze.

'Never thought I'd hold an Olympic medal,' she said, handing me the box back. 'Thanks for letting me do that. I've got goose bumps now.' She ran her hands up and down her arms and I had a strong desire to wrap my arms around her until she'd warmed up, but I could hardly do that after my reaction to her hug earlier.

'Your tea will warm you up,' I said, returning the box to the drawer and closing it. 'Back downstairs?'

We collected our drinks from the kitchen and Zara sat down on the sofa with hers while I put on a couple of lamps and lit the log burner. I could have plonked myself down at the far end of the sofa but I didn't want the distance between us. I hadn't wanted it in the gym either – I'd just been taken by surprise.

'I love log burners,' Zara said, staring into the flames.

'Me too. Although nothing quite beats the fire pit outside.'

It was the sort of comment I'd have expected her to pick up on, but she remained silent. Something had happened after I showed her the medals. She seemed a little melancholy.

'Are you okay?' I asked.

'Just thinking.'

'About anything in particular?'

She finally turned her gaze back to me. 'How much fun I've had in the gym this afternoon and on Friday. Are you really sure about coaching me?'

'It would be a pleasure.'

She smiled but it didn't quite reach her eyes. Something was definitely wrong.

'Why did you stop going to gymnastics?' I asked.

'I told you the other day. I'd fallen behind and I lost interest.'

Her answer was a little too quick. Too rehearsed. I could see the pain of the lie in her eyes before she turned her gaze back to the flames.

'And what was the real reason?' I said gently.

'What makes you think there's something else?' The averted eyes and the catch in her voice confirmed my suspicions.

'I'm not trying to analyse you or pretend I've got you sussed after so little time with you, but you've been like an open book until now and it's as though the book has just been closed on a painful part.'

She released a slow shuddery sigh. 'You're right. I never lost interest. It's an excuse I told everyone. Including myself.'

29
ZARA

Fifteen years ago

We'd only been back at the gym after the Christmas break for four sessions when my coach, Margo, asked me to stay behind for a chat.

'Don't look so worried,' she said, sitting down on one of the benches beside me once the others had gone. 'You're not in trouble. I wanted to talk to you about your future as a gymnast. I wasn't sure you were going to catch up on the missed time but, last term, I was really impressed with your progress. I wanted to see whether you still had that same fire burning in your belly when we returned after Christmas and it seems you do. I'm particularly excited about your progress on the bars, so I have a question for you, Zara. What sort of gymnast do you want to be?'

My heart leapt. I'd dreamed of her asking me that question. The answer was the difference between staying with Margo and doing gymnastics for fun and fitness or moving into Carlos and Andrea's class and properly going down the competitive route. They were tough coaches but they were brilliant.

'I want to compete,' I said, bursting with excitement.

Margo smiled. 'Although I'll be sad to lose you, I was hoping you'd say that. I can see great potential in you and I believe the bars are going to be your best friend. But if you do join Carlos and Andrea, it's a big increased commitment. You'll need to train every Saturday and three nights a week, which ups to four nights in the approach to competitions. Then there's the competitions themselves, which means time and travel.'

I nodded.

'Before I speak to your mum or Owen about the increased costs, I'd like you to think hard about whether this really is the route you want to take because the focus will change.'

'Okay.'

'Off you go then. If you have any questions, bring them to me next time.'

I smiled and thanked her then ran back to Owen.

'Margo thinks I've improved loads,' I told him as he drove me back home. I wished it was his home too but he wasn't going to move in until he and Mum got married in September. Mum said he was *an old-fashioned gentleman about things like that*, whatever that meant, so he'd return to his flat when Mum got back with Roman.

'Is that what she wanted to talk to you about?' Owen asked.

'Yes. She thinks I'm ready to go up a class.'

'That's fantastic. Would that class still be the same nights?'

'Yes, and on another night and a Saturday.'

He kept his eyes on the road but his hands gripped the steering wheel tighter and I could tell I'd said something bad because Mum gripped the wheel like that when she was about to tell me off.

'We'd have to talk to your mum about that,' he said with a sigh. Owen was normally really positive but he sounded sad. Did he think Mum would say no? Because that was my fear too.

* * *

Mum didn't even ask what going up to Carlos and Andrea's class would mean to me. As soon as she heard that I'd need to go twice as often and that it would cost more money, she said it wasn't an option and I wasn't to mention it again.

But I had to mention it again. Andrea stopped by my class the following week and watched me on the uneven bars and I knew she was impressed because she actually smiled when I landed my routine and she hardly ever smiled.

'Have you thought any more about moving up?' Margo asked when Andrea left.

'Lots. I want to do it, but Mum said no. Can you talk to her?'

'It's a bit difficult to do that when it's not her who brings you. Do you think there's any chance she could come one night? If she could see how good you are, she might think differently about you moving up.'

I shook my head. 'She won't come. She's only interested in Roman and his football. Can you ring her and tell her I'm good enough?'

'I don't usually.'

'Please!'

'Okay. But I should warn you that I'm not great at talking parents round. She'll probably still say no.'

I grinned at her. 'But she might say yes!'

* * *

The following Monday, I was in bed when Mum and Roman returned from football.

'You're in trouble,' Roman cried in an irritating sing-song voice as he burst into my bedroom.

'Why?'

'You got your gym coach to ring Mum and she's really mad with you about it. Wouldn't like to be in your stinky shoes right now.'

'Bog off!' I cried, grabbing a cuddly sheep and tossing it in his direction. It bounced off the door as he closed it.

I hated him. He'd just turned fifteen and he should have grown up a bit by now, but he acted more like a five-year-old round me, teasing and tormenting, always telling me I was in trouble with Mum. I usually was and it was obvious he loved every minute of it.

I curled up on my side and waited for Mum's footsteps but, instead, I heard raised voices downstairs. Or rather I heard Mum shouting and the pauses in between were presumably Owen trying to quietly reason with her. It seemed that I was in trouble because of the phone call. *Too many nights. Too much money. Too much effort. Not happening.* Message received loud and clear.

Mum didn't come up to say goodnight and she didn't say anything to me over breakfast the next morning either. The silence was deafening and I couldn't bear it. I only managed half my breakfast then left the house early, shivering in the bus shelter as I waited for the bus to senior school and wishing it wasn't so cold and wet.

When I got home, Mum asked me about my day but she didn't mention gymnastics and I didn't dare raise it, sloping up to my bedroom to do my homework.

A few nights later, I was in for a surprise when Owen turned up as usual but announced that he was taking Roman to football.

'I'm taking you to gymnastics tonight,' Mum said, her voice tight. 'I hear you want to go up to the next class.'

'Yes, please.'

'I've been instructed to watch you.'

I couldn't wait to show Mum how well I was doing but, as she drove me to the gym, my confidence seeped away. Mum was clearly still annoyed with me, which didn't make sense to me because I'd have thought she'd be pleased that I'd finally caught up and was showing potential for the next level.

If she'd continued to give me the silent treatment all the way, I might have been all right but, when we were halfway to the gym, she lectured me instead on whether I realised what a huge commitment it was going to be. And then there was that killer final comment.

'You'd better be good after all this. Because if this is just that gym club trying to squeeze more money out of me, I won't be impressed and there's no way I'll consider moving you up.'

I was so nervous by the time we arrived at the gym that I felt sick. We warmed up and then I did a floor routine where I stumbled once and fell twice. The bits I did right weren't very good. My vault was only okay and I didn't land it very well, the beam was hit and miss and the bars were a disaster, not helped by the fact that I was crying throughout my routine, knowing I'd already fluffed up my big chance.

Margo gave me a hug afterwards. 'Don't be too hard on yourself,' she whispered. 'We all have bad days.'

True, but my bad day had been when it really counted.

While I was putting my tracksuit and trainers on, Margo had a word with Mum. Margo did lots of pointing at the apparatus and gesturing with her hands. Mum did a lot of shaking of her head. And all I did was cry.

'I'm sorry,' I said in a quiet voice as I pulled on my seatbelt a little later, ready to go home. 'I got nervous having you there.'

She sighed. 'I'm sorry it didn't go how you wanted but, if you get this nervous in front of me and it affects your performance like that, how on earth would you manage in front of a crowd of strangers in a competition?'

'It was only because you never come to see me and I really wanted to show you how good I was.'

'Isn't that the point of competitions, though? To show the audience and judges how good you are? I'm sorry, Zara, but I don't think you're ready for this.'

'I am! I really am!'

'I don't think you are.'

'It was just tonight. Please, Mum!'

She sighed again. 'Truth is I can't afford the extra classes.'

'Then why did you come tonight?'

'Because I thought that if you truly were a gifted gymnast like your brother's a gifted footballer, I'd have a word with your dad and see if there's any chance of him paying for the extra classes. But, after today, I can't passionately fight your corner. You must be able to understand that.'

'Can't you come again on Monday?'

'I'm sorry, but no.'

I cried myself to sleep that night. I was so disappointed that I'd messed up and ruined my chance to progress but what hurt the most was what Mum had said about Roman and the thought that she might be right.

* * *

Roman couldn't help himself. Over the next few days, every time he passed me, he either made a snide comment about me being a failure or he pretended to fall over. I wished he really would fall and hurt himself. It would serve him right for being so nasty.

After lunch on Sunday, I told Mum I'd been invited to Suzie Thomas's house. I hadn't been. Suzie and I had drifted apart when we'd started senior school last September and she'd found a new group of friends. I wandered round the village for a while but it started drizzling so I reluctantly returned home. I called out to Mum to let her know I was back but she didn't respond so I went up to my bedroom.

Not long after, I heard a car pulling up on the drive and peeked out the window, surprised to see it was Dad. I hadn't seen him for weeks and wondered why Mum had let me go out when he was expected. Unless it was a surprise visit. Or he wasn't here to see me. He knocked on the door and I heard Mum inviting him in and telling him that Roman and I were both out so they could talk freely.

'What's up?' he asked, after turning down her offer of a coffee. 'You sounded stressed on the phone.'

They moved away from the door and into the lounge. Something told me I was going to want to hear this conversation so I crept out of my room. Our stairs ran straight down into the lounge and I could hear them but stay hidden if I crouched down at the top.

'Zara has her heart set on progressing with her gymnastics,' Mum said. 'It means more sessions at the gym and lots of competitions, but her coach claims she's good enough.'

'Claims?' Dad said. 'You haven't seen her?'

'I usually do the football runs. You know that. Anyway, it's a big hike in fees. You know I've never asked you for anything since the divorce, but it isn't easy for me. My job doesn't pay that well and it's not enough to cover everything for the kids.'

'Jenna! We agreed a more than fair maintenance payment.'

'I know, but it doesn't stretch far enough to cover both their clubs. Have you seen the price of football kits and leotards?'

'Can't Owen help out?'

'Esther bled him dry in the divorce. Please, Bryson! You should have seen how upset she was when I told her no.'

'If you've already told her no, why are we having this conversation?' Dad asked, sounding exasperated. 'She's twelve this year. She'll get over it.'

'But her coach thinks—'

'I don't give two hoots what her coach thinks. What do *you* think? Have you seen her do gymnastics recently because, back when I used to take her, she was just a little kid doing roly-polys.'

There was a silence and my heart thudded, wondering whether she'd tell Dad about last week.

'Her coach invited me on Thursday so, yes, I've seen her recently.'

'And?'

'And it wasn't good, but it was only because I was there and she got nervous, wanting to impress me.'

'It wasn't good? So we return to my earlier question. Why are we even having this conversation?'

There was a pause before Mum said, 'She was so upset about messing up.'

'I get that so let's put it another way. Do you think, hand on heart, that she's got what it takes? Roman has lived and breathed football since he could walk but I've never had that same sense of passion from Zara. Do you think this is what she really, truly wants and that she has the desire and talent to make it worth the investment?'

Another pause and I willed for Mum to fight my corner although I knew, deep down, that she wouldn't push any further. I was surprised she'd gone as far as she had.

'She's not like her brother,' she said eventually. 'Her enthusiasm comes and goes and I haven't seen any evidence of the talent her coach spoke about. She's not good enough.'

'There's the answer then. Kids need to learn that they can't have everything, especially things that suck up so much time and money. Things are tight for us too. The wedding wiped us out and I wasn't going to announce it yet but Charlotte's expecting again.'

My stomach flopped. Dad and Charlotte were having a third baby?

Another person Dad would love way more than me. Another reason for not spending time with us.

'Congratulations,' Mum said. 'I'm pleased for you both.'

'Thank you, but I'm sure you'll understand why I can't help financially. We agreed a generous settlement, Jenna, and I haven't got anything else to give.'

I shuffled back across the landing on my hands and knees, quietly closed my door and curled up on my bed, silent tears raining down my cheeks. *She's not like her brother. I haven't seen any evidence of the talent her coach spoke about. She's not good enough.* I clung onto my pillow, reeling from those words. *Not good enough.* Would I ever be?

30

ZARA

Present day

'That was the moment I disengaged,' I said to Snowy as I watched the flames leaping in the log burner. My throat had steadily tightened as I told the story and I was so close to breaking down. I couldn't bring myself to avert my gaze as a sympathetic look or a nice word was going to tip me over the edge.

'My parents didn't believe in me so I stopped believing in me too. Checked out. Gave up. Stopped aiming high because if nobody is expecting greatness, you're not going to disappoint them when you don't achieve it. In some ways, it was good. Pressure was off. I could do gymnastics and trampolining for fun and it *was* fun until I was the only teenager in a class of primary school kids who were doing better and going further than me. I couldn't take the humiliation or disappointment anymore.'

'What about your stepdad?' Snowy asked. 'Didn't he believe in you?'

Feeling like I was in control of my emotions once more, I looked at Snowy again. 'Owen was and still is my one-man cheerleading squad. Later that night, after I overheard Mum and Dad's conversation, I told Mum I'd changed my mind about moving up a class – said she had a good point about crumbling under pressure – but it obviously didn't fool

Owen. When he drove me to my class the following day, he kept telling me that I was brilliant and was I sure about giving up on my dreams? I hated lying to him, but what choice did I have? I honestly don't know what I'd have done without that man. He's always been there for me.'

'We all need an Owen in our lives. Mine was Grandpa. No matter how spectacularly I screwed up, he was always there, believing in me.'

'Your grandpa's lovely.'

'He's the best.' He paused as he added another log to the burner. 'I don't know whether it helps or makes it worse, but I can tell from what you've done in the gym so far that you were trained well and you have some skills. They're rusty, obviously, but they're good. Would you have progressed to a high level if you had moved up a class? There's no way of knowing. You came to an impassable barrier and there was nothing you could do about it, especially at your age, and it's something I saw all the time in my clubs. There are gymnasts like you who want to and could succeed but can't progress because of the time and money needed. There are those who have the time and money but don't actually have the ability or the right mindset. And sometimes circumstance or injury take it all away. That's what happened to my wife, Eliza. She was brilliant and I'm sure she could have gone all the way but she had a freak fall from the beam and broke both her wrists. She never got her confidence back to try again on any of the apparatus.'

'She must have been devastated.'

'She was when it happened, but Eliza was one of those people who are always sunny and positive. She changed sport and got into swimming instead. She was too late to consider the Olympics but she could still swim competitively and she loved it.'

It was obvious from the warmth in his voice and the shine in his eyes that he'd loved her very much. How must it feel to find someone to love who loved you back and to lose them at such a young age? It was touching how, in a short space of time, Snowy had gone from being wary around me to opening up about his family. Would the next step be opening up about his bad decisions?

Eddie and Harrison arrived home, drawing a natural end to our conversation. Harrison was delighted with his large pack of pens and asked if I could show him my scrapbooks to give him ideas for filling his. The four of us sat round the dining table as I worked through the pages of my original precious pages, pointing out my first gymnastics certificate and my report from leaving primary school. I hadn't looked through it for years and had forgotten what was in there. As I opened a page containing several Polaroid photos – me striking a pose in my leotard, bending over backwards on the beam and paused in a handstand on the bars – I felt all choked up.

I glanced at Snowy. 'Owen took these a couple of weeks after my routine went wrong to prove to me that I had what it takes. Forever my cheerleader.'

I hoped Owen knew how much he meant to me. For his birthday each year, I spent ages searching for a card containing a poem which conveyed how much I cared. I wondered if Mum ever noticed that I didn't do the same for her, but how could I buy a card which talked about always being there for me when she hadn't been? I was sure my life would be very different today if Owen hadn't been in it. And not in a good way.

31

SNOWY

Harrison gave Zara a goodbye hug and thanked her again for his gifts, making me glow with pride. We'd raised such a well-mannered young boy. Grandpa gave her kisses on each cheek and, as she faced me, ready to leave, my arms twitched to grab her in a bear hug, but I was very aware of Grandpa and Harrison watching and said I'd walk her out instead.

Had I really talked to her about Eliza? It had felt so natural and I'd managed it without any tightening in the throat or burning in my eyes. If Grandpa and Harrison hadn't arrived home at that point, might I have opened up further? Might I have told her the truth? Something told me she'd understand.

'I've just realised we never made it into the woods,' I said after I'd closed the door behind us and stepped out into the cold night air. 'I know you're heading up to Scotland next weekend but, if you have any time free before you go, we can have a tour and hopefully see a little owl or a short-eared one. If you're really lucky, we might even spot both.'

'That would be amazing. We're driving up on Sunday but I'm free on Saturday. Can I come back to you later about a time?'

'That's fine. We've got no plans so whatever suits you best.' As I said that, it struck me that we hardly ever had plans. I was okay with that, but was Harrison?

We'd reached her car. 'I'm really sorry you didn't get the support you needed from your parents,' I said, 'but I'm glad you had your stepdad in your corner. We're a bit late for LA 2028 but, if we knuckle down, we could be ready for the Owl's Lodge Summer Olympics. Way more prestigious than anything else in the competitive calendar. And if you'd rather wait until the Owl's Lodge Winter Olympics, then you're in for such a treat because the medals are made of chocolate coins. We even tape ribbons to the back.'

I loved that I could make Zara laugh. 'No expense spared, eh?' she said.

'No expense at all. Don't be fooled by the mild-mannered inventor we live with. He might have made his fortune but it doesn't stop him being a kleptomaniac. He's like a magpie, drawn to those gold coins on the supermarket shelf. Next minute, he's filled his pockets and he's off sprinting across the car park, security alarms blaring in his wake.'

She was still laughing. 'Oh, so Eddie's an athlete too?'

'Hell, yeah! East Yorkshire's answer to Mo Farah, you know.'

I couldn't keep a straight face any longer at the thought of Grandpa sprinting out of Sainsbury's, his pockets stuffed full of chocolate coins. The more I laughed, the more Zara laughed and the pair of us soon had tears running down our cheeks.

'The thought of your granddad shoplifting gold coins...' Zara wiped her cheeks as she struggled to catch her breath. 'That's brilliant, Snowy. I swear that image will keep me going all week. I had a difficult start to the New Year and I needed that pick-me-up. Thank you.'

'New Year's tough for us too. We lost Eliza on New Year's Day so I find January a challenge. You probably picked up on that vibe. I'm sorry I wasn't more welcoming.'

'Don't be. You've more than made up for it since.'

She was standing so close to me, looking up with a tender expression on her face, and I imagined pulling her into my arms and kissing her – a thought which both thrilled and terrified me.

'How about Tuesday for your first coaching session?' I asked.

She screwed her nose up. 'I can't. It's my friend Phoebe's birthday and she's having a party. What about Wednesday?'

'Works for me.'

We both stood there for a moment, neither of us saying anything. Should I hug her? Was she going to hug me? No, there was no way she'd try that again after my reaction from earlier. *And now we've been standing here for too long hug-free so to do it now would make it weird.* Not that it wasn't weird already.

Zara opened the back door and placed her bag behind the driver's seat, taking the tension from the situation.

'See you on Wednesday,' she said, getting into the front and starting the engine.

I waved as she pulled away, cursing myself for being so inept. Eliza and I hadn't gone through all these shenanigans. We'd been friends and, when I was fifteen, I'd asked her if she wanted to be my girlfriend instead. She said yes and that was that. Simple.

* * *

Harrison liked to have a bath on a Sunday night and I could have placed money on Grandpa taking that opportunity to quiz me about Zara.

'When are you seeing her again?' he asked, looking up at me from his book as I joined him in the lounge with a glass of water.

'She's coming back on Wednesday evening for a coaching session.'

'You seemed a lot more relaxed around her today.'

'I felt it. She's good company – easy to be relaxed around.'

He closed his book and adjusted position. 'You seemed extra relaxed after we got back from town, so did something happen while we were out?'

I couldn't resist teasing him. 'Like what?'

'You know exactly what I mean.'

'No, it didn't.'

'Is that why you didn't hug her goodbye?'

He missed nothing! 'I didn't hug her because she hugged me earlier and it was a bit awkward. I froze and didn't respond.'

Grandpa winced.

'Yeah, I know! Not one of my finest moments, so that's why we didn't have a goodbye hug.'

'Why did she hug you earlier?'

'A thank you, I think, so don't read anything into it.'

He studied my face for a moment. 'But you wished it had meant something more. You like her. I knew it!'

'I do like her, but it scares me.'

Grandpa put his book down – *very* serious conversation cue. 'Firstly the hug. It's the first female contact you've had since Eliza so I can't say I'm surprised by your reaction. Secondly, you have no idea how happy it makes me to hear that you're thinking about the possibility of someone else.'

'Am I, though? I've only just met her and those tentative feelings might fade.'

'They might deepen.'

'I never expected to feel anything for anyone again and I feel guilty about it.'

'Why?'

I raised my eyebrows at him. 'Do you really need to ask that?'

'I know Eliza was the love of your life, but it's been five years. How long do you need?'

'Says the man who's been widowed for fifteen years and hasn't so much as looked at another woman.'

'That's different.'

'How?'

'Because Shirley and I had our life together. I wished we'd had longer. I wish she was still here, but I'm forever grateful for the time we did have. I was nearly seventy-eight when she died. Why would I want to find someone else at that age? It's not like I was craving companionship. I had you and Eliza here.'

'And I've got you and Harrison.'

'True, but we both know how delicate life can be, here one minute, gone the next. I'm still determined to reach my century, but I won't be here forever and I want to bid you farewell knowing you've found love again.'

'Nobody mentioned love!' I cried. 'We're talking a few butterflies here.'

'And that can lead to love. All right, stop shaking your head at me. Maybe it will, maybe it won't. Maybe it won't be reciprocated but, whether it's Zara or someone else, you're only thirty-four. You're in your prime. You've got your whole life ahead of you. Make it count.'

'It's good advice,' I admitted, 'but how do I stop feeling guilty?'

'You think about the kind of woman Eliza was. If she'd come round in hospital and had known her time was at an end, her dying wish would have been for you and Harrison to be happy. She'd even have ordered you to find someone new.'

I couldn't argue against that. It was Eliza through and through – selfless to the core.

Grandpa wasn't finished. 'As for feeling guilty about her death, only you can make your peace with that. I've told you a million times that you're not to blame and it was a tragic accident, but I know that's fallen on deaf ears. So here's a thought. What if Eliza sent Zara to you? What if she knew you needed some time to heal and, when she felt you had your strength back, she sent you an owl-bearing angel?'

Grandpa's eyes sparkled with unshed tears and I felt the most enormous lump blocking my throat. I couldn't respond to that because there was a part of me that so wanted to believe he was speaking the truth. Especially when it was exactly the sort of thing Eliza would have done.

32

ZARA

The thought of Eddie as a chocolate coin-stealing nonagenarian was still tickling me as I drove through the darkness back to Bumblebee Barn. What a strange, reflective, wonderful, funny, emotional afternoon I'd just had. The change in Snowy's behaviour around me was astonishing and I was loving his quick sense of humour – something I'd never have guessed lurked beneath the sullen surface when we first met. Although now that he'd told me his wife had died on New Year's Day and January was a struggle, was it any wonder he'd been a bit moody?

Pulling into the farmyard at Bumblebee Barn, I was surprised to see Joel's car. My headlights picked up Joel himself, by the open door. He waved as I parked.

'Can't stay away from the place?' I asked, getting out of my car.

'Something like that.'

'Coming or going?'

'Going. I'm on an early shift in the morning.'

His voice was flat and, in the glow from the security light, he looked tired.

'Everything all right?' I asked, tentatively.

He sighed. 'You might as well hear it from me. Marley and I have split up.'

'Oh, no! Oh, Joel, I'm so sorry.' I genuinely was sorry. My feelings for him were neither here nor there. He was a friend who was hurting and that was what was important right now.

He closed his door and came round to join me, leaning against the passenger side of his car as he spoke. 'She phoned me earlier to say that she's been thinking a lot about her future and she doesn't want children in it, so it has to be over for us.'

He looked heartbroken and there was no way I couldn't hug him. We stood there for ages, clinging onto each other. Joel eventually stepped back.

'I want to say something but everything feels so trite,' I said, shrugging apologetically. What was the point in dishing out platitudes like *it'll be all right* because I knew from experience that, at the point of being dumped, it never felt like that?

'Barney and Amber said pretty much the same thing,' he said, shrugging. 'It's crap but it is what it is and it's best that I know now. At least Imogen never met her and got attached.'

'I can't believe she didn't say anything right at the start. It's not like you've ever hidden the fact that you're a dad.'

'I threw that at her but she said she thought she could cope with a partner's child and it was only when Tilly said it was okay for her to meet Imogen that reality hit.'

'I am sorry.'

'Me too. God, my dating history reads like a who's who of unsuitable choices, although I should be grateful that Marley didn't steal the crown from Tilly as Queen of Bad Endings. A fortnight before walking up the aisle really takes the biscuit. One of these days I'll get it right.'

'I keep telling myself the same thing. Did I tell you about my romantic weekend in the Cotswolds to celebrate my birthday last year? Declan was a no-show and he finally messaged me to say it was over but to enjoy the weekend on him as he'd settled the bill as a birthday gift. So I did. Except he hadn't paid after all. That was a fun birthday.'

'What a gent!'

He shared a couple of his other bad relationships and I could completely relate to that confusion around being drawn to the wrong partners.'

'I feel your pain. There's not a single boyfriend in my past who had long-term potential. Freud would probably have a field day with me, always drawn to the bad boys.'

'He'd have a field day with me too. My main weakness is women who want to friend-zone me.'

We rolled our eyes at each other, laughing at our shared tragic dating history.

'I can't believe how badly you've been treated by your exes,' Joel said. 'Their loss.'

'Right back at ya.'

'No more bad boys for you. You need someone who'll see you for the lovely person you are and treat you right. Someone more like me.'

'And no more women who don't want children and just want to be friends for you,' I said, smiling at him. 'Someone more like me.'

'We should have got together instead,' he said. 'We're nothing like each other's exes.'

It was a joke, some banter, completely typical of the exchanges that we had every time we met. But on my part, it was how I felt and from the look on Joel's face, it was as though he'd suddenly realised that it would have been a good idea. He narrowed his eyes, his mouth slightly parted, as though he wasn't sure whether to say anything else. I had no words. We continued to hold eye contact for what felt like minutes but was probably only seconds, then we both looked away, laughing awkwardly.

'I should go,' Joel said at the exact time I said, 'I'd better go in,' and we laughed about speaking over each other.

'See you later,' I said, grabbing my bag from behind my seat and scuttling towards the farmhouse, my heart pounding, feeling totally unnerved.

Amber was in the kitchen emptying the dishwasher while the kettle was boiling. 'Hi,' she said, smiling at me. 'You've just missed Joel.'

'I saw him outside. He told me about Marley. Do you think he'll be all right?'

'Yeah. He'll be licking his wounds for a couple of weeks but he'll soon bounce back. Even if it hadn't been for the kids thing, he was already doubting their future. Marley's a strong personality and he'd noticed how she has to have her own way. While Joel's pretty chilled and likes to keep the peace, it doesn't mean he should have to give in to her every time. There has to be some compromise, but it seems that's not a word in Marley's dictionary.'

Amber made us both a mug of tea and we sat at the table.

'You know what's funny?' she said. 'When we were filming *Love on the Farm*, I thought you and Joel were going to get together. I remember you telling me how hot you thought he was the first time you saw him and... Oh, my God! You still fancy him!'

It was evidently written all over my face so there was no point in denying it. 'I've had a little thing for him since that first day, but there was so much drama going on that there wasn't a chance to do anything about it and then filming was cancelled and we left and...' I tailed off with a shrug, not wanting Amber to feel any guilt for us leaving early and taking me away from Joel.

'Aw, Zara, I wish I'd known. It must have been difficult for you seeing him with Marley.'

'Not my favourite way to pass time but what could I do about it? I liked her so I wasn't going to let on to anyone that I had feelings for him.'

'And now?'

'And I'm not going to let on now either. Rebound relationships don't work and there's no way I want to be Joel's rebound. He'll need space and who knows what will happen after that? I'm not holding out any hope. I think our opportunity has already passed.'

I was still thinking about that when I settled into bed later. When I'd heard that there was trouble in paradise, I hadn't felt elated and, now that it was officially over, I didn't feel thrilled either. I still had feelings for Joel. My heart had been pounding while we'd hugged and there'd been a fizzing moment between us when he'd joked about us being a couple, but could I see us in a relationship together somewhere down the line? I wasn't sure I could and that surprised me. What I'd said to Amber about our opportunity having already passed had been an off-the-cuff comment, but there might well be some truth in it.

33

SNOWY

'Is Zara coming tonight?' Harrison asked, joining me for breakfast on Tuesday morning.

'Tomorrow. She's at a friend's birthday party tonight.'

'I've never been to a birthday party. Can I have one this year?'

The first thought that sprung to mind was – *and invite who?* – but I didn't voice it and offered a woefully non-committal, 'It's early to be thinking about your birthday.'

'It's only ten weeks away.'

'That's still ages. And we've got Pops's birthday before that so we're not discussing plans for yours now.'

'But Pops never wants to do anything for his birthday.'

'Harrison! What did I just say?' It was extremely rare for me to be sharp with him and I hated myself for using that tone now when I was in the wrong. The big, sad blue eyes which met mine made me feel even worse.

'We'll talk about it again after Pops's birthday,' I said, my voice softer. 'For now, just focus on eating your breakfast.'

'Okay. Sorry.'

Sorry? What did he have to apologise for? This was all my fault.

* * *

I went to The Roost on my own as dusk fell. I wasn't surprised that Harrison didn't want to join me. We'd had a subdued day which Grandpa had naturally picked up on. I'd told him about Harrison's birthday party request and his response had been, 'It seems you've got some big decisions ahead. And not just about Harrison's birthday.' He wasn't wrong there.

I stared up at the rafters. A heart-shaped face appeared in the entrance to the nesting box, followed by a pale body. The barn owl paused, looking around, before taking off in soundless flight. His mate appeared in the entrance and watched for a while, then disappeared back inside.

Most of the time, I could push everything out of my mind when I was in The Roost but there was far too much going on today and it was time to put my thoughts into actions. I heaved myself up, left the barn and took my mobile out of my pocket. There weren't many numbers saved on it. I'd deleted nearly all the contacts from my old life – especially those who'd spoken to Parnell – but I'd kept Ashley's number. He'd never let me down.

My heart raced as I listened to it ringing. It might not even be his number anymore. It clicked into voicemail. 'Hi, this is Ashley Bennett. I can't take your call at—'

I hung up without leaving a message. A two-way conversation was going to be hard after four and a half years. Leaving a *Hi, it's me, sorry it's taken forever to return your calls but I need a favour* voicemail wasn't going to cut it.

It was nearly half nine and Harrison was settled in bed when Ashley's name flashed up on my phone. I'd told Grandpa that I'd made the call so I showed him the screen and he gave me a thumbs up as I stepped out onto the veranda.

'Hi, Ash,' I said, realising too late that it was a FaceTime call.

Ashley's face appeared on the screen. I could see a foam pit in the background so he was obviously still at the gym.

'Snowy!' he said, grinning at me. 'I've been expecting your call for a while.'

He didn't sound pissed off with me and he definitely didn't look it, so that was a good start. Although was that a dig about me not returning all his calls after Eliza's funeral?

'I know. I'm sorry. I didn't mean to shut you out. It was—'

'I don't mean about that. I meant about your lad. If I've done my maths right, he must be approaching ten. You need him affiliated to a gym so he can start competing and you thought where better to start than your old gym. Am I right?'

'Yes, but...' When he put it like that – even if it was said in his usual warm tone – it made me sound so mercenary. Was that who I was now?

He laughed. 'Your face! I'm winding you up, mate. It's good to hear from you. I've missed that ugly mug of yours and I know you've missed me because, well, who wouldn't?'

'Because you're an absolute legend,' I said, smiling as I used the term he jokingly used to describe himself.

'Too right I am! So is it about Harrison joining the gym?'

'Yes, but I wanted to say sorry too.'

'We could do that over a coffee sometime. As for Harrison, I'm really sorry but I can't give him a place.'

My stomach sank. 'You're full?'

'We're closing.'

I searched his face for a sign that he was winding me up, but his expression was deadly serious.

'Why? I thought gymnastics was more popular than ever. I was worrying about waiting lists and hoping... Why?'

'Because Fred's retiring and there's nobody in his family to pass it down to, so he's selling up.'

Campion's Gymnastics Club had been around for decades. It was the first club I attended, alongside Ashley and, later, Eliza. Fred Campion had coached us all and, when Ash and I had moved on to a bigger club in Leeds, we'd stayed in touch with him. Ashley was a brilliant gymnast but not quite Olympic standard and he'd returned to Campion's as a coach in his mid-twenties.

'What are you going to do?' I asked.

He scrunched his face up and shrugged. 'No idea. We only found out last week.'

'Has he found a buyer?'

'There's a leisure chain who want to turn it into a recreational gym. It's obviously not what he wants but, as there's been no other interest, it looks like he might have to go with them. I offered him my life savings but apparently twenty-seven pence won't even buy me a foam block.'

Someone in the background shouted something. Ash turned away from the camera for a moment and nodded before turning back to me.

'Sorry, Snowy, I've got to shoot. We should properly catch up, you know.'

'Yeah, I'd like that.'

'Give me a shout when you're free.' And, with that, he disconnected the call.

I sank down onto one of the chairs with a heavy sigh. Fred was really retiring and selling up? The Olympic dream for Harrison was impossible without following the competition route and that was impossible without gym affiliation. I'd always assumed that Harrison would join Campion's at some point this year or next and move on to Leeds in his teens – the same route I'd taken. The comfort of going to Campion's was Fred's zero-tolerance approach to bullying and threats – the opposite to the coaching style Dad had used on me. I wanted a safe space for Harrison to develop his skills and Campion's would have been it. If a new regime came in, they might not operate the same philosophy, although it sounded like that wasn't going to happen and it was more likely a change of use.

There was a club in Whitsborough Bay which used to have a good reputation. I could look into it, but it was an unknown and that worried me. Would Harrison need to start in Leeds instead? It was a ninety-minute commute each way, which would be exhausting for him at his age, and there was no way I could consider moving over there and leaving Grandpa all alone. I raked my hands through my hair. Here was me thinking the big problem would be me letting go and it turned out there was something way bigger than that.

'If you can't see the obvious solution, then I'm not sure you should be home schooling your son,' Grandpa said, laughing after I updated him on my conversation with Ashley.

'Are you calling me thick?'

'If the cap fits. Honestly, lad! Fred needs a buyer who'll keep the place running as a gymnastics club. That person would need a passion for gymnastics, knowledge of the sport and quite a few pennies. If only we knew an Olympic gymnast whose grandpa had a shedload of money from inventing stuff. Hmm.'

'You can't invest your life savings in a gym.'

'I wouldn't be. You would.'

'But...'

'But nothing! Who's going to get the money when I die? You and Harrison. Who needs it now? You and Harrison. No brainer.'

'Even if I accepted the money, what makes you think I'd want to run a gym?'

'What's stopping you?'

'The responsibility. The people.' I shuddered at the thought. 'I've barely seen or spoken to anyone in years. I'm not about to suddenly thrust myself out into the world and run a people-focused business.'

Grandpa closed his owl care book and stood up. 'That's your head telling you that and you listen to it far too often. It drowns everything else out. Do yourself a favour and listen to your heart for once. Trust it. You have the heart and soul of a beautiful gymnast but you have the head of your father. Your wings aren't broken, you know. They're not even clipped. If you really wanted to, you could fly. I believe your heart and soul want to do that and they just need to convince your head to take that leap of faith.' He patted his hand on the front of the book. 'I'm going to read this upstairs. Night, lad.'

'Night, Grandpa.'

And he headed up the stairs, leaving me reeling with his wise sage words. Or should that be wise owl words? Very wise because I couldn't help thinking that everything he'd said was right. My head *was* the problem. Was I strong enough to do something about it – something as huge as investing in my old gym?

34

ZARA

'Fizz really hasn't given you any clues?' I asked Barney as he drove Amber and me towards Hedgehog Hollow on Tuesday evening for Phoebe's party.

'None. She says Phoebe swore her to secrecy.'

The instructions had been around what to wear – comfortable clothes, layers, trainers and a coat. Amber had guessed a treasure hunt in the dark and the layers could be so we could remove something if we got too hot. I wasn't convinced as Fizz had asked to borrow my Polaroid camera, which was better suited to daylight and indoor photos.

We pulled into the car park where there was quite a crowd gathering.

'That's Mum's van,' Barney said, spotting the van Natasha used for her events management business. 'She never said she was involved.'

'She's invited, though?' I asked, thinking that surely Phoebe's invitation would have included her girlfriend's mum.

'Yes, but she'd have come in the car. She only uses the van if she's shifting kit.'

We grabbed the bags containing Phoebe's gifts and wandered over to the crowd. There was no sign of Phoebe or Darcie but I recognised most of the faces – Samantha, Josh and members of their extended family, volunteers from the rescue centre, and friends of Phoebe and

Fizz. Phoebe had generously extended the invitation to Matt, Jackie, Shane and Ishaan and they were huddled together, chatting, their breath hanging in the cold night air. There was no sign of Fizz or Barney's parents. I craned my neck, looking for Joel, but I couldn't see him either.

Amber must have realised who I was looking for. 'He had to work late, but he'll be here soon,' she whispered and my heart did a flip-flop.

A loud whistle from Fizz brought the chatter to a close.

'Welcome to Phoebe's twenty-third birthday party,' she shouted. 'The birthday girl and Darcie are down in Wildflower Byre putting the finishing touches to a fun-filled evening for you all. On New Year's Day four years ago, Phoebe and Darcie arrived at Hedgehog Hollow under really difficult circumstances. They both had January birthdays and Samantha and Josh did something special for each of them that year to show that there were people who cared. The thing we did for Phoebe's birthday was so much fun that we decided to scale it up and repeat it again this year. Those who were there will now know what's in store, but please don't tell the others as we walk down. Follow me and let the fun commence!'

I loved the dramatic way in which Fizz delivered her little speech and was now even more intrigued as to what was in store for us. We filed into Wildflower Byre, where Phoebe and Darcie were waiting in front of a curtain screen so we still couldn't see anything. There was a table laid out for cards and gifts and another one with jugs of water and juice alongside sports bottles with our names written on them.

Once everyone was inside, the curtains lowered and I clapped my hand across my mouth. The room was full of giant inflatables – a bungee run, a boxing ring with giant sumo suits, a rodeo and a surfboard.

Natasha was standing on a small stage with a microphone. 'Welcome to Phoebe's birthday party! Are you ready for some fun?'

The group cheered and, after an explanation as to how the evening would work, along with some safety rules, we were off.

I was waiting by the bungee run, laughing at Amber and Barney racing each other along the inflatable tracks, seeing who could Velcro their bean bag to the furthest point before being yanked back by the bungee rope attached to a harness round their waist, when an arm slipped round my shoulder.

'What have I missed?' Joel asked, releasing me. 'Sorry I'm late. Work stuff.'

'You look happier today,' I said, taking in his smile and sparkly eyes.

'Who wouldn't be happy with all this to play on?' he said. 'Although, seriously, I'm feeling good about things. Nothing like a bit of reflection for spotting all the red flags in a relationship. I think Marley might have done me a favour by ending it.'

'It's good to see you so positive. So, what are you going on first?'

Although the emphasis was on fun, there was a competitive element to the evening and I felt a long-lost desire to win flowing through my veins – that same feeling I'd had fifteen years ago when Margo took me aside and said I had potential. There was a leader board running for the individual events, capturing the longest time staying on the rodeo bull and surfboard. Samantha's dad Jonathan was the rodeo champion and Phoebe's friend Leo won the surfing.

The pairs events culminated in a final in which I somehow found myself, pitched against Joel. The rest of the partygoers had to vote on which inflatable to use and they chose the giant sumo suits, which I was pleased about. Joel had the weight and size advantage but I was quick and agile – even in a giant inflatable. It was the best of three and one–all after the first two matches, but I managed to fell Joel in the third match and was declared the winner, hoisted onto Josh's and Barney's shoulders, and carried round Wildflower Byre in a victory lap.

'To a worthy winner,' Joel said, clinking his bottle of lager against mine as we huddled on benches round an enormous fire pit later that evening, full from a delicious barbeque.

'That was the funniest thing I've ever done,' I said. 'I could barely breathe for laughing at one point.'

We moved back inside for a disco, mainly consisting of old party tunes with routines like 'Y.M.C.A.' and 'The Time Warp', which was exhausting but great fun. Not usually a big drinker, it didn't take me long before I was tipsy but that made the evening even more fun, completely taking away my inhibitions both on the dance floor and with Joel. I didn't think of myself as a flirt. If I liked a guy, I usually told them (Joel being an exception) or they asked me out before any flirting was needed, but Joel made it so easy and he was definitely flirting back. The sensible voice in my head kept reminding me that I didn't want to be a rebound girlfriend and that I'd already concluded that our time had long passed. The not-so-sensible voice told me that the sensible voice was a bore.

As the evening drew to a close, Take That's 'Rule the World' started playing. Joel activated the torch on his phone, grabbed my hand and raised my arm in the air. We swayed in time to the first verse but, when the chorus kicked in, he waltzed me round the room. We were soon dizzy from the spinning and had to slow it down. He drew me into his arms and I rested my head against his chest as we shuffled in a circle.

The track changed to Lady A's 'Need You Now'.

'I love this song,' I said.

'I do too.' Joel's hold tightened and I responded by doing the same.

'I probably shouldn't say this,' he said, 'but I nearly asked you out.'

I lifted my head from his chest but kept the rest of my body close. 'When?'

'When you first came to Barney's farm.'

'Really? What stopped you?'

'You weren't going to be around for long so I talked myself out of it. Bad decision.'

I smiled at the unexpected revelation. 'I wish you had. I'd have said yes.'

Joel gulped and I rested my head back against his chest, feeling his heart pounding as he tightened his hold even further and we swayed to the rest of the song. The title of the song was apt. 'Need You Now'. That's how I felt about Joel, and him staying over at Barney's tonight gave the perfect opportunity for an impulsive 'now'. But what about tomorrow? He might have said he'd nearly asked me out and I might have admitted I'd have said yes, but that had been at the start of last June and a lot had happened since then. Was it really a good idea to get involved with Barney's best mate – even if only for one night – when Barney provided me with a home and Amber provided me with employment? But my lager-addled brain told me to hush and just go with it.

The track was coming to the end. 'Home time,' I whispered, reluctantly pulling away, but not leaving Joel's side.

'Ready to go?' Amber asked, joining us with Barney.

Several guests had already left but we did a round of goodbyes to those who remained and I gave Phoebe a huge hug, wishing her a happy birthday again and thanking her for such a brilliant night.

'Are you Joel's girlfriend now?' Darcie asked after I hugged her goodnight.

'No. Why?'

'You looked like you were going to kiss each other on the dance floor and you've been flirting with each other all night.'

'Darcie!' Phoebe cried, gently placing her hand over Darcie's mouth.

'It's okay,' I said, smiling at them both. 'No, I'm not Joel's girlfriend. We're friends.'

When Amber, Barney, Joel and I reached the car park, Joel headed for the back door. 'I'll get in the back with Zara,' he said and my stomach did another flip.

On the journey home, we talked about the amazing evening, laughing at Barney's playful teasing that I'd bested Joel in the sumo final when he was a full foot taller than me. And all the while, Joel's fingertips kept contact with mine on the back seat and I could feel the air between us buzzing with anticipation.

When we returned to Bumblebee Barn, I'd wondered if we'd have the awkwardness of everyone staying up for coffee, but Barney announced he was off to bed.

'You know where the spare bedroom is,' Barney said to Joel as he left the kitchen. 'Make yourself at home.'

Joel was filling a glass of water from the tap and didn't hear Amber adding in a quiet voice directed at me, 'He probably won't need it, though.' She raised her eyebrows at me. 'Be careful.'

She followed Barney upstairs and Joel handed me a glass of water which I gratefully gulped down. He scrolled through his phone and placed it down on the worktop with a smile as the opening bars of 'Need You Now' sounded.

'I'm sure I've heard that song recently,' I said.

'Thought we could pick up where we left off.' He put his arms out but his expression was hesitant. 'If that's okay with you.'

I gave him a reassuring smile. 'It is, although it's a bit bright in here.' I flicked the under-cupboard LEDs on and the main switch off, bathing the kitchen in a softer light.

We resumed our position from earlier, his arms round my back, mine round his waist, my head against his chest, and shuffled in a slow circle to the first verse. The kitchen didn't have the same atmosphere as the dance floor but it wasn't a bad substitute. During the first chorus, Joel's hold tightened and my heart pounded faster. I looked up at him. He gave me a gentle smile as he lowered his head. I rose up on my tiptoes and closed my eyes as our lips met.

Seven and a half months had passed since I'd first thought about this moment and I expected to completely lose myself in it. What I didn't expect was someone else's face to appear in my mind. I pulled away, shocked.

'That bad?' Joel asked, wincing.

'No. Sorry. It wasn't you. Let me just...'

But as we kissed again, Joel's face wasn't the one I pictured. And there was something else wrong. I'd expected my heart to pound even faster, my legs to feel weak, my body to call to his and none of those things were happening. This didn't feel right at all.

We both pulled back and stared at each other, the confusion I felt mirrored on his face.

'That didn't...' Joel began, scrunching up his nose.

'No, it wasn't...' I agreed. 'You're not feeling it, are you?'

'No. Sorry. But neither are you, are you?'

I felt completely bewildered that I'd got what I'd dreamed of for months and it was nothing close to what I'd expected. It wasn't that Joel was a bad kisser. It was just that Joel and me... not right together.

'I'm not,' I admitted, 'which is super weird because I've had this crazy little crush on you since I first met you.' I steepled my fingers to my lips, shaking my head. 'I know you say women always friend-zone you but, somewhere along the way, I think we might have friend-zoned each other.'

He laughed. 'I think you're right. Wow! Didn't see that coming.'

'Me neither. But it was fun imagining it could be different.'

'It was.'

We smiled at each other and started laughing.

'Oh, well,' I said. 'No harm done.'

Joel nodded. 'No hard feelings but probably a good lesson learned for both of us.'

'What's that?' I asked.

'When you meet someone you're attracted to, it's a good idea to do something about it before too much water passes under the bridge. If I'd asked you out when we first met – just went for it instead of finding excuses why it might not work – who knows what would have happened?'

'It's a good lesson but, do you know what I think? If we were *really* meant to be together, it would have happened tonight, even with all the water under the bridge. It hasn't happened because that's not our plan. There are still two people out there destined for you and me and we just haven't met them yet.'

Or perhaps one of us had.

'I want to believe that,' Joel said, sadness in his tone.

'Do you know what's stopping you?' I said, drawing him into a hug and whispering in his ear, 'You are.'

'And on that note,' I said, voice back to normal as I released him, 'I need my beauty sleep. Night, Joel.'

'Night, Zara. Thanks for everything tonight.' He broke into a grin. 'Except maybe whipping my arse in the sumo final. Barney's never going to let me live that one down.'

Socks sauntered through the cat flap and followed me upstairs. What an unexpected evening. Turned out that Joel wasn't the person I wanted to be with after all. Snowy was. Definitely hadn't seen that coming.

35

ZARA

Things could have been awkward between Joel and me the following morning. I felt a little nervous walking into the kitchen but he greeted me with, 'Morning, Friend-zone,' and we both laughed about it and agreed it was the best almost-relationship we'd ever had.

Amber joined us in the kitchen and it was obvious she was dying to find out what had happened between us. We tried to wind her up with some innuendos around what an amazing night it had been but ended up laughing too much and giving the game away.

'Just friends,' I told her. 'Yes, we kissed, but neither of us felt the thing.'

'And you've got to feel the thing,' Joel said, and the pair of us burst out laughing again.

Amber groaned. 'So, are you ready to retrieve your car, Joel? And I'm assuming I don't need to ask whether you're travelling with me or Zara?'

Joel put his arm around my shoulders. 'With my new bezzie mate, of course.'

* * *

After a successful day's filming, Amber drove back to Hedgehog Hollow and I went to Owl's Lodge. I hadn't been able to stop thinking about Snowy and, when I turned onto the track, the butterflies in my stomach which had flitted on and off all day fully took flight. I felt completely out of my depth with him. He was a widower with a young son and a difficult past which added several layers of complication I'd never experienced before and, although I didn't want to turn them into excuses not to act on my feelings, I couldn't ignore that I'd need to tread really carefully with him.

Snowy had messaged me to say he'd meet me in the gym so I parked in the passing space by The Roost. I was ten minutes early but, as I could see the lights on in the gym, I crossed the road and went down the steps, wishing I could get a grip on my nerves. Taking a deep breath, I pushed open the door and quietly slipped inside, not wanting to disturb Snowy. He was on the high bar and I watched, completely captivated by his artistry as he pirouetted and changed his grip and direction before doing a double twist dismount into the foam pit. I had no doubt he could have landed it perfectly on a mat but the pit was there for safety with him being alone.

'I hope you're not expecting me to do something similar on the uneven bars,' I called to him as he scrambled out of the pit.

He looked over and smiled. 'You saw that?'

I set off to join him. 'I saw it and loved it.'

'It's been a while since I've done the high bar but it was calling me. Haven't done the rings for ages either.'

'Then you'll have to rectify that.' I'd reached him and my heart leapt as I gazed into his beautiful eyes. 'I'd love to see it.'

'Okay. I'll see what I can do. How was your friend's party?'

'Brilliant! Barney's mum's an events planner and she had all these giant inflatable games which were hilarious, followed by a barbeque and party tunes disco. I barely left the dance floor all night.'

'Sounds fun.'

'It really was and it was so lovely being around so many friends. It's weird to think that, until recently, I didn't have any close friends other than Amber. The *Countryside Calendar* team are great, but we don't meet up outside of filming or anything. I got to know the Hedgehog Hollow gang when we were filming here last summer and I've finally got a good group of friends.'

'I'd have expected you to have a huge circle of friends. You're so warm and friendly.'

'Aw, thank you, but no. My best friend from primary school drifted away from me at senior school and I never found any close friends to replace her. I've spent the last six years travelling with work so I'm not usually in one place long enough to build new friendships. What about you? Big friendship group?'

Just because he'd said he wasn't used to visitors, it didn't mean he didn't have friends who he met up with away from home, although there was an air of loneliness about him so I couldn't help thinking that I'd already met all the important people in his life.

'My friends were all gymnasts and we lost touch. Or rather *I* lost touch with them, some because of those bad decisions I mentioned, others after Eliza died. The one who hung on the longest was Ashley but there were only so many times he could keep pushing on a closed door.'

He looked wistful and I wondered once more whether he was going to open up about what had happened in the past.

'I hadn't spoken to Ash for four and a half years but we spoke last night and...' He paused and smiled. 'I think that's a conversation over a cuppa. How about we crack on with your session and I'll tell you about it afterwards? I could do with your objective opinion on something.'

'Sounds intriguing. I'll help if I can.'

'That'd be good, thanks. Right! Let's get warmed up and start your first coaching session at Snowy's Gymnastics Club.'

36

SNOWY

Snowy's Gymnastics Club? Had I just said that to Zara? It had a ring to it. This morning, Grandpa had asked me if I'd thought about his proposal overnight and I'd told him I'd thought of nothing else but I couldn't do it and it had never been part of the plan. He'd pushed back on that, reminding me that it had been part of the original plan for after I retired from professional sport. I was going to qualify as a coach and either set up a gym of my own or buy-in to a partnership.

'Plans change all the time because unexpected things happen,' he said. 'I didn't plan to buy a farm but I got made redundant, invented some things and here we are with a better existence than I'd ever dreamed of. You didn't plan to injure yourself, you didn't plan to retire so early, but it happened. You still became a coach and there's nothing to stop you renewing your qualifications and reverting to the original plan. Because maybe everything you've been through since your accident was the plan for you all along.'

Maybe it was, but I'd still welcome another perspective and Zara was the only person I could ask. It was no good going to Ashley as he was involved and I didn't want to get anyone's hopes up. It wasn't just his job on the line. His wife Kendra also worked at Campion's – or she had before we lost touch.

After Zara warmed up, I asked her to show me some basic floor movements. I wanted to ensure her technique was spot on for those skills before we moved onto anything more complex. She was a good listener, completely open to feedback, and I liked how she didn't apologise constantly for mistakes, as though she accepted that this was a learning environment and errors were part of the process. She was also fearless on the floor, which I hadn't expected after so long away from the sport.

'We'll focus mainly on the floor and trampoline,' I said, 'but I don't want the apparatus to be something to fear so I'd like to tackle that early on. I don't mean by doing tricks as we'll go back to using a harness for that. I just want you to get familiar with the apparatus again, starting with your favourite piece.'

We moved over to the bars at the end of the session.

'All I want you to do is hang. You didn't think you'd be able to support your body weight but I don't think that'll be a problem. You've got strong arms and you're petite. Are you ready to give it a try?'

Zara drew in a deep breath and I could tell she was nervous, but she smiled and nodded. She rubbed some chalk into her hands and stood under the high bar. I placed my hands on her hips and lifted her up but she slipped straight off and into my arms.

'I've got you,' I said, my heart pounding with the closeness of her body against mine.

She looked up at me, eyes wide, and I swear there was electricity fizzing in the air between us. Or was it just fear because she'd slipped?

'Ready to try again?' I asked gently.

'I think so.'

'You won't hurt yourself if you fall. I'm right here for you.'

37

ZARA

You won't hurt yourself if you fall. I'm right here for you. Might be too late to stop myself from falling and I didn't mean off the apparatus. I'd only slipped because I'd been so distracted by how amazing Snowy's hands on my hips felt. When he'd said *I've got you* just now, his face so close to mine, it had taken all my willpower not to kiss him. I'd never felt such a yearning for someone before.

'Ready,' I whispered, melting inside as his strong hands clasped my hips once more.

'I won't let go until you say so,' he said, his voice reassuring.

'I'm fine. I've got it.'

'Fantastic! See if you can swing a bit. Nothing more. No hand movements – just gentle swinging back and forth.'

The feeling in my muscles was so familiar as I swung my body back and forth. I'd no idea I'd missed this quite so much.

'That'll do for now,' Snowy said, taking me by the hips once more and guiding me down onto the mat. 'Feeling okay?'

He still had his hands on my hips and I was feeling a whole lot of things, but none of them I could share with him. Not yet anyway.

'Yes, absolutely okay. Thank you.'

'First lesson over,' he said, smiling at me as we headed over to the benches. 'How was it?'

'It was the best.'

'So you'll come back for more?'

'If it wasn't for work, I'd be here every night. You'd soon be sick of me.'

He held my gaze and my heart leapt.

'I don't think that would ever happen,' he said, his voice husky. 'It'd be the other way round.'

'Not a chance,' I said, but it came out as a whisper.

He liked me. I was absolutely certain of it, but I could sense his fear. I didn't want to rush him into anything, but I wanted him to know that whatever he was feeling was reciprocated. How? Telling him outright that I fancied him was pretty full-on, and kissing him was way beyond that. The kind of playful flirting Joel and I had undertaken last night didn't feel appropriate. Snowy didn't strike me as the sort who played games. He had a sense of humour but he had a serious side and, actually, I really liked that. Not a single one of my exes had been serious and I'd received the message loud and clear from all of them that I was just a bit of fun. I didn't want to be anyone's *bit of fun*. I wanted to be their world.

* * *

Harrison and Eddie had eaten earlier, but they joined Snowy and me at the dining table and talked to us while we ate. They were keen to know how my coaching session had gone and Harrison told me he'd wanted to watch but Snowy had said no.

'As I told you, it's not fair on Zara,' Snowy said. 'You get one-to-one time and so does she. It's a fairer and quicker way for her to get her confidence back and rebuild her skills, so no trying to meddle with the plan, thank you very much.'

He had such a lovely way with Harrison, giving clear explanations in a friendly way which also made it clear that the subject wasn't up for debate. It certainly beat the 'no' I'd repeatedly heard during childhood.

Eddie asked me about Phoebe's party and Harrison wanted me to describe all the different activities.

'Could I have something like that for my birthday?' he asked Snowy.

'What did we discuss just yesterday?' Snowy replied, eyebrows raised in question.

'It's too early and Pops's birthday is first,' Harrison murmured.

'Exactly. Now, it's getting late so it's time you said goodnight to everyone and went upstairs to read for a bit.'

Harrison did as he was told and, after hugs all round, headed off to bed. Eddie made us all a cup of tea then said he was off up to bed to read too and I felt bad that my presence had pushed everyone away, while also feeling a little pleased that it meant more alone time with Snowy.

'He often goes up early,' Snowy said, as though reading my thoughts.

'You wanted my objective opinion on something?' I prompted as we settled on the sofa with our drinks.

'Yes. My conversation with Ashley. I've known Ash for years. We met at a gym called Campion's. He transferred to Leeds with me and we did the competition circuit together, although he wasn't quite strong enough for Team GB. Anyway, he returned to Campion's as a coach. I need to get Harrison into a club and I've been putting it off because…'

'Because you've built a safe life for him here?' I suggested when he tailed off.

Snowy nodded slowly, his expression sad. 'Yesterday he asked about having a party for his birthday in April and all I could think about was the tiny guest list – Grandpa, me and next door's grandkids. I thought I was doing the right thing keeping him home and protecting him from idiots like Parnell – the one I told you about who called me Freak Show – but I can't do that forever. I might be keeping him safe from the bullies, but I'm depriving him of friendships and that isn't fair.

'I stand by my decision to home school as far as learning goes and I don't think I want to change that – or at least not while he's at primary school age – but I *do* want him to start making friends, and the gym is where I found my people.'

'And that's why you spoke to your friend Ashley?' I said.

'Yes, except Ash told me that Campion's is up for sale as the owner, Fred, is retiring. A leisure centre chain wants to buy it but Grandpa thinks I should.'

'Oh, wow! That's big.'

'Isn't it?' He sighed. 'I told Grandpa I wasn't interested because it wasn't part of the plan, but he said it used to be my plan for when I retired from competition. But that was before it all fell apart.' He grimaced. 'I've just realised I'm being really cryptic. You don't know what happened and I *will* tell you, but just not quite yet.'

I lightly touched his arm. 'Like I said before, there's no pressure on that from me. When and if you're ready. So, as an outsider who knows nothing about what happened and the long-term impact on you, I can't help thinking Eddie has a point. If this was *always* part of the plan, what's stopping you? If you have the finances to buy your old gym, that sounds like a lovely full-circle situation. You've maybe arrived at the destination in an unexpected way, but you've still got there. And if the problem is that you don't want to run the place, you don't have to. Get a manager in or make Ash your manager if he's got the skills. Just because you invest in the place, it doesn't mean you have to be actively involved. Unless the problem is that you want to be active and whatever happened is making you fearful of that.'

Snowy raked his hands through his hair and stared into the log burner.

'Have I said too much?' I asked, worried I might have overstepped somewhere.

He whipped his head round to me. 'God, no! I don't know how you've managed it, but I think you've got to the crux of the problem. I *can* buy the gym, but that's the easy part. The hard part is that I *can't* be the silent investor. If I get a sniff of that world again, I'm going to want to be part of it and I don't know if I'm ready.'

'Then have a word with the owner. Tell him that you're interested but you need more time to fully think it through. Ask him if there's any way he can hold back on doing something rash like selling it to the leisure chain. I'm assuming he knows your story so he's going to understand why you can't rush straight into it. This *is* huge, Snowy, and so is everything that's led you to this point. You've only just made the decision to enrol Harrison in a club and that obviously hasn't been easy for you. You've just reconnected with someone from your past to make that happen – also difficult for you – and you've only just found out that your old club's up for sale. You don't have to make a decision on it this week. Something like this is life changing. Give yourself time to make the decision that's right for you and your family. Be kind to yourself.'

I longed to hold him tightly and tell him that whatever he decided would be fine. But I also wanted to tell him to just go for it because, if not now, when? No matter what he'd been through, this had been his original dream. He'd likely never imagined he'd have the opportunity to do it with his old club so could it be more perfect? And if he was thinking that Harrison's home schooling might end when he hit senior school age – something that was clearly on his mind – then what was he going to do with himself then? This would keep him occupied.

As an outsider, I definitely leaned towards if not now, when? But that was the problem. I *was* an outsider and I had no clue as to what happened in the past and I refused to let my mind wander and speculate. Could it be too much for Snowy to recover from? Could doing something this monumental break him?

38

SNOWY

Zara kept doing it, kept amazing me. Everything she said made sense and spoke to my soul. She didn't know about my past but she was perceptive and had rooted out the issue before I'd fully got to grips with it myself. The issue was me. The issue was *always* me or, as Grandpa said, my head drowning out what my heart wanted. Yes, I wanted Campion's Gymnastics Club. Absolutely 100 per cent. It was a dream of an opportunity and I couldn't help thinking it was always meant to be. Why else had I chosen now of all times to pick up the phone to Ash?

'I don't know if I've been any help,' Zara said, her tone uncertain.

'More than you could ever imagine,' I assured her. 'It doesn't have to be dive in right now or walk away. You've given me a third option and I'm going to take it. Thank you.'

We sat in silence for a couple of minutes, sipping on our drinks. My head felt so much clearer than it had done earlier. Zara had been exceptionally helpful and I wanted to return the favour. I thought back to her confession on Sunday about how she'd had to pack in gymnastics in favour of her brother. I couldn't imagine that was conducive to a great sibling relationship. Maybe she'd like to offload about that?

'You mentioned your footballer brother,' I said. 'Do you have any other siblings?'

She shook her head. 'One's more than enough. You?'

'Only child. I don't think my parents quite knew what hit them so one was enough.' We could easily go down a rabbit hole with that one and it wouldn't help her at all. Focus!

'Do you see much of him?' I asked.

'Only when I have to. I know it sounds awful saying that, but it's a mutual thing.' She finished her tea, placed it down on the side table and picked up a scatter cushion which she cuddled to her stomach. 'It was bad but it would have been even worse if Owen hadn't been around. As well as getting me back into gymnastics, he was the voice of reason and peacekeeper. Without him, I'm fairly sure Mum and I wouldn't be on speaking terms. He helped me separate out the Roman fandom and focus on the positive parts of her relationship with me and that saved us. Now that she's accepted that Roman and I are never going to be close, my relationship with Mum has already improved. It makes me sad, though. Amber has a brother and sister and Barney has a sister and they have amazing relationships. I wish Roman and I could have that, but the hurt runs too deep for me now and Roman's too self-involved to care.'

I could hear the pain in her voice.

'Comes with the territory sometimes,' I said gently. 'When you're at the top of your profession and you're a public figure, it's easy to get sucked into the hype and believe that you're more special than you are.'

'I can't imagine you being like that.'

'I wasn't at the time, but I was hideously self-involved after my injury. Back to your brother, though. I don't know him and I don't follow football but my guess is that he has people around him who make him feel like he's the dog's bollocks.'

'I've met several of them and yes, they do. And it's not just the people he sees regularly – it's the eleven billionty adoring fans who follow him on social media.'

'Eleven billionty?' I said, laughing. 'That's an interesting number.'

'It's real! Didn't you learn it in maths?' She grinned at me. 'Okay, slight exaggeration – it's a few million followers. He probably wouldn't have that many as a League One player, but he's been on social media since forever and he's really savvy with it. He's got a YouTube channel and him and a group of mates do a mixture of commentary on key moments from other matches, re-enacting goals, and footie tricks. Mum watches every piece of content he puts out and she often sends me links but I never watch them. Gosh, that makes me sound awful.'

'You're not awful,' I said gently.

'I *am* proud of him for what he's achieved and, even though I wouldn't admit it to him, I do keep an eye on the scores, but I don't go to matches and I don't follow him on the socials. I often beat myself up about it thinking that I should be more supportive, but then I ask what he's ever done for me. All I see is an arrogant bully who made my childhood hell, who my parents didn't think I was a patch on, and who doesn't care enough to know anything about me.' She sighed. 'Feel free to look him up and see for yourself what he's like.'

Zara told me about his New Year's Eve party and the conversation she'd had with her mum a few days later. I was relieved for her that her mum seemed to finally understand how she felt about her brother and was going to stop pestering her to play nicely with him when he didn't sound like he deserved her in his life.

'Did you ever feel like you'd disappointed your parents?' she asked, tears in her eyes.

'My mum left when I was three and I have no idea where she is. I don't even know if she's still alive. As for my dad, I felt like I disappointed him pretty much every day so I know how it feels and I know how it eats away.'

'I'm sorry about your mum,' she said. 'Did you tell your dad how you felt?'

'No but, when I was thirteen, Grandpa did. It kicked off big time and life was never the same after that, but Dad never had been capable of taking feedback, even from his coach back in the day. From what you've said about your mum, it sounds like she is receptive to feedback now so, for your sake, it might be time for her to hear the full story.'

'All I ever wanted was for her to say she's proud of me,' she said, tears tumbling. 'She's still never said that.'

I shuffled along the sofa and took her in my arms, cradling her while she sobbed. Dad had never once said he was proud of me either and I knew how deeply that cut. Even when I won the silver, he said, 'It's not gold, is it?' And that from a man who'd 'only' won bronze.

* * *

'What time is it?' whispered a voice. I felt a nudge in my side and opened my eyes, blinking in the dim lamp light. The room was cold and I shivered.

'Oh, my God! It's quarter past two,' Zara exclaimed. 'We must have fallen asleep.'

I rubbed my eyes, feeling totally disorientated. 'I'm sorry. It was so warm and comfortable.' I shivered once more. 'It's not now.'

'It's okay. I was warm and comfy too.'

'We've got a spare bedroom,' I said, concerned about her driving while she was sleepy.

'Thanks, but I should get back to the farm. Socks won't be impressed if I stay out all night.'

'Socks?' I asked.

'One of Barney's cats. He's taken a shine to me.'

I could relate to that. Campion's Gym wasn't the only thing my heart wanted. It wanted Zara too – that *owl-bearing angel* who'd burst into our lives just a week ago and yet felt like she'd been part of my journey forever. But to have either or both, I needed to dig deep and muster all the courage I could find because the future I was facing now felt even scarier than standing in the stadium at Beijing aiming for Olympic success.

Zara put her trainers on while I retrieved her coat.

'You don't need to come out with me,' she said as I pulled on a pair of heavy-duty boots. 'It's freezing out there.'

'And that's exactly why I'm coming out with you. The veranda's icy and those steps will be too, so I need to make sure you don't slip.'

It was just as well I insisted on accompanying Zara as, the moment we stepped onto the veranda, her feet slipped and she grabbed me. She linked her arm through mine and slipped again.

'And the award for the most useless pair of trainers in icy weather goes to...' She lifted her leg up and twisted her foot left and right. 'You might need to carry me to my car.'

'Your wish is my command!'

Before she had time to object that she'd been joking, I'd scooped her up and carried her down the steps.

'My hero!' she said with a smile as we reached her car.

Much as I'd have loved to keep hold of her, I gently placed her back on her feet. 'All part of the service, ma'am. Let's get this car defrosted. Do you have a scraper?'

Zara whacked the heating on full to clear the windows and warm the car while I set to work with the scraper she'd handed me.

'The track should be okay,' I said, handing her the scraper back when I was done, 'but the gritter doesn't usually do the roads around here.'

'Thanks for the heads up. I'll drive slowly.'

'Will you message me to let me know you're home?' I said with an apologetic shrug, hoping that didn't sound overbearing, but Zara smiled at me.

'Are you still okay for coming over on Saturday for a tour of the woods?' I asked.

'Definitely.'

'Do you want to try and squeeze in another coaching session before then?'

'I can't. We're doing some evening filming over the next couple of nights.'

'Okay. Well, we can do a coaching session on Saturday as well if you have time.'

She smiled. 'Sounds perfect.' She opened the car door, but closed it again and fixed her eyes on mine.

'I wish it could be sooner,' she said, her voice soft. 'Because I know I'm going to miss you.'

My stomach did a backflip. The way she was looking at me and the emphasis she'd placed on those words suggested she didn't mean as a friend or a coach. I could already feel the ache of loss and she hadn't even gone.

'I'm going to miss you too.' I hoped she saw and heard that whatever she was feeling was reciprocal.

The air crackled between us and, despite the freezing temperatures, all I could feel was heat. I don't know whether she made the move, if it was me or if it was mutual but, next moment, she was in my arms and we were kissing. A tidal wave of emotions consumed me. There was desire and happiness but there was guilt and fear too. I heard Grandpa's voice in my head telling me to listen to and trust my heart instead of my head and I thought about Zara on the trampoline, living in and loving the moment. *Be the bear!* As Zara's arms slipped round my waist, pulling me closer, I shut out all the voices and completely lived in that moment. And loved every single second of it.

I went up to bed after Zara left but there was zero chance of me settling until I heard from her. I've never been so relieved to hear my phone beep as I was when her message came through.

> **FROM ZARA**
>
> Made it back safely. Thanks for everything, especially that amazing goodbye. Hoping there's more where that came from but completely understand if it was a momentary lapse of concentration x

I smiled as I typed in my response.

> **TO ZARA**
>
> No lapse at my end. We can try for an equally amazing hello on Saturday x

A reply came through immediately with four emojis – a thumbs up and three blowing kisses. I replied with 'ditto' before switching my phone to silent and settling down to sleep. Only sleep wouldn't come. I couldn't stop thinking about that kiss and the giant leap of faith I'd just taken. I pictured Grandpa's delight when he found out and imagined him saying, 'It's about time too!'

I never thought I'd be ready to let another woman into my life. I wasn't sure I was fully ready now, but I had to take that chance. I knew that Grandpa was right that it was what Eliza would have wanted for me, but that didn't mean it was going to be easy. Up until tonight, the only woman I'd ever kissed was Eliza – first and only girlfriend, first and only love. Feeling fear taking hold once more, I switched my thoughts to the conversations Zara and I had had this evening and how, albeit in a completely different way, her family sounded as complicated as mine. That New Year's Eve party sounded like a nightmare and it was good that she'd been able to tell her mum how she was feeling and find a way forward. It had clearly taken guts to do that. I often wondered if things would have been different for me and Dad if Grandpa or I had said something to him sooner.

39

SNOWY

Twenty-two years ago

My thirteenth birthday fell on a Sunday and I lay in bed wondering what it must feel like to wake up on your birthday feeling excitement rather than dread. Grandma and Grandpa always made a fuss of me with presents and a cake, but it was hard to enjoy their attention with Dad stomping round like a lion with a thorn in its paw, wondering when he was going to lash out. He blamed me for Mum leaving – my fault for being born, for making her turn back to drink, for her walking out on my third birthday.

If anyone needed evidence showing why alcoholics shouldn't date while in recovery – and especially why they shouldn't date each other – they only needed to look at my parents. My grandparents had met in church. They had a lovely story of Grandma dropping a glove on her way out, Grandpa bending down to pick it up, their fingers touching as he returned it and a thunderbolt hitting them both. My parents' story wasn't quite so wholesome. They met in an Alcoholics Anonymous meeting when Mum, shaking from alcohol withdrawal, spilt her coffee on Dad. The thunderbolt which hit them was more destructive. They knew they shouldn't date, but they did. They knew that a long-term relationship was risky, but they exchanged their wedding vows three years later. They knew that having a baby could bring stress and pressure which might make them want to return to the bottle, but they had me a year after their wedding.

My grandparents repeatedly assured me that it hadn't been me, no matter what Dad said. I hadn't been more of a crier, more demanding, more sickly or difficult than the average baby, but having a small human completely dependent on them was too much for two addicts and it wasn't long before Mum relapsed.

I had no memories of Mum, which was probably just as well. It was only 9.30 a.m. a few days before Christmas when the police pulled her over for erratic driving. She blew twice the legal limit and it got messy with Social Services because I was in the back of the car – only eighteen months old – and clothed in nothing more than a towel. She apparently told Dad it was the wake-up call she needed to stop drinking. She didn't stop. She just got better at hiding the evidence. On my third birthday, she left a note to say that she couldn't do it anymore and not to come looking for her. Nobody did.

Dad showed the determination of an elite sportsman in staying sober but it didn't make him a better person than her. It might have been better for all of us if he had turned to the bottle or dipped out of our lives like Mum, because his way of coping without her was to stay in control. Not just of his abstinence but of everything and everyone, especially me and especially on my birthday.

A bang on my door made me jump. 'It's past seven!' Dad shouted. 'Get your lazy backside out of bed.'

Happy birthday to me! I pushed the duvet back and shuffled across the landing to the bathroom, getting washed and brushing my teeth as quickly as I could, then pulling on my gym gear. It didn't matter that it was a Sunday, that it was my birthday or that the Beijing Games were five years away. If Dad said I had to train, I had to train. I'd learned not to question him.

* * *

'No!' he barked as soon as I'd landed my vault. 'Again!'

I'd done the same vault twenty times in a row now with no clear feedback as to what I was supposedly doing wrong. Every time I asked him for some pointers, he shut me down. How was this helping me?

'Should I try a different one?' I asked.

'You can try a different one when you've perfected this one. Again!'

I executed the front handspring with a one and a half twist once more with a solid landing.

'Rubbish! Again!'

I wanted so badly to shout back at him that it was far from being 'rubbish' but he was in a darker mood than I'd seen him in for a long time and I feared for the repercussions. But how was I supposed to please him if he wouldn't tell me what was wrong? I wiped the sweat from my eyes, took a swig of my drink and swallowed my anger and frustration before trying again. It still wasn't good enough for him.

'There's six-year-old girls at that gym of yours who can vault better than you,' he snarled.

I wasn't standing for that. 'Fred says I'm the best in the club.'

'*Fred* says...' he mimicked. 'What the hell does he know? Has he got an Olympic medal?'

'No, but—'

'Wait till you start at Leeds in September. Then you'll realise how bad you are.'

'If I'm that bad, why do you bother coaching me?' I could hear the anger in my voice now.

'I ask myself that same question every day. Again!'

'No!' I strode over to him, fists clenched by my side. 'Not until you specifically tell me which part needs work.'

He narrowed his eyes at me, curled his lip up and gave me a shove so hard that I stumbled back several paces and fell. Fuming, I scrambled to my feet and lunged at him, intending to shove him too and see how he liked it, but he was too quick for me and grabbed my arm, twisting it behind my back.

'Apologise to me right now!' he snarled.

'No!'

'Apologise!'

'Not until you apologise to me.'

He released my arm and started laughing. It crossed my mind that perhaps this was some sort of weird test of my manhood, pushing me so that I actually stood up to him. But it wasn't. The laughter stopped and his face contorted in an expression that could only be described as hate. He drew his fist back.

'Stop!' Grandpa shouted from the direction of the entrance, but it was too late. Dad's fist collided with my nose and there was a sickening crunch and the most intense pain before I collapsed onto the mat, blood pouring down my face and soaking into my white leotard.

Grandma sank to her knees by my side and pressed my towel to my nose. She was speaking to me but whatever she said was drowned out by Grandpa. My grandpa was the kindest, softest man I knew and I'd never heard him raise his voice. He'd give advice, share his opinion and even express his displeasure but always in a calm, measured way. But not today. He unleashed everything on my dad. I felt sick and dizzy so I couldn't catch it all but I got the gist. *Angry, bitter, a bully, shameful behaviour.* It was harsh, but every single word he spoke was the truth. Surprisingly, Dad said nothing in return. He stood there and took it all until Grandpa finally ran out of steam.

'Finished?' Dad snapped, glaring at him. 'Hope you feel better now, old man.' Then he stormed out of the gym.

Grandma helped me to my feet and Grandpa draped my tracksuit top over my shoulders as they both led me towards the entrance.

'Mind the mess,' Grandma said, steering me to one side.

I looked down to see what she meant. Splatted on the wooden floor was a large gooey chocolate cake and several broken candles. Lucky they'd chosen that moment to surprise me with a birthday cake because I dread to think what else Dad might have done to me if they hadn't.

My thirteenth birthday was memorable for all the wrong reasons. It was a day of stops and starts – the day Dad stopped coaching me, the day I stopped believing he had anything to offer me, the day I thought my nose would never stop bleeding, and the day Dad started drinking again. Seventeen years of sobriety gone in a three-day bender.

40

ZARA

I couldn't stop thinking about Snowy and that kiss. Everything about yesterday had been so perfect and that goodbye had been the cherry on the top of the cake. Saturday couldn't come fast enough for second helpings but, for now, I had work to do. I was really excited about this evening's filming as we were releasing a vixen. After last night's heavy frost, it had been touch and go as to whether it would go ahead, but the temperature had risen during the afternoon and stayed in plus figures, so it was all on.

A local villager had found the vixen with her leg tangled in some sofa springs at the end of a lane which had become popular for fly tipping. The springs themselves had cut her badly but Samantha and Fizz believed that she'd also been gnawing at her own leg in a desperate bid to escape, causing further injury. She'd therefore been a patient at the rescue centre for quite some time while her wounds healed but was now ready to be released where she'd been found, the rubbish having been cleared. Fly tippers made me so mad. It was a growing problem we'd seen all over the country and we'd covered it a couple of times on *Countryside Calendar*.

Samantha and Fizz always gave their rescues names and, to help with creativity, worked within a theme. When the vixen had been admitted before Christmas, they were working through characters in classic festive films so she'd been christened Aurelia after the Portuguese housekeeper in *Love Actually* who fell for Colin Firth's character. Aurelia was such a pretty name, deserving of a beautiful animal.

'Do you think animals know they're going to be released?' I asked Fizz as the crew filmed Samantha taking Aurelia's carrier out of the barn and strapping it into her jeep.

'I like to think so. That first sniff of the fresh air after so long inside is going to tell them that something's different. I hope she has a mate waiting for her.'

We drove to the country lane just outside Little Tilbury, twenty minutes from Hedgehog Hollow. I'd seen the heartbreaking photos of the piles of rubbish dumped there and Aurelia trapped among it and it was so good to see the lane clear.

When the crew were ready with the cameras and sound equipment, Samantha removed the carrier from her jeep.

'Can we all step back to give Aurelia space, and stay nice and quiet?' she asked. 'Once I've opened the door, she'll probably take a moment or two before she feels safe enough to come out of the carrier and, once she's out, she'll probably sniff the air for a bit first before taking off.'

I stayed well back so that there was no danger of getting into the shot. I therefore couldn't see the vixen inside the carrier but I'd have a clear view when she emerged. Exactly as Samantha had predicted, Aurelia stayed in the carrier for a while, then poked her head out, sniffing the air with her pointed nose. She tentatively emerged, body tense, still sniffing. I wondered if she knew that this was where she'd been injured. She stopped, her head turning left and right, her ears rotating, nose in the air. Twenty, maybe thirty, seconds passed and then she scampered off down the lane but, just before she disappeared into the darkness, she stopped and looked back at us for a moment. She dipped her head, then turned and ran off into the night. I pressed my hand to my chest, tears flowing.

'It was as though she was saying thank you,' Amber whispered, voicing my sentiments exactly. 'That was beautiful. I could cry.'

I pointed to my wet cheeks. 'So special,' I whispered back as Amber drew me into a hug.

Given the sniffing and subtle wipes of the eyes, we clearly weren't the only ones affected by Aurelia's release. I thought about Portia calling nature programmes boring. Perhaps they were to her but, to me, moments like this were an honour and a thrill.

* * *

We were debriefing in the barn back at Hedgehog Hollow when Josh arrived with several boxes of takeaway pizzas. What a perfect end to the evening, sharing pizza and listening to Samantha, Fizz and Josh sharing tales of their most favourite and memorable releases.

It was past eleven when Amber and I arrived back at Bumblebee Barn so we said goodnight and headed up to bed. I took my phone out to message Snowy and did a double take at the screen. There were six missed calls from Mum and a message to call her as soon as I could, no matter how late it was. Had something happened to Owen? My heart pounded as I paced my bedroom floor, waiting for my call to connect.

'Mum! What's happened? Is it Owen?'

'Owen's fine,' she said. 'It's Roman, but he's fine too. Well, he's not really, but it's not what you might think and—'

'Mum!' I cried, cutting across her gibbering. 'What's happened?'

I heard her deep intake of breath. 'Your brother went out drinking and he got into an altercation and, well, he got arrested. It's nothing to worry about. He got a split cheek so he needed stitching up, but it could have been worse. I wanted to let you know before you see it splashed all over the front page of the papers tomorrow. The main thing is he's all right.'

'Where is he now?'

'A night in the cells.'

I winced and bit my tongue so that nothing flippant like *serves him right* spilled out, especially when I didn't know what had led to the altercation.

'Are you okay?' I asked.

'A bit shocked, but these things are sent to try us. As I say, I just wanted you to know before it hits the papers. Might even be on the socials already. I can't face looking.'

I could tell from the high pitch of her voice that she was way more worried about him than she was letting on and that she was far from all right, but there was nothing I could do.

'I'm drained, Zara. I need my bed. Do you want to speak to Owen?'

'Yeah, you can put him on.' I might get more out of him.

'I'll speak to you later,' she said. We said our goodbyes and, moments later, Owen came onto the phone.

'How's she *really* doing?' I asked.

'Not so good. It's been a fraught evening.'

'I can imagine. Why does Mum think this will be front-page news? I'd expect it to be in the papers, but not front page.'

'It probably wouldn't have been, but the fight was with Kai Casper.'

'Oh!'

'Exactly.'

Kai Casper. Lincolnshire son, former model and lead singer of Britain's hottest boy band, reVerb. That'd *definitely* be front-page news.

'Dare I ask what happened?'

'Roman took Portia to some event – not sure what – and reVerb were the special guests. Roman had VIP tickets and Kai took a shine to Portia. You can guess the rest.'

I closed my eyes, shaking my head. My brother had repeatedly flirted with other women in front of Amy and slept around behind her back, but another man showed his girlfriend some attention and out came the fists. Oh, the double standards!

'Sounds messy. Give Mum my love and let's hope it isn't as bad as she's anticipating tomorrow.'

We bid each other good night and ended the call. Not as bad as she was anticipating? I suspected it would actually be worse. I couldn't imagine Lincoln City FC being too impressed with Roman's behaviour as they'd see him as a representative of their club, and I couldn't imagine the legions of reVerberators, as the band's devoted followers were known, reacting positively to one of their five heroes being thumped by a footballer. Roman could well lose his job, social media status and his girlfriend in one drunken night. I didn't like him, but I certainly didn't wish any of that on him.

41

SNOWY

That kiss from Zara carried me through Thursday with a big smile on my face and a determination to get a grip on the way I lived my life – for Harrison's sake and also for mine. It didn't take long to find the sale particulars for Campion's Gymnastics Club online. I scrolled through the gallery on the club's website for additional photos of the interior, spotting several changes since my time there, and noted down the membership numbers and how many staff they had. Once Harrison had gone to bed, Grandpa and I went through the figures. I'd need to visit the gym to do a proper assessment but I could tell from the photos that some updates were needed and the asking price was a bit steep on that basis. I was confident I'd be able to bring Fred down. After all, if the leisure centre chain were the only other interested parties, they'd be paying for the building only as opposed to the business so he was better going with me as long as my offer was more than theirs.

Grandpa was thrilled that I was considering it and I had to remind him that it wasn't a done deal – just tentative feelers at this stage.

'You keep telling yourself that,' he said, laughing.

This morning, I'd phoned Fred. He was clearly shocked to hear from me and even more surprised when I said I might be interested in buying the gym. We arranged for a tour a week on Sunday when the gym would be closed, but I swore him to secrecy. There was no way that I wanted any of the staff, especially Ashley, to have a sniff of my interest in case I didn't go for it. I told Fred it wasn't fair to get anyone's hopes up – including his – as this was just a possibility I was exploring at the moment and no firm commitment. I FaceTimed Ashley after that.

'I wasn't sure I'd hear from you again,' he said.

'Yeah, well, first step was the hardest. Is that coffee still on offer?'

'You name the day and I'll be there.'

We agreed on Wednesday. 'While I've got you,' I said, 'I've a favour to ask. I know the future of the gym's in jeopardy, but I'm really keen to expose Harrison to Campion's. Is there any chance of him joining, even if it's only a short time?'

'It might be a *very* short time.'

'I'd still like him to do it.'

Ashley rolled his eyes at me. 'Argh! What the heck! It would be great to see the little man and give him some coaching. Future me can have the honour of saying *I used to coach that Olympic gold winner*. Bring him along on Monday at four.'

'You're a legend.'

'I know! And you're paying for the coffees on Wednesday as a thank you.'

I smiled at him. 'Thanks, Ash. Harrison and I will see you on Monday.'

* * *

For the rest of the day, it was so hard containing the news about Harrison joining Campion's on Monday. I knew how excited he'd be and there was no way he'd concentrate on his school work if I told him. Besides, I wanted Grandpa to be there when I gave the news but he was at Desmond's doing some planning for their May fishing trip.

My opportunity came while our tea was in the oven. 'I have some news,' I announced, joining Harrison and Grandpa on the sofa.

'Scroll through these photos,' I said to Harrison as I passed him my iPad. 'This is the very first gym I went to in Wilbersgate, before I moved to the one at Leeds. It's where I met your mum. My friend Ashley is a coach there and I've arranged for you to go for a trial session with him on Monday. Would you like that?'

Harrison's head whipped round. 'Will there be other kids there?'

'Yes. You'll be in a class with other children of a similar ability.'

The enormous grin and the shine of his eyes nearly broke me and I had to look away as he added, 'Does that mean I'll finally have some friends?'

'It looks good, doesn't it, Harrison?' Grandpa said, giving me a moment to compose myself.

'It looks awesome.' He scrolled through the photos once more then passed the iPad back to me. 'If I like it, do I get to keep going?'

'Yes, you can.' There was no point adding in a complication about the club being up for sale when I was 99.9 per cent sure I was going to buy it.

His face fell. 'But will that mean you don't coach me anymore?'

'No. I'm always here for you and we'll still have the gym here for practice.'

He launched himself at me for a hug. 'Good, because I love you coaching me.'

I held him tight. I might have doubted my decision about keeping him home but that one statement told me I wasn't a bad dad. I could never have imagined saying those words to my dad. I'd made plenty of mistakes and I'd mirrored some parts of him in my dark moments, but I'd never ever treated my son the way my dad had treated me.

* * *

While Harrison and Grandpa were watching television after tea, I messaged Zara.

> **TO ZARA**
> Hope filming goes well tonight. Just wanted to let you know I've got a busy week next week – Harrison starting at the gym on Monday, coffee with Ash on Wednesday and a gym viewing with Fred on Sunday. None of those things would have happened if it wasn't for you! Thank you. Can't wait to see you tomorrow x

I'd deliberately worded it in a way that she wouldn't feel any pressure to reply, knowing she'd be working. I was therefore surprised when her name flashed up with a FaceTime request at quarter past eight.

'Hi!' I said, accepting the call.

'Hi, you! I started typing in a response and thought it'd be easier to call. I'm on a break so I haven't got long but I just wanted to say I'm so chuffed for you and Harrison. What a fantastic day you've had!'

'I meant what I said. I'd never have done any of that without you. I owe you big time.'

She grinned at me. 'I accept payment in kisses.'

'I think that can be arranged. How's your day been?'

'Urgh!' She scrunched up her nose and shuddered. 'Awful!'

'Shoot going badly?'

'No. Filming's all good. It's my brother. Stupid muppet was papped last night, roaring drunk and in a fight with Kai Casper.'

'Who?'

'Lead singer of reVerb – huge boyband of the moment. It's all over the papers and the socials. It got caught on camera, of course, and it's clear that Roman started it all and the only punch Kai threw was in self-defence. The reVerberators – the band's fans – are like a lynch mob and he's had some horrendous abuse online and even death threats. Obviously the death threats are hot air from angsty teens but Mum's completely hysterical about it. I spent an hour on the phone this morning trying to convince her that today's news is tomorrow's cat litter tray lining but it's harder to make the same argument when it's all online. Owen has had to confiscate her phone and disconnect the broadband to stop her scrolling.'

'That sounds like a nightmare.'

'Sounds like Roman,' she said, rolling her eyes. She turned and looked behind her. 'Sorry, we're ready to go again. I'll tell you more tomorrow, but if you're at a loose end this evening, feel free to go online and see for yourself. Roman Timmins and Kai Casper. It's trending so you won't have to search hard. Congratulations again on your good day and I'll see you in the morning.'

She blew me a kiss and disconnected. Getting papped fighting was not good and I could well imagine the lynch mob mentality in defence of a boyband favourite.

Once Harrison was settled in bed and Grandpa had his feet up with a book on birds of prey, I scrolled through my iPad and immediately found the story of last night's scuffle. I paused before reading it, feeling like I was intruding, but Zara had specifically said I was welcome to look and, as I was sure she'd want to offload about it tomorrow, I could be more supportive if I'd done some research.

It felt weird being back on social media. My accounts were still active but I hadn't posted anything for years. Roman's story was indeed trending and it made for gruesome reading. Although the death threats themselves seemed to have been removed, there were screen shots of them. Nothing shared on the socials ever truly went away. The reVerberators were certainly a passionate lot and several of the posts included a peculiar language which had passed me by. What the hell was stanning? Roman's followers were fewer but they fought back just as hard and I cringed at the number of homophobic comments directed at Kai Casper which, aside from being disgusting, didn't make sense when the fight had been triggered by Kai's attention towards Roman's girlfriend.

Each article I clicked into brought up another and the algorithms soon picked up that I was more interested in reading about Roman than Kai. Before I knew it, I'd gone down a rabbit hole and found my way onto his YouTube channel. I shoved my EarPods in and watched video after video, going further back in time.

Several hours later, with Grandpa long gone to bed, I tore my tired eyes away and closed the iPad, a knot of tension in my stomach. Something wasn't right with Roman and it hadn't been for a long time. It wasn't just the injury. Things had been falling apart way before that. Most people wouldn't notice but most people hadn't been where I'd been. They didn't know the signs. Did Zara know? I'd put money on it that she didn't.

42

ZARA

After a second late night of filming at Hedgehog Hollow, I had hoped for a lie-in but my phone ringing at half seven on Saturday morning put paid to that. I probably should have put it on silent but I hadn't liked to with Mum being in such a state.

'Hi, Mum,' I said, answering it.

'Portia's dumped him,' she said without greeting me.

The first thought that sprung to mind was, *Is that such a bad thing?* Not because I hadn't warmed to her but because, from the pre-fight footage I'd seen, she'd clearly been flirting with Kai Casper.

'How did Roman take it?' I asked.

'Not good. Especially as she's front-page news today, all over Kai Casper in some London club. I never liked that girl.'

That was news to me. I could recall several occasions where she'd waxed lyrical about what a wonderful girlfriend Portia was.

'It never rains but it pours,' I said, not able to think of anything more helpful.

'I saw him last night. Right state he looked, all bruised and sorry-looking. And you should have seen his flat. Empty cans and bottles everywhere and the whole place reeked like a brewery. Could have done without spending a couple of hours cleaning up for him.'

How peculiar to hear Mum criticising Golden Boy. I'd have expected to feel smug that he'd finally slipped from his pedestal but, instead, I felt sorry for him. His life was falling apart spectacularly and being played out in all the tabloids. As well as watching the videos, I'd scrolled through a few posts yesterday and they'd been vicious. As somebody who obsessively checked his stats and read everything about himself, there was no way Roman wouldn't have read them so it was hardly surprising he'd decided to drown his sorrows with alcohol for a second night in a row.

'Are you at work today?' I asked.

'No. I should have been but I've swapped weekends with Howard. I'm going to lie on the sofa, close my eyes and wish this sorry situation away.'

'I know it's hard, but try not to get yourself too upset about it,' I said gently. 'The best way to do that is to stay away from the Internet. I know you want to help Roman, but reading every article and comment isn't going to do that. It's just going to torture you. You know that, don't you?'

'Yes. I just… Yes, I know. I can't help myself.'

'Then surrender your phone to Owen again and take some time to relax. Roman's going to need you more than ever, but you're no good to him if you've made yourself sick worrying about all this. What do you think?'

There was a pause and a sigh. 'Yes. I can do that.'

'Good. I hate to say it, Mum, but I need to go and get ready as I'm meeting someone. Call me if anything else happens.'

'Okay. Thanks for being the voice of reason.'

I had just enough time for a quick shower. As I was walking to the car, I sent Snowy a message.

TO SNOWY

> Just about to leave. Much as I'd love to take you up on that amazing hello, I'm guessing you won't want to tell Harrison about us just yet so I'll restrain myself and will be counting down the minutes until we can say hello properly x

His reply came through before I set off, making me smile.

> **FROM SNOWY**
>
> I think you might be an even wiser owl than Grandpa. You're right and I love that you understand. Harrison has appointed himself as woodland tour guide but Grandpa is taking him swimming afterwards so we'll have our moment then x

* * *

My tour around the woods at Owl's Lodge was worth the wait. There were different areas, some filled with evergreens, others with deciduous trees. Harrison excitedly showed me the clearing they used for forest school and it was amazing. A large stone circle in which they built fires was surrounded by logs to sit on and there were several dens built in between the trees and a couple of treehouses.

Harrison pointed out nesting boxes for owls, hedgehog houses and bat boxes and kept pretty much a constant commentary going about nature and wildlife. Snowy looked at me a couple of times with a smile and mouthed 'sorry' but there was nothing to be sorry for. Harrison's knowledge and enthusiasm was heart-warming.

I told them about Whisby Nature Park back home and how I loved to lean out my bedroom window and listen for owls, which usually got me told off for letting the cold in.

My highlight of the tour was seeing a couple of owls. The first was a short-eared owl on a post at the edge of the woods and it was lucky Snowy spotted him as I'd have walked straight past. He was quite small, completely still, and his mottled brown feathers blended perfectly into his surroundings. Not long after, we were walking along the border between Owl's Lodge and a field which Snowy had told me had been part of the original farm when Harrison pointed out a little owl. It was roosting in the top corner of a dilapidated shelter.

'They love abandoned buildings like that,' Snowy said. 'They can see everything going on around them but, if they sense danger, they can scoot back inside.'

As though on cue, a rook cawed loudly and the owl disappeared, reappearing moments later.

'They've got the funniest faces,' Harrison said. 'They look really grumpy like this.' He frowned at me. I had no idea if it was a good impression of a little owl or not, but it made me smile.

'They've got yellow eyes too,' Snowy told me. 'The eye colour's connected with when they hunt. Yellow for diurnal – daytime – owls, orange for crepuscular – dawn and dusk – and it's dark brown or black for our predominantly nocturnal friends.'

'And what about blue eyes?' I asked, having seen photos online of blue-eyed owls.

Harrison and Snowy exchanged looks and both started laughing.

'Photoshop,' Harrison said.

'Or AI,' Snowy added. 'There aren't any blue-eyed owls in real life. Only online.'

'And on your socks,' Harrison added, which tickled me.

* * *

Shortly before 11 a.m., Eddie took Harrison swimming as planned, telling us they'd be back for a late lunch. Snowy and I stood side by side on the veranda and waved them off and, the moment the car disappeared from sight, we were in each other's arms. Last time, we'd both been sleepy and perhaps a little tentative, although it had still been a fantastic kiss. This time, there was confidence and, for the first time ever, I knew what it meant to get lost in a kiss. Everything was gone from my mind except a longing for this kind but complicated man.

'I've wanted to do that all morning,' Snowy said, hugging me tightly.

'Me too, but it was worth the wait.'

He kissed me once more before taking me by the hand and leading me into the lodge.

'Even though it meant a delay in collecting that amazing hello, I have to say that Harrison's company is great,' I told Snowy as we settled onto the sofa together. 'You must be so proud of him. He's such a credit to you and Eddie.'

'Thank you. We couldn't be more proud of him. He's a great kid.' He entwined his fingers with mine. 'And just in case you hadn't realised, he adores you.'

'Which is a relief because this could be a bit awkward if he didn't like me.'

'I can't imagine anyone not liking you,' he said, the expression in his eyes so tender.

'Oh, I dunno,' I teased. 'I don't think a certain Olympic owl rescuer was too keen on me when I first turned up with Zorro.'

Snowy scrunched up his face and shook his head. 'I'm so embarrassed about that.'

I laughed lightly. 'Honestly, don't be. I completely understand why you were like that and, if we're talking about embarrassing, I had my moment too, giggling at you for stuffing that owl up your jumper.'

Snowy laughed. 'That was funny, and I'm glad you did it because it's what made me properly look at you for the first time. You made a strong impact on me right from the start and I'm sorry for all the moments I was rude or stand-offish. I hope you know it was never about you.'

'Was it about Eliza?' I asked softly.

He nodded. 'I didn't want to meet anyone else. I didn't think I deserved to, but I guess fate had other ideas.' He grinned at me. 'Fate and Grandpa. I could have throttled him the day he invited you to help release Tufty and stay for tea, but he knew what he was doing.'

'Your grandpa's adorable and, yes, I might have spotted some of the meddling.'

We kissed again, but something was niggling at me. Snowy was wary about visitors and trusting people was clearly an issue for him. I needed him to know he could trust me implicitly.

'There's something I want to tell you,' I said when we drew apart. 'It's how I realised I wanted to be with you and I think it's important you know it because I wouldn't want it to come out later and you think I've been keeping things from you.'

'Okay.' He looked apprehensive and I assured him it was nothing to worry about.

'In the spring, I came to the area to film a new reality TV show called *Love on the Farm*...'

I watched Snowy's expression carefully as I recounted how I felt when I first met Joel through to the kiss we'd shared where all I could think about was Snowy. It was a risk sharing something so personal which might evoke jealousy in some men, even though I was making it clear that Joel carried no threat.

'I genuinely don't think Joel and I were meant to be, but it was a lesson in not wasting time. I know you have a past we haven't spoken about and that the ripples from that still affect you, but I want to be here for you and help you navigate that when you're ready because, if not now, when?'

Snowy gently ran his hand down the side of my face and I nuzzled against it. His lips met mine with such tenderness, my insides felt like they'd turned to liquid.

'You know what I said earlier about fate and Grandpa?' he said, holding my gaze. 'Grandpa says you're an "owl-bearing angel". He believes that Eliza sent you to us.'

Tears rushed to my eyes and I pressed my hand against my heart. 'What do you think?' I whispered.

'That he could be right. It would be a very Eliza thing to do.'

'She sounds wonderful.'

'She was.'

We hugged tightly, our connection deepening further. I wanted him to feel that he could talk to me about Eliza. She was part of his past but his love for her and the memories of their time together were part of his future too and something to be celebrated rather than threatened by.

43

SNOWY

Zara continued to amaze me. I appreciated how honest she was telling me about Joel and I loved how she didn't look uncomfortable when I spoke about Eliza.

'How are your brother and your mum doing?' I asked.

She brought me up to speed with the latest headlines, the end of the relationship with Portia, how it seemed as though her mum's rose-tinted glasses had come off in regards to her brother and how that had unexpectedly made her feel sad.

'That's because you're a lovely person,' I assured her. 'From what you've told me, it was never about wanting your mum to stop championing him. It was about her having a balance and supporting you too.'

'That's a good point.'

I needed to broach my fears about her brother. 'Does your brother drink a lot?' I asked, a ripple of nerves flowing through me. It was a big thing to ask her, and it meant a big revelation was needed from me too.

'I'm not sure.' She pondered on it for a moment. 'Possibly. I hardly see him but, when our paths have crossed, he usually has had a drink in his hand. Why? Do you think I should be worried?'

I hated to answer a question with a question. 'Do you think your mum's worried?'

'She's never come out directly and said anything but she did say something really cryptic when she came to apologise after New Year. She was on about him being complicated and things not being what they seem, but she wouldn't expand on it. I don't think Owen knew what she was referring to.'

'Is it possible your brother has a drink problem?'

She bit her lip, her brow furrowed. 'I don't know. It sounds like he's drinking too much at the moment although that's probably because he's injured. Mind you, he has had injuries in the past – nothing big like this, of course – and he's always maintained the *my body is a temple* philosophy.'

I needed to tread carefully here as, no matter what Zara said about her brother, he was still family and I could upset her. I also didn't know Roman but I knew the behaviour. Very well.

'What do you know about his injury?' I asked.

'Bad tackle, nasty break. Mum told me the name of it at the time, but I haven't retained it. Talk to me about farming and nature and it stays in. Tell me something medical and it's in one ear and out the other.'

'I did what you suggested and I looked up the fight online, but I went down a rabbit hole. I found the name of the injury and did some digging. Did you know that it's highly likely he'll never be able to play professionally again?'

She gasped. 'Nobody's mentioned that to me. I knew he was out for this season, but I thought he'd be playing again next season.'

'Of all the injuries a footballer could get, it's up there with the worst and there's no way your brother hasn't been told that. They tell it to us straight. Yes, there's always hope, but athletes are given the worst-case scenario. My guess would be that your brother is drinking to avoid facing up to his career as a professional footballer being over.'

Her face had paled. 'It'll kill him,' she whispered. 'It can't be that.'

'I'm so sorry.'

She pressed her hands to her lips and scrunched her eyes tightly for a moment. 'Those cryptic comments from Mum make sense now. She knows but she's been trying to protect him.'

'Sounds like it. I hate being the bearer of bad news.'

'I'm glad you told me. I did wonder about the drinking recently. As I said, any other injury and he's been *my body's a temple*. I figured it was just different this time because the injury would take longer to heal.'

'When the athlete's injured, sometimes a drink will take the edge off the pain or the fear. Or three drinks. Or ten. And before you know it, you can't get through the day without it.'

Zara held my gaze and I could tell from the way her eyes widened that she'd connected a few dots.

'You sound like you're speaking from experience,' she said gently.

I released a deep shaky breath. 'My name's Nathan Edward Oakes, Snowy to my friends, and I'm an alcoholic.'

44

SNOWY

Thirteen years ago

I didn't think anything could top the elation I'd felt when I heard that I'd be representing Team GB at the Beijing 2008 Olympic Games, but being confirmed for London 2012 did. What an honour to be representing my country in a home Games, being able to defend – and hopefully exceed – my medal haul, knowing I was even better mentally and physically prepared this time around. And, of course, making Eliza and Grandpa proud was a privilege. If only Grandma had still been with us, but she'd died in the November a year after Beijing.

I wasn't a drinker. I'd seen and felt the impact of living with an angry, bitter recovering alcoholic and I'd watched him push the self-destruct button when he fell spectacularly off the wagon on my thirteenth birthday. He hadn't bothered to stick around while I prepared for Beijing, buggering off to Mexico at the start of 2008 to lose himself in (less expensive) bottle after bottle with a parting quip of, 'You won't win, anyway and, if you do, it won't fill the void.'

He didn't share what his void was and none of us asked. I personally didn't believe I had a void that needed filling. Yes, I hoped for medal success but I wouldn't feel empty if it didn't happen. I had so much else that was amazing in my life.

So, I wasn't a drinker but I wasn't teetotal either and occasionally had a couple of drinks when there was something to celebrate. After making Team GB for London 2012, there was a lot to celebrate and it didn't take many drinks out in Leeds with Ashley and my gym buddies to get me completely hammered.

I don't remember who said it as we left our fourth pub of the evening and made our way towards the club. It probably wasn't even a serious suggestion but the challenge was out there. Could I do my pommels routine on one of those green boxes which housed electricity cables? It seemed like a good idea at the time. These things usually do. Until they go wrong. With my mates – and a handful of strangers who'd tagged onto us – surrounding me, chanting my name, whooping and clapping, I felt invincible as I mounted the box and did a couple of turns.

And then my hand slipped.

One stupid challenge, too many drinks, and my Olympic career was over. Damage to the back and neck which would be an inconvenience to most people but were a disaster for an elite gymnast.

My coach, Grandpa and Eliza were all there with me when they delivered the prognosis, but the words didn't sound real. I had this sensation like I was floating above myself, waiting for the punchline, at which point I could re-join my body and we'd all be able to get back to training. The surgeon, doctor, consultant – whatever he was – would say something and I'd say, 'But I'll still be on Team GB,' and he'd say something else, and I'd respond, 'I know, but I'm still competing in London.'

I could see them all exchanging confused glances and wondered why. They were the confused ones, not me. I'd be representing my country at the thirtieth modern summer Olympics in London. Why did nobody seem to understand that?

* * *

I didn't make a conscious decision to start drinking. Does anyone? Or perhaps I did because I did it sneakily and it was vodka I bought. No smell. No odour. I only bought a small bottle so I didn't mean serious business.

It was proportionately cheaper to buy a bigger bottle than a small one and everyone loves a bargain. That was the only reason I went for the bigger one next time.

I had an excuse for everything I did – the miniatures were for a treat, the many different supermarkets and off-licences visited were to support all the businesses rather than just one, and the bottles of lager or occasional glass of wine I had at mealtimes with my unsuspecting family were just me being sociable.

Because I'd lived with my dad as a relapsed alcoholic for four years before he abandoned us, I knew all his tricks. Not only that, but I knew where he'd messed up so I knew how to be 'better' than him. It came easy to me. After all, he'd 'only' got an Olympic bronze whereas I'd attained a bronze *and* a silver. Better than him at everything.

I'd proposed to Eliza on her birthday last year, but we'd made the decision not to start planning the wedding until after London 2012. With the Olympics no longer on the cards, Eliza suggested we get married in the early September so that I had something to look forward to which would help take my attention away from what I couldn't have. She meant well. It was a great idea and I loved her for it. But nothing could take my attention away because it wasn't a case of not having – it was a case of me throwing it away, flushing my career down the toilet, ruining my life's work.

And, really, could I ignore the Olympic Games when the UK was the host country? That ten-day period across late July and early August was hell. I practically welded myself to the sofa watching every single artistic gymnastics event. It was torture. Of course I was delighted for my team mates and I screamed at the television with each fantastic performance and the medal wins, but inside I was dying because I should have been there. And the only thing that took the edge off the pain and regret was a drink. Or several.

45

SNOWY

Present day

Zara shook her head, her eyes full of sorrow after I'd told her how my career ended, my problems with alcohol started, and about my own parents' battle with addiction.

'I can't even begin to imagine what you must have been feeling that summer,' she said, her voice soft and understanding. 'I'm so sorry. And your family didn't know about your drinking?'

'They made a few comments about easing back on the beers, but they hadn't a clue that it was the bottles of vodka stashed in the woods that they needed to worry about. All they saw was someone they cared about cheering his team on and having a few melancholy moments about what could have been. It was natural, expected. Besides, Eliza was distracted with planning our wedding and Grandpa was struggling to rebuild his life without Grandma in it. It had been three years but you can't put a timescale on grief, especially when they'd been together that long and were as devoted as they'd been.'

Zara squeezed my hand, conveying her sympathy.

'When did your family find out?' she asked. 'Presumably they did realise?'

'It was the following summer. Grandpa had ventured into the woods, looking for interesting fungi to draw, so he didn't stick to any of the tracks. He spotted the sun glinting on something and found a bottle of vodka hidden among some tree roots. He assumed it was one of Dad's from years before so he got rid of it and never thought to mention it to anyone. When I went to find it, I assumed I'd drunk it so I bought a replacement. When Grandpa found that, he realised someone else had a problem. I denied it, of course. Said some awful things about his mind going and challenged why he'd think I was capable of secret drinking after the hell Dad put us all through. I was even more careful after that. Made a big show of not drinking anything and returning to the gym. My intake did massively reduce, but it didn't stop. I thought about drinking all the time. There's something about elite athletes and addiction. In order to progress, we have to be extreme with our training and that can make us extreme in other parts of our life. We can be susceptible to drinking, gambling, drugs, which is why I find myself wondering about your brother. I've been there.'

I raked my hands through my hair and closed my eyes, taking in the enormity of having shared my story for the first time since Eliza's passing. Or part of it, anyway.

'There's more, but do you mind if we leave it there?' I said.

Zara shuffled closer to me, cupped my chin and lightly kissed me. 'Thank you for telling me. That can't have been easy for you.'

'It wasn't, but I feel I can trust you. I've been sober for four years and twenty-five days now and I'd love to say it's been a walk in the park, but there've been plenty of moments of temptation. Every time the drink calls, I think about Harrison and I think about my own dad. I'd never want Harrison to go through even a small fraction of what I went through so, for my son and my own hero – Grandpa – I've ignored that siren call.'

'And you really think that Roman might be hearing that call?' Zara asked.

'I do. I could see a change in him across his YouTube clips way before his injury and alarm bells started ringing. Is he an alcoholic? It would be doubtful if he only started drinking after he broke his leg but, if it started long before that – and I think it did – he could be in trouble. To my knowledge, footballers are subject to random drugs tests, but they're not tested for alcohol so it would be possible to have a problem and hide it. From what you've said about your mum, it does sound like she knows more than she's letting on.'

Zara sighed. 'I need to speak to her, but this isn't a phone conversation. If she's hiding something, I'll be able to tell. Argh! Why do I have to be heading to Scotland tomorrow?' She picked up her phone and checked the time. 'I hate to say this, especially when I'm going away for a fortnight, but would you mind if I took off after lunch? I need to see her. Amber's not planning on setting off until after lunch tomorrow so I could always come here for a bit in the morning.'

'Of course I don't mind, but I've got a suggestion. What if Harrison and I come with you? I can take him to that nature park you were telling us about while you spend some time with your mum. If you find you need to stay longer, Harrison and I can get a train back or, if you want to stay overnight, I can check Harrison and me into a hotel and come back with you in the morning. No pressure if you'd rather do this on your own.'

'I don't want to do this at all! The company would be brilliant.'

'I'll throw some things into a bag. We've got spare toiletries and I can lend you a T-shirt to sleep in and a fresh one for tomorrow.'

Zara cuddled up to me. 'Thanks for this. You pack that bag and I'll let Amber know what's happening. Mum's already told me she's staying home all day so I'm not going to tell her I'm coming. She'll only want to know why and it might get messy.'

46

ZARA

Harrison was delighted by the prospect of a road trip and didn't seem fazed by the uncertainty around coming back or staying overnight. Although Snowy had packed a bag for him, he raced upstairs to get his book and a few other items to entertain himself with if they did end up checking into a hotel, which gave Snowy and me the opportunity to properly explain what was going on to Eddie.

We set off after lunch and, after dropping Snowy and Harrison off at the nature reserve, it was 3 p.m. when I pulled onto the drive in Thorpe on the Hill. Even though I still had my key, it didn't feel right letting myself in now that I no longer officially lived there.

'Zara! What are you doing here?' Owen asked as he hugged me on the doorstep.

'I wanted to see how Mum's doing.'

The expression on his face told me it wasn't good. 'It's knocked her for six. She's meant to be relaxing in front of a film, but I know she's not watching it.'

I followed him into the lounge where Mum was lying on her side on the sofa with a throw over her legs, staring at the floor rather than the TV.

'Hi, Mum,' I said. 'I wanted to check you're okay.'

She took one look at me and burst into tears. I rushed over to her and knelt down on the floor, hugging her. It was heartbreaking and worrying to see her in such a state.

'I've made your lovely jumper wet,' she said, pulling away, sniffing.

'Don't worry about that,' I said, sitting beside her when she moved her legs. 'Is there any more news?'

'Nothing new. I've done as you said and stayed off my phone, but I spoke to Roman a few hours ago and he promised nothing else has happened. We're going to see him tonight.'

'There's something I want to ask you about Roman,' I said, butterflies flapping anxiously in my stomach. 'Please don't get mad at me, but does he have a drink problem?'

'Of course not!' she cried, that familiar defensive tone in her voice. 'He's very—'

'Jenna!' Owen's voice, cutting across her, was stern.

Mum's shoulders slumped and she sighed. 'Yes, he does. But he swears it's nothing to worry about. He assures me he's not an alcoholic. He's just going through a rough patch.'

I winced. 'That sounds like the sort of thing an alcoholic would say.'

She sighed once more. 'I suppose so, but I believe him. He talks to me about things – things that he wouldn't share with other people. People judge and they make assumptions but they don't know what's really going on.'

'You've said something like that before. What *is* going on? Talk to me, Mum.'

She glanced across at Owen, who gave her an encouraging nod. Presumably Mum had now opened up to him.

'Your brother has other problems,' she said. 'He needs to be adored – by his coach, his teammates, women, strangers. I wish I could say I don't know where it stems from, but that would be a fib. I might have created a monster by pandering to him from the start and building him up way too high. Social media feeds into it and doesn't help. I can track his subscriber levels by his moods. If he's on a high, he's gained a load of followers, but a downer means he's lost loads. A viral post has him on cloud nine, and not going viral has him in the doldrums.'

She nibbled on her thumbnail before continuing. 'When he started out on YouTube, he was one of the first, but now there are so many others doing what he does and the truth is that many are doing it better. He's forever comparing himself and it's having such a negative effect on him. It's affecting him mentally but it's also affecting his content. What made him such a social media star was that what he and the boys did was natural and spontaneous. They weren't trying to be slick or clever, but now everything seems contrived and forced. That spontaneity has gone and his followers have noticed and disengaged so he tries even harder and... well, you can imagine how that's gone.'

I knew he'd basked in the adoration, having previously boasted to me about how many followers he had, but I had no idea he'd gone this extreme with it.

'You say he talks to you about this?' I asked.

'About the follower numbers and how that affects his mood, yes. He's also talked about other content creators, but what I said about the lack of spontaneity is my own observation. I haven't said that to him as I don't want to bring him down even further. After his injury, he got himself all worked up about how many followers he'd lose when he couldn't do any of the physical challenges they love. Sure enough, the numbers dropped and, thanks to his fight with Kai Casper, they've tanked again. He's trying to be positive, saying a break might be good and he can come back next season with fresh content once he's playing again.'

I winced. 'So Roman does expect to be playing again in August?'

'Absolutely. He might be eased in gently, but he'll be back on the team.' She frowned at me. 'What's that look for? Do you know something I don't?'

'I've discovered that his injury is a career-ending one. He's never talked to you about that?'

Mum gasped, clasping her hand to her throat. 'He's always said he'll be back.'

'I've got a friend who got an injury which ended his Olympic career. He started drinking heavily to numb the pain of everything he'd ever worked towards being over. I can't help but wonder if Roman's doing the same.'

Mum looked down at the floor, chewing her lip, evidently considering that possibility.

'This friend of yours,' she said, looking up at me eventually. 'Was he an alcoholic?'

'Yes.'

'And did he admit it?'

'No. He hid it from the people he loved because that's what alcoholics do.'

'I don't think Roman's...' But she tailed off, shaking her head.

'None of us want to think that,' Owen said, his voice gentle. 'But, with Roman, he's either there or he's close. Whether he agrees is another matter.'

* * *

I stayed for about an hour, most of that time spent discussing ideas for how Mum could raise the issue of Roman's drinking and also his future in football. She invited me to stay overnight but it didn't make sense to be in on my own while Mum and Owen went to Roman's so I said goodbye and asked her to keep me posted.

Snowy had messaged to say they'd had a good walk round Whisby Nature Park and had decamped to a pub to warm up. I found them inside and, over a drink, listened to Harrison's excitable recount of everything they'd seen and heard.

'You look drained,' Snowy said when Harrison nipped to the toilet.

'I feel it. I don't fancy the drive back.'

'I can sort insurance and drive if you like, or we can check into a hotel and get some rest. Obviously we'll get you a room of your own.'

'Let's stay. We can have a nice meal and relax for a bit and, if Mum needs me, I'm not far away.'

We managed to book adjoining rooms in a lovely hotel near Lincoln city centre. Going out for a meal in a quiet pub was exactly what I needed and I couldn't help smiling to myself that my first date with Snowy included his son.

When Harrison settled down to sleep later that evening, we left the adjoining door ajar and settled on my bed to talk without disturbing Harrison. I filled Snowy in on the conversation with Mum but also shared more about my childhood and our deteriorating relationship. It brought up lots of difficult memories and I found myself in tears on several occasions.

'I couldn't stand him,' I told Snowy as we lay on top of my bed, my head resting on his chest. 'And now I feel ashamed of that. All these years I've dismissed him as being an absolute arse, but it sounds like he's been fighting a mental health battle.'

He gave me a gentle squeeze. 'From what I've learned about him, he *is* an absolute arse so don't beat yourself up about it. And remember that his shitty behaviour towards you started when you were only eight. Did he have mental health problems then? Was he drinking? Was he obsessed with building his social media presence? No to any of that. I agree with you that he turned your relationship into a competition and, because of your mum's choices, he was always going to be the winner. Most kids grow out of the one-upmanship but it sounds like he never did. He gave you every reason to dislike him and don't get me started on the New Year's Eve party. There was no excuse for any of that.'

'Mum admitted something about the party this afternoon. Roman didn't cancel his holiday because he didn't want a long flight with his leg in plaster. He cancelled it because he was craving adoration. He desperately wanted some validation that he was still relevant and three hundred adoring guests and a free bar was his way of doing that. Turns out he didn't want me there because I don't suck up to him like everyone else.'

'Whatever his reasons, he still had no right to treat you that way.' He lightly kissed the top of my head and it felt so good to have someone other than Owen in my corner.

Snowy entwined his fingers with mine. 'Whether your brother's an alcoholic or not, and whatever his mental health issues are, don't forget that he's still a grown adult who makes his own choices. If those choices were made under the influence, they probably weren't good ones but they were still choices which *he* made and which had a major impact on you. Just because you know some of the behind-the-scenes stuff now, it doesn't take away the pain, it doesn't wipe the slate clean, and it doesn't make you guilty of anything other than being human. Sorry. Am I lecturing you?'

'No. You're making so much sense, especially as you've been through this yourself.'

Mum's cryptic comment about Roman being complicated was an understatement. But weren't we all, some to lesser and some to greater degrees? Snowy was right that I couldn't take on the guilt. My brother had treated me badly and feeling sorry for him right now didn't take away years of hurt. I wanted him to get help but did that mean I directly wanted to help him, to be back in his life? Did what I'd discovered about him change how I'd felt on New Year's Eve that our relationship was beyond repair and it was time to accept that? Probably not. For now, I'd focus on being there for Mum and she could deal with Roman.

'You know what you were saying about Eliza sending me to you when you needed me? I think she might have sent you to me when I needed you too.'

47

SNOWY

Having never met him, there was no way I could categorically state that Roman Timmins was an alcoholic but I was fairly certain from what Zara's mum had told her that he was and that Jenna knew it too.

'Your mum is going to encourage him to get some help, isn't she?' I asked.

'Yes. She's hoping that, when the dust settles on the fight and the split with Portia, he'll realise he's hit rock bottom and want to do something about it.'

'It's not easy admitting that you have a problem and it's not easy admitting you need help, but I cannot emphasise enough how vital that help is. Living and breathing proof of that right here.'

I told Zara about the support I'd had, but it made me realise I should have kept it going for longer. I might have got control of the drink, but I hadn't got control of my whole life.

It was time for me to open up and tell Zara the full story, but not tonight. She was worried about her family and it would be hard enough for her to spend the next fortnight in Scotland with that on her mind without knowing my entire backstory. We'd talk about it when she returned.

***

Zara drove us home after an early breakfast, declaring that she wanted the journey to be fun so it was going to be quick-fire questions all the way. You name it, we talked about it, including several obscure categories, mainly courtesy of Harrison, like favourite dragon, favourite magic spell and favourite gross thing. After an emotional evening, it was great to see Zara laughing and I was in awe of her resilience in bouncing back.

She couldn't stay long at Owl's Lodge as she needed to finish packing for Scotland, but she nipped inside to say hello and goodbye to Grandpa. While Harrison told Grandpa all about our trip, I took Zara over to The Owlery to say farewell to Zorro.

'I'm gutted I'll miss his release,' she said, smiling at him, 'but thanks for agreeing to film it for me. Aw, you're so gorgeous, Zorro. You take care.'

She rested against the desk and took my hands in hers. 'Thanks for yesterday, especially back at the hotel. I've kept so much of that bottled up and I can't tell you how good it felt to get it all off my chest. You're a good listener and you give good advice too.'

'If you need to offload again while you're away, you know where I am.'

'I might take you up on that. And thanks for telling me about your drinking. I know you were going to tell me at some point but I suspect you might have shared it a little sooner than anticipated.'

I smiled at her incredible perception once more. 'I trust you and I'm ready to tell you the rest when you're back from Scotland. I want to be completely honest with you about who I am, who I've been, and what you're letting yourself in for before either of us get in too deep.'

She squeezed my hands and planted a gentle kiss on my lips. 'I already know who you are and, as for who you've been in the past, nothing you could possibly tell me is going to change how I feel about you. But I do appreciate that you want to share it with me. As for that last part about telling me before either of us get in too deep, it might be a bit late for that from my end.'

My heart pounded as she snaked her arms round my neck and kissed me again.

'I'd better go,' she said, her tone apologetic as she pulled away and glanced towards the door.

We left The Owlery and walked to her car in silence.

'First time ever I haven't wanted to go away,' she said, her eyes watery as she looked deep into mine.

'I don't want you to go either,' I said, my voice hoarse with emotion. 'I'm going to miss you so much.'

'I know they might be watching but you can explain away a hug, can't you?' she said, launching herself at me before I could answer.

She released me with a shaky sigh then jumped in her car and sped off down the track. I felt incredibly emotional as she disappeared from sight, as though a part of me was missing. I needed to compose myself before I saw Grandpa and Harrison so I strode back over to The Owlery and stood for several minutes staring at Zorro, feeling closer to Zara just by being near her namesake. How had she changed my life so much in such a short space of time? How was it possible to ache for someone who I'd only just met? Zara wasn't the only one for whom it was too late. I was in deep too.

48

ZARA

Work had been pretty full-on since filming started for *The Wildlife Rescuers* at Hedgehog Hollow because, alongside my responsibilities for the docuseries, I also had preparation for filming *Countryside Calendar* in Dumfries and Galloway, and future episodes of both programmes. There'd been limited time for a non-work catch-up with Amber, but the long car journey to Scotland finally gave us that opportunity.

Amber already knew about Roman's fight and the split with Portia, but I filled her in on my visit to Mum and the concerns that he might be an alcoholic in denial.

'That explains so much,' she said.

'Doesn't it?'

'It was good of Snowy to go with you. Would I be right in thinking he's become a bit more than your owl fixer and gymnastics coach?'

I couldn't stop smiling. 'It's taken us both by surprise. You know how Joel and I kissed after Phoebe's party and we didn't *feel the thing*? Well, the reason I didn't feel it was because, when I kissed Joel, the person I pictured was Snowy.'

'Hold that thought. There's a service station two miles away so we're going to stop there and you can tell me all about it. I want to be able to listen properly because I can tell from your voice that Snowy's something special.'

'I'm so chuffed for you both,' she said, beaming at me across the table of the services café after I'd given her the full story. 'After all these years of being single or in crap relationships, who'd have predicted that the answer for both of us was to move to East Yorkshire?'

* * *

Amber and I were staying in a gorgeous barn conversion in a pretty village called Glentrool on the edge of Galloway Forest Park. Most of the filming for *Countryside Calendar* would be taking place in the national park – a massive 300 square miles of forest, lochs, rivers and mountains – which I couldn't wait to visit.

During our first day of filming, I learned about a project to increase the number of breeding pairs of barn owls in the area. I FaceTimed Snowy that evening to find out how Harrison's first session at Campion's had gone and he put Harrison on who was practically bursting with enthusiasm. When Snowy took the phone back, I told him about the barn owl programme and reminded him I meant what I'd said about being a sponge and eager to lap up all his owl knowledge. He suggested we start now and take an owl at a time, beginning with the tawny owl in honour of Zorro's release on Friday. Shortly after the call, some YouTube links came through and, the more I learned, the more I wanted to learn.

On the second night, we filmed a dark skies experience which was breath-taking. I'd experienced many clear night skies but the remoteness of Galloway Forest Park took it to a different level with over 7,000 stars and planets visible to the naked eye. As I stood there, head tilted back, captivated by the beauty, I wished Snowy, Harrison and Eddie were there with me. They'd have loved it so much. Although it wasn't the same as being there in person, I messaged them some video links when I returned to the cottage.

On Wednesday evening, Snowy FaceTimed to update me on his coffee catch-up with Ashley. He apologised that he couldn't give me much detail about how their conversation had gone when I didn't know the full story yet.

'It went well,' he concluded, sounding positive. 'There were a couple of awkward moments, but the main thing is we're in touch again. He's gutted about the gym closing and it was so hard not to tell him I've got a viewing booked for Sunday.'

The following evening, Harrison sent me a video of a new twist on the trampoline which was looking amazing and Eddie had messaged me on Snowy's account to say that his drawing of Zorro was progressing nicely. He'd taken a photo of a tiny section to give me a teaser and the detail in it was incredible. I couldn't wait to see the full sketch.

Across the week, Mum was in regular contact. I was pleased to hear that Roman was fine about the break-up with Portia but not so pleased to hear that he was still drinking heavily and refusing to acknowledge it as an issue. All Mum could do was keep voicing her concerns and hope that Roman would come round and want to do something about it. These things couldn't be forced. I spoke to Owen too while Mum was at work one evening to make sure she was holding up okay and he assured me that she was much better after getting over the initial shock of it all. He said my involvement had been invaluable. I'd got through to her how fruitless it was to keep scrolling through all the comments online and I'd got her to properly accept that Roman was going through more than a 'rough patch'. I'd never thought I'd see the day where my counsel was sought and welcome, although I wished for my brother's sake that it hadn't taken his downfall to make that happen.

On Friday, Snowy messaged me to say he wouldn't forget to film the release, but then he surprised me by FaceTiming me later so I could watch it live. We'd just finished filming for the day so it was perfect timing. Amber and I huddled together in her car with the heating on, watching the video on my iPad. Just like Tufty and Aurelia the vixen, Zorro was hesitant at first – so hesitant that Snowy had to remove him from the crate and rest him on his glove, arm outstretched. Zorro looked around him as if not quite believing that he was seeing an entire paddock instead of the restricted insides of an aviary.

I could hear Harrison in the background saying, 'Come on, Zorro! You can do it. Fly!'

And fly he did. What a spectacular sight and how special to see it live rather than on a video afterwards.

'That was so considerate of him,' Amber said after we'd both thanked him and said goodbye. 'You've bagged a keeper there.'

'Certainly feels like it.'

I'd never experienced a relationship like it and wondered what the heck I'd been doing with previous boyfriends. None of them had ever made me feel important or special like Snowy did. I'd never had the sense that they were thinking of me when we were apart. I'd received the occasional *missing you, can't wait to see you* message from Declan, but I didn't believe he'd meant it – it had just been a way of keeping me sweet. By comparison, Snowy *showed* me he was missing me by sending photos of the patients in The Owlery, owls he'd spotted in the grounds and GIFs he thought I'd like. I'd met him a little over a fortnight ago and he already knew me better than Declan during our six months together.

* * *

Saturday arrived and, after a busy week of filming, Amber and I were looking forward to a day off. We'd bought the ingredients to cook a full Scottish breakfast followed by a visit to Wigtown – Scotland's National Book Town and a book lover's haven.

I'd been snoozing my alarm for the past half hour, too cosy beneath my duvet, but had just accepted that it was time to get up when there was a knock on the bedroom door.

'Come in!' I called.

Amber opened the door and I was about to greet her with a cheery *good morning* but the dark expression on her face told me it wasn't a good one at all.

'I hate to start the day this way,' she said, passing me her iPad, 'but you'd want to know.'

My eyes widened as I clocked a photo of Snowy on a tabloid website. And me. Me! Who the hell had been taking photos of us together?

The headline read:

Fallen Olympian Falls Again

'You've read it?' I asked, looking up at Amber. 'Is this about the past? He was planning to tell me when I get back.'

'Looks like someone's beaten him to it.'

I closed my eyes for a moment and drew in a deep breath, then reluctantly read the article. The early part hauled over what I already knew – alcoholic father with a bronze medal, bronze and silver Olympic success for Snowy, a disastrous fall which ended his London 2012 hopes and his career, as well as triggering his alcoholism. What I hadn't known – and what was clearly the part he was going to share with me after Scotland – was what had happened to Eliza.

I pressed my hand to my mouth as tears tracked down my cheeks. 'That poor family.'

'I know. It's devastating.'

'Why's this in the papers now? It isn't new news. My name isn't even in there. It's like they've been waiting to pap Snowy with a woman just to drag it all out again. Who writes this crap?'

I scrolled up to the byline. 'Elliot Parnell.' The name was familiar. 'No way! This is the guy who bullied Snowy at school. He called him Freak Show! No wonder it reads like a one-man vendetta.'

I grabbed my phone and called Snowy but there was no answer.

'Do you think he's seen this?' I asked Amber.

'Does he read the papers?'

I shrugged. 'I don't think so, but he's bound to know someone who does.'

'Get yourself dressed while I look up some train times.'

'I can't abandon you.'

'You can and you will. You need to be with Snowy right now. Don't worry about work. Some things are more important. I can use a runner to help while we're filming and there's nothing I need you to do that you can't do from home or I can't get someone else to do if it comes to it. Not that I'm saying you're dispensable.'

and Grandpa that I'd try to cut down and I hadn't had anything to drink yet today.

'Why don't you take your hat off?' Eliza said, her voice low.

'You know why.'

'Nobody's looking at you. They're with their kids. They're looking at the lights and decorations.'

'They might not be looking now but they will be. The minute they see the hair, I'll be recognised and the whispering will start.'

I slipped my jacket off and draped it over my arm.

'Seriously, Snowy, take your hat off.'

'I'm hot too!' Harrison announced and whipped off his bobble hat. I crouched down, intending to push it back on his head, but he grabbed my hat and ran along the aisle, giggling, a hat in each hand.

'Harrison!' I yelled and everyone in the queue turned to look as I chased after my four-year-old son.

And soon they weren't just looking. As predicted, they were whispering. I heard my name and various words which proved that it wasn't just me being paranoid – *medal, gymnastics, drinker, disgrace.*

I caught up with Harrison and scooped him into my arms. He could wriggle, kick and squeal as much as he liked, but he wasn't getting free and he wasn't seeing Santa Claus.

'You can't do this!' Eliza cried, running after me as I stormed across the car park, Harrison limp in my arms, his squeals now cries.

'I can and I am,' I snapped.

'He's not you, Snowy! He doesn't understand why that was wrong. He's just a little kid. Don't punish him because of something you did.'

I stopped dead, heart pounding as I turned to face her.

'You still have no idea what it's like, do you? I messed up. I know that and I have to live with it, but this bloody hair is the bane of my life. I can *never* be allowed to forget about my screw-up for one single day because, everywhere I go, I'm recognised. They whisper, they laugh and they judge.'

'So let them! They're strangers. They're nothing to you. The people who love you don't do that.' She swiped at the tears streaming down her cheeks. 'Focus on the ones who love you. Come back to us. Please.'

I didn't trust myself to speak. Eliza didn't deserve my anger and neither did Harrison, but I was too embarrassed and fired up to find the words to express that. And I needed a drink.

'Why don't you sit in the car and listen to some music?' she said, her voice pleading. 'I'll take Harrison in to see Santa and then we can all go home together.'

I lowered Harrison to the ground. 'Do what you want. I'm going to the pub.'

I ran out of the car park, ignoring her calling my name and the cries of my son.

* * *

The atmosphere at Owl's Lodge that Christmas was tense and I couldn't bear it. I knew I'd caused it but I couldn't do the one thing they wanted me to do to make it better. I couldn't stop drinking. I'm not sure how many hours I lost, staggering through the woods, drinking straight from the bottle. I'd sometimes hear my name being called, although it could have been the wind or the echoes of the past taunting me from when the crowd had chanted my name in adulation. Nothing to adore me for now and that hurt, but the drink took the edge off it. It numbed the memories, helped me forget, cushioned that pit of blame and despair.

I was diagnosed with depression six months after receiving confirmation that professional gymnastics was not my future. I had meds but I preferred the way drink made me feel. As the end of each year approached, my depression weighed down more heavily on me. Another wasted year gone by. Another year of zero achievements approaching.

Three days after Christmas, with torrential rain making the woods an uncomfortable and undesirable hideout, I caught a taxi into Wilbersgate. I settled into a dark corner in a pub with my long-term drinking buddies Guilt, Hate, Bitterness and Regret and drank my way across the optics.

'You know what they say about people who drink alone?'

Of all the people! I squinted up at Elliot Parnell's smug expression. 'Cheaper bar bill?' I deadpanned.

'Oh, very droll,' he said, slipping into the chair opposite me. 'Mind if I join you?'

'Yes, but you're going to anyway. Thanks for that pile of crap you wrote about me,' I slurred. 'Hope you're proud.'

'Oh, come on, Snowy! That was nearly seven years ago and it was true. Well, most of it. If you decline to comment, you can't get upset when someone has to fill in the blanks. You can't still be annoyed with me for that.'

I necked back the shot of dark liquid in front of me and tried to focus on him, but my eyelids were heavy and there seemed to be more than one of him.

'You'd be surprised at how long I can stay annoyed with you,' I murmured.

I wiped my mouth, pushed my chair back and staggered past him, but he followed me out of the pub. There was a large beer garden out the front with wooden benches and raised flower beds, heaving in the summer, but empty on a wet winter's day like today.

'I wish you'd think of me as a friend,' Parnell said, an *I'm-so-misunderstood* whine to his tone. 'Come back inside. I'll buy you a drink and we can have a nice little chat.'

He leaned forward and reached for my arm. No way was I going back into the pub with that lowlife.

'Go screw yourself,' I snarled, yanking my arm away but, as I did that, I staggered backwards and tripped over one of the low metal chains marking out the beer garden. Next minute, I was sprawled across one of the raised flower beds, the puddles of dirty rainwater soaking into my jeans.

The last thing I remembered was Parnell leaning over me with his phone out, laughing. 'Oh, this is good! You look like you've pissed yourself. So appropriate for someone who pissed his career away.'

* * *

I woke up the following morning face down on the sofa, a blanket tangled round my bare legs. I smacked my cracked lips together several times, my mouth as dry as a desert, and rubbed my eyes. Becoming aware of being watched, I squinted across the gloomy room to where Eliza was fully dressed and sitting cross-legged in an armchair.

'Do you think you can walk?' she asked in a hushed voice.

'Yeah, why?'

'I don't want Harrison to find you like this. Go upstairs while I get you some water.'

I rolled off the sofa, wincing. I felt like I'd gone through several rounds in a boxing ring. I lifted my T-shirt and frowned at a couple of dark bruises on my side. I remembered the pub and Parnell. I winced again, recalling my tumble into the planter. After that...

'How did I get home?' I asked, but Eliza was in the kitchen with the tap on.

I stumbled several times on the stairs, unsteady on my feet, still drunk from the night before, and sank wearily onto our bed. Eliza was seconds behind me. She closed the door softly and thrust the glass at me with an instruction to drink. I downed the pint of water and placed the glass on the bedside cabinet, expecting Eliza to sit beside me, but she sat down on her dressing table stool instead.

'We have a son, Snowy,' she said. 'We have a beautiful, clever, cheeky four-year-old who is starting to ask questions and I don't know what to tell him.'

Eliza was petite but she looked even smaller than normal today, her face pale, her shoulders stooped.

'What happened yesterday?' she asked.

'I went to the pub.'

'You didn't tell any of us you were going. Eddie and Ashley spent three hours searching the woods for you. They were scared you might have...' She released a shaky breath and looked up at the ceiling, blinking rapidly.

'How did this happen?' She picked up her phone from the dressing table, swiped the screen and held it out for me to see.

My stomach lurched at the photograph of me splayed out in the planter.

'I tripped.'

'I can see that. Plus, it's the only thing you said all the way home.'

'You picked me up?' I couldn't remember that at all.

'The landlord phoned demanding I collect you, so that was fun. You threw up in my car. That was fun too.'

Her tone was so weary and I felt the disappointment in me dripping from every word.

'I'll clean it up.'

'I've already done it.'

'I'm sorry.'

'Are you?' She shrugged. 'I don't mean about the vomit or the flower bed or even disappearing without telling anyone. I mean about all of it. I don't recognise you anymore. I feel like we've lost you and I'm scared you'll never come back. I'm so tired.' She shook her head slowly, her forehead creased with a deep frown. 'What do you want, Snowy?'

'To turn back time.'

'You and me both. But, seeing as we can't do that and we don't have a magic lamp and a genie to grant us wishes either, what do you want now and for the future?'

'I don't know.'

She pressed her lips together, her watery eyes fixed on mine. 'Oh, wow! And here was me foolishly thinking you might have said your family.'

'Eliza, I... It's hard.'

'I know it is and I do understand. I understand more than anyone what it's like to have the future you dreamed of snatched away from you because it happened to me. And I do get that it's bigger for you than it was for me because you were so much further down the line. But sometimes bad things happen. That doesn't mean we have to stop dreaming – just that we need to find a different dream. I thought Harrison and I were...' She broke off, her voice catching in her throat. 'I'm taking Harrison and we're going away for a few days.'

'Where?'

'I'm not sure yet. It doesn't really matter. What matters is that I'm giving you three days to think about what you want because I refuse to believe that this is it. It's certainly not what I want and it's not what I want for Harrison. We'll come back in the morning of New Year's Day and I'd like you and me to talk about how next year is going to work for us because we can't have a repeat of this one.'

She stood up slowly and I did the same.

'So you're leaving me?' I asked.

'I never said that. I'm giving you some time and begging you to take it for all our sakes.'

'I want to see Harrison.'

'No. Not like this.'

'Like what?'

'Don't make me spell it out.'

I glared at her.

'You're covered in mud and bruises, your T-shirt's ripped and you reek of sick. Clear enough for you?'

She crossed the room and embraced me, but I stood rigid in her arms. She was leaving me. She was taking my son and walking away and she wouldn't even let me say goodbye to him. But how could I fight that when everything she said was fair? I was failing them both. They'd be better without me.

'I love you, Snowy,' she whispered. 'I always will. Please come back to me.'

She kissed my cheek then walked out, closing the door behind her.

51

ZARA

Present day

'You don't have to continue,' I told Snowy, placing a reassuring hand on his thigh. 'We can take a break and you can tell me the rest later.'

He placed his hand over mine. 'It's easier that I get it all out. At least you haven't run yet.'

'You know I'm not going to do that.'

'Eliza left with Harrison. She stayed with a friend but she kept in touch with Grandpa that whole time. He knew she needed some space so he told her I was still drinking but I was home and safe. Thing is, he didn't have a clue where I was.

'After they left, I showered and I tried to get some focus but my head was a mess and all I could think about was where I'd stashed the nearest bottle because I was going to need it soon. When I put my coat on to go out in search of a drink, I discovered my phone was still in my pocket. There were missed calls from Eliza, Grandpa and Ashley the previous day and a stack of unknown numbers from that morning – reporters. And there was a message from my dad. He'd get in touch every so often, joking that he was checking we were all still alive.'

Air quotes across *joking* indicated that Snowy didn't rate his dad's sense of humour.

'Contact with him was never particularly pleasant so I should have known better than to open his message. He'd attached the photo from the papers of me in the planter. He'd photoshopped a gold medal round my neck and added the words *Snowy Oakes bags the gold in fucking up spectacularly.*'

'Ooh, that's nasty.'

'That's my dad for you. Oh, and it was accompanied by about twenty laughing emojis. If Eliza hadn't walked out, maybe I'd have been able to ignore it, but he'd put in his own colourful way what she'd effectively told me in her understanding, sweet way. The truth hurts and what does an alcoholic do when they're hurting?'

'Drink to numb the pain,' I said, squeezing his hand.

'I disappeared on a bender. I couldn't tell you where I went. Pubs, alleyways, bus shelters, more pubs. I woke up on New Year's morning on a sticky, smelly carpet with a slice of pizza stuck to the side of my face. I looked around the room and I had no idea where I was or who any of the sleeping strangers were and I wondered what the hell I was doing. I picked my way through the empty bottles and left the flat. I couldn't call a taxi because my phone was dead and, even if I'd had some charge, I didn't know where I was.

'I walked aimlessly for a while in the most horrendous storm. Eventually I stumbled across a mini-market. It was a tiny shop and the alcohol was behind the counter. The shop assistant was obviously not happy about working on New Year's Day and she glared at me and demanded *What do you want?* The exact words Eliza had said, although in a completely different tone. And I had this moment of clarity. What *did* I want? I wanted my family, of course. So I asked the assistant where I was, bought a bottle of water and a Twix, and called a taxi.'

He released a heavy sigh and nervous butterflies lurched in my stomach because I knew what happened next. He might have finally seen the light but he wasn't about to get his happy ending.

'I'm so sorry,' I whispered.

'Me too.'

52

SNOWY

Five years ago

The taxi driver who picked me up outside the mini-market that stormy New Year's Day morning took one disgusted look at me and I could tell he was about to refuse me access to his car.

'I'll give you a twenty quid tip,' I said and he reluctantly indicated with a toss of his head that I should get in.

I must have reeked because, despite the rain battering at his window, he opened it.

The journey back to Owl's Lodge seemed to take an eternity, not helped by floods across the road and debris from trees everywhere.

Eliza had said she'd be back in the morning so, when we pulled onto the track just after eleven, I expected her to be there. As we travelled towards the lodge, I felt sick with nerves. I was about to have the biggest conversation of my life and I couldn't be less ready for it.

There was no sign of Eliza's car. I thrust several notes at the driver, leapt out and sprinted up the steps.

'Eliza?' I shouted, running inside. 'Grandpa?'

Grandpa appeared from the kitchen, wiping his hands on a towel. 'Where the hell have you been?'

'It doesn't matter. Has Eliza been back yet?'

'Yes, and she's gone out to look for you.'

'In this weather?'

'I told her to give you a bit longer, but she said she couldn't sit around doing nothing.'

'Where was she going?'

'I don't know. She took Harrison and—'

But Grandpa didn't finish that sentence. The colour drained from his face as he stared past me. I spun round to see what had caught his attention and my stomach plummeted to the floor as a pair of uniformed officers exited a marked police car and looked up at the lodge.

* * *

Present day

'A tree had come down in the storm right on top of Eliza's car,' I told Zara, shaking my head. 'It struck Eliza but missed Harrison. They'd already taken him to hospital where he was being checked over and there were paramedics with Eliza on the roadside. She was still alive but it wasn't looking good. They were certain she'd have internal bleeding but they couldn't get to her. The fire brigade needed to cut up the tree and the car to do that.'

'You must have been terrified.'

'Like you wouldn't believe. It's the most horrific thing I've ever experienced. Grandpa rushed to the hospital to be with Harrison and I went to Eliza but I couldn't get close. There wasn't the room and I couldn't risk them delaying their work for even a second. I shouted to her...'

I crumbled at that point, tears tracking down my cheeks with the rawness of the memories that I hadn't shared with anyone. Zara was openly sobbing too and we leaned into each other and held on tightly.

'I shouted to her that I loved her and I was sorry,' I said when I felt strong enough to pick the story up again. 'They said she was unconscious by that point so I don't know if she'd have heard.'

'Even if she didn't, she'd have known it anyway,' Zara said. 'She'd have felt it.'

'I hope so. Because she was loved. So very loved by everyone she met.' I took another deep breath. *Nearly there.* 'They got her out of the car and the air ambulance took her to hospital, but her internal injuries were too great. She died on New Year's Day at 2.34 p.m. and I never got to say goodbye.' I paused and swiped at my wet cheeks. 'The year that followed was a blur. I knew I needed to be strong for Harrison, but I was so consumed with guilt. A million if onlys spun around my mind. If only I hadn't disappeared on that bender after Christmas, if only I hadn't let Parnell get to me, if only I'd answered her question with what was really in my heart.

'I managed to stay sober until the funeral but putting Harrison to bed that night, knowing we'd just cremated Eliza and he'd go through his whole life not knowing his mum, I poured myself a drink. And another. And another.'

'I can't even begin to imagine what you were going through then,' Zara said, dabbing her eyes with a scrunched-up tissue. 'Such a tragic loss. I'm so sorry, Snowy.'

'Eliza was cremated but Grandpa refused to let me scatter her ashes until I was properly sober but there was no way I could get sober when all I could think about was how I'd still have a wife and Harrison would have a mum if it wasn't for me.

'Grandpa and Ashley begged me to get help, but I told them it was too late. I was awful to Ash. I pushed him away again and again, refused to see him, ignored his calls, and eventually Grandpa had to tell him it was time to let it go because it was making Ashley ill. More guilt for me.'

'So how did you get sober?'

'I found a letter from Eliza. It was under the lining of one of the bags she'd taken with her when she spent those few days with her friend. I say letter but it was more like a three-part essay about our past, present and future. She'd listed all these happy memories from the friendship years and when we first got together, along with why they were so special to her. The second part was after my accident and, again, it was full of special moments that had still been there among the dark days including getting married and having Harrison. And, finally, she wrote about the future she imagined once I got sober because she wholeheartedly believed that it would happen.'

My voice cracked once more as I recalled sitting on the floor with my back against the bed, smiling, laughing and crying as I read through those pages. Her zest for life, her optimism and her love for me emanated from every word.

'It was like having one last conversation with her and it was exactly what I needed to get control back. I got a therapist, joined AA and, on New Year's Day a year after she died, I had my first day of sobriety.'

'I bet that was hard, especially being the anniversary.'

'I don't know how I managed it, but I knew I had to. Harrison was five and he needed a parent. A year after that, we scattered Eliza's ashes in the paddock and we go there on New Year's Day every year and say a few words at the exact time she left us. There's a bench on the tree line which Grandpa made. When we release the owls in the paddock, I imagine her flying with them as they do their laps, soaring free, healed at last.'

Zara grabbed another tissue and wiped her cheeks. 'That's beautiful.'

'So now you have the full story. I don't know what Parnell wrote – I don't want to – but he'll have sensationalised it. That's his style.'

'He seemed to really have it in for you.'

'Hated me from the moment he met me and it got worse in our teens. He had a thing for Eliza. I'd imagine her choosing me – *Freak Show* – over him was an ego-bruising and only added fuel to his hatred.'

We sat in silence for a few minutes.

'How do you feel now that you've shared that with me?' Zara asked.

'Lighter. And it's confirmed something for me too – that I haven't fully let go of the guilt and it's time I booked a few more sessions with my therapist to help me do that. So that's the truth in its painful, tragic colours. I'm sorry for making you cry.'

'I appreciate you being so honest with me.'

My eyes searched hers. 'You're still here,' I whispered.

'I was never going anywhere. Like I told you before I went to Scotland, there's nothing in your past that could have made me change my mind about you. Alcoholism's a disease and a mental health issue and I know –

just like Eliza did – that the person struggling with it wasn't the real you. The real you is right here right now.'

As she wrapped her arms round me and held me tightly, I felt the heavy weight of my past ebbing away and hope for a positive future seeping in.

* * *

Zara was quiet during tea and, as we settled onto the sofa afterwards, she could barely keep her eyes open. I suggested she put her head down for a bit in the spare bedroom.

'An hour or so should sort me out,' she said, settling under the duvet.

'Take as long as you need. You look exhausted.'

'I feel it. It's been a big day.'

Harrison and I peeked in on her when he went to bed a few hours later, but she didn't stir. I looked in again at eleven and she was still dead to the world so I left her to sleep.

* * *

'I can't believe I slept right through,' Zara said, joining me in the kitchen the following morning, dressed in a hoodie I'd left in her room. 'I set my alarm for an hour and I remember switching it off thinking I'd get up in a minute. Next thing I knew, it was morning.'

'You obviously needed the sleep,' I said, smiling at her. 'I'm meeting Fred in an hour. Grandpa's taking Harrison swimming because we don't want him to know about the gym unless I go for it. Would you like to come with me?'

'I'd love to. You don't mind?'

'There's a danger of me being a bit too nostalgic, so it would be good to get an objective viewpoint.'

We did a detour via Bumblebee Barn so Zara could change into some fresh clothes.

'That's Barney,' she said as we pulled into the farmyard.

A tall man wearing wellies and a boilersuit was hosing down a red quad bike, watched by two Border collies. He looked up and waved.

'Do you want to say hello?' Zara asked as we parked.

I instinctively pulled my beanie down over my ears.

'It's okay if you'd prefer to stay in the car,' she said, her voice full of reassurance. 'He'll understand, although Bear and Harley might not be so forgiving. They're such an attention-seeking pair of divas.'

The thought of a couple of farm dogs being divas relaxed me and I smiled at her. 'I'd love to meet him.'

'He's lovely,' she said. 'You'll be fine.'

My nerves weren't so much about meeting a stranger, but about meeting someone who was important to Zara. I didn't want to mess things up, but I needn't have worried. Barney came straight over, shook my hand and introduced me to the dogs. A black and white cat shot out from a large barn and made a beeline for Zara. I guessed it had to be Socks. Zara scooped him up and showered him with kisses. 'I've missed you,' she said, cradling him like a baby. The loud purrs from Socks confirmed the feeling was mutual.

She said I was welcome to join her in the farmhouse but I decided to challenge myself and stay with Barney. If I was going to buy Campion's and get involved in running the business, I'd need to get better at engaging with strangers and making small talk, so this was a practice opportunity.

'How big's the farm?' I asked as Zara headed off to the farmhouse with Socks.

Barney gave me an overview and asked me about Owl's Lodge. By the time Zara returned, I'd been invited back with Harrison to meet the animals and ride on the quad bikes.

'How did it go?' Zara asked as we set off down the farm track shortly after.

'Good. He's easy to talk to.'

'Yeah, he's great and so's Amber. I can't wait for you to meet her, but there's no pressure on you to meet any of my friends. We can take it slowly when you're ready. So, are you excited about a tour round your old gym?'

***

When Harrison had been for his first class on Monday – the first time I'd stepped inside Campion's in over a decade – I'd introduced him to Ashley then left them to it, conscious that I'd be looking around constantly if I stayed and potentially giving the game away. Today's tour was therefore my first time for a proper explore.

It was great to see Fred again although he completely threw me as, after I'd introduced Zara, he offered his condolences about Eliza. I stupidly hadn't been expecting that, although why wouldn't he say something? He'd been her coach in this very gym. He'd been there when she had her fall and he'd gone over and above trying to rebuild her confidence. Zara had evidently picked up on my discomfort as she told Fred that she'd been a gymnast when she was younger and how much she was enjoying rediscovering her skills. The deflection gave me the time I needed to compose myself.

Fred gave us a quick tour, talking about various upgrades he'd made over the years. He then sent us for a wander round on our own while he made drinks. It was really helpful doing that, opening doors and cupboards and knocking on walls. Zara jotted down several notes on her phone for areas that needed attention.

'So what's the verdict?' Fred asked when we were finished.

'It's great being back and I'm very interested, but I can't make a decision today.'

'Wouldn't expect you to.'

'I need to talk it over with my grandpa and look at some figures. I noticed some damp so, if I do make an offer, it wouldn't be the asking price.'

Fred nodded. 'Fully expecting that. I'll level with you, Snowy. You know what this gym means to me and my family and I don't want to sell it to the leisure chain because I don't want it to stop being about gymnastics. Their offer isn't good because they don't want the apparatus or the business, but it's the only one I've got and it's better than nothing, especially when I'm more than ready to retire. It would be a dream to sell it to you. I love the idea of you coming full circle, owning the place where it all started for you, so don't be shy with the offer. I'm open to suggestions and I know you'll be fair.'

We thanked him and said our goodbyes, with me reassuring him I'd be in touch as soon as I could.

'I've got a question,' Zara said as we pulled out of the car park. 'I love the full-circle thing and I can see how special this place was to you, but I need to play devil's advocate here. Why would you need to buy a gym when you already have an incredible gym on your own land with state-of-the-art apparatus?'

'Grandpa and I have talked it over, but it's not viable. It's too remote and there's not enough parking without taking some trees down, which is a deal breaker for me. I'd need to upgrade some apparatus, put in more toilets and install showers, which would need money and space. But the real biggie is there'd be no separation from home and work. This is our family home. I don't want to share it with the general public.'

'Completely understand.'

We arrived back at Owl's Lodge and, as Grandpa and Harrison weren't back yet, we went over to The Owlery first to check on my two newest patients – a short-eared owl and a little owl who'd both sustained leg injuries.

'They're so gorgeous,' Zara said. 'Will they be here long?'

'No. I should be able to release them next week.'

She perched on my desk looking around the room while I fed them.

'I love it in here,' she said. 'I love the woods, the lodge, the gym. It's got a good vibe – calm and happy.'

'It's been my sanctuary,' I replied, as I washed my hands.

'I can see why. I love how it's a place where owls come to heal but also where you've healed too – or started to, anyway. It's had the same effect on me. This place, you, your family...' She smiled and shook her head. 'Am I making any sense?'

'Perfect sense.' I cupped her chin and gently kissed her, warmth flowing through me.

'There's another reason why I don't want to turn the gym here into a business,' I said. 'I want it to remain somewhere special where my son did his first forward roll and discovered his love for gymnastics, where Eliza recovered her confidence, where you rediscovered the joy of trampolining.' I paused and took a deep breath, trying to quell my nerves. 'And where I started to fall in love with you.'

'You're falling in love with me?' she asked, her eyes shining.

'I am.'

'Was it the owl socks?'

I laughed. 'They're pretty special, but I can pinpoint the moment. It was when you were being the bear.'

'Living in and loving the moment,' she said, smiling at me.

'I'd forgotten how to do that until you arrived and now look at me. I've reconnected with Ashley and enrolled my son in the gym that I'm thinking of buying.'

'It's so amazing. Seeing as we're living in and loving the moment, I'm falling for you too. I've already told you the moment I realised that I was interested but, watching you with the owls just now, I've realised that the seeds were planted before then. Something happened to me the moment you stuffed Zorro up your jumper.' Her shoulders bounced with laughter. 'Honestly, Snowy, that was the most unexpected but loveliest thing I've seen in a long time.'

'In that case, you're just going to have to up your visits because there's plenty more where that came from.'

53

ZARA

Assured that Snowy was in a good place with better things to focus on than Elliot Parnell's stupid articles, my thoughts turned to work. I couldn't help feeling I should return to Scotland to support Amber, but I wasn't sure I could face that long journey again. Snowy and I returned to the lodge where I FaceTimed Amber to give her an update and make sure she really was okay with me not being around in person.

'Please don't even think about coming back,' she said, shaking her head at me. 'It'd be different if I was here for another fortnight, but I'm home on Saturday.'

'Okay, I'll stay here, but is there anything you need me to do because I reckon I only have a couple of days' work? And don't say relax because I'd feel like I was skiving.'

There was a pause. 'Not really, but I might have an idea. Leave it with me and I'll come back to you later.'

Eddie and Harrison returned in the meantime and had just finished telling me about their session at the swimming pool when Amber called back so I excused myself and settled into one of the high-backed chairs in the book nook.

'How would you feel about doing some work for Natasha this week?' she asked.

'I'd love to.' I adored Barney's mum and would be more than happy to help her out with anything she needed for her events planning business.

'Perfect. She'll meet you at the farm at ten in the morning and explain what's needed.'

'Can I visit your farm?' Harrison asked when I told them all I wasn't returning to Scotland and would be working for Barney's mum next week.

'It's my friend Barney's farm so it's up to him, but I think your dad might have already bagged you an invitation.'

Harrison looked up at Snowy, eyes wide.

'I do. We haven't sorted a date yet but Barney says we can go and meet the animals and have a go on his quad bikes.'

After a tough day for him yesterday, it was lovely seeing Harrison back on form, eager to know all about the farm animals and the pets at Bumblebee Barn and excited about riding a quad bike. I'd have a word with Barney when I got home and see if we could confirm a day for a visit next week.

* * *

'I'm so glad you can help me this week because I've had a bit of a shocker,' Natasha said when I met her at the farm the following morning. 'I've got a silver wedding party on Saturday and the function room roof has caved in after a leak.'

'Oh no! That's not good.'

'The manager says there's a room they haven't used in years which they could clear out and, with a bit of imagination, might be suitable so I need to check it out, but I have a stack of other urgent tasks...'

I was buzzing after Natasha left. I had such a varied week ahead of me with emails to send, a stocktake to complete, orders to place and themed items to source. I put my coat and boots on and headed across to Events Barn – the former milking barn where Natasha stored everything. I'd first seen it when we were filming *Love on the Farm* and there was a group activity for Barney and his three potential matches to paint a horse-drawn cart in Christmas colours. I'd been really impressed with the way everything was divided into bays, organised by theme or occasion, and had longed to explore further.

The small stock items which I needed to count were spread across a couple of bays fitted out with strong metal racking, kept in labelled crates or boxes. Although the shelves were tidy, there was an area where surplus items had been dumped so I returned them to their rightful homes before I could commence the stocktake. All the while, I was watched by Socks, Radley and Pumpkin.

I wasn't seeing Snowy tonight as he was taking Harrison for his second gymnastics session. I wouldn't see him tomorrow night either as Natasha had asked me to help her with an evening event. I knew it was good to have some time apart after an intense weekend, but I missed him so badly already.

'Just as well I don't have to return to Scotland,' I told the cats. 'Although I will be away again later in the month. Not sure how I feel about that.'

I recalled returning from Northumberland just before Christmas when Amber had observed that our trip had felt so much longer than a fortnight. My response had been, *It's since you met Barney. You've got someone to rush home to now.* That was going to be me from now on, longing to return from our travels. I was convinced more than ever that Amber wouldn't want to continue after we'd wrapped *The Wildlife Rescuers* and I was fairly sure I wouldn't want to either. I wasn't even sure I wanted to wait that long. When Amber returned, we needed a talk about the future.

* * *

Barney proposed Wednesday for Snowy and Harrison's tour of the farm and suggested that Harrison might like to spend a full day with him as his apprentice. When they came across on Wednesday morning – the first time I'd seen Snowy since Sunday – it took a heck of a lot of restraint not to throw myself at him. While I helped Harrison into a boiler suit and wellies, Barney had a quick word with Snowy. I already knew what he was going to suggest – that the three of them spent the first hour or so together and, if that went well, Snowy could leave Harrison with Barney for the rest of the morning. Having watched how Harrison reacted to Bear and Harley and the additional excitement when he was shown the quad bikes, I didn't think there'd be any issues at all.

Sure enough, I was in Events Barn when Snowy joined me an hour later.

'They don't want me anymore,' he said, pretending to look dejected.

'Oh no!' I said in mock horror. 'If only there was someone nearby who did want you.'

He pulled me into his arms and kissed me with a passion that left me breathless.

'Where did that come from?' I said, when he released me.

'I missed you.'

'I missed you too, although I think we should spend more time apart if that's the quality of your welcome back kisses.'

He laughed. 'I'd better give you another one then.'

After another mind-blowing kiss, I took him over to the farmhouse to make us some drinks.

'Have you made a decision about Campion's?' I asked as we settled side by side at the kitchen table.

'Decision to go for it not only made but also executed,' he said, eyes shining. 'You're looking at the new owner, subject to paperwork. That circle is complete.'

'Oh, Snowy, I'm so pleased for you. Have you told Harrison?'

'Not yet. It's only right that Ashley knows first, especially as I want him to be the head coach and manager.'

'What's your role going to be?'

'Silent owner at first,' he said. 'I'd ultimately love a more hands-on role, but it would be too much to do that from the start. I've spent nearly thirteen years retreating from the world and the past five barely interacting with anyone. I need to be sensible about what I can do and how quickly I can do it.'

'I'm so proud of you,' I said, cupping his face and gently kissing him. 'What you're doing is amazing. So much strength and courage. You've bought a gym.'

'I know! Can you believe it?'

'Actually, I can, and I think it's going to be the making of you.'

He evidently liked me saying that because he gave me another one of his epic kisses. That man knew what he was doing. But as I melted into him, I realised that it wasn't just him being a good kisser. It was about me and how I felt about him. I'd liked Declan and previous boyfriends a lot but I'd never been in love. I'd felt lust, desire, passion but never that deep and meaningful connection and, boy, was it a game-changer.

54

SNOWY

The short-eared owl – who Harrison had named Velma after the *Scooby Doo* character – was ready for release on Saturday. As Zara was keen to continue her owl education, this was the ideal chance for her to get hands-on. I explained how to safely transfer Velma into the carry crate and watched as she executed the transfer perfectly, ready to step in if the owl got spooked.

'She's lighter than I expected,' Zara said as she closed the crate.

'They've got a long wing span which makes them look bigger than they really are.'

Grandpa and Harrison were waiting for us in the paddock. When I opened the crate, Velma's feathered ear tufts were up, indicating her wariness.

'She's not sure, is she?' Zara whispered. 'Gosh, I love her eyes.'

They were yellow but with large black pupils and a black rim. I started to say that she looked like she had eyeliner on, like Zara, but she made the same observation at the same time, making us both laugh.

'Oh, she's going!' I said, as Velma took off. She flew round the edge of the paddock once in a clockwise direction.

'Look where she's stopped,' Grandpa said, handing me his pair of binoculars.

I smiled and nodded. 'That feels apt.'

I passed the binoculars to Zara and pointed to the top of the field so that she knew where to look and Harrison could adjust his.

'Is that Eliza's bench?' Zara asked.

'It is!' Harrison cried. 'Mum's bench.'

Zara handed them back to me and I took another look. I swear Velma stared straight at me and held my gaze for several seconds before spreading her wings and taking off once more, disappearing over the neighbouring field.

Zara squeezed my hand, as though understanding that I needed a moment. We'd talked about Eliza a lot over the past few evenings and her attitude was beyond touching.

'Eliza will always be a part of your life,' she'd said, 'and you're always going to love her. I know that doesn't diminish how you feel about me now or in the future because it's not the same thing. So any time you want to talk about her or have a moment on your own to think about your life with her, just be honest with me. I'll get it.'

And she'd just proved it once more by handing me back the binoculars and giving me that space.

We hadn't needed to tell Grandpa about us. It had been obvious to him after her dash down from Scotland that something had shifted and he'd been delighted. All three of us agreed that we'd give Harrison a bit longer. He clearly adored Zara and welcomed her presence but there was so much going on at the moment that it didn't feel right to throw something else into the mix. There was already the excitement of him starting gymnastics and me buying the gym (serious cool-dad points there) but we'd had a couple more moments of upset and confusion as he came to terms with everything Parnell's article had opened up. We'd tell him about us but, for now, Zara was 'just a friend'.

* * *

Even though it was the second week in February, it wasn't particularly cold and there was no breeze so Grandpa suggested we light the fire pit in front of the lodge after tea and toast some marshmallows. Harrison gave a whoop and sped off to find the long sticks.

'This is so special,' Zara said, turning her stick above the flames. 'Would you believe, I've never done this before?'

'Never?' Harrison asked. 'It's the best.'

'I can't wait to eat it,' she said. 'And it's so beautiful out here. You're so lucky to have this.'

'You'll be able to do this all the time when you move in,' Harrison said.

'What?' I cried. 'Who said... what?'

'Zara's your girlfriend, isn't she? So she'll move in and you'll get married and I'll have a brother or sister.'

I glanced at Zara, worried that she might panic at Harrison having us married and expecting, but she was doubled up laughing, as was Grandpa.

'Did you say something?' I asked Grandpa.

'Dad!' Harrison cried. 'I'm nearly ten. I'm not stupid.'

I shrugged. Seemed we didn't need to find the right timing after all. 'Yes, Zara's my girlfriend,' I said. 'As for the rest of it...' I wasn't sure how to end that sentence because, while we hadn't talked about that far into the future, it didn't scare me. It felt right.

'One step at a time for us, Harrison,' Zara said, smiling at him. 'Just living in and loving the moments right now.' But the adoring look she gave me told me she was thinking about the future too.

55

ZARA

I stayed over at Owl's Lodge on Saturday night, keen to give Barney and Amber some alone time after nearly a fortnight apart. As I kissed Snowy goodnight, my mind wandered into what it would be like to spend the night in his bedroom instead of the spare one but we'd agreed that we didn't want to rush that side of things. I suspected that wouldn't stay the case for long.

The next morning, I returned to Bumblebee Barn. Amber and I had spoken briefly across the week but this was a chance for a proper catch-up.

'It's so good to see you so happy,' Amber said after I'd updated her on the past week, including Snowy's big decision to buy Campion's. 'I can't wait to meet the man who's captured your heart. Barney thinks he's amazing. I can't believe he met him before me!'

'We'll sort something out soon so you can give him your seal of approval.'

'Good! I really missed you this past week. It was ridiculously quiet without you in the evenings, so I found myself doing lots of thinking.' Her smile faded. 'There's something I need to talk to you about, but it's... it's not easy to say.'

'Go on,' I encouraged when she faltered, biting her lip. I was pretty sure I knew where this was heading and could soon reassure her we were both on the same page.

'We've got the rest of this year and the start of next mapped out with *Countryside Calendar* and *The Wildlife Rescuers* and I'm excited about our plans and the places we'll be visiting, but being away from Barney and the farm is getting harder and harder. I love my job, but the truth is I love my life here more, so I've made a big decision. I don't want to continue beyond *The Wildlife Rescuers*. But if I step down, that means—'

'I'll be out of work too,' I finished for her.

'I'm so sorry, Zara.' Her eyes sparkled with unshed tears and I knew how much it was hurting her, thinking she might be hurting me.

'I'll be fine,' I assured her. 'Don't worry about me.'

'I can't help it. It feels so unfair that what I want affects you so much. Matt and I had dinner together last week and we got talking about the future. When I told him I'm ready to step back he said he'd employ you in a heartbeat. Could you see yourself working for Matt instead of me?'

'That's really flattering,' I said, giving her a grateful smile. 'Matt's great and he'd be easy to work for, but I've been doing lots of thinking this week too and I've reached the same conclusion as you. This job – whether working for you or for Matt – requires long stints away from Snowy and his family and I don't want that. Even before I met him, I was feeling ready to settle in the area, and now that's stronger than ever. So it really is fine. Stepping back is the right decision for you and Barney, but it's also the right decision for me.'

Amber clapped her hand to her heart. 'I'm so relieved to hear you say that. I felt awful about letting you down.'

'You're not letting me down and it's not like it's come out of nowhere. You and Barney want a family so change was always on the cards.'

'Any idea what you'd do instead?' Amber asked.

'I'm not sure yet. I've really enjoyed working with Natasha this week, so if she could use me more... What are you grinning at?'

'You saying that. I might have a solution. Natasha was super impressed with you this week. Her business is expanding and she *does* need more help, although only part-time initially. However, she and Barney have been talking for ages about organising school visits for the farm, running a petting zoo and setting up a farm shop. Between them, they've struggled for time to progress anything, but if they had an extra pair of hands...'

'You think they could have a job for me?' I asked, my heart pounding with excitement. I'd loved working with Natasha and my mind had been bursting with ideas, but I hadn't wanted to overstep the mark by blurting them all out. If there were some projects to run alongside the admin work, it would be a dream job, playing to the strengths I used working for Amber, but without the travel.

Amber smiled. 'Let me talk to her and Barney, but I'm fairly sure they'd love to have you.'

I knew that Amber couldn't promise anything as it wasn't her decision to make, but I couldn't imagine Natasha and Barney not going for it. What a gift it would be to live at Owl's Lodge and work at Bumblebee Barn. I smiled to myself. Living at Owl's Lodge? That was Harrison's fault when he'd called out our relationship round the fire pit. It was too soon at the moment, but I could definitely see it happening, along with everything else Harrison had said. My Christmas wish had been to get over Joel and find someone decent, but I'd never dared to imagine all of this too.

56

SNOWY

It was Valentine's Day the following Friday. I was conscious that, after nearly three weeks together, Zara and I hadn't been on a proper date – we couldn't exactly call the pub meal in Lincoln a date when Harrison had been with us. I could cope with a quiet pub but I wasn't ready for a crowded restaurant, surrounded by people drinking, and there was no chance anywhere would be quiet on a Valentine's evening. Zara said staying in didn't bother her, but she deserved something more special.

The temperature had dropped and it was too cold to sit on the veranda and it was hardly romantic anyway with Grandpa and Harrison on the other side of the glass. But I had come up with something.

'I've got you a Valentine's gift,' Grandpa said, giving Zara a welcome kiss on each cheek when she came over that evening. He passed her a cardboard envelope and she removed the contents, a smile lighting her face.

'You finished it! It's beautiful.'

He'd completed his pencil drawing of Zorro and, I have to say, he'd excelled himself. Zara hugged him tightly, thanking him profusely.

'I enjoyed it,' he said. 'Handsome owl, that one.'

Harrison wanted to show her his progress with his scrapbook. The rolls of washi tape Zara had ordered online had arrived earlier in the week so he'd been in his element sticking everything in.

'Harrison and I have got something for your scrapbook too,' I told Zara, handing her a certificate we'd created on the computer for an *Owl Level 1, Certificate of Knowledge – The Tawny Owl*.

'This is amazing!' she cried. 'Thank you both so much. This and my picture of Zorro will be getting a page each in my precious pages tomorrow.'

'Zara and I have somewhere special to go,' I said, picking up her coat and helping her back into it. 'So we'll both say goodnight and I'll see you tomorrow.'

After hugs all round, Zara and I left.

'We're going out?' she asked as I guided her towards my car. 'But I thought…'

'We're going out, but we're staying in too,' I said, mysteriously. 'All will be revealed.'

'Hedgehog Hollow?' Zara said as we pulled onto the farm track a little later. 'Plot twist.'

I laughed. 'I'm not saying anything.'

We stopped in the farmyard and I took her hand as I guided her round to the holiday cottages, pausing by the smallest one, Meadow View. A wreath of pink roses in the shape of a heart hung from the door.

Inside, Samantha and Natasha had done an incredible job of creating a restaurant ambience without the restaurant. Romantic music played softly, flameless candles flickered in the gentle lamplight, and the table for two was beautifully decorated with a white rose across each place setting. A bottle of sparkling fruit juice was chilling in a bucket of ice and the beef stroganoff in the slow cooker smelled divine.

'Going out, but staying in too,' Zara whispered, looking round the room with a smile.

'Is it okay?'

'It's better than okay. I can't believe you went to all this effort.'

'It was Samantha and Natasha really, but my brief so—'

'Shut up and take the credit,' she joked, pressing her lips against mine.

I handed her a card.

'You made this?' she asked, waving it at me. 'As in you drew this?'

'Yes, with the help of a stack of online tutorials.'

I'd recreated a cartoon version of the bear bouncing on the trampoline GIF with #BeTheBear beneath it. Inside, I'd written:

Living in and loving every moment now that you're by my side.

'It's perfect. But do you know what's really funny?'

She handed me a card which I opened, laughing. It showed Winnie the Pooh and Tigger bouncing on a trampoline and she'd added the same hashtag as me underneath.

We settled at the table for our meal. The stroganoff, accompanied by rice which had been staying warm in a rice cooker, was delicious. Natasha was an exceptional chef.

'Until tonight, my most memorable Valentine's Day was being dumped,' Zara said, placing her cutlery down on her plate when she'd finished eating. 'The bar wasn't high but it's right up here now after this.' She raised her hand high above her head. 'I reckon going out but staying in is the new going out.'

'Pressure's on for next year,' I said.

'I've got a birthday first. Thirteenth of April. Just saying.'

We moved onto the sofa, deciding on a break before the cheesecake dessert in the fridge.

'I had a visitor this afternoon,' I told her. 'Mike Sunning dropped by.'

'Your contact at the police station? Everything okay?'

'He was off duty so it was an off-the-record visit but he thought I might be interested in hearing that a certain Elliot Parnell was about to have a taste of his own medicine. I don't know whether it'll make the national news but the local papers will be reporting that their friendly local investigative journalist isn't so friendly after all. He's been done for stalking and harassing three different women.'

'Oh, my God! What a piece of work!'

'I don't know any details and I feel sick for the women involved, but he's going to spend some time at His Majesty's Pleasure and, frankly, it couldn't have happened to a nicer person.'

'He won't be pestering you again.'

'No. No more *Come on, mate, I only want to tell your side of the story*. As if he was ever interested in that.'

Zara adjusted position so she could fully face me. 'Have you ever thought about doing that? Telling your side of the story, but in a book rather than to a journalist. Maybe not yet, but down the line – how you came full circle and saved the gym. Your story's inspiring. It might help people and it might be cathartic for you to write it.'

'A book?' I mulled it over. 'I'm not sure about that, but there is this podcast I listen to – *CLASS*. It stands for "Creating a Life After Sporting Success" and the researcher once contacted me about being a guest. I didn't respond. I didn't think I had anything to offer.'

'Snowy, you have *everything* to offer. I know you're still on a journey and there'll still be bumps ahead, but you'd be perfect for a podcast like that.'

I thought about all the episodes I'd listened to and how inspiring I'd found them. Now I'd finally taken that inspiration and channelled it into something.

'I'll email the researcher tomorrow and sound them out,' I said.

'You don't have to commit if it doesn't feel right for you. They're your steps at your pace and I'll be cheering you on every step of the way.'

As we cuddled up on the sofa, I marvelled again at the positive impact Zara had had on my life – on all our lives – in so little time and the way she wasn't pushy about anything. My steps, my pace. I loved that. Could I see myself writing a book one day? My full story wasn't ready to be told yet because it was still a work in progress and, even though things were going swimmingly right now, Zara was right about those bumps in the road. Running a business, being back in the world I'd fled from, being surrounded by people – these were all huge things for me and any one of them could knock me off course.

If I did ever get to that point where I felt stable enough to tell my story, the reality was that it wasn't just *my* story – it was Harrison's too. Did I want to immortalise our history in a book? Harrison needed a say in that and he wouldn't be ready to do that until he was further into his own story. If he wanted it out there, maybe it would be when he'd secured his gold or whatever else he achieved, depending where his journey took him. It might not be the Olympics. It might not even be gymnastics. The difference between Dad and me was that I only wanted Olympic success for my son for as long as he wanted it for himself. I had no void I needed to fill. I went for an Olympic medal and came back with two. I'd already won. And with Grandpa, Harrison and now Zara in my life, I'd just won gold.

57

SNOWY

Seven weeks later

I drove into the car park on Sunday afternoon, pulled into the space where Fred used to park and twisted round to face Harrison in the back seat.

'Are you ready for your party?' I asked him.

'I'm so excited!'

Harrison had settled into Ashley's gymnastics class with ease and made friends so quickly that I'd agreed to him having a birthday party, confident that he'd now have a decent guest list. I wasn't ready to open up our home to a load of people I didn't know but, with the purchase of Campion's completed three weeks ago, we had an alternative venue.

He'd actually turned ten on Wednesday so we'd had a birthday cake at home then. Today, he was expecting a trampoline party and I couldn't wait for his reaction when he saw what was inside.

'The sign looks awesome, Dad,' Harrison cried as we got out the car.

I still couldn't quite believe I owned my old gym and seeing 'Snowy's Gymnastics Club' emblazoned across the side and above the door – freshly installed yesterday – was so surreal. I wondered how long it would be before I stopped referring to it as Campion's.

Ashley had been flattered by my job offer but said he couldn't accept it until we cleared the air properly because he'd hate anything unsaid to build up and bubble over at some point in the future. That made sense as I was aware that we'd only scraped the surface during our original coffee catch-up. We had a lengthy honest but difficult conversation about everything that had happened and I was mortified to discover that, a month after Eliza died, Kendra had had the first of two miscarriages. Ashley hadn't got the strength to keep fighting for me when they were experiencing their own tragedy and he was on the brink of a breakdown so, when Grandpa asked him to stop calling, he didn't argue. They now had two boys under three, both of whom were showing an early aptitude for gymnastics. I felt terrible that I hadn't even known Kendra was pregnant, let alone that they'd gone through such a tough time. Ash felt like he'd failed me, but I wouldn't hear of it. I was the one who'd made the bad decisions back then and he'd stuck around way longer than most would have done when treated so badly.

I cried when he stopped by Owl's Lodge a couple of days later to say that he felt so much better for offloading all the hurt and for seeing how much progress I'd made so, if the offer was still on the table, he'd love to accept it. Kendra was officially on maternity leave but, if I had a vacancy for a coach from September, she'd be delighted to have her old job back too. It felt so good to have my best mate back in my life.

'I want you to close your eyes when we go inside,' I told Harrison. 'Zara will get the door for us.'

He closed his eyes and shuffled forward cautiously until we were fully inside the gym.

'Open them!' I declared.

His jaw dropped open as he looked round in wonder, lost for words for once. I'd arranged for Natasha to bring the giant inflatables for the kids to play on, although we'd still be using the trampolines.

'They're the ones my friend Phoebe had at her party,' Zara said. 'You're going to have so much fun.'

Harrison hugged me, Zara and Grandpa before rushing over to Natasha. Grandpa followed him and Natasha took them on a tour round the different items.

'Half an hour to go,' Zara said. 'How are you feeling?'

'So nervous. I keep telling myself they're all here for Harrison and it's not about me, but it doesn't do much to calm me.'

She put her arms around me and held me tightly. 'Just do what you can and don't put yourself under any unnecessary pressure. Harrison will have an amazing time whether you're here for five minutes or the full thing.'

I took a deep, calming breath as she released me.

'I'm going to see if Natasha needs any help. Will you be okay?'

'I'll be fine. I'll go into the office and check my emails.'

The office had a couple of knackered old desks, four threadbare chairs and a row of battered filing cabinets. It needed a major overhaul but it wasn't a priority for now. Feeling hot and shaky as I sank down on one of the chairs, I pulled my hat off and gulped down a bottle of water before scrolling through my phone. My heart leapt as I spotted an email from the *CLASS* podcast researcher. I'd had an acknowledgement from them several weeks back but then it went quiet so I'd assumed they'd changed their mind about featuring me. This email said that Brent and Kimberley loved my story, they definitely wanted me on the show and that they were booking up for June and July if I wanted to pick a date. I replied immediately, picking the first date they had available – less time to fret about it.

'Cars have started arriving,' Zara said, poking her head round the door a little later. 'Are you ready?'

I stood up, grabbed my beanie and pulled it on.

'You've got this,' Zara said, smiling warmly.

And, at that moment, I felt like I had. I slid my beanie off my head and tossed it onto the desk.

Zara's eyes widened.

'I need to stop hiding under my hat. My name's on the building. They all know who I am. And if I'm going to share my story with thousands of listeners on the *CLASS* podcast in June, I need to be prepared for a few whispers and curious glances.'

'They've confirmed you for the podcast? That's brilliant, Snowy. I'm so proud of you.'

I took another deep breath and followed Zara into the gym where several children were greeting Harrison and handing over gifts. No matter how uncomfortable I felt today, it wasn't about me. This was about my son and I could do it for him.

58

ZARA

One week later

Snowy amazed me every day and I'd never felt more proud of him than at Harrison's birthday party last weekend. I knew how hard it was for him, but he'd only taken one time out while the kids were eating and who could blame him for that? I'd wanted to escape from the noise and mess myself!

I think it helped that most parents hadn't stayed and, those who had, he already knew, like his next-door neighbour, who'd brought her grandkids with it being the start of the Easter holidays, and Phoebe and Joel, who'd brought Darcie and Imogen respectively after Harrison had made friends with them during visits to Bumblebee Barn.

Across the past couple of months, Snowy had met all of my friends, starting with Amber, and they all adored him. I'd been slightly apprehensive about introducing him to Joel, with him knowing the two of us had kissed, but the pair of them hit it off immediately.

The only people he hadn't met were my family. We hadn't been able to coordinate a good time around Mum's shifts and Snowy's commitments to building works at the gym, so I'd been down to Lincolnshire a few times on my own. It was my birthday today and they were visiting

Owl's Lodge this afternoon. I had no worries about Owen, but I hoped Mum was on her best behaviour. She'd already made comments about our relationship moving fast after I told her I stayed at Owl's Lodge several nights a week. When I'd shared the plans I'd agreed with Amber, Barney and Natasha to have a phased handover across the next twelve months, continuing my work on *The Wildlife Rescuers* including the travel to the other rescue centres being filmed, but working on *Countryside Calendar* from home while Amber used an intern for the onsite responsibilities, Mum had proffered an unwelcome opinion – *but you're throwing away your career in television*. I hadn't appreciated the comment, but I'd let it go as I knew she was under immense stress with the Roman situation.

Early last month, Mum had insisted on accompanying my brother to hospital for a check-up and the consultant had confirmed that he wouldn't play professional football again. She told me that Roman had been in denial so she'd asked the consultant to repeat the prognosis several times to make sure it went in. Roman's reaction to that was to go on a massive bender. He got into another fight, although not with a famous boy band member this time, and without an arrest.

A couple of weeks ago, wishing to be more supportive to Mum, I'd joined her when she visited Roman. She'd warned me that I wouldn't recognise him, but it was still a shock seeing my immaculately groomed cocky brother looking so dishevelled as he stared silently at the television, stony-faced, drinking. Snowy had told me I could share his story if I thought it would help and had even offered to talk to Roman himself, but he wasn't interested. *I'm not an alcoholic so why would I want to be lectured by an alcoholic failed gymnast?* It was the most he said for the hour we were there.

When I spoke to Mum a few days ago, she'd shared that there was a small chink of light. Amy had reached out to Roman after his fight with Kai Casper. She'd admitted she still loved him but wasn't willing to consider trying again while he was in self-destruct mode because there was no way it would work. But she'd given him her friendship and support and we all hoped it would be enough. If anyone could get through to him, it was Amy. Despite all the crap he'd put her through, he'd never stopped loving her either so maybe they could have a second chance. It wouldn't be quick or easy, but I wanted to believe it could happen.

* * *

'They're here,' I said to Snowy as I spotted Owen's car approaching the lodge shortly after two. Eddie had taken Harrison over to his workshop so that the moment Snowy met Mum and Owen wouldn't be overwhelmed by introductions.

'You look nervous,' Snowy said.

'I feel it. My mum can be...' I shook my head. 'You know. I've told you already.'

He cuddled me to his side. 'Whatever she says, I'm here for you and so are Harrison and Grandpa. Owen's not your only cheerleader anymore. You've got a squad now. Give me a Z! Give me an A...!'

I gave him a playful shove as he pretended to wave pompoms in the air, and stepped onto the veranda to welcome them.

'Happy birthday!' Mum and Owen called as I waved down to them.

'This place is stunning,' Mum said, gazing round her while Owen removed some gift bags from the boot. 'I can see why you love it so much.'

They ran up the steps and both hugged me before following me into the lodge. With Mum not being a hugger, I expected her to smile at Snowy or perhaps even shake his hand, but she put her arms out and hugged him too.

'I'm so sorry we haven't met sooner,' she said. 'Life's a bit complicated at the moment.'

'It's okay. I understand. Great to meet you both at last.'

The two men hugged and I sank down onto the sofa, relieved that the introductions had gone well. Snowy made drinks and Eddie returned with Harrison just as we were finishing them.

'Do you want to see my treehouses?' Harrison asked after we'd done another round of introductions.

'You have more than one treehouse?' Mum asked.

'I've got two and lots of dens.'

I'd expected Mum to say no but she stood up. 'I loved building dens when I was your age, but I never had a treehouse. Let's go on a tour, then.'

So we all went on a tour round the grounds, culminating with going into the gym.

'This takes me back,' Owen said, gazing round the apparatus. He pointed to the uneven bars. 'That was your favourite, wasn't it?'

'Yes.'

'And the trampoline.' He pressed his fingers to his lips. 'I can picture you – my little Tigger – bouncing on there as though it was just yesterday.'

I slipped my arm round his waist and cuddled into his side. 'Still your little Tigger and still bouncing most days thanks to Snowy.'

'Would you like to see my routine?' Harrison asked.

He'd expanded Eliza's original routine with several flips and twists and astonished me with his skill and fearlessness. Mum and Owen were clearly impressed too, giving him a huge round of applause.

'I'd love to see you on the trampoline again,' Owen said. 'Will you?'

'Okay, but I'm not at Harrison's level.'

I'd been working on a short routine with Snowy so I slipped off my trainers but, as I handed my jewellery to Snowy, panic gripped me. Last time Mum saw me in the gym was the time I messed it all up. The words she'd said to Dad flooded into my mind. *She's not like her brother. I haven't seen any evidence of the talent her coach spoke about. She's not good enough.*

'Don't talk yourself out of it,' Snowy said, fixing his eyes on mine. 'You've done this loads of times and you're brilliant at it. Forget anyone's watching. Be Tigger. Be the bear.'

He kissed me on the tip of my nose – such a tender gesture – and I scrambled onto the trampoline, feeling strong from his belief in me.

I didn't mess up, grinning widely as I landed the routine to whoops and cheers. I glanced at Owen, who looked like he might burst with pride, wiping tears away between claps. Then I glanced at Mum and she was clapping and cheering too.

'That was amazing,' she cried. 'I can't believe you can do all that after such a long break.'

Snowy hugged me as soon as I'd lowered myself to the floor. 'Uneven bars?' he whispered.

'I'm not sure.' Snowy was an exceptional coach who, as well as teaching me loads, had given me the confidence to build up a short routine on the bars.

'You've always regretted falling apart in front of your mum and this is the perfect chance to show her that you are talented. If it doesn't go well, she'll understand because you're learning, but I don't think it will go wrong. I think this is your moment. And if not now, when?'

He was so right. I'd gone back and forth as to whether to tell Mum that I'd overheard the conversation she'd had with Dad. She already knew from her visit after New Year how much she'd hurt me so did I need to keep rubbing salt in the wound? Our relationship had improved immeasurably so I'd decided I was happy to draw a line in the sand and leave the past in the past. Even so, it had still niggled that her opinion of me was that I hadn't been a talented gymnast. It was one thing doing a simple routine on the trampoline, but the uneven bars were a different beast. My nemesis. And there would never be a more perfect opportunity to prove to Mum that my brother wasn't the only one with a gift. Perhaps I did need to show her that so that I could fully close the door on the past.

'Okay. I'll get changed and do it.'

'Zara's going to show you something else that she's been working on,' Snowy said to Mum and Owen. 'We've only been working on this for a month, but what she's achieved in that short space of time shows what an amazing gift she has.'

I smiled to myself as I grabbed a leotard from the spare kit locker and headed to the toilet to change. Snowy's words were chosen carefully and conveyed with such enthusiasm that I doubted Mum would have any idea they were directed at her.

After several more words of encouragement from Snowy, I chalked my hands and took a deep breath as I paused beneath the bars. *All you have to do is fly!*

And fly I did, releasing a squeal of delight as I dismounted into the foam pit after completing my routine better than ever before.

'Yes!' Snowy cried, rushing over to me and swinging me round in a circle once I was free from the pit. 'That was incredible!'

As soon as he put me down, Mum rushed at me.

'I'm sorry I didn't believe in you,' she said, clinging on tightly.

She released me and took both my hands in hers. 'You did have talent. You *do* have talent. I'm so proud of you.'

I'd waited years to hear those words and had expected to feel different, but nothing shifted inside me. The hurt from that overheard conversation didn't miraculously disappear and I realised that it didn't really matter whether Mum was proud of my gymnastic ability or not because I was proud of it. I had nothing to prove except to myself.

'And I don't just mean about what you've shown us here,' Mum added. 'I mean I'm proud of everything – how you've been there for me these past few months, how you've been trying to help your brother after everything he's done to you, for the life you've created here, and for everything you've done with your career. You know who you are, what you want, and you've made it happen. I'm so impressed with you.'

Those words really did mean the world to me because they were about the woman I was now rather than the child I used to be. I hadn't opened up my presents yet but, whatever was in those gift bags, it wouldn't match the amazing birthday gift Mum had just given me. After a lifetime of feeling inferior and invisible, my mum finally saw me.

* * *

Mum and Owen stayed for tea, then drove back to Lincolnshire. Snowy suggested we light the fire pit and finish my birthday in style with toasted marshmallows. Although I loved listening to the sounds of nature, it was my birthday so music was called for and I pulled up a playlist of uplifting songs on my phone.

As the sky changed from blue to orange and yellow, Eddie and Harrison headed back inside, leaving Snowy and me to cuddle together beside the fire and enjoy the sunset. I pointed at a barn owl passing overhead in silent flight, thrilled to see it on such a special day.

'Good birthday?' Snowy asked.

'The best. Thank you for everything – for being wonderful with my parents, for encouraging me on the bars, for that amazing cake and, most importantly, for being you.'

He kissed me, his hands running across my face and through my hair, taking my breath away. Every day, I fell more deeply in love with him and I felt it back in return. I'd never expected this to happen to me and it was amazing to think that I had an owl to thank for it.

'I've been thinking,' he said. 'When you asked me why I didn't run the gym here as a business, one of the reasons I gave was to separate work and home. It strikes me that, now that you're working part-time at Bumblebee Barn, you don't have that work and home separation, so I was wondering how you'd feel about making Owl's Lodge your permanent home instead.'

My heart leapt. 'You want me to move in?'

'I'd love you to. Do you want to?'

'Does the invitation extend to Socks? Assuming Barney is happy for me to steal him?'

'Of course. Socks is more than welcome here.'

'In that case, yes! I love this place and I love you. Yes, yes, yes!'

I flung my arms round him and hugged him. Michael Bublé's version of 'Feeling Good' started playing and as he crooned about a new dawn, day and life making him feel good, it struck me that it could be our song. This year had brought a new dawn for us both. We'd helped each other to face up to the past and were looking forward to embracing the future together. And it really did feel good.

AUTHOR'S NOTE
THE 'NEXT' OLYMPIC GAMES

Although this book was released in 2024, it's set in 2025. Part of this story involves the Olympic Games and, although my characters are fictional, I can't fictionalise the venues and years of the Olympic Games.

The 2024 Olympic Games are in Paris and the 2028 Games are in Los Angeles. For anyone reading this story around its release in May 2024, Paris 2024 will be the next Olympics for you. However, because this book is set in 2025, Los Angeles 2028 is the next Olympic Games as far as my characters are concerned.

Thank you xx

ACKNOWLEDGEMENTS

I hope you've enjoyed your second visit to Bumblebee Barn in the Yorkshire Wolds, catching up with a few friends from the first book and finding some new friends... and lots of owls!

I love owls and built up quite a collection of owl merch while I was a Brown Owl for a local pack of twenty-four Brownies for seven and a half years. It was always my intention to write a story one day which heavily featured owls and, as I was writing *Healing Hearts at Bumblebee Barn*, I could see potential for a sequel where I could do exactly that. But that story was meant as a standalone and we had no idea how readers would respond to it after so much disappointment expressed at me ending the Hedgehog Hollow series. Thankfully readers loved it and asked for more, so *A New Dawn at Owl's Lodge* was my opportunity to tell my owl story and there'll be one more tale out next year featuring Joel and his search for his happy ever after.

I knew straight off that Zara would be the main character in this second book and she'd encounter an aloof reclusive owl rescuer called Snowy but I wasn't sure what his story was. I'm a huge fan of the ITV show *Dancing on Ice* and have watched every series. In 2023, Olympic gymnast Nile Wilson was crowned deserved champion. During the show, he shared some of his mental health battles when an injury meant he could no longer compete and I knew then that Snowy would be an Olympian who'd had his career cut short. His story isn't Nile's but I have taken aspects of Nile's experiences in both Snowy's and Roman's stories. For more information on Nile's journey, you can find his documentary on mental health and addiction in pro sport – *The Silent Battle* – on YouTube.

Which brings me onto gymnastics. I knew nothing about the world of gymnastics or the Olympics (sport of any sort really isn't my thing!) but I know somebody who does. Huge thanks to author and blogger Karen Louise Hollis for sharing her extensive knowledge with me through copious messages, emails and even a video call. I'm so very grateful. If there are any gymnasts reading this, please bear in mind that this is a work of fiction rather than a technical guide to the sport, so I might have made some adjustments to language or simplified certain aspects in order to make this a story that can be universally understood and which flows. As an extra thank you, Socks was named after Karen's cat. Thanks also to my brother Chris for his knowledge on talent academies and my husband Mark for answering lots of questions about football divisions.

Onto owls, which I did know something about, it has been a pleasure to learn so much more about these beautiful birds. If you're curious, I highly recommend Wild Owl TV on YouTube with owl conservationist Ian McGuire. His videos about each of the five owls native to England had me captivated. If barn owls particularly appeal, I recommend a stunning book called *The Book of the Barn Owl* by Sally Coulthard. Thanks to Ann Day from Wolds Hedgehog Rescue (the 'real' Hedgehog Hollow) for talking me through the process needed for rescuing the hedgehog admitted in the bucket.

I often turn to my Facebook group, Redland's Readers (do come and join us!), when I need inspiration. I was struggling for a name for Snowy's son and would like to thank Hayley Whittlesey for suggesting her nephew's name – Harrison. Thanks to Samantha Luke, Jan Clark, Rebecca Bush and Lesley Pay for making the same suggestion. Thank you also to author Margaret Amatt who came up with reVerb for my boyband, from which I created the reVerberators. Great name, Margaret!

Thank you to Jaimie Pattison, who attended a writing course I ran through RNA Learning. She'd recently lost a friend, Karen, whose motto was *If not now, when?* That motto resonated for Zara's and Snowy's stories so I really appreciate Jaimie sharing it with me and send hugs to her and to Karen's family and friends.

As always, thank you to my exceptionally brilliant editor, Nia Beynon.

This is our twenty-third novel together and I couldn't do this without her encouragement, belief and fantastic editing guidance. It takes a team to pull a book together so thank you to Cecily Blench for the copy edits, Susan Sugden for the proofread, Lizzie Gardiner for another stunning cover and our amazing in-house production team. Thanks to Rebecca Norfolk and Jon-Paul Rowden for bringing Zara and Snowy to life in the audiobook, and to ISIS Audio and Ulverscroft for the recording and distribution. Thanks also to the fabulous Claire Fenby, Head of Marketing, and her team for all the marketing support and gorgeous promotional materials, and our amazing CEO and Founder, Amanda Ridout, for being such an inspiring and enthusiastic leader. Thank you to Rachel Gilbey and the wonderful reviewers who've participated in the blog tour for *A New Dawn at Owl's Lodge*. I really appreciate all the kind comments.

Hugs of gratitude to my husband, Mark, and our daughter, Ashleigh, for their continued support and encouragement, and my lovely mum, who never misses an opportunity to champion me. You're the best, mummy bear xx

Writing can be a lonely profession and I'm so grateful for the friendship and support of so many writing friends including my bestie, Sharon Booth, Eliza J. Scott, the Write Romantics, all the other Boldwood authors and my wonderful friends from my writing group, The Beverley Novelists. I started a list of specific shout-outs to various author friends but it became very long and I feared I'd miss someone important out so I thought I'd better avoid the list. Grateful hugs to you all.

Massive appreciation to The Friendly Book Community, Riveting Reads and Vintage Vibes and the various other Facebook groups who champion my work, as well as all the lovely members of Redland's Readers who lift me every day. And thank you to you for reading this book and any others you might have dived into. The love and enthusiasm shown by my readers for the worlds I've created means everything to me and keeps me writing.

Finally, I want to mention my dedication. *Healing Hearts at Bumblebee Barn* was dedicated to my Auntie Mary. Sadly, she passed away at the grand age of ninety-two while I was working on my edits for *A New Dawn at Owl's Lodge* so it felt appropriate to dedicate this sequel to her daughters (my cousins) Christine and Gillian and their families on the loss of a wonderful woman. Quick-witted with a lovely laugh, she will be greatly missed. RIP Auntie Mary xx

Big hugs
Jessica xx

ABOUT THE AUTHOR

Jessica Redland writes uplifting stories of love, friendship, family and community set mostly in Yorkshire where she lives. Her Whitsborough Bay books transport readers to the stunning North Yorkshire Coast and her Hedgehog Hollow series takes them into beautiful countryside of the Yorkshire Wolds.

Sign up to Jessica Redland's mailing list here for news, competitions and updates on future books.

Visit Jessica's website: www.jessicaredland.com

Follow Jessica on social media:

- facebook.com/JessicaRedlandAuthor
- x.com/JessicaRedland
- instagram.com/JessicaRedlandAuthor
- bookbub.com/authors/jessica-redland

ALSO BY JESSICA REDLAND

Welcome to Whitsborough Bay
Making Wishes at Bay View
New Beginnings at Seaside Blooms
Finding Hope at Lighthouse Cove
Coming Home to Seashell Cottage

Hedgehog Hollow
Finding Love at Hedgehog Hollow
New Arrivals at Hedgehog Hollow
Family Secrets at Hedgehog Hollow
A Wedding at Hedgehog Hollow
Chasing Dreams at Hedgehog Hollow
Christmas Miracles at Hedgehog Hollow

Christmas on Castle Street
Christmas at Carly's Cupcakes
Starry Skies Over the Chocolate Pot Café
Christmas Wishes at the Chocolate Shop

The Starfish Café
Snowflakes Over the Starfish Café
Spring Tides at the Starfish Café
Summer Nights at the Starfish Café

Escape to the Lakes
The Start of Something Wonderful

A Breath of Fresh Air

Standalones

The Secret to Happiness

All You Need is Love

Healing Hearts at Bumblebee Barn

Christmas at the Cat Café

A New Dawn at Owl's Lodge

LOVE NOTES
LOVE IN EVERY CHAPTER

WHERE ALL YOUR ROMANCE DREAMS COME TRUE!

THE HOME OF BESTSELLING ROMANCE AND WOMEN'S FICTION

WARNING:
MAY CONTAIN SPICE

SIGN UP TO OUR NEWSLETTER

https://bit.ly/Lovenotesnews

Boldwood

Boldwood Books is an award-winning fiction publishing company seeking out the best stories from around the world.

Find out more at www.boldwoodbooks.com

Join our reader community for brilliant books, competitions and offers!

Follow us
@BoldwoodBooks
@TheBoldBookClub

Sign up to our weekly deals newsletter

https://bit.ly/BoldwoodBNewsletter